P9-CEH-478

Praise for
Jenny Colgan

"I love this book! It's funny, page-turning and addictive . . .
just like Malory Towers for grown-ups."
—Sophie Kinsella

"I have been waiting twenty-five years for someone
to write a bloody brilliant boarding school book,
stuffed full of unforgettable characters, thrilling adventures,
and angst, and here it is."
—Lisa Jewell

"A wonderful first novel that had me in tears and fits of
laughter. Definitely an A+!"
—Chris Manby

"If you were a fan of Malory Towers or St. Clare's
books in your—ahem—youth, you'll love this modern
boarding school based tale. . . . Top of the class!"
—*Closer*

"This brilliant boarding school book, with its eccentric
cast of characters and witty one-liners, should prove an
unmissable dose of nostalgia. Whether you've recently
left school, have rose-tinted memories of it, or are a
teacher looking for some escapism from classroom
dreariness, this book will certainly score A+."
—*Glamour*

"Good old-fashioned fun and escapism. . . .
A fabulously fresh and fun read."
—*Heat*

"This is Malory Towers . . . for grown-ups."
—*Company*

"If you're looking for delightful childhood
reminiscing or perhaps are the person who fantasized
about being in a boarding school as a youngster,
then this is the book for you!"
—BookPleasures

Welcome to the School by the Sea

Also by Jenny Colgan

Welcome to the School by the Sea

The First School by the Sea Novel

Jenny Colgan

AVON

An Imprint of HarperCollinsPublishers

WELCOME TO THE SCHOOL BY THE SEA. Copyright © 2008 by Jenny Colgan. Excerpt from RULES AT THE SCHOOL BY THE SEA © 2009 by Jenny Colgan. All rights reserved. Printed in the United States of America. No part of this book may be used or reproduced in any manner whatsoever without written permission except in the case of brief quotations embodied in critical articles and reviews. For information, address HarperCollins Publishers, 195 Broadway, New York, NY 10007.

HarperCollins books may be purchased for educational, business, or sales promotional use. For information, please email the Special Markets Department at SPsales@harpercollins.com.

Originally published as *Class* in Great Britain in 2008 by Sphere.

FIRST U.S. EDITION

Designed by Diahann Sturge

Library of Congress Cataloging-in-Publication Data has been applied for.

ISBN 978-0-06-314171-1
ISBN 978-0-06-321276-3 (hardcover library edition)

22 23 24 25 26 LSC 10 9 8 7 6 5 4 3 2 1

For my mother

Characters

Staff

Headteacher: Dr. Veronica Deveral
Administrator: Miss Evelyn Prenderghast
Deputy Headteacher: Miss June Starling
Cook: Mrs. Joan Rhys
Caretaker: Mr. Harold Carruthers
Physics: Mr. John Bart
Music: Mrs. Theodora Offili
French: Mademoiselle Claire Crozier
English: Miss Margaret Adair
Maths: Miss Elia Beresford
PE: Miss Janie James
Drama: Miss Fleur Parsley

Governors

Dame Lydia Johnson
Majabeen Gupta
Digory Gill

Characters

Pupils

Middle School Year One

Sylvie Brown
Imogen Fairlie
Simone Pribetich
Andrea McCann
Felicity Prosser
Zazie Saurisse
Alice Trebizon-Woods
Astrid Ulverton
Ursula Wendell

A Word from Jenny

H ello, hello!
  I know, a pre-introduction, that is WEIRD. Sorry. But
I wanted to write a quick note to explain what this book is all
about.

A few years ago, I wanted to read a boarding school book,
having loved them when I was younger. But I couldn't find one
for grown-ups. So I wrote a couple. We then decided, we being
my publishers and I, to release them under a different name.
I can't remember why now. It SEEMED like a good idea at the
time.

Anyway, regardless, *Class* and *Rules* came out and they had
lovely reviews. But as it turned out, absolutely nobody bought
them at all, having never heard of Jane Beaton, which was perfectly understandable, but also made me very sad as I loved
writing them and was very proud of them.

As the years have gone on though, people keep finding their
way to them, little by little, and finally last year somebody wrote
the publishers a letter saying "do please let me know what happened to Jane Beaton, as I kept checking the obituaries in case she
died," at which point we thought, okay, ENOUGH IS ENOUGH.

A Word from Jenny

So we are now bringing them out again as Jenny Colgan novels this time, and hopefully I'll get to finish the series (there are going to be six, of course), and hopefully everything will all work out nicely this time.

They are a couple of years old, but I haven't changed anything except one thing: when I wrote them originally I had in my mind for Simone, the scholarship girl, a pretty unusual surname I'd heard on a little-known lawyer back in a nineties trial and stored away.

For obvious reasons since then, we've decided to change the name "Simone Kardashian." She will now be Simone Pribetich in honor of one of my dearest friends, Anouch, who is also Armenian.

Everything else—including "Jane's" original introduction, which are, of course, my feelings too—remains exactly the same, and I so hope you enjoy reading the School by the Sea books as much as I loved writing them. Do let me know on Instagram @jennycolgan, or track me down on Facebook, of course. As Jenny, probably, not Jane :)

WITH LOVE,

Jenny X X X

Introduction

When I was growing up, attending my normal, extremely bog-standard Catholic school, I was obsessed with boarding school books. All of the Malory Toweres and St. Clare series *Frost in May*, *Jane Eyre*, *The Four Marys*, *What Katy Did at School*, the Chalet School books.

It's not difficult to understand why: the idea of a bunch of girls all having fun together, working, playing, and staying up late for midnight feasts, as opposed to the tribal, aggressive atmosphere of my own school, exerted a powerful pull on a swottish, awkward child. None of these books, for example, had playground meetings that decided which girls were going to be "in" or "out" that week, cruel nicknames, long hours of Catholic instruction (OK, apart from Antonia White), or compulsory tiny miniskirts for gym for the boys to line up and jeer at.

So I lost myself in pranks played on French mistresses; school plays (unheard of at my lackadaisical state school); lacrosse (whatever that was); and the absurd fantasy that you could speak English, French, and German on alternate days. Incidentally, has there ever been a school on earth that makes you do that?

Introduction

When the Harry Potter books came out, obviously their wizard lore and storytelling were a huge draw—but part of me still wondered how much of their success was down to the idealized boarding school life of Hogwarts, filled with delicious meals and having great fun with your wonderfully loyal friends, *sans* fear of parental intervention. The fact that boarding school applications rose sharply with each book published seemed to indicate that I might be right.

Of course in my adult life I've met plenty of people who did go to boarding school, every single one of whom has assured me it was absolutely nothing like the books at all—they know this because, oddly, my dormitory-bound friends seem to have read just as much boarding school fiction as the rest of us.

Perhaps it's the certainties of these schools—their rock-solid concepts of nobility, self-sacrifice, "the good of the school"—as opposed to the reality of the lives of most adolescents and pre-adolescents: shifting sands of loyalties; siblings cramping your style; and the gradual, creeping realization that your parents are just feeling their way and don't really have all the answers. Whereas boarding schools, of course, always have strict yet kindly pastoral figures—like Dumbledore, Miss Grayling, or Jo at the Chalet, who always know what to do and are liberal with their second chances. The repetitive rhythm of the terms provides solid ground, endlessly comforting to children in an ever-changing world.

As a voracious adult reader, I realized a couple of years ago that I still missed those books. The prose of Enid Blyton jars a little these days (and they do horribly gang up on and bully Gwendoline, for the sole sin of crying when her parents drop her off), although Curtis Sittenfeld's marvelous book *Prep* is a terrific contemporary account.

To Serve Them All My Days by R. F. Delderfield, though inevitably dated (which adds a wonderfully bittersweet twist to his stories, knowing how many of his boys were unwittingly bound for the battlefields of World War II), appeals to the adult reader, but as for my beloved girls' stories, there were none to be found.

So I decided to go about writing one myself. *Welcome to the School by the Sea* is the first in a projected series of six books about Downey House (Of course! There must always be six. Well, unless you're at the Chalet school, in which case there can be about seventy-five). *Rules at the School by the Sea* will be the second.

Although I'm writing this series for myself, when I've chatted about it I've been amazed by the number of people (all right, women) who've said, "I've been waiting for a book like this for such a long time." I hope I don't disappoint them—and us, the secret legions of boarding school book fans.

Jenny Colgan

Welcome
to the School
by the Sea

Chapter One

Purple skirt *no*. Gray suit *yes* but it was in a crumpled ball from an unfortunate attack of dry cleaner phobia. Black, definitely *not*. Ditto that Gaviscon-pink frilly coat jacket thing she'd panic-bought for a wedding and couldn't throw away because it had cost too much, but every time she came across it in her wardrobe it made her shiver and question the kind of person she was.

Job interviews. Torture from the pits of hell. Especially job interviews four hundred miles away which require clothing that will both look fantastic and stand up to seven hours in Stan's Fiat Panda, with its light coating of crisps. Oh, and that would do the job both for chilly Scotland and the warm English riviera. God, it sucked not being able to take time off sometimes.

Maggie Adair looked at herself critically in the mirror and decided to drive to Cornwall in her pajamas.

FLISS WAS HAVING a lie-in—among the last, she thought, of her entire life.

I can't believe they're making me do this, she thought. I can't believe they're sending me away. And if they think they're fooling me with their jolly hockey-sticks utter bloody bollocks they can think again. Of course Hattie loves it, she bloody loves anything that requires the brain of a flea, a tennis racket, a boys' school on the hill, and eyelash curlers.

Well, I'm not going to bloody love it. I'll sit it out till they realize how shit it is and they'll let me go to Guildford Academy like everyone else, not some nobs' bloody hole two hundred miles away. Why should I care about being sent so far from London just as everyone else is getting to go to Wembley concerts and on the tube on their own? I'm nearly fourteen, for God's sake. I'm a teenager. And now I'm going to be buried alive in bloody Cornwall. Nobody ever thinks about me.

I'll show them. I'll be home after a month.

Breakfast the next morning was even worse. Fliss pushed her All-Bran round her plate. No way was she eating this muck. She'd pass it on to Ranald (the beagle) but she didn't think he would eat it either. She patted his wet nose, and felt comforted.

"And I don't know for sure," Hattie was saying, "but I think they're going to make me prefect! One of the youngest ever!"

"That's wonderful, sweetie," their mother was saying. "And you can keep an eye out for Fliss."

Fliss rolled her eyes. "Great. Let everyone know the big swotty prefect is my sister. NO thank you."

Hattie bit her lip. Even though she was eighteen months older, Fliss could still hurt her. And she wasn't *that* big.

"Behave yourself," said their father. "I don't want to hear you speaking like that."

"Fine," said Fliss, slipping down from the table. "You don't have to hear me speaking *at all*. That's why you're sending me away, remember?" And she made sure the conservatory doors banged properly behind her as she mounted the stairs.

"Is she really only thirteen?" said her mother. "Do we really have to put up with this for another six years?"

"Hmm?" said her father, buried under the *Financial Times*. Selective hearing, he reckoned. That's all you needed. Though he couldn't help contrasting his sweet placid elder daughter with this little firecracker. Boarding school was going to be just what she needed, sort her out.

DR. VERONICA DEVERAL couldn't believe they were still interviewing for staff three weeks before the beginning of term. It showed a lack of professionalism she just couldn't bear. She glanced in the mirror, then reached out a finger to smooth the deep furrow between her eyes. Normally she was without a hint of vanity, but the start of the new school year brought anxieties all of its own, even after thirty years, and Mrs. Ferrers waiting for the very last minute to jump ship to Godolphin was one of them.

So now she was short of an English teacher, and with eighty new girls soon turning up—some scared, some weepy, some excited, some defiant, and all of them needing a good confident hand. She put on her reading glasses and turned back to the pile of CVs. She missed the days when she didn't need CVs, with their gussied-up management language, and fancy euphemisms about child-centered learning, instead of simple common sense. A nicely typed letter without spelling mistakes and a quick once-over to see if they were the right stuff—that used to be all she needed.

Still, she mused, gazing out of the high window of her office, over the smooth lawns—quiet and empty, at least for a few more weeks—and up to the rocky promontory above the sea, which started just beyond the bounds of the school, it wasn't all bad. These ghastly "inclusiveness" courses the board had suggested she attend—no one would ever instruct Veronica to do anything—had been quite interesting in terms of expanding the range of people the girls could work with.

They had such hermetic upbringings, so many of them. Country house, London house, nannies, and the best schools. Oh, there was divorce and absent parenting, and all the rest, but they still existed in a world in which everyone had help; no one had to worry about money or even getting a job. Now, wasn't there an application somewhere from a woman teaching in a Glasgow housing estate? Perhaps she should have another glass of mint tea and look at it again.

"LA DEE DAH."

"Shut it," Simone said.

"La dee dah."

"Mum! He's doing it again!"

"Joel!"

"I'm not doing *anyfink*."

Simone tried to ignore him and concentrate on an early spell of packing, which was hard when he wouldn't get out of her tiny bedroom. And, even more irritating, she could kind of see his point. Even she'd winced at the straw boater and the winter gloves on the uniform list, though at first she'd been so excited. Such a change from the ugly burgundy sweatshirt and optional (i.e., everyone wore them if you didn't want to get called a "slut") gray trousers and black shoes at St. Cat's.

She tried to ignore her annoying younger brother, and bask once again in the memory of the day they'd got the letter. Not the months and months of long study that had gone on before it.

Not the remarks from her classmates, which had got even more unpleasant the more she'd stayed behind and begged the teachers for extra work and more coaching—most of the third years were of the firm conviction that she'd had sex with every single teacher in the school, male and female, in return for the highest predicted GCSE grades the school had ever seen, not that there'd been much to beat.

She'd tried her best to keep her head high, even when she was being tripped in the corridor; when she couldn't open any door without glances and whispers in her direction; when she'd spent every break-time and lunchtime hiding in a corner of the library (normally forbidden, but she'd got special permission).

No, she was going back to the day the letter came. In a heavy, thick white envelope. *"Dear Mr. & Mrs. Pribetich . . . we are pleased to inform you that your daughter Simone . . . full scholarship . . . enclosed, clothing suppliers . . ."*

Her father hadn't said very much; he'd had to go out of the room for a minute. Half delighted—he'd never dreamed when he'd arrived in Britain that one day his daughter would be attending a private school—he was also annoyed that, even though it was a great opportunity for Simone, he wasn't paying for it himself. And he worried too for his sensitive daughter. She'd nearly worked herself ill for the entrance exams. Would she be able to keep up?

Simone's mum however had no such reservations. She flung her arms around Simone, screaming in excitement.

"She just wants to tell everyone," said Joel. But Simone hadn't cared. She'd been too busy taking it all in. No more St. Cat's. No more burgundy sweatshirts. No more Joel! No more being paraded in front of Mamma's friends ("No, not pretty, no. But *so* clever! You wouldn't believe how clever!"). Her life started now.

It HAD TO be around here somewhere. Just as she was ferreting with one hand for the last of the Maltesers in the bottom of her bag, Maggie crested the hill in the car. And there it was.

The school most resembled a castle, perched by the sea. It had four towers—four houses, Maggie firmly told herself, trying to remember. Named after English royal houses, that was right. Wessex; Plantagenet; York, and Tudor. No Stuart, she noted ruefully. Maggie mentally contrasted the imposing buildings with the wet, gray single-story seventies build she'd left behind her up in Scotland.

Uh oh, she thought. What was it Stan had said? "The second you get in there you'll get a chip on your shoulder the size of Govan. All those spoiled mimsies running about. You'll hate it."

Mind you, it wasn't like Stan was exactly keen for her to broaden her horizons. He'd been in the same distribution job since he left school. Spreading his wings wasn't really in his vocabulary. But maybe it would be different for her. Let's face it, there had to be more out there than teaching in the same school she grew up in and having Sunday lunch round her mum's. She had to at least see.

VERONICA DEVERAL RUBBED her eyes. Only her third candidate, and she felt weary already.

"So," she asked the wide-eyed young woman sitting in front of her. "How would you cope with a difficult child . . . say, for example, one who doesn't think she should be here?"

The woman, who was wearing pale blue eyeliner that

matched both her suit and her tights, and didn't blink as often as she should, leaned forward to show enthusiasm.

"Well," she said, in refined tones that didn't quite ring true—junior acting classes, thought Veronica—"I'd try and establish a paradigm matrix of acceptable integral behaviors, and follow that up with universal quality monitoring and touch/face time. I think non-goal-orientated seeking should be minimized wherever appropriate."

There was a silence.

"Well, er, thank you very much for coming in, Miss . . ."

"Oh, I just like the kids to call me Candice. Promotes teacher–pupil sensitivity awareness," said Candice sincerely.

Veronica smiled without using her lips and decided against pouring them both another cup of tea.

GETTING CHANGED IN a Fiat Panda isn't as much fun as it looks. Maggie tried to imagine doing this in the car park of Holy Cross without getting a penknife in the bahookie, and couldn't manage it. But here, hidden out of sight on the gray gravel drive, it was at least possible, if lacking in the elegance stakes.

She put her makeup on using the car mirror. Pink cheeks, windswept from having the windows open for the last hundred miles, air-con not quite having reached Stan's mighty machine. Her dark, thickly waving hair—which, when properly brushed out by a hairdresser was really rather lovely but the rest of the time required lion taming—was a bit frizzed, but she might be able to get away with it by pulling it into a tight bun. In fact, frizzy hair in tight buns was exactly what she'd expect a boarding school teacher to wear, so she might be right at home. She smoothed down her skirt, took a deep breath, and left the car.

Straight ahead of her, the sun glistened off the choppy sea. She could probably swim here in the mornings, lose the half stone caused by huddling in the staffroom ever since she'd left college two years before, mainlining caramel wafers in an attempt to forget the horror that was year three.

Maggie stepped out onto the gravel drive. Up close, the building was even more impressive; an elaborate Victorian confection, built in 1880 as an adjunct to the much older boys' school at the other end of the cove, the imposing building giving off an air of seriousness and calm.

She wondered what it would be like full of pupils. Or perhaps they were serious and calm too. At the very least they were unlikely to have police records. Already she'd been impressed by the amount of graffiti on the old walls of the school: none. Nothing about who was going to get screwed, about who was going to get knifed . . . nothing at all.

No. She wasn't going to think about what it would be like to work here. This was just an experiment, just to see what else was out there before she went back to her mum and dad's, and Stan, in Govan. Where she belonged. She thought of Stan from weeks earlier, when she'd talked about applying.

" 'Teacher required for single-sex boarding school,' " she read out. " 'Beautiful location. On-site living provided. English, with some sports.' "

Stan sniffed.

"Well, that's you out then. What sports are you going to teach? Running to the newsagents, to get an Aero?"

"I'm trained in PT, thank you!" said Maggie sniffily.

"It'll be funny posh sports anyway, like polo, and lacrosse." He snorted to himself.

"What?"

"Just picturing you playing polo."

Maggie breathed heavily through her nose.

"Why?"

"You're frightened of horses, for one. And you'd probably crush one if you keep on eating bacon sandwiches like that."

"Shut up!" said Maggie. "Do you think being Scottish counts as being an ethnic minority? It says they're trying to encourage entries from everywhere. Apply in writing in the first instance to Miss Prenderghast . . ."

"A girls' school with free accommodation?" said Stan. "Where do I sign up?" He thought she was only doing this to annoy him, even when the interview invitation arrived.

"Dear Ms. Adair," he'd read out in an absurdly overexaggerated accent. "Please do us the most gracious honor of joining us for tea and crumpet with myself, the queen and . . ."

"Give that back," she'd said, swiping the letter, which had come on heavy cream vellum paper, with a little sketch of the Downey school printed on it in raised blue ink. It simply requested her presence for a meeting with the headmistress, but reading it had made her heart pound a bit. It did feel a little like being summoned.

"I don't know why you're wasting your time," Stan had said, as she'd worried over whether or not to take the purple skirt. "A bunch of bloody poncey southern snobs, they're never going to look at you anyway."

"I know," said Maggie, crossly folding up her good bra.

"And even if they did, you're not going to move to Cornwall, are you?"

"I'm sure I'm not. It's good interview experience, that's all."

"There you go then. Stop messing about."

But as they lay in bed in the evening, Stan snoring happily

away, pizza crumbs still round his mouth, Maggie lay there imagining. Imagining a world of beautiful halls; of brand-new computers for the kids that didn't get broken immediately. Books that didn't have to be shared. Bright, healthy, eager faces, eager to learn, to have their minds opened.

It wasn't that she didn't like her kids. She just found them so wearing. She just wanted a change, that was all. So why, when she mentioned it, did everyone look at her like she'd just gone crazy?

THE MAIN ENTRANCE to the school was two large wooden doors with huge circular wrought-iron door knockers, set under a carved stone lintel on which faded cut letters read: *multa ex hoc ludo accipies; multa quidem fac ut reddas*. Maggie hoped she wouldn't be asked to translate them as one of the interview questions. The whole entranceway, from the sweep of the gravel drive to the grand view out to sea, seemed designed to impress, and did so. In fact it hardly even smelled of school—that heady scent of formaldehyde, trainers, uneaten vegetables, and cheap deodorant Maggie had gotten to know so well. Maybe it was because of the long holiday, or maybe girls just didn't smell so bad, but at Holy Cross it oozed from the walls.

The doors entered onto a long black-and-white tiled-corridor, lined with portraits and photographs—of distinguished teachers and former pupils, Maggie supposed. Suddenly she felt herself getting very nervous. She thought back to her interview with James Gregor at Holy Cross. "Good at animal taming, are you?" he'd said. "Good. Our staff turnover is twenty percent a year, so you will forgive me if I don't take the trouble to get to know you too well just yet."

And she'd been in. And he'd been right. No wonder Stan

was bored with her looking at other options. After all, college had been great fun. Late nights out with the girls, skipping lectures, going to see all the new bands at King Tut's and any other sweaty dive where students got in free. Even her teaching experience had been all right—a little farm school in Sutherland where the kids didn't turn up in autumn (harvest) or winter (snowed in), and had looked at her completely bemused when she'd asked the first year to write an essay about their pets.

"What's a pet, miss?"

"My dad's got three snakes. Are they pets, miss? But he just keeps them for the rats."

Then she'd come back to Glasgow, all geared up and ready for her new career, only to find that, with recruitment in teachers at an all-time high, the only job she could find was at her old school, Holy Cross. Her old school where the boys had pulled her hair, and the girls had pulled the boys' hair, and it was rough as guts, right up till that moment in fifth year when big lanky Stanley Mackintosh had loped over in his huge white baseball boots and shyly asked her if she wanted to go and see some band some mate of his was in.

The band sucked; or they might have been brilliant, Maggie wasn't paying attention and no one heard of them ever again. No, she was too busy snogging a tall, lanky, big-eared bloke called Stan up at the back near the toilet and full of excited happiness.

Of course, that was six years ago. Now, Stan was working down the newspaper distributors—he'd started as a paper boy and had never really gone away, although it did mean he was surprisingly well informed for someone who played as much Championship Manager as he did—and she was back at Holy Cross. They never even went to gigs anymore, since she left college and didn't get cheap entry to things, and she was always knackered when she got home anyway, and there was always marking.

Back in Govan. And it didn't matter that she was still young, just out of college—to the students, she was "miss," she was ancient, and she was to be taken advantage of by any means necessary. She'd ditched the trendy jeans and tops she'd worn to lectures, and replaced them with plain skirts and tops that gave the children as little chance to pick on her as possible— she saw her dull tweedy wardrobe as armor. They still watched out to see if she wore a new lipstick or different earrings, where-upon they would try and turn it into a conversation as pro-longed and insulting as possible.

Once she'd dreamed of filling young hearts and minds with wonderful books and poetry; inspiring them, like Robin Williams, to think beyond their small communities and into the big world. Now she just dreamed of crowd control, and keep-ing them quiet for ten bloody minutes without someone whack-ing somebody else or answering their hidden mobiles. They'd caught a kid in fourth year with a knife again the other day. It was only a matter of time before one got brandished in class. She just hoped to God it wasn't her class. She needed to learn another way.

THE ELEGANT TILED corridor leading off the grand entrance hall at Downey House toward the administrative offices was so quiet Maggie found she was holding her breath. She looked at the portrait right in front of her: a stern-looking woman, who'd been headmistress during the Second World War. Her hair looked like it was made of wrought iron. She wondered how she'd looked after the girls then, girls who were worried about brothers and fathers; about German boats coming ashore, even down here. She shivered and nearly jumped when a little voice piped, "Miss Adair?"

A tiny woman, no taller than Maggie's shoulder, had suddenly materialized in front of her. She had gray hair, was wearing a bright fuchsia turtleneck with her glasses on a chain round her neck, and, though obviously old, had eyes as bright as a little bird's.

"Mrs. Beltan," she said, indicating the portrait. "Wonderful woman. Just wonderful."

"She looks it," said Maggie. "Hello."

"I'm Miss Prenderghast. School proctor. Follow me."

Maggie wasn't sure what a proctor was but it sounded important. She followed carefully, as Miss Prenderghast's tiny heels clicked importantly on the spotless floor.

Veronica glanced up from the CV she was reading. Art, music, English . . . all useful. But, more importantly, Maggie Adair was from an inner-city comprehensive school. One with economic problems, social problems, academic problems—you name it. So many of the girls here were spoiled, only interested in getting into colleges with good social scenes and parties, en route to a good marriage and a house in the country . . . sometimes she wondered how much had changed in fifty years. A little exposure to the more difficult side of life might be just what they needed—provided they could understand the accent . . . she put on her warmest smile as Evelyn Prenderghast knocked on the door.

Oh, but the young people were so *scruffy* nowadays. That dreadful suit looked as if it had been used for lining a dog's basket. And would it be too much to ask an interviewee to drag a comb through her hair? Veronica was disappointed, and it showed.

Maggie felt the headmistress's gaze on her the second she entered the room. It was like a laser. She felt as if it was taking in everything about her and it made her feel about ten years old. You wouldn't be able to tell a lie to Dr. Deveral, she'd see through you instantly. Why hadn't she bought a new suit for the interview? Why? Was her mascara on straight? Why did she waste time mooning at all those portraits? She knew she should have gone to the loos and fixed herself up.

"Hello," she said, as confidently as she could manage, and suddenly decided to pretend to herself that this *was* her school, that she already worked here, that this was her life. She gazed around at the headmistress's office, which was paneled in dark wood, with more portraits on the wall—including one of the queen—and a variety of different and beautiful objects that looked as if they had been collected from around the world, set on different surfaces, carefully placed to catch the eye and look beautiful. Just imagine. Maggie looked at a lovely sculpture of the hunting goddess Diana with her dogs, and her face broke into a grin.

Veronica was quite taken aback by how much the girl's face changed when she smiled—it was a lovely, open smile that made her look nearly the same age as some of her students. Quite an improvement. But that suit . . .

VERONICA WAS FRUSTRATED. This girl was very nice and everything—even the Glaswegian accent wasn't too strong, which was a relief. She hadn't been looking forward to an entire interview of asking the girl to repeat herself. But so far it had all been chat about college and so on—nothing useful at all. Nothing particularly worthwhile, just lots of the usual interview platitudes about bringing out children's strengths and independence of thought and whatever the latest buzzwords were out there. She sighed, then decided to ask one question she'd always wondered about.

"Miss Adair, tell me something . . . this school you work at. It has dreadfully poor exam results, doesn't it?"

"Yes," said Maggie, hoping she wasn't being personally blamed for all of them. She could tell this interview wasn't going well—not at all, in fact—and was resigning herself to the long trip back, along with a fair bit of humble pie dished up by Stan in the Bear & Bees later.

Dr. Deveral hadn't seemed in the least bit interested in her new language initiatives or her dissertation. Probably a bit much to hope for, that someone from a lovely school like this would be interested in someone like her from a rough school. Suddenly the thought made her indignant—just because her kids weren't posh didn't mean they weren't all right, most of them. In fact, the ones that did do well were doing it against incredible odds, much harder than the pony-riding spoon-feeding they probably did here. She suddenly felt herself flush hot with indignation.

"Yes, it does have poor results. But they're improving all the—"

Veronica cut her off with a wave of the hand. "What I wonder is, why do you make these children stay on at school? They don't want to go, they're not going to get any qualifications . . . I mean, really, what's the point?"

If anything was likely to make Maggie really furious it was this. Stan said it all the time. It just showed he had absolutely no idea, and neither did this stupid woman, who'd only ever sat in her posh study, drinking tea and wondering how many swim-

15

ming pools to build next year. Bugger this stupid job. Stan had been right, it was a waste of her time. Some people would just never understand.

"I'll tell you the point," said Maggie, her accent subconsciously getting stronger. "School is all some of these children have got. School is the only order in their lives. They hate getting expelled, believe it or not. Their homes are chaotic and their families are chaotic, and any steadiness and guidance we can give them, any order and praise, and timekeeping and support, anything the school can give them at all, even just a hot meal once a day, that's what's worth it. So I suppose they don't get *quite* as many pupils into Oxford and Cambridge as you do, Dr. Deveral. But I don't think they're automatically less valuable just because their parents can't pay."

Maggie felt very hot suddenly, realizing she'd been quite rude, and that an outburst hadn't exactly been called for, especially not one that sounded as if it was calling for a socialist revolution. "So . . . erhm. I guess I'm probably best back there," she finished weakly, in a quiet voice.

Veronica sat back and, for the first time that day, let a genuine smile cross her lips.

"Oh, I wouldn't be so sure about that," she said.

SIMONE HELD HER arms out like a traffic warden's, feeling acutely self-conscious.

"We'll have to send away for these," the three-hundred-year-old woman in the uniform shop had said, as all her fellow crones had nodded in agreement. "Downey House! That's rather famous, isn't it?"

"Yes, it is," said her mother, self-importantly. Her mum was all dressed up, just to come to a uniform shop. She looked totally stupid, like she was on her way to a wedding or something. Why did her mother have to be so embarrassing all the time? "And our Simone's going there!"

Well, obviously she was going there, seeing as she was in getting measured up for the uniform. Simone let out a sigh.

"Now she's quite big around the chest for her age," said the woman loudly.

"Yes, she's going to be just like me," said her mum, who was shaped like a barrel. "Look—big titties."

There was another mother in there —much more subtly dressed—with a girl around Simone's age, who was getting measured for a different school. As soon as they heard "big titties," however, they glanced at each other. Simone wished the floor would open and swallow her up.

As the saleslady put the tape measure around her hips, Simone risked a glance out of the window. At exactly the wrong time: Estelle Grant, the nastiest girl in year seven, was walking past with two of her cronies.

Immediately a look of glee spread over Estelle's face, as she pummeled her friends to look. Simone's mum and the lady were completely oblivious to her discomfort, standing up on a stool in full view of the high street.

"Can I get down?" she said desperately, as Estelle started posing with her chest out, as if struggling to contain her massive bosoms. It wasn't Simone's fault that she was so well developed. Now the other girls had puffed out their cheeks and were staggering around like elephants. Simone felt tears prick the back of her eyes. She wasn't going to cry, she *wasn't*. She was never going back to that school. Nobody would ever make her feel like Estelle Grant did, ever again.

"Now, your school requires a boater, so let's check for hat

size," the lady was saying, plonking a straw bonnet on her head. This was too much for the girls outside; they collapsed in half-fake hysterics.

Simone closed her eyes and dug her nails into her hands, as her mother twittered to the saleslady about how fast her daughter was growing up—and out! And she got her periods at ten, can you imagine?! The saleslady shook her head in amazement through a mouthful of pins, till Estelle and her cronies finally tired of the sport and, in an orgy of rude hand signals, went on their way.

Never again. Never again.

Chapter Two

Maggie Adair was making the long trip a second time, but now she was a little more organized, and didn't mind at all. She kept glancing at the heavy card envelope on the seat beside her, as if it were about to disappear if she didn't keep it under constant attention.

When it had arrived, just two days after she'd returned from Cornwall ("Did you make friends with any sheep while you were there?" Stan had said, and that was all he'd asked her about it), she'd gotten a huge shock. Then she'd assumed that anything arriving this quickly could only be a rejection, which was belied by the size of the envelope. Sure enough:

"... we would be pleased to offer you the post of junior English mistress ..."

AND THAT WAS all she read before dropping it on the floor. "Oh," she said.

"What is it?" said Stan, lumbering down the stairs with his polo shirt buttoned up wrong and sleep still in his eyes.

"Uhm . . . uh . . ." She looked up at him, realizing she was about to drop a bombshell. "I got that job."

"What job?" said Stan. He wasn't quite himself before two cups of builder's tea in the morning. Then, as he reached the kettle, he stopped suddenly and turned round. "The posh job?"

Maggie nodded. Her hands were shaking, she just couldn't believe it. Dr. Deveral had given nothing away at all and she'd driven the whole evening back convinced she'd wasted her time—the woman next in line for the interview looked like Gwyneth Paltrow in a netball shirt, for goodness' sake.

Stan stared at her. She wondered how long it had been since she'd really looked at him—really taken in the person she'd been with since the last night of school. He'd put on weight, of course, they both had, and they'd never again be as skinny as they were then, at seventeen. But his spiky hair still stuck up in all directions, and he still looked a mess whether in his work clothes, his pajamas, or his kilt. Even now she could feel toast crumbs compelling themselves toward him from all corners of the kitchen. Her daft Stan.

"But you can't take it," he said, doggedly, staring at her.

Maggie stared back at him and realized that, up until that moment, she hadn't been quite sure what she was going to do.

"But I want to," she said, slowly.

SIMONE WATCHED AS her mother piled the car high with silver foil packets.

"Mum, you know, they feed us there."

"Yes, but what kind of food, huh? Bread and jam! Cup o' tea!"

"I like bread and jam."

"Too much," said Joel. "You look like a jam roly-poly."

"Shut up! Mum, tell Joel to shut up."

Her mum raised her heavily painted eyebrows, sighed, and continued packing the car. It was a five-hour drive, but her mother had enough stashed away for a full-scale siege. There were cottage cheese doughnuts, meatball soup, pickled cabbage in jars . . . It looked like a toss-up for her mother: was she going to starve to death at school, or were they all going to succumb on the drive?

"Jam roly-poly! Jam roly-poly!"

Simone concentrated very hard on her Marie Curie biography. Perhaps she'd had a small, very annoying brother whose constant torments had strengthened her resolve to become a great heroine of science.

Dad was already sitting in the driver's seat. He'd been ready to leave since seven a.m., even though they didn't have to be at the school until teatime. He was wearing a suit and tie, even though he normally went to work in overalls. The tie had teddy bears all over it. She and Joel had bought it for him for Father's Day years ago. It didn't look very good, but she wasn't going to say anything. He was in a right mood. He should be happy for her, she thought. It wasn't like he would miss seeing her—most days he was out the house to work before they'd gotten up for breakfast, then he got back after eight o'clock, ate his dinner, and fell asleep on the sofa.

Simone glanced at her suitcase. She wished it wasn't so tatty. It had been her grandfather's, and her dad had brought it over from the old country. It had been made to look like leather but here and there where the fabric was torn you could tell it wasn't really, there was cardboard poking through. Bogdan Pribetich was stenciled on the top of it, and it smelled musty—like it had been put in the attic with someone leaving some old socks in it.

Still, inside were her new clothes—she couldn't think of them without being pleased. She knew the "Michaelmas term" list by heart:

Navy blazer with school crest
Bedford check winter-weight skirt
Navy V-necked jumper with school crest
4 x white short-sleeved blouse
2 x T-shirt with school design for Drama lessons
2 x white polo shirt with school crest
Navy games skirt
Navy felt hat with school crest
Navy cycle shorts
Navy sweatshirt with school crest
Navy tracksuit trousers with school crest
Royal blue hockey socks
Navy swimming costume with gold stripe
Navy swimming cap

She'd tried everything on, but only once, so she didn't get it crushed. Her mother had invited lots of her aunties round (they weren't all her real aunties, but she'd called them aunty for so long sometimes she couldn't even remember who she was actually related to) and they'd made her do a fashion show for them in the living room, as they ummed and ahhed and talked about the quality of the cloth and the weight of the material and Simone had done the occasional slightly clumsy turn, as her mother warned people eating the *mamaliga* not to get their fingers on anything and Joel played up like a maniac, running around being a very noisy Dalek, desperately trying to regain some of the attention.

Now, ironed a second time, it was all tightly packed up in the suitcase, with underwear, tights, and socks squeezed in the gaps in between. Simone had wanted to ask whether or not she'd be getting a new bra; just one wasn't really enough, but her mother hadn't mentioned it and it hadn't come up, so she kept quiet. Her father had looked at her, navy blue from top to toe, and smiled, a little sadly.

"You look quite the little English lady," he'd said. Simone supposed it was meant to be a nice thing to say, but she wasn't 100 percent sure.

"WHAT'S THE MATTER with everyone?" Maggie had said to her sister as she was preparing to leave. "It's just a job."

"I don't know," said Anna. "I suppose I just always thought you'd be teaching Cody and Dylan, you know? That they'd always grow up with their auntie in the school."

But Cody, the eldest, was only three, Maggie thought, even if, with his shaved head and Celtic football club shirt, he looked like her year 2 troublemakers already. But that meant in nine years' time everyone thought she'd still be exactly where she was. She didn't want that to happen. She wasn't going forever. She was going to get some experience, somewhere excellent, then come back to Glasgow and apply it where it was needed, that was all.

Anna had passed over a glass of warm white wine; it was after hours in the salon, and she was putting navy blue streaks in Maggie's hair. She'd been experimenting on Maggie for so long Maggie hardly noticed anymore—in fact it had helped at school, made her a bit more trendy having a hairdresser for a sister who used her as a free guinea pig, despite the occasional results that made her actually resemble a real guinea pig.

"I'd better be able to wash this out before I go," she warned. Anna ignored her.

"And the thing is, Maggie, kids round here, they need good teachers. They need people like you who are dedicated, who care about things. What do you want to go wasting your time with a posh bunch of nobs who already have everything and are only going to leave school and sit around on their arses waiting for a rich man for the next fifty years?"

Maggie looked at her glass. "Well, I want to . . ." she said. Then she tried again. "If I stay here . . ." That didn't sound right either. "The thing is, Anna, I just want to get out a bit. If I keep on here . . . it's not that it's bad or anything . . ."

"But it's good enough for all of us," said Anna.

"That's not what I mean. But I think I'll just get jaded and a bit bitter . . . I won't be a good teacher. I won't be good for the kids, I'll just turn into one of those rancid old harridans, like Fatty Puff. Mrs. McGinty. Just shouting all the time. I think it'll be good for me to work in a different place for a while, just get some more experience. Then come home."

"And Stan agrees with that, does he?" Anna slapped on some color with what felt like malice. Maggie wondered if it was time for a chop. What did southern teachers look like?

VERONICA SMOOTHED DOWN her soft gray cashmere cardigan. She supposed pearls weren't exactly fashionable anymore, but then what was fashionable was just so horrific she could hardly bear to think about it—in fact, if she could stop the upper sixths coming back from holiday with tattoos she'd be delighted. Didn't their parents even mind? Half of them were so busy working or having affairs they probably didn't notice. All those little butter-flies and fairies on their shoulders or down their backs. Surely they'd live to regret them. Veronica tried to imagine having a tattoo when she was at school, but she couldn't. It wouldn't even have crossed her mind; she might as well have been told not to fly upside down. She'd forbidden them time and time again, but it didn't seem to make any difference; they got to the Glastonbury Festival and every sensible thought flew right out of their heads.

So, her pearls might not be fashionable, but they had been her mother's best. She remembered so vividly her mother getting ready for a night out. She'd wear stiff petticoats under her skirt—satin was a favorite. She liked ice cream colors: pistachio, pale pink. And she wore Dior by Yves St. Laurent. You didn't get that much these days either; for years Veronica hadn't been able to smell it without being taken straight back to her childhood. She'd crouch down by the dressing table (her mother wouldn't let her on the bed in case she creased the counterpane) and watch in awe as her mother deftly applied powder, lipstick, and a block mascara. She'd thought she was the most beautiful woman in the world.

All of that was before, of course. In fact, those were the only happy memories she had of her mother, painted and pretty, heading out with her father, with his hair scraped down with oil.

Later on, it had been snatched meetings in Lyons Corner Houses, her mother having told some lie to her father to get out of the house, as Veronica's belly got bigger and bigger. On one of these wet and rainy occasions, as they sat over scones and tea with damp coats and dripping umbrellas, both trying to avoid looking at the empty third finger of Veronica's left hand, her mother had handed her the small box, wrapped in cloth.

"Just," she muttered, "something to pass on. If it's a girl I mean. Your father won't notice."

That night, back at the convent—the grim home for unmarried mothers she'd been dispatched to—sitting stoically as she always did after the nine p.m. curfew, while other girls sobbed their hearts out on the cold, greasy-blanketed cot beds that lined the walls, or talked defiantly about how their men would come for them, she had let the pearls run over her hands like water, feeling their perfect smoothness and cool beauty.

Veronica shook her head briskly to clear her brain, and focused on what she'd say to the new parents this afternoon. In fact, the pearls would help there. They normally did. They said, this is what our school is about: class, family, traditional values. That was what the school was about. The pearls were from somewhere else altogether.

It had not been a girl.

FLISS WAS IN her favorite spot, underneath the cherry tree in a far corner of the old orchard. No one could see you there from the house, unless they stood on the roof. She had the new Jacqueline Wilson, Ranald, and a bag of cherries she'd filched from the kitchen, but it wasn't doing the trick. All she could think of was that they were sending her away. OK, so she hadn't exactly covered herself in glory at Queen's middle; she winced as she thought back to her report cards. "Felicity has plenty of ability but tends toward laziness." "If she focused, she'd do as well as her big sister." "Felicity's conduct does occasionally give cause for concern." And so on and so on, blah blah blah. She didn't care. School was stupid, and now they were sending her somewhere even stupider. Great. She obviously didn't come up to her parents' high standards, so they were just chucking her out like rubbish. She cuddled Ranald.

"It's easy for you," she whispered into his panting neck. "You don't have to go to bloody school. I wish I were a dog." Ranald whimpered his agreement, as the grass ruffled gently in the breeze.

And she wondered what would be the best way out of there. Not expelled—too much trouble. Just a way of showing them that the local school, with her real actual friends and not some of Hattie's horrid swotty cast-offs, would be best. At the local school in Guildford they were allowed to go into London when they were fifteen, *and* they didn't have to wear a uniform. So completely the opposite of Downey bloody House then.

"Hurry up!" she could hear her mother shouting. "We have to go or we'll get stuck on that bloody A303 again, and I'm quite old enough as it is."

FINALLY ENSCONCED IN the car, Fliss flicked through *a fashion magazine* and sighed loudly for the nine hundredth time.

"I *told* you," said her dad. "We're nearly there."

"I don't give a . . . crap . . ." said Fliss, wondering how strong a word she could get away with when they were on the motorway with nowhere to stop, and she was leaving for ever anyway, " . . . how far it is to go. You can just keep driving as far as I'm concerned. Why couldn't we bring Ranald anyway?"

"Because I didn't want the window open the entire way," said her mother, looking crossly out of the window. Hattie had her head well and truly down and was supposedly reading one of her swanky upper-fourth books but Fliss could tell she hadn't turned over a page in nearly twenty minutes. She'd considered instituting back-of-the-car territory wars, but that really did make the parents stop so it probably wasn't worth it. It didn't look like they'd had any last-minute changes of heart.

"So last night," she said airily, staring at the pylons flicking

27

past, "you didn't, say, have some kind of psychic dream that said how awful it was to lose a child when they were very, very young?"

Her parents both ignored her, only glancing at each other. After the sulks and the door slamming had had no effect, she was doing what an advice columnist suggested and presenting logical sides to her problem.

"You know, studies show that marriages are at very great risk from empty nest syndrome when the children leave home. Of course, for *most* families this doesn't happen for years yet. Think what a higher risk you must have trying to do it so early."

Fliss's mother turned round awkwardly in the front seat of the Freelander.

"Darling," she said. She'd had her roots done, Fliss thought. She used to be really proud that her mother looked after herself— she was more in shape than Hattie was, that was obvious. But now she wasn't sure; her mother spent half the blooming day at the hair salon or getting her nails done, and Fliss wondered if she didn't have to bother with all that crap, maybe she'd have more time for not having to send her away to school. She thought of her friend Millie's mum, who had long gray hair. Millie always said it was a huge embarrassment and that her mum made her feel absolutely skint whenever she turned up anywhere because she looked a million years old, but Fliss liked going round there. Millie's mum was always cooking something for dinner and taking lovely bread out of the Aga or playing with the dog in their big messy kitchen. Fliss sometimes thought this was how mummies were meant to be. Mind you, when Millie came round to her house she liked to go upstairs and secretly try on some of Fliss's mum's makeup.

Fliss's mum didn't cook much. She heated stuff up for them, with a big sigh, as if it were a terrible chore to take the wrapping off a Waitrose packet. She let them have a lot of ketchup with their veg, though. She was always dashing out and complaining about being tired, though she still found plenty of time to go out in the evenings or have dinner with their dad or do a million things that seemed a bit more important than making soup or something.

It wasn't that she wasn't fun, though. Sometimes they'd all go to London and hit Selfridges and Harvey Nicks and their mum would buy them cool clothes and say, "Oh, this is too naughty" when she got her credit card out, and then take them for smoothies—Hattie and Fliss would rather have gone to McDonald's, but if they mentioned it their mother would say, "Got to watch those hips, girls!" so they didn't mention it anymore.

They'd also do their best not to fall out on those trips. Falling out meant fewer goodies. So they'd go to Oxford Street, and Hattie would get posh face cream for her spots, and Fliss would get lip gloss, and they'd try on loads of things in Top Shop, which was miles better than the one in Guildford, and when they got home their dad would cover his eyes and go, "Oh my God, how have my girls been trying to bankrupt me today," but he didn't mean it really, he was actually quite pleased. Then they'd do a fashion show with all their new kit unless they'd got anything too short, when their dad would call them a Geldof girl and make them hide it away.

Fliss sniffed hard. There wouldn't be much more of that. She bet there wouldn't be a Top Shop in the whole of Cornwall, not even a tiny concession one. She thought back over her hideous school uniform, all heavy navy blue, which didn't really work with her blond hair, and the stupid hats and elasticated gym knickers. She hated it! She hated it. She hated it.

She let out another long sigh. So did her mother.

"It's ONLY CORNWALL," Maggie had said, for what felt like the millionth time. "It's not the moon! There's not even a time difference! It's only for ten weeks at a time, they get loads of holidays."

The only person who'd been completely sanguine about the whole thing had been her headmaster, funnily enough. "Jumping from the sinking ship?" he'd said on the phone, as she nervously steeled herself to say she was leaving not long before the start of term. "Don't blame you. Don't worry about notice, there's enough wee lasses kicking around at the moment who'll jump at your job."

"Right then." Maggie had felt quite insulted. OK, she hadn't exactly thought that everyone would be standing on their chairs like in *Dead Poets Society*, but it would have been nice to think that her headmaster would remember her name.

On the home front, though, she thought as she traveled through Birmingham and down toward the west, the Fiat Panda making its displeasure known with suspicious little grunty noises, it hadn't been like that at all. Although no one would say it out loud, it seemed to be the general consensus that she'd gone all snobby on Govan and thought she was too good for them all, especially Stan.

"You know I'm not leaving you," she'd whispered, late at night, after another evening of Stan studiously ignoring her while eating a fish finger sandwich in front of *A Question of Sport*.

"So, just moving out of the house to the other end of the country. I'm so glad that's not leaving me," Stan had said.

"It's only for a few weeks at a time! You can fly down to Exeter for weekends!"

"Well, I'll have to, won't I? You're taking the car."

"I need the car."

"You need, you want, your job, your things," said Stan, turning over. "Yes, Maggie. I know it's all about you."

They hadn't even made love since she'd got the job offer. Maggie was worried. Why wasn't she more upset?

Chapter Three

Veronica stood up at the lectern and surveyed the hundreds of girls and their parents, crowding out the long hall. Part of the original cathedral structure, the long hall retained its original features—two rows of stern-looking carved stone angels, punctuating the tall arched windows that lined both sides. They seemed to be gazing down on the girls, kindly, but with a look in their eyes that suggested they'd not be amused by any mischief. That's what Simone had thought anyway. Her own mouth had been permanently open since their old car had drawn up on the sweeping gravel drive. She'd seen the pictures—*pored* over the pictures, of course—but nothing had really prepared her for the scale of the great gray towers, silhouetted against the blue sea and sky. She simply couldn't believe this was her new home, her place. Even Joel had been temporarily stunned into silence.

"Zoiks," he'd said finally. "It looks like Hogwarts."

It didn't really. It looked like a castle from long ago, set against the wind and the waves. Simone, whose tastes in reading were running quite quickly in advance of her age, was lost in a Daphne du Maurier dream, looking at the oriel windows set in the towers, and the ivy clambering up the north side.

She came back to earth with a bump as her dad, who'd been quiet the whole journey, followed the temporary signs pointing toward the "parents car park." Simone's heart started to pound even harder. This was it! She was here! She looked at the other cars entering the car park. There wasn't a single other ancient, creaky old beige Mercedes-Benz there, and there certainly wasn't one with a gold-encrusted tissue box holder in the back seat. The car park was full of 4x4s, new shiny Audis and BMWs, huge creamy Volvos, and even a couple of Bentleys, which she only recognized when Joel went, "Fffooo! Bentleys! They cost, like, a million squillion pounds!!! And the insides are made out of gold and diamonds and stuff." And when their mother told him to be quiet, in an uncharacteristically nervous-sounding voice, he was for once.

The car rolled to a stop.

"Let's get on with it then," growled her father.

OH GOD, WHAT the hell was that? Fliss squinted at the big ugly car blocking their way to the entrance.

"Great," she said. "I see they run a minicab service."

"Felicity," said her father, in his "trying to tell her off" tone of voice, which never worked. Hattie had already jumped out of the car, spying several thousand of her very closest friends and screaming at them at the top of her voice. Fliss rolled her eyes. She'd met Hattie's friends before, when they came up to visit, and she thought they were all ridiculous. As slowly as she dared she drew her hockey stick out of the boot, and turned round to see a dumpy girl emerging from the hideous brown car.

The girl was plump, with rather sallow skin and hair tightly pulled back in a ponytail. She was already wearing her full

33 🐦

school uniform; didn't she know you got to wear your home clothes on your first day?

She looked over at Fliss with a brave, friendly smile on her face. Oh great, new girls time. Better luck next time, podge, thought Fliss viciously. She didn't want friends here. She had her friends. In Guildford. Where she was going back to, just as soon as she'd figured this place out. As she turned round to pick up her suitcase, a large woman, obviously the girl's mother, and dressed in what looked like evening wear—a lot of black and sequins—clambered out of the front of the car.

"Simone! Simone!" she screeched at the top of her voice. The entire car park turned round. "We've got a present for you!"

Simone, as the plump girl must be called, gave an embarrassed-looking half-smile and turned round as her mother handed over a small package and then looked directly at Fliss's mum.

"It's an extra bra," she announced proudly, out of the blue, just like that, as if it was the kind of thing you would say in normal conversation to everyone in the world. "They grow up so fast, no?"

"Yes, they do," said Fliss's mum, with the smile she got on her face whenever she wanted to get moving somewhere down the street and they got stopped by someone who wanted them to sign up for charity.

"I am Mrs. Pribetich, Simone's mother. This is Simone's first day."

No kidding, thought Fliss, looking at Simone's skirt, which hung way down below her knees. Fliss was already planning on rolling hers up as far as she could get away with. And then a bit further.

"Caroline Prosser. Hello."

Her mother gave a rather limp handshake. Mrs. Pribetich raised her eyebrows looking at Fliss and Hattie.

"I think maybe our girls will be friends, yes?"

Not in a million years, thought Fliss, digging her hockey stick into the gravel.

Not in a million years, thought Simone, catching the look of disgust on Fliss's face. And on her mother's, come to that.

"WELCOME," VERONICA SAID. It was nice to have the whole school quiet; that wouldn't happen again for another year. "We're very pleased to welcome you here to Downey House; for our returning girls, and our new ones."

She addressed the little ones—she knew they were thirteen, not exactly babies, but they looked so young, with their scrubbed faces and long hair. Not like the older girls, who were affecting to slouch against the back of the hall, as if assembly was just too unutterably dull for words. The school—a middle and upper school—started at year three when the girls were going on fourteen, and ran up to an upper sixth. There were just over three hundred and fifty students.

Of course they were just as nervous, she knew—they had their new haircuts; their new experiences of whatever the summer had brought them, ready to be shared and picked over with the other girls. Would they still be friends? Would someone have a boyfriend when they didn't? Would they pass their exams? The jutting lips, cutting-edge outfits, careful hairstyles, and overuse of makeup (the rules about that didn't kick in till the next morning) betrayed just as many nerves as the little plump sallow-skinned girl just in front of the lectern, whose right knee was jiggling so hard she wanted to put her hand on it.

* * *

MAGGIE SPIED THE little girl jiggling too. Her heart went out to her. She didn't mind sitting up at the front of the room with all the other teachers—she was used to that. She was just a little unnerved by the level of scrutiny going on. At Holy Cross you got a quick once-over while the pupils worked out the best nicknames they could for you, so if you had a big nose, or big breasts, or anything else about you whatsoever, so much the better. Then they went back to either ignoring you or working out persecution tactics.

Here, it felt oddly like being judged by a group of your peers. You didn't need to glance too long at the girls here to realize just how big the poverty gap in Britain was. Very of these girls were overweight—there were a couple plump with puppy fat, but it was a healthy, pink-cheeked big-bummed horse-riding look, thought Maggie, not the gloopy rolls that accumulated on so many of the girls at her old school through endless processed meat and pastry and no fruit and veg. And regardless of the cover of the school's prospectus—which looked like those old Benetton ads—there was a lot of homogeneity; blond hair, pale skin. One or two staggeringly beautiful black girls who looked like (and probably were) African princesses of some kind; some Middle Eastern girls too, but nothing like the ragtag mix of Polish, Hindi, and patois she'd been used to.

Her mind jumped to the surprisingly comfortable suite of rooms in the East Tower that Miss Prenderghast had shown her to. There was a pretty sitting room with a lovely view out to sea (currently rather gray and imposing), a floral sofa, and a round dining table. She also had a small bedroom at the back with a single bed covered by a toile counterpane. Maybe when Stan came down they could book a bed-and-breakfast somewhere. Nobody had asked about her marital status, but there'd been a few glances at her empty ring finger, which was quite funny. She was also to share a small office, though with whom she didn't yet know, where she was expected to meet the girls and take seminars for the older ones preparing for university.

Bringing herself back to the assembly, she glanced round at her fellow teachers; she'd only had ten minutes to try and meet as many of them as possible. The deputy head, and head of English—in effect her immediate boss—was a pinched woman, far too thin for her age, called Miss Starling. Not Ms. The Miss was unmistakable. She'd obviously been at Downey House for about nine thousand years and wasn't intending to look on Maggie as anything else but an interloper till she'd been there three generations, probably. From first glance (or rather, the first time Miss Starling had said, "Now, I know that modern com-pre-HEN-sive teaching doesn't emphasize discipline, but here, Ms. Adair, we like SI-lence in the classroom," overemphasizing odd syllables and making, not for the last time, Maggie figured, reference to her more humble beginnings), Maggie had guessed that Miss Starling might be a teacher the pupils respected, but not one they liked or enjoyed. Which felt like such a shame; if you couldn't have a bit of fun and interest in English, you were unlikely to get it anywhere in the curriculum.

Then there was Mam'selle Crozier, the French mistress. Maggie had liked her immediately. Tall and slender—*mais bien sûr*—she looked like she too might be quite stern but in fact had immediately let out an infectious giggle and said in a low voice how "*superrr*" it was to have someone around her own age, and that they must go out for a drink, which cheered Maggie immensely; she'd had images of lots of long dark evenings in her room on her own, correcting papers and worrying about whether Stan had eaten any vegetables.

"Do not worry," the French teacher had said. "Some of them are leetle sheets, but that is simply teaching, *non*? And the rest are superrr."

Maggie was sitting in the front row on the stage, waiting to be introduced to the school. She felt a shot of adrenaline run through her and a distinct shiver of nerves.

VERONICA HOPED SHE'D done the right thing employing Margaret Adair. She looked so nervous sitting there, and quite out of place in the same old suit—she'd really need to have a word. She knew students had debts and so on these days, but this was quite ridiculous, there was no excuse for not grooming yourself. She hoped the girls would understand her and not start laughing the moment she opened her mouth (this hadn't occurred to Maggie)—the accent really was very Glaswegian. However. Nothing ventured, nothing gained.

"I'd like to introduce our new English teacher, replacing Mrs. Ferrers," she said. "Ms. Adair has come to us all the way from Glasgow. She's worked in different types of schools that have given her a real view of life at the sharp edge, which I think is going to make her a huge asset here at Downey, so please give her your warmest welcome, girls."

"SINK," SAID A voice next to Fliss. They were sitting cross-legged on the floor. Fliss didn't think she could keep it up for much longer—what was it, some kind of prison camp torture? Nobody else seemed to mind, but her calves were killing her.

"What?" she whispered. She was sitting next to a beautiful black-haired girl, with dark blue eyes and a slightly supercilious expression.

"She's a sink teacher, isn't she? Obvious. 'Life at the sharp edge.' They must be getting desperate."

Fliss glanced sideways with some admiration, not only for the girl's obvious prettiness. She was obviously annoyed to be here too.

"Do you know lots about the school?" she whispered, as Maggie stood up on stage, thanked everyone nicely, and said how much she was looking forward to . . . blah blah blah. She sounded like that politician who made her dad swear whenever he came on the radio. Oh God, if the teachers were going to be crap too, that was all she needed. She looked about Hattie's age.

"Enough to know I don't want to be here," said the girl. "Hello. I'm Alice."

"Fliss. I don't want to be here either."

"Excuse me," came a voice. "Are you two chatting?"

It was Miss Starling. She was their head of year so they'd met her already. Fliss felt a thrill of fear.

"No, miss," said Alice contritely, looking innocent.

"A teacher is talking," said Miss Starling. "Not a peep out of you two please. On your first day too!"

MAGGIE FELT HER face burn up. She was furious. How dare another teacher impose discipline when she was talking? She'd immediately been shown up as an amateur in front of the whole school. She shot a quick glance at Miss Starling, a glance not missed by Veronica. Interesting, thought Veronica. Quite the little spark of temper in there. But she was quite right; June Starling had absolutely no business telling off girls in front of other teachers; it was sheer showing off. Perhaps it was time for the school song, the rousing "Downey Hall," named after the original building. She nodded to Mrs. Offili, the hearty, beefy, and universally adored head of music, who banged down on the piano with a rousing hand.

We are the girls
The Girls of Downey Hall
We stand up proud
And we hold our heads up tall
We serve the Queen
Our country, God, and home
We dare to dream
Of wsider plains to roam
We are the girls
The Girls of Downey Hall.

SIMONE, HAVING LEARNED the song off by heart before she arrived, had jumped up with pride when she heard the piano start up. Quickly, she'd realized she was first up, and that her enthusiasm was being met with sniggers from some of the surrounding girls. She felt her face flame pink, before the teachers all stood up too and there was a general shuffling of chairs being pushed back and feet clomping up on the dusty wooden floor.

To Simone, used to a *laissez-faire* comprehensive environment, everything so far had passed in a whirr of queues and laundry bags and a blur of girls running all around. Quite a lot of the girls, it seemed, already knew each other from their "prep" schools. Simone didn't know what a prep school was, exactly. And they were all so . . . they were so small, and petite, and pretty. Or, the ones who weren't small were tall and willowy, like reeds, with long limbs lightly tanned by the sun. One or two were even wearing sandals showing painted toenails.

Miss Starling, the head of Plantagenet House, to which she'd been assigned, had terrified her—simply glancing up briskly, saying, "You're the scholarship girl, are you? Well done. Well, we hope to see a lot of work out of you. Not just for yourself, but to inspire the other girls. In fact, I don't expect to have to pay you much attention at all. You know what will happen if you don't get your act together, don't you? There's a lot of girls from backgrounds like yours that would kill for the opportunity. Don't mess it up."

"No, miss," Simone had said, her head pointed directly toward the floor.

"No, Miss Starling," Miss Starling had said.

"No, Miss Starling."

They were called in to meet the headmistress too before her parents left. Simone just wanted them to go. She could see they didn't belong, and they felt it too. The other mothers were all chic and sleek-looking; they had short blond hair and wore gently draping things in soft colors, or smartly tailored suits, or even slim-cut trousers. Nobody was wearing a large black dress with sequins at the neck, nobody, even if Simone's mum had announced that she thought everyone would dress like Princess Diana so she was going to too.

Simone was in awe of the headmistress's office immediately. It was so beautiful. The far wall was covered with a heavy old-fashioned print wallpaper, but nearly obscured by paintings, which, although different in styles—some abstract, some figures, a large oil painting of a horse that Simone adored immediately—all seemed to blend together well. The other wall was filled with floor-length windows that looked straight out over the cliffs and out to sea. Many had been the badly behaved girl who'd sat there, staring and wishing herself on a boat, far, far away!

Veronica looked up from her desk. She was aware—more than any of the other teachers or students knew, or ever would—of the difficulties of coming from one world into the next. Many of the scholarship girls they got were what she thought of as the "genteel poor": middle-class girls whose parents had fallen on hard times, but still knew the value of an excellent education. Some of them went through the school quite happily with no one even knowing; the school gave a grant for uniforms, and families scraped together for the rest, so it was only the lack of Easter suntans and talk of new cars at seventeen that would give the game away, and then only to a close observer.

From her first glance at Mrs. Pribetich's hair, however, she realized that this was something else—a genuine girl from a difficult background. Her heart softened as soon as she looked at Simone, whose body was pasty from too much time in with her books, and fat from too many sweets and biscuits, no doubt given as well-intentioned treats. She needed lots of fresh air, exercise, good food, and encouragement of the right sort; she sensed the problem might be prying Simone away from her books, rather than the other way around.

"Welcome," she said. Over the years Veronica's voice had become incredibly genteel. Simone might have felt more at home if she'd known how it started out. "Welcome to Downey House."

"Thank you," said Simone. Her mother nudged her. "I mean, thank you for the opportunity to attend your, ehm, august seat of learning, and I hope that I'll be a credit to you and this institution for many years to come."

Veronica stifled a smile. Actually she could do with more girls coming in with that attitude, even if they were forced to learn a rote speech.

"Well, good. Thank you. That's nice to hear."

"We're just so proud of her," said the mother. "You know, she's such a good girl, and so obedient and never stops studying . . ."

Veronica ignored her, but in a positive way.

"Simone," she said. "We're very pleased to welcome you here. Many girls aim for a scholarship to Downey, and very, very few succeed. It's a great achievement."

Simone went bright pink and stared at her lap.

"But, now you're here, I want you to take advantage of everything we can offer you. Downey House isn't just about books and exams, although those are part of it. It's about becoming a confident, rounded young woman. It's about being able to take on the world. So I don't want you to chain yourself to the library. I want you to get out there; to enjoy the fresh air; to make good friendships with the other girls; to participate in as many sports and societies as you can, and to throw yourself into everything with as much enthusiasm as you've thrown yourself into getting in here."

Simone nodded mutely. The idea of her becoming a confident young woman like the ones she'd seen standing around the assembly hall, so terrifyingly beautiful and self-assured—well, she'd never be like that in a million years, about as long as it would take her to . . . get on a pony. But she knew she always had to agree with what the teacher said.

"You'll get a lot out of Downey House—as long as you give a lot back."

Simone looked up through her glasses. What an unprepossessing child, thought Veronica. Just one big bundle of nerves.

She really did hope the school would knock some of it out of her, and not drive her more into herself.

"Yes, miss," said Simone.

SIMONE'S MOTHER HAD finally been persuaded to get back into the car, howling and wailing, just as the very last of the parents were setting off. Simone watched her, her insides clenching with embarrassment. Not one of the other mothers had clung to their daughters, weeping huge tears, and certainly none of the other fathers had had to pull off the mothers and practically fold them into the car.

From above, though, through one of the dormitory windows, the girls were watching.

Each spacious dorm took four girls and had its own bathroom, comfortable single beds that the girls brought their own duvet covers for, and a cupboard, desk, and bedside cabinet for each one. Fliss Prosser looked down from her assigned room into the car park below (sea views were reserved for older students).

"Look at this," she scoffed to Alice, who was in the same dorm. "God, if my mother did that I'd be so embarrassed."

"So's she," pointed out Alice. "But still—eww."

They both looked over to the still empty bed in their room. The third was taken by a quiet student called Imogen, who'd unpacked her belongings immaculately and immediately sat down at her desk with her back to the room and started to cram for their maths course. But the fourth was ominously empty.

"Oh God," said Alice. "That means . . . she's ours! The hippopotamus!"

"Ssh!" said Fliss. It wasn't nice, really it wasn't. But Alice was so pretty and funny and lively, it was impossible not to want to be her friend.

"What if she makes big snuffling heffalump noises at night? And cries all the time? And leaves hairs all down the sink? It'd be *terrible*."

Fliss couldn't help herself. She snuffled up her nose and did a pretty good imitation of grunting.

"Snorty . . . I'll just sleep here . . . SNORT."

"Got any turnips I can eat?" said Alice. "That's what we have back in my country."

"Yes," said Fliss. "My mum had some decorating her hat!"

The girls collapsed into fits of giggles that suddenly went silent. There, framed in the doorway, pale and scared-looking, was Simone.

Fliss's first instinct was to apologize. Simone looked like a wounded animal, like Ranald with a thorn in his paw, and her instinct was for kindness, and to look after the weaker person. But she felt Alice's eyes upon her, sizing her up to see what she would do. And Fliss remembered how cross she was to be there, and how she certainly wasn't going to worry about anyone else.

"Oh, hi," she said, in a disdainful tone of voice. "I suppose that's your bed then."

MAGGIE SAT ON her bed with her hands clasped. It was odd; she felt like she didn't know what to do. She tried ringing Stan again, and this time she got him. She had the weird feeling that he wasn't picking up his mobile before. It was odd, that sense that she felt he was there, but deliberately not answering the phone. It wasn't like him; normally he was thrilled to hear from her in the day.

"Hiya," he said, in a neutral tone.

"Hi, sweetie," she said, trying to sound as normal as possible. "How are you? How are you doing?"

"I'm not in hospital," said Stan irritably. "I'm just having my life as normal, remember? It's you who's disappeared."

"I haven't disappeared," said Maggie, rolling her eyes. She didn't want an argument, just a friendly voice when she was hundreds of miles away, in a tower of a castle filled with four hundred people she didn't know.

"Hmm," said Stan. He was eating.

"Are you having chips?" she asked him. Dinner had been perfectly serviceable, but undeniably plain, lamb chops, green beans, and mash. Some chips from the Golden Fry down the road suddenly felt like a fabulous idea.

"Uh huh," said Stan.

"Are they good?"

"Why, are youse somewhere too poncey for chips now?"

"I am actually," said Maggie. "There must be some at the seaside. But I think the school is a chip-free zone. That's what you pay for."

"People paying to be deprived of chips," scoffed Stan. "Sounds a pretty stupid setup to me."

Maggie found herself agreeing with him—anything to hear his voice soften.

"So, how is it then?" he asked grudgingly. "Do you live in a castle now?"

"It is a bit like a castle actually," Maggie admitted. "It's very formal, much more than I thought. All the girls have to stand up when the head passes, that kind of thing."

"Bloody hell. Do they still get caned and stuff?"

"No, not here. Apparently the boys' school over the hill still does, but only for real transgressions. And even that's only because the parents like it, apparently—they never do it really, they just put it in the prospectus."

"Sick," whistled Stan.

Maggie wanted to tell him about all the new teachers she'd met, and the grand hall, and her neat little suite of rooms, and how excited and trepidatious she was about the next morning and taking her first class. But she knew deep down that he wouldn't—couldn't—share her enthusiasm and that it wasn't really fair to try and make him.

"So, how was your day?" she asked, timidly.

Stan paused. "It was the same as every day," he said, as if surprised she'd asked. "Same old jerks, same old distribution problems. Oh, no, hang on, I came home to an empty house with no dinner. That was a bit different."

Maggie didn't take the bait. She was so tired anyway, it had been such a long day. "I'll be back soon," she said soothingly. "And you must come down. We'll find chips, I promise."

Stan made a noncommittal grunt, then there was a silence.

"Well, I'd better get to bed," Maggie said. "Big day tomorrow and everything."

"Yeah," said Stan. "Well, you have a big day tomorrow. Mine is pretty small, I expect."

"Hmm," said Maggie, feeling tired of his whingy tone, and then guilty for being annoyed. "Well, goodnight then . . ."

Stan either didn't hear the appeal in her voice—for him to say something nice, to say he loved her or he missed her; anything at all. He either didn't hear it, or he ignored it.

VERONICA COULDN'T BELIEVE it had taken her all day to get round to opening the post. Yes, she was terribly busy, but even so . . . Miss Prenderghast would have taken care of much of it this morning, but would still have left out the pieces she felt Veronica should see—invoices to initial; letters from concerned parents or applicants; and government circulars trying to interfere with things, which she generally binned immediately.

This was different, however. It was from the charities commission—many private schools were registered charities and, as such, didn't pay tax—talking about an assessment.

Veronica's school was exempt from goverment inspections, belonging as it did to the private sector. However, there were "voluntary" assessments that could be carried out, which worked in roughly the same way. They were becoming less and less voluntary as parents became more and more savvy about standards and league tables, and Veronica knew, deep down, that she wasn't going to be able to refuse—she'd put them off in the past, and if she put them off again, it would start to ring warning bells.

Sitting up in bed, she smoothed her neat gray hair behind her ears. If she hadn't ruthlessly trained it out of herself, she would have sworn. The last thing she needed was people picking over the school, nosing their beaks into her affairs. This was a wonderful school and she ran it very well. And beyond that was nobody's business.

Chapter Four

Maggie woke up blinking at the unfamiliar sunlight glancing off the rough white painted ceiling of her small bedroom. At first she had no idea where she was. Then she remembered, and a sharp bolt of excitement ran through her. She, Maggie Adair, was assistant head of English at one of the smartest girls' schools in the country! She was going to take fine young minds and fill them with words, and creativity and learning and . . .

A loud bell roared and Maggie jumped out of her skin. It sounded like a fire alarm, but didn't last. She looked at her phone. Seven o'clock! Did the bells really start ringing at seven o'clock in the morning? Every morning? This she was not going to like.

Still, she was up now. She went to the window and opened it wide, inhaling the lovely salt air off the sea. Why had she never lived by the sea before? Why had she always looked out on housing estates and not the little white hulls of trawlers bobbing off in the distance? Because she couldn't afford it, she supposed. Well, she was coming up in the world now. As she gazed out in a reverie, she heard a frantic cursing next to her in what sounded like French. She leaned over and looked to her left. Sure enough, there was Mademoiselle Crozier and, tumbling from her fingers, a lit cigarette.

"Hello," she said. Mademoiselle Crozier was wearing a black satin robe that looked incredibly luxurious for a teacher. Maggie instantly swore to finally get rid of her old terry cloth dressing gown that Stan had repeatedly pointed out made her look like the Gruffalo.

"*Merde*," said Mam'selle. "Oh, it's you. I 'ave dropped my cigarette."

"Won't they think it's one of the girls?"

"*Mais oui*, and then there will be a grand inquisition, *non*?" She stared gloomily at the grass below. "Perhaps it will all catch on fire and the evidence will be gone."

"We could sneak down and pick it up," offered Maggie. "I won't tell anyone."

"Sank you," said Mam'selle. "It is strictly *non* here, *non*?"

"*Oui*, Mam'selle" said Maggie smiling. "Shall we go for breakfast?"

Mademoiselle rolled her eyes. "You have not tried the coffee. No breakfast for me. But please, call me Claire."

Maggie felt pleased. She thought she was going to like Mam'selle. Then she thought about her first class, and her chest tightened uncomfortably. It was one of the first forms, or what she thought of as year three—there were four forms, one from each house, so hopefully they'd be as nervous as she was and not inclined to try and trip her up. She *hoped*.

She had her lesson plan set out, based on what had worked well with her smarter pupils at Holy Cross, and had chosen for her first years a book she'd found the most terrifying thing she'd ever read when she was a teenager, *Brother in the Land*, about a young male survivor of a nuclear holocaust in England. She found it worked perfectly by being so scary that, if you got it as your first book, you also assumed that the teacher was very scary and might well bring down Armageddon on your head at any time. Almost as effective as displaying lots of strong discipline, and vastly easier. Obviously there was the odd complaint from parents when their thirteen-year-olds started wetting their beds again, but surely they were made of sterner stuff at boarding school.

Pulling on a jumper over her pajama bottoms, she decided it was too beautiful a morning to waste; and that there wasn't much point in not living on a housing estate anymore if she didn't get out and enjoy it.

The main hall, with its plaster angels, was eerily quiet—the girls were all in their towers, she assumed, brushing teeth and getting ready for the day. She padded across the hall in her Birkenstocks—ugly, but incredibly useful—and out into the dewy morning.

Goodness, but it was beautiful. The crests of the distant waves were whipped white, the morning with its last streaks of pink in the air. A fresh pure salty wind was blowing that felt as though she was getting her brain washed.

First, Maggie rounded the East Tower and peered at the grass. Sure enough, there was a handful of butts, some with lipstick around them. Surely Claire didn't wear lipstick to bed? Well, maybe the French did that kind of thing—Maggie had never had a friend from another country before. She took a bag out of her pocket and started lifting them up.

"Ah," came a voice. Maggie looked up. It was Miss Starling, immaculate in a purple tweed suit. Maggie smiled nervously,

Jenny Colgan

conscious of her old University of Strathclyde sweatshirt and pulled-back hair.

"Good morning," she said. She had to get it into her head that this woman was a colleague, not her teacher. Her boss, yes, but not her housemistress.

"Miss Adair. Good morning!"

She stared at Maggie with the cigarette butts in her hand.

"I don't know if it was made clear at the interview, and I know things are different in . . . our more *deprived* parts of the country, but we don't tolerate smoking at this school. At all. It's against the law and it's a bad example for the girls. When you're in town, I suppose, if you must, but it's *completely* forbidden on school property . . ."

"I don't . . ." stuttered Maggie, looking at the butts in her hand. Miss Starling raised an eyebrow. Maggie considered dropping Claire in it, but realized she couldn't. "Uh, all right."

"Well, let us say no more about it. Off for an early morning walk?"

Maggie nodded, not knowing the right answer.

"Very good. Helps the constitution. Good day!"

Maggie watched her stalk off, feeling a little weak and trembly. This was ridiculous. She couldn't be frightened of her boss. She thought of her old head of English, Mr. Frower, invariably known as Percy, even though the children weren't old enough to remember how he'd gotten his nickname. He'd nipped out for fags in the middle of lessons and was regularly to be found sticking on videos of shows only roughly connected with the topic and wandering off for a sit-down. The time two of his children fluked their way to B's, they practically had to have a party for him. Oh yes, things had changed.

Maggie struck out for the clifftops, feeling, despite her telling off, that the world belonged to her. The only soul she could see was a gardener, down in the far end of the grounds. There was a whole team of gardeners. "I have a whole team of gardeners," Maggie thought to herself with a grin, and almost broke into a skip as she headed toward the garden gate.

"LOOK AT THAT," said Alice scornfully, looking out of their dormitory window as the small figure of Maggie could be seen, wandering over the grounds. "What on earth is she wearing? What does she think she looks like? Are those *pajamas*?"

Fliss had never seen a teacher in pajamas before. She couldn't resist taking a peek.

"God," Alice said. "Look at the arse she's displaying to the world! That is rude, man."

Fliss looked at herself in the mirror. Then she looked at Alice, who was combing out her long dark hair and looked beautiful and extremely confident. She needed a bit of that. She'd love to be so sure of herself. So she nodded and joined in.

"Isn't it true they all eat deep-fried Mars bars in Scotland?" she said.

"I don't know," said Alice. "It's impossible to understand a *word* they say. I think they all have heart attacks, though. Which should get us out of double English."

Quietly, as if trying to make herself as small and unnoticeable as possible, Simone shuffled past into the bathroom. She was wearing huge pink pajamas covered in little pictures of dogs. She'd noticed that the other girls wore slinky Calvin Klein bottoms and tiny little tank tops to bed, which showed off their little Keira Knightley tummies and high round breasts. How did they know what to wear to bed? Was there some sort of a memo sent round? Her mum had bought her these pajamas be-

Jenny Colgan

cause they'd both thought they were cute, and they were cheap in Primark, and nice cozy flannel, because Mrs. Rishkian down at the laundrette had heard that these boarding schools weren't heated and she'd need to be nice and warm.

Alice regarded her steadily in the mirror.

"Nice pajamas," she said in a neutral tone.

"Thanks," said Simone, coloring and looking for her toothbrush.

"Primark?" Alice asked.

"Yes!" said Simone, amazed that this gorgeous girl seemed to be making reasonable conversation with her.

Alice looked at Fliss. "I'd never have guessed."

Fliss felt bad. "I'm going to go and get dressed," she said. "Your pajamas are cute, Simone."

Alice rolled her eyes.

The blowing blustery clifftops brought some of Maggie's confidence back. She felt exhilarated by the whipping waves and the clouds racing over the sky, as the sun steadily warmed her back.

"*I wandered lonely as a cloud!*" she shouted into the head of the wind. "*That floats on high o'er vales and hills . . .*"

Getting into it now she started to declaim louder and louder, enjoying the sensation of roaring into the wind and being so very far away from everything she found familiar.

"*. . . And then my chest with pleasure fills,*" she concluded, throwing out an arm to a hovering audience of gulls and cormorants, and imagining her new class applauding and being inspired and moved by poetry. "*And dances with the daffodils!*"

"Oh, very good," came a voice, and, from almost directly beneath her feet, a man emerged from the undergrowth, clapping.

54

"Shit!" shouted Maggie and jumped back, almost losing her footing.

"Sorry, sorry!" said the man, putting up his hands to make it clear he wasn't a threat. As well he might, thought Maggie, hiding in the undergrowth next to a girls' school. She fumbled in her pajama pockets for her mobile phone. Maybe she'd have to call the police. She hadn't brought it. Shit. Shit. She felt her face flush.

"It's OK," he said. "I was on the path, see? It goes just below here. I was walking my dog."

As if to prove this to her he whistled and a lovely mongrel bounded up, hopping joyously.

"Oh what a nice dog," said Maggie, unable to help herself. She was fairly sure that pedophile perverts didn't have nice dogs. "What is it?"

"A bitter," said the man. "Bit o' this, bit o' that, you know?"

She smiled, despite herself. "I was just . . ."

"Yes, what *were* you doing? I can see you're questioning my motives, but I'm afraid you are *much* more suspicious. Out shouting loudly in your underwear?"

Oh God. Maggie felt her face get even redder. "I was just practicing some poetry. And these are perfectly decent pajamas, thank you."

"Well, you obviously haven't seen the hole in the back. And a bit of Wordsworth. Very nice. Although I think you'll find it's 'my *heart* with pleasure fills.'"

"I'm the new English teacher at Downey House."

"*Are* you?" His face split into a wide, slightly manic grin. "Well, very nice to meet you, New English Teacher at Downey House. I'm your opposite number."

He stuck out his hand. Maggie stuck hers out to meet it before realizing it was covered in cigarette ash from picking up Claire's butts. She quickly pulled it back and scratched the dog's neck instead. The man didn't seem to mind.

"What do you mean?"

"I'm David McDonald. Head of English at Downey Boys."

Maggie still didn't know what he was talking about.

"The boys' school? Over the headland? Downers? That's what the boys call it. Or Downey's Syndrome, if they're in the mood to be really horrid, which as we know all boys are. You'd think they'd use a bit of imagination . . ."

Maggie wasn't entirely sure how to get him to stop talking.

"Oh," she said, just pitching herself in in the middle. "Wow. Hello then!"

"We'll be seeing a bit of each other then," said David. Maggie realized to her horror that she was meeting a new professional colleague (and possible ally—though his grin was a bit loopy, she liked his dog) while still in her damn pajamas. She was going to bin these things asap. "Inter-school debates, that kind of thing. Are you interested in drama?"

"Uh, yes, definitely."

"I think I could tell by your excellent presentation. Well, good. We should talk about that sometime."

"Uh huh," said Maggie, embarrassed now by her wild hair bushing around her face and her nicotine-stained fingers.

"Well, I'd best get going. The brutes will be going feral. And as for the boys . . ."

"OK then," said Maggie, smiling. "OK. Bye."

"Come on, Stephen Daedalus!" It took a minute for Maggie to realize he was shouting on his dog. "See you around!"

"Uh, yeah OK!"

But her voice was swept away on the wind as she watched him descend back along the cliff path.

BACK AT THE school, things were much, much busier, even though Maggie hadn't been away twenty minutes. She realized immediately one of her worst fears—who on earth had she thought she was, dashing out onto the moors without a second thought? Catherine from *Wuthering Heights*? Yes, probably. Impetuous behavior; always a fault in her, she knew, particularly unsuited to being a teacher.

The front courtyard was teeming with girls looking for their classes. Oh no, Maggie thought crossly. She was going to have to go through the whole courtyard, full of girls, in her pajamas. Which possibly had a hole in the back—she wasn't 100 percent sure she believed the rather mischievous-looking Mr. McDonald. On her very first morning. This kind of thing, she knew, could ruin a teacher's rep forever. At her old school a new recruit, Mr. Samson, had turned up on his first day with a stain on his tie. He'd spent the rest of his career as Bird-shit Samson, and never knew why. She had such a short time to make a good impression—she was already going to seem so strange and foreign to most of them, at least if it worked the other way as to how strange and foreign they felt to her.

Stupidly, she found herself hiding behind her parked car. What was she going to do? What? Wait until they all went into lessons? But then she'd be late! That wasn't much better, Miss Starling would doubtless have a thing or two to say about it. Who was she less afraid of, the girls or Miss Starling? She wasn't sure.

* * *

Jenny Colgan

VERONICA REPLACED HER teacup thoughtfully as she considered drawing down the blinds. Was that her new teacher hiding out in the car park? *Surely* not. Obviously she'd gone out on a limb with the appointment, but it was rare that her judgment was quite as poor as that. Oh, that would be all she needed, a new headache to add to the other things they were going to have to go through this year. She returned her gaze to the pile of paperwork on her desk. Examiners were suggesting commencing over a three-week period during which they would sit in on classes, talk to selected pupils (selected by whom? Veronica wondered drily), look at the school accounts, and generally poke their big noses into everything. Including, Veronica worried, herself.

Goodness me, what *was* that ridiculous Scottish girl doing? The whole point of this school was to teach young ladies calm and order, not how to run about in their underwear, something half the sixth form needed almost no practice in anyway. She would definitely have to have a word.

"PSSST," CAME A voice. On the verge of panic, Maggie cut her eyes to the side. There, sidling through the car park and squeezing through the very small spaces between the cars with an elegant swing of her hips, was Claire.

"What are you doing? *Qu'est-ce que vous faites?*" she demanded, obviously so used to teaching in two languages she didn't really let it go at any other time. As she got close Maggie could smell the cigarettes on her breath.

"I can get out but I can't get back in," whispered Maggie frantically. "I've never taught at a school where there were people *all the time* before."

"That ees no problem," said Claire. "Follow me."

And she sidled off (Maggie found it difficult to get through some of the smaller spaces between the parked cars) all the way round the building, via the hedges, to a small door round the back of their turret that Maggie hadn't even noticed.

"Fire exit," explained Claire. "It should not be open from the outside, huh, it will encourage the girls to misbehave. But for one morning only . . ."

"I think," said Maggie, "you behave worse than any of the girls here."

Claire smiled. "You cannot get a reasonable loaf of bread from here to Le Touquet," she said. "One must do sometheeng for fun, *non*?"

Maggie made it upstairs, showered, changed, and went into assembly with mere moments to spare. She was ready.

Chapter Five

Fliss looked at the card as she stood by the old-fashioned wooden pigeonholes, trying to ignore all the older girls shouting and gossiping with one another. Alice had disappeared and she felt entirely on her own. Half of it made her want to sneer and rip it up. Half of it made her want to cry.

Our darling Felicity, the card said. *We know this is the first day of a great adventure for you. You may not think we are doing the right thing, but we think you will thrive and grow up into the wonderful young woman we know you can be.*

Fliss's throat had got a lump in it just then. She was glad no one else was around to see.

So do what you can to make us proud and we know you'll be happy too.

All of a sudden she felt a whirl in her stomach as someone picked her up and spun her round.

"All right, baby sis?"

It was Hattie. She was wearing her prefect's badge proudly on her blazer and her navy jumper tied loosely over her shoulders in a way Fliss couldn't help finding extremely irritating.

"Hey," said Hattie, grabbing the card out of Fliss's hands. "Is that from home?"

"Give it back!" said Fliss. "It's private mail! It's MINE!"

"Don't be silly," said Hattie, who'd never had the faintest problem with bursting into Fliss's room at odd times of day, or flicking through her diary (which Fliss kept out in the stables now). "What could they possibly be writing to you that they wouldn't want me to see?" She scanned the note quickly. "Oh yeah. They sent one just like this to me." She sniffed.

"Did they?" Fliss felt immediately crestfallen. She'd thought she'd detected Daddy's hand in the card; that he had wanted to send her some reassurance, try and suggest that he hadn't really wanted her to go at all, that they loved her too much.

"Yeah, yeah. It's just meant to make you work hard. Mind you, did the job for me."

"What do you mean?" said Fliss, red-faced and upset.

"Oh yeah, I didn't want to come here either. Thought you'd get to stay behind having all the fun. But I did what they said, and it's been the making of me," said Hattie. "I might even make captain of netball this year. So. Listen to them. They know what's best for you." She gave a patronizing smile. "And so do I. Even if you don't think so at the moment." She bustled off importantly.

Fliss's fists clenched by her sides and she felt fury burn up inside her. So everyone knew what was best, did they? Well, they'd see about that! She wasn't going to turn into a useless busybody suckbutt like Hattie, no way.

"Hello, Fliss," said Alice, wandering up, looking pristine in an oddly impertinent way—her uniform was a little too tidy; her shirt a little too white. It looked as though she was challenging you to say something about it. "Want to pretend we got lost and be late for class?"

Fliss realized one of her fists was clenched, and slowly let it unfurl.

"Sure," she said.

SIMONE LOOKED ROUND the empty classroom. Where was everyone? Was she in the right place? Her skirt button was rubbing. She shouldn't have had that extra slice of bacon this morning. But the breakfast had been brilliant; fried bread and sausage and yogurt and fresh fruit. No coffee, like she got at home, except for sixth formers, but she'd had tea with four sugars and there was no one to tut like her mum did. Plus she'd heard the girls say they only got a top-up feed on the first morning so she should make the most of it.

The refectory was a high-ceilinged paneled room, with high-set windows, long wooden tables, and benches that sat eight or ten; the room's bad acoustics meant that while the clanging of knives and forks was always loud, it was sometimes difficult to hear even your neighbor. Hence everyone shouted.

From where she'd been sitting on the end of the row by herself, Simone couldn't believe all the other girls seemed to have coupled up already. How was that possible? It wasn't that she wasn't used to eating by herself; God, at St. Cat's it had happened all the time. But how had all these girls managed to fit in so quickly? Even their haircuts were similar. Was there some memo that went round that said you had to have long silky straight-cut hair without a fringe, as well as the PE kit and a boater? Had she missed it? She'd stroked her fuzzy plaits nervously. Simone didn't realize that a lot of these girls came from the same small number of "feeder" schools that educated them to take the exam. Half of them had already met at pony club, or their mothers were friends, having been to the same school twenty years before.

Sitting at the end of the row she'd watched them enviously as she stuffed two sausages inside a sandwich and covered it liberally in ketchup.

"Oh, this food is great," one girl was saying.

"Heavenly." But, oddly, neither of them was actually eating. Carefully, one of the girls had fished a piece of kiwi fruit out of the fruit salad and popped it in her mouth.

"I'm stuffed," she said. "Huge supper last night."

"Ya, me too," said another.

"And my stash is just to die for," said a third. "My mother sent me an entire bloody fruitcake. I think I ate the whole thing."

Simone had stuffed down the rest of her sandwich and sidled away as quickly as she could, to puzzled glances from the others. As soon as she was nearly out of earshot, naughty Alice had said, "I just can't make up my mind—transfer from Roedean or, perhaps . . . *scholarship*?" And the whole table had dissolved in laughter.

Now Simone sat alone in the English classroom, trying to figure it all out.

ASSEMBLY AND ROLL call over—a lengthy and tedious allocation of classrooms, timetables, groupings, and house leaders—Maggie was at last ready to teach her first lesson. All her classes were Plantagenets, and she had a pastoral role toward Middle School 1. So, thought Maggie, running it through her head. Pregnancy, skag, fighting, and usually the first time they got thrown out of the house and temporarily rendered homeless.

63

Oh, no, hang on. It wouldn't be like that here. With any luck it would only be periods and missing tennis rackets.

She looked through it all nervously in the staff room. Some modern poetry, nothing too frightening, plus the novel. She was looking forward to *Wuthering Heights* and *Tess* for the older ones; she'd never been able to teach those before, as the boy halves of her classes, even the small senior ones, groaned and rolled their eyes laboriously whenever they came out, whereas the girls could just float away on a cloud of doomed romance. Although, she wondered, maybe all the girls here would have read those books already? They were going to be way ahead of what she was used to. What if this was the equivalent for them of Noddy stories?

Well, it was on the curriculum, so that was what they would have. The A-level students, who came in in the afternoon, were doing Chaucer. She cursed. She hated Chaucer, always had. So hard to interpret and not that funny when you finally managed it. Still, Miss Starling had just told her, before dashing out to get over to Tudor, that the A-level students were quiet, studious girls in this house, expected to do extremely well and good self-starters. The way she'd said it left Maggie in no doubt that the reason they were such paragons of virtue was because of Miss Starling's immaculate regime, which she had no wish of changing.

Well, we'll see, thought Maggie, smoothing down her checked jacket in the ladies and checking she didn't have any grass in her hair, just as the bell tolled again, loud and clear. Maggie took a deep breath and headed out to her classroom.

"Hello," she said cheerily to the lone girl, a chubby lass who seemed to be eating. "I'm Miss Adair. The new English teacher."

"Hello, miss," mumbled Simone, embarrassed that she'd been caught out. Her mother had sent her some *mamaliga* cakes in the post—she must have mailed them before they'd even left yesterday. The grease had stained through the wrapper, but they tasted of home, so good she didn't care. Even the smell made her think of them all sitting on the big brown settee, watching *X Factor* and bugging their dad to let them phone in again. She even missed Joel kicking her in the ankle when he thought she was taking up more than her fair share of the cushions. She had a lump in her throat. What was she doing here?

"Are you eating?" asked Maggie, thinking as she always did, how much saying this made her sound like a teacher.

"Yes miss," said Simone, turning a deep shade of purple. In trouble! On her first day.

"Well, are you allowed to eat with your other teachers?"

"No, miss."

"So why do you think I'm going to be any different? Give me that please."

Sniveling, Simone handed up the parcel of home. Maggie debated throwing it in the bin—it looked like soggy bread and smelled very peculiar—but she could sense with this girl she probably wasn't going to have to be too tough.

"You can pick it up after school," she said. Simone nodded numbly.

Great, thought Maggie. Been here ten seconds and have already reduced my first pupil to a dumbstruck sodden mess.

"What's your name?" she asked kindly.

"Simone."

"Do you need a tissue, Simone?"

Simone nodded quietly, while Maggie retrieved one from the packet no sensible teacher did without in her handbag. She was about to ask if the girl was all right, when suddenly, with a noisy chatter, the main river of schoolgirls burst into the room.

Chatting, yelling, giggling, they were making a lot of noise, Maggie knew, to cover up their essential nerves at this, the start of a new school, with new girls and new ways of doing things. Although the way this lot threw themselves about, it was as if they'd known one another for years. She was used to first years being a little more cowed than this, if only because the ones at Holy Cross weren't sure whether they were going to get mugged at break time for their mobile phones.

Maggie gave them a couple of minutes to choose their seats and settle down. The desks were the old-fashioned kind she hadn't seen in years—wooden, with proper lids and inkwells, scored and scratched with years of discussion about who loved whom and which pop group was the best, etched by compasses.

Then she wrote her name up on the board and turned round to face them all.

"Hello," she said. "I'm Miss Adair. For those of you who are new here, I'm also new here, and very happy to be. Here. Now, who can tell where my accent is from?"

Maggie had expected to be able to start some friendly banter, but no one said a word. She looked around the class until a few people tentatively raised their hands. She picked a dark-haired girl at random.

"Scotland?" said the girl, as if slightly puzzled that she'd asked such a stupid question.

"That's right," said Maggie. "Have you been there?"

"Well, my family owns an estate there," said the girl, looking bored.

"OK, well done," said Maggie, trying not to show that she was flustered. "Who else has been to Scotland?"

Pretty much the entire class raised their hands. Maggie wondered if she'd have gotten the same response if she'd said the Caribbean, or America, or France. Probably. Thirteen years old and they'd done it all. She noticed her little muncher hadn't raised her hand yet. She'd have to keep an eye on her.

"Well," she said. "I thought, just for us to get acquainted, we could start with a Scottish poem, from the land of my birth. A great poet, called Liz Lochhead. Then we can discuss it, see what you think, and open up the floor."

The girls opened their jotters obediently, with only one low groan from the back. Maggie's heart sank a little. Maybe she'd just ignore this one. She knew she needed to flaunt her authority at an early stage, but maybe not just yet.

"It's called 'The Choosing,'" she said. And she read the beautiful verse, of two girls growing up, one to go on to study and do well for herself, one forbidden by her father to continue her schooling, the first spending all her time in the library, running into her pregnant friend upstairs on the bus, "her arms around the full-shaped vase that is her body." Maggie remembered so well the first time she'd heard it; how clearly she had identified herself with the two girls on the estates. That she would be the one in the library, with the prizes there for the taking. Was it having the same effect? She cast half an eye in their direction. Perhaps this was wrong. There wasn't a choice for these girls. Of course they would succeed. Effortlessly. Failure wasn't an option when you could pay thousands of pounds a year to buy your girls the best education possible.

But they listened politely enough, and she tried to elongate her vowels and not roll her *r*'s too much to give them a fair shot.

"So . . ." she said, leaning back, trying to look cool and collected and utterly unfazed by the new world she found herself in. "Any thoughts?"

There was a long moment when nobody moved a muscle in the class and Maggie had that thought she sometimes got that she should have done primary teaching after all and they could have just pulled out some coloring-in books at this point.

Fliss sat at the back, and glanced at Alice, whose eyes were dancing, full of mischief. Alice nodded. "Go on," she whispered. Fliss rolled her eyes. Alice giggled.

"You two," came Maggie's voice firmly. "Do you have something to say?"

"Well, the thing is," drawled Fliss, quite amazed at where on earth she'd found the courage. "I'm afraid I didn't really understand what you were saying."

Maggie felt the class stiffen.

"Was it English?" Fliss went on, scarcely believing her own daring.

Maggie stared at her. "Well, you'll find out," she said. She rifled through her file, scarcely able to believe she was doing it, and pulled out another poem.

"Why don't you read this to the class, if your diction is so much better."

She stared at Fliss, who stared back. She couldn't mean it, could she? She couldn't possibly be expecting her to read something out loud?

Maggie was doing her best inside to look steely. That was the only way, she kept telling herself. Be tough, and you only had to do it once. And never, ever let them get to you.

She held up the paper. "Out at the front, please. What's your name?"

"Felicity Prosser," Fliss mumbled, her cheeks going scarlet.

Maggie was surprised to see her blushing. Obviously not quite as shameless as she liked to pretend. Still, she wasn't going to back down now.

"Out you get then."

For a short period nobody moved a muscle. Then, gradually and as sulkily as she could manage, Fliss pushed herself out to the front of the class.

"What's this?" she asked.

"Some foreign poetry," said Maggie. "Read it to the class, please."

The class stared at Fliss, looking awed and amazed. She felt her face burn but didn't feel she had any choice.

Gradually, haltingly she began:

"Go fetch to me a pint o' wine,
An' fill it in a silver tassie,"

Felicity kept her head down and muttered into the paper.

"That's a cup," said Maggie. "Speak louder, please."

"That I may drink, before I go,
A service to my bonnie lassie."

"That means 'girl,'" said Maggie.

"I know," said Fliss.

"OK. Sorry, it's just you said you didn't understand foreign."

"I'm sorry, miss."

"Keep reading, please."

As Fliss stumblingly reached the second verse, even she could see it was quite exciting, and the class was looking interested as she intoned,

69

"The trumpets sound, the banners fly,
The glittering spears are rankèd ready;
The shouts o' war are heard afar,
The battle closes deep and bloody;"

And when she reached the end, Maggie checked and saw the class was listening intently. Good. It had worked.

"That's Robert Burns," said Maggie. "One of the greatest poets that ever lived. Do you think you're still going to have trouble understanding Scots? I have lots more poems here that we can move on to if you don't."

"I'm sure I'll be fine, miss," said Fliss, still feeling sick with the humiliation.

"All right. Sit down please."

Maggie turned back to her class.

"Right. Now where were we? On Liz Lochhead. Does anyone have any trouble with translation?"

Everyone else fervently shook their heads.

"All right. Comments, please. The sheets are on your desks."

There was a long, long wait while it seemed as though no one was going to speak. Until, finally, a small girl tentatively raised her hand.

"Yes. You," said Maggie, in a much friendlier voice, pointing her out. "Can you say your names too, when you answer? Makes my job easier."

"I'm Isabel," said the girl, and Maggie jotted it down on her seating chart.

"What did you think, Isabel?"

"Well, she kind of feels sorry for the other girl, but a bit jealous too, doesn't she?"

After that the class relaxed and went much better. Except

for one girl, sitting at the back. I will never forgive her, thought Fliss. Never.

"SIMONE?" ASKED MAGGIE. "Who do you empathize with in the poem?"

Simone had loved the poem. That was her. All those other girls at school could just go out and get pregnant and she was going to go and do something else. She had to articulate it. She had to get it out. Flushing horribly in front of everyone, she stuttered.

"The poet," she said. "I mean, she was going to the library and getting on with her life and . . ."

"Not the vase?" came a voice from behind her. The whole class sniggered. Simone was by far the heaviest one there. Immediately her face turned bright pink and she stared down at her desk.

"Who said that?" said Maggie, annoyed. Fliss was delighted. It wasn't just going to be her who hated this teacher.

As always happens in schoolrooms, the girls imperceptibly moved away from the culprit, leaving her encircled. Maggie glanced at her chart.

"Alice Trebizon-Woods?"

Alice was a pretty, blank-faced girl with long dark hair and an innocent-looking expression Maggie didn't trust for an instant.

"Yes, miss."

"Did you interject?"

"Did I what, miss?"

Maggie waited a couple of seconds.

"Did you want to say something to Simone?"

"I was just adding to the debate, miss. About whether she felt like the other woman. I thought we were opening up the floor."

There wasn't much Maggie could say to that.

"Well, keep things out of the realm of the personal, please."

Alice opened her eyes wide and blinked them.

"I wasn't, miss."

"Continue, Simone," said Maggie, but Simone couldn't, and stared hard at her desk. Maggie stared hard at Alice and made a mental note to mark her card. The other girls too, all new, stared at the bold girls in the back desk, impressed.

"HI, STAN."

There was a long pause.

"Yeah, hi, Maggie."

There was another long pause.

"It was my first day in the classroom today."

"Oh yeah?" he said. "Sorry, I haven't been keeping an eye on my academic calendar, you know."

"That's OK," said Maggie. "It went . . . fine. Not great. Not bad."

"So they haven't immediately twigged you're just a schemie girl frae Govan and chucked you out on your bahookie."

Maggie stiffened. "Was that supposed to be funny?"

Stan wasn't sure. "Uh, yes."

"Well, it wasn't. There's no earthly reason I can't be a teacher here." She thought back to Clarissa Rhodes. The tall, beautiful, elegant sixth former who looked like a young Gwyneth Paltrow, with her clear blue eyes and shiny mass of hair, had flawlessly recited six stanzas of the Chaucer, then deconstructed them with a skill and elegance that left Maggie gasping her admiration.

"I'm not sure," Clarissa had said afterward when Maggie had taken the time to meet the girls individually. "I was thinking of discussing it at my Oxford entrance. But I've also got an offer from the Royal College of Music for the cello and Mr. Bart—that's the physics teacher—he thinks I should really take this offer from Cambridge seriously." She'd blinked her large blue eyes. "It's hard being a teenager, Mrs. Adair."

"It's 'Miss,' actually," Maggie had said, feeling about two feet tall.

"I deserve to be here," she said now to Stan, but it was as much to convince herself as anything.

"Course you do, love," said Stan then. "We just miss you, that's all."

"I miss you too," said Maggie. "Tell me the gossip."

Stan thought for a while. Gossip wasn't really his thing. He thought of it as a totally female thing. Football for blokes, gossip for girls, and he wasn't about to feign an interest now. "Your dog got sick," he said suddenly.

"Muffin? What happened?" Suddenly Maggie felt a homesick wrench.

"Oh, Dylan and Cody were feeding him turkey twizzlers. And he took up and spewed all over the carpet. It was hilarious."

"Is he all right?"

"Well, he ate the sick," said Stan.

A bell rang loudly.

"I have to go," said Maggie. "We've a dinner meeting."

"Whenever I bring up spew, you always have to go," said Stan.

Maggie paused. "I do," she said.

"Yeah yeah yeah," said Stan. "Right, I'm off to find the bleach."

And he hung up. Maggie had been hoping for a bit more interest and support on her first day. But she supposed other people's lives were still going on.

She made her way to the headmistress's office, where they were having a small reception so all the teachers could meet, along with the staff of their brother school over the hill. She wondered if the crazy man from that morning would be there. Well, be nice to see a familiar face. She felt as nervous as . . . who was that terribly awkward girl in the first form? Simone. Yes. She dipped into the staff toilets to rub a piece of lipstick on, and smelled smoke as she got in there.

"Claire? *C'est vous*?" she said.

The French mistress appeared from the cubicle she'd been hiding in.

"Ah, no. Well, of course. Yes. We must go to a boring cocktail party and still they say, no, you must not smoke. But for sure, teachers always smoke. It is unusual and cruel punishment."

"It's horrid, Claire. And it's bad for the girls."

"Ah, *oui oui*, OK." She threw her butt down the toilet and came over and inspected her perfectly made-up face in the mirror.

"*Mon dieu*, I shall rot in this place."

"You look beautiful," said Maggie, truthfully.

"And what about you, you have a boyfriend?"

Suddenly Maggie wasn't desperately keen, for some reason, to talk about spew-obsessed Stan and his grumpy ways. She couldn't see him coming here and making small-talk with Claire, who was wearing a beautiful white blouse under a gray cashmere sweater, which somehow didn't look boring at all, but perfectly chosen and fitting. What would they talk about? Would Stan sneer as they went through the courtyard? What would he eat? She felt disloyal, even as she said, "Oh, kind of, you know?"

Claire nodded her head fervently. *"Bien sûr,* I understand."

Maggie smiled.

"He is married, yes?"

"No!"

"Very old and very rich?"

"Don't you think we should go?"

MAGGIE WAS GLAD she was with Claire as she walked into the office. The place was full of teachers and the noise level was high. Sixth-form girls were helping the staff handing round canapés and drinks. Maggie wasn't sure this was a good idea. Giving the girls access to alcohol and the potential to overhear teachers' gossip. There was loud chatter and several animated conversations were going on. Maggie saw Miss Starling bending the ear of an elderly-looking chap with whiskers who was either half-deaf or just politely nodding at random intervals. Dr. Deveral was deep in conversation with a rather charming older man, dressed tweedily in the Oxford style, with a waistcoat and patches on the elbows of his jacket. On seeing Maggie, she beckoned her over.

"Yes, Margaret. Let me introduce you to some of the staff from across the way. This is Dr. Robert Fitzroy, headteacher of Downey Boys, just over the hill. It's a stunning Georgian building, you must make an effort to visit as soon as possible."

"Nice to meet you," said Maggie, unsure about what to do, but gratefully accepting the outstretched hand. She was a little wary of the English tradition of kissing strangers.

"Of course, you're Veronica's social experiment," said Robert, smiling kindly.

"Of course she isn't, Robert," said Veronica, a little pink spot appearing on her cheeks. "She's a much valued new member of staff."

"So, do you speak any of your beautiful languages from up there?" said Robert. *"Ciamar a thathu?"*

Maggie decided his face wasn't that kind after all. "No," she said.

"What about lallans?"

"I know some Burns," she said.

"Some Burns! Well, that's a relief."

"Robert," said Veronica, reprovingly.

"I'm sorry, my dear," said Robert to Maggie. "I'm just making a comment on the state of comprehensive schooling, that's all. I'm so pleased you're here."

"There are plenty of good comprehensive schools," said Maggie, angry and prepared to be outspoken.

"My school," said Robert, "has two computers per boy, and fifteen acres of football pitch. Don't you think every child deserves access to those kinds of facilities?"

"I think one computer is probably enough for anybody," said Maggie.

Robert raised his eyebrows. "A socialist on our hands."

"Robert, stop being annoying," said Dr. Deveral, with more charm than Maggie had seen before. "Maggie, do ignore him, he's teasing you."

"All right," said Maggie. But it hadn't particularly felt like teasing. She looked around to see if there was anyone else she could talk to. Her gaze fell suddenly on David McDonald, who was standing on the periphery of some sports masters and mistresses who appeared to be demonstrating rounders pitching. He looked bored. But as soon as he saw her his face broke into a wide, slightly manic grin and he raised his glass. Then, seeing she didn't have one, he strode over.

"Hello! Where's your wine?"

"Of course," said Veronica, looking round for one of the sixth formers, who stepped forward immediately. Maggie took a glass of white and hoped she wouldn't be asked to comment on the vintage.

"Margaret, this is David . . ."

"We've met," said David, grinning broadly. "Both fans of early morning walks."

"Oh, good," said Veronica.

"I think we should introduce compulsory cold early-morning walks for the pupils," said Robert. "What do you think? Blow the cobwebs away before classes."

"Well," said Veronica. "One, they're hard enough to shift as it is. Two, they'd probably take us to the European court of human rights. And three . . ."

"Boys and girls out together in the early morning is just asking for baby-shaped trouble," said David, draining his glass. "What about those cold showers, Robert?"

"Well, yes, that too . . ." started Robert, as David guided Maggie away.

"He's a dinosaur," said Maggie.

"Oh, he's all right. Just old-fashioned. Bit set in his ways. Thinks school was better when there was a lot more whacking in it. The parents love him."

"I'm not surprised—he looks like he walked out of the pages of the *Daily Mail*."

"The boys love him too. He's all right. Anyway, if you're that dead set against the *Daily Mail*, what are you doing teaching in a private school in the south of England?"

"I wanted to learn some good techniques to take back to Govan."

"Is that all?" asked David.

Maggie looked at her wineglass for a moment.

"And well, I just . . . I wanted a change. To see a bit more of the world, I think. I mean, I was teaching at the same school I went to, having to make small talk with my old teachers, can you imagine?"

David made an appropriate face.

"It just seemed a good opportunity. Robert's right in a way. The school I was in was kind of getting me down." She looked up. "Why are you here?"

"Holding the line against the philistines," said David, gesticulating rather wildly with his wineglass. "Against a world full of texters and magazine addicts and people who think punctuation is for pussies and only care about trainers and would beat you up if you liked poetry. Hearts and minds."

"Hear hear," said Claire, who was standing nearby.

"And also, I'm on the run from the French Foreign Legion."

Maggie smiled. "Really?"

"We had a misunderstanding." He whirled off to get some more drinks.

"What a very peculiar man," said Maggie to Claire.

"The boys they love him," said Claire.

"I bet they do."

"I CAN'T BELIEVE the teachers are downstairs getting pissed," said Alice to Fliss, as they mounted the stairs of their tower to prep. It was still light outside. Fliss was used to going to bed when she liked, pretty much. Her parents would try and pick their battles, and bedtime was no longer one of them. This was inhumane. Prep till seven-thirty, then television till nine, lights out at ten! Surely they could sue someone over it.

"This is why they send us to bed so bloody early," said Alice.

"So we don't stumble on them completely half-arsed, throwing up on the lawn."

Fliss laughed. "And copping off with each other."

Alice looked at her thoughtfully. "Have you ever been pissed?"

"Course," scoffed Fliss, although in fact, apart from the champagne they were allowed at Christmas and a few slugs of an alcopop Hattie had once lowered herself to letting her try, she hadn't at all. Hat was so bloody perfect all the time, far too busy with her sports clubs and guiding to get caught up in any kind of "nonsense' as her father called it. So there wasn't any illicit vodka swilling all round the house, like Fliss had heard other girls talk about. Some even claimed to be going to nightclubs already, though she wasn't sure if this were true.

"What about . . ."

"What?"

But Fliss knew what was coming next, and wasn't looking forward to the question. She thought she'd better lie.

"Have you ever . . . snogged a boy?"

"Of course," said Fliss, fiercely jumping in.

She thought back over the last summer. She'd had the biggest crush on Will Hampton, the eldest son of their near neighbors. He was tall and slim with floppy brown hair, was going up to Oxford in the autumn and went out with one of the local girls who was emo and gorgeous, really skinny with her huge eyes outlined in black liner. Fliss used to hang around the village shop just in the hopes that she'd catch him going in to buy *The Times* (she'd vowed to take *The Times* when she was older, even if boring old Mummy got the *Mail* and Dad liked the *Financial Times*) and he'd grin and say hello to her and that would be enough to last her the whole day. Once, he'd patted Ranald.

Her hopes were high when her parents had his round at Christmas for a couple of glasses of wine, but he showed up for five minutes, then scooted off to a party in town. How she'd wished he'd turn round to her, in this totally stupid dress her dad had wanted her to wear, and ask her to come with him. Of course he hadn't. Still, at least he hadn't asked Hattie, that would have been too mortifying. Hattie pretended she didn't care that she wasn't asked. Everyone would like to be asked somewhere by Will Hampton. But *this* Christmas . . . surely she'd be out of this dump by then.

Apart from that, opportunities for snogging were pretty limited, although Fliss was absolutely riven with curiosity. She'd read *Cosmo* and so on, but they were terribly graphic. And everyone had chattered at school when Faith Garnett had reportedly tongue-smashed one of the jockeys up at the pony club and Faith had briefly been the most interesting and popular girl at school as they'd all queued up for details (sloppy and a bit wet was the consensus), then some of the girls had started saying nasty things and it had ended up with Faith in floods in the toilets surrounded by concerned onlookers and Miss Mathieson giving them all a strict talking to on the perils of gossip, most of which had gone completely over Fliss's head.

"Oh," said Alice. "Have you got a boyfriend?"

Fliss would have given anything to be able to answer "yes" to that question: "Yes . . . he's going up to Oxford . . . his name is Will Hampton."

"No," she said. "I'm too young."

"I've been asked out a lot," said Alice. "Most people think I look older than thirteen. When I'm not wearing stupid effing knee socks."

"I know, it's harsh," agreed Fliss vehemently. "You do, you look loads older."

"Thanks," said Alice. "I think I have a mature face. Though it's ugly."

"No, you're beautiful!" said Fliss. "I'm disgusting."

"You're beautiful," said Alice immmediately. "I'm so disgusting."

"You're not, you're gorgeous," said Fliss.

Alice started getting undressed for bed with a sigh. "We're never going to meet boys here. What do you think, Imogen?"

Imogen was still studying, her face toward the wall, her back toward the room. She just shrugged. Alice turned to Fliss with a merry look.

"God, Imogen, do you have to be so noisy all the time?"

Simone trooped in from the bathroom in her big pajamas and slippers.

"What about you, Simone?" said Alice, sitting on the bed.

"What?" said Simone, coloring again. Fliss thought what a shame it was she was carrying so much weight; there was a very pretty face in there. If only she wasn't so heavy.

"Got a boyfriend?"

"No," said Simone shortly, taking her book and climbing into bed.

"Well, I was only *asking*," said Alice. "You don't need to be so touchy."

"Sorry," said Simone, in a miserable voice.

"Maybe she likes women," whispered Alice to Fliss quietly. "Better watch out for yourself."

"Stop it, Alice," said Fliss. And the bell came, ringing for lights out.

* * *

BACK AT THE drinks party Veronica eyed two women sidling in, both wearing wildly unflattering trouser suits. One was carrying a clipboard. Not, thought Veronica to herself, the most elegant of accompaniments to a drinks party. Neither of them was smiling. Veronica checked her hair (perfect, as ever—not a strand would dare defy her bobby pins) and glided over toward them.

"Liz, Pat," she said. "Thanks so much for coming to join us."

"We just found our way," said the older of the two women. She had very short hair, unflatteringly layered along the side of her head, clear glasses, pale lipstick, and a couple of chins too many. Veronica didn't want to see what the stretched seat of her trousers must look like. "It's not easy to get here." She said this in an accusatory tone.

"No," said Veronica. "I think when it was built it wasn't particularly easy to get anywhere, so it didn't really matter. And I've always thought our location and views are so worth it, don't you think?"

"All right for some," said the other woman, who had gray hair that looked like it was standing as a rebuke to other, lesser women who dyed theirs.

Veronica's heart sank. She knew the school had to be inspected, she'd just hoped she'd get some people sympathetic to what they were doing here, not ex–local government-class warriors. She gave the second lady, Pat, a cool stare. "You are here to examine the school's facilities? So of course you're hoping everything will be as good as possible?"

"Yes, good for the kids whose parents can afford it."

"I realize that," said Veronica, bristling. "But that's the world as it is. And you're here to see that we're doing as well as we can for the girls, isn't that right?"

The first woman grunted, and looked around to see where the girls were with their canapés. She beckoned them back and took a handful, cramming them into her mouth. Veronica privately thought that if one of her girls ate like that in company she'd have taken her outside and had a quiet word. Then she started considering her strategy. What a shame that scholarship girl was so timid this year. That's what they needed to be pushing; how Downey House could be a force for good in poorer communities and bring out potential that would get squashed elsewhere. She must keep an eye on that girl.

And that outspoken Scottish teacher should impress them too. They could share the chips on their shoulders.

Veronica smiled at Pat and Liz and asked them if they'd like more wine. They would, of course.

"BETJEMAN," SAID DAVID disconcertingly.

"What?"

"We should add some Betjeman for the Christmas concert. He's fallen so far out of fashion; we could remind people just how good he is. It's a great poem. Got bells, vicars."

"I know the poem," said Maggie, impatiently. "I come from Scotland, you know. Not classical Mesopotamia."

"But you've heard of classical Mesopotamia," said David, with an engaging grin. "Everyone in Scotland is a genius anyway, it's a well-known fact. So. Your predecessor, incidentally, was a ninny, who never wanted to get herself involved in cross-school work. Or work of any kind in fact. Are you like that?"

"I'd have to check with Miss Starling," said Maggie, thinking that being involved in the Christmas concert would be such a huge treat for the girls and really fire their enthusiasm. At Holy Cross they'd had talent shows at Christmas, which had usually become sexy dancing and rap competitions. They were good fun, rowdy affairs but not the same thing at all. And it would have to be with the younger girls; the older ones had mock exams coming up and wouldn't have time for rehearsals.

"Ah, the fire-breathing Miss Starling," said David. "Moral guardian of our humble state. Although you know she's all right really."

"Miss Starling? Are you serious? She's terrifying."

"She's a poppet."

"A *poppet*?"

"A poppet,"said David decisively.

Maggie glanced at June Starling, who appeared to be giving short shrift to some messy-looking women with sour faces. Their trouser suits looked shabby and cheap next to Veronica's immaculate twinset. With sinking heart Maggie knew she probably looked more like the women than the head. She really must reconsider her wardrobe. The girls had all looked like off-duty models in their home clothes from the first day, so there was no point trying to compete on the casual end of things. Could she look classic without looking like a gran? It would be nice to stand out a bit for . . . for any men that might be around, not that she was looking.

"What are you thinking?"

Maggie spluttered a little into her drink. "Nothing. I just . . . she doesn't seem like a poppet at all."

"I would have thought you were quite hot on not judging a book by its cover."

Maggie smiled. "I know. Just settling in I suppose."

"Well, watch this."

David left Maggie hovering by the punch and sidled up to the group.

* * *

OH, THANK GOODNESS, thought Veronica to herself. That young English teacher from over the hill was something of a maverick, but a good example. There weren't anything like enough smart men going into teaching these days. Too many nebulous accusations from a Childline-savvy generation. She'd have liked to poach him, actually, but there were too few male teachers these days to risk a tall skinny one with quick dark eyes and a wide grin—she didn't want anyone flunking their A-levels because they'd gone puppy lovesick for a master, and, equally, she knew how beautiful and eloquent her eighteen-year-olds were, because she'd worked incredibly hard to make them that way. Best not tempt fate.

"David," she said, graciously. "Would you like to meet Patricia and Elizabeth? They've agreed to survey the school for Centrum Standards."

"Oh, that's great!" said David.

Pat and Liz smiled a little.

"Where are you from?"

"Reading," said Pat.

"I live in Hackney," said Liz. "Everyone else has moved out, you know, like 'white flight,' but I believe it's important to stay in local communities."

"I couldn't agree more," said David. "In fact, maybe you could come over to the boys' school one day and talk to them a bit about where you live? Share a bit of experience about your environment?"

"Reading is very mixed too," said Pat, eagerly. Liz shot her a dirty look. "We might be too busy," she said. "We have a lot to do. We're always really incredibly busy."

Pat took the opportunity to refill her glass for the fourth time.

"Well, if you can," said David. "It's been a real pleasure to meet you."

"Thank you, David, that's a very interesting offer," said Veronica, slightly irritated that it took a man to get a smile out of these two self-professed feminists.

"Anytime," he said. "June, I was just talking to your very nice new English teacher Margaret, and we were thinking of putting some of her girls up for the Christmas show."

Dear me, thought Veronica. I hope that one doesn't run away with itself. But it certainly was time they had a good turnout again. Mrs. Ferrers had always had lots of excuses as to why she couldn't quite put her girls up this year.

Miss Starling sniffed. "Maybe," she said. "What were you thinking of?"

"Christmas poetry and prose set to music," said David. "Lots of Dickens and Eliot and so on. Huge fun."

"I think Eliot is terribly elitist," said Pat.

"Good," said David.

"That sounds suitable," said June Starling, ignoring Pat completely. "I expect you'll be wanting our auditorium."

"You do have the proscenium arch."

"We do," said Veronica, smiling at him, and wondering how many good kudos points they'd get for doing it. "Well, the third formers don't often get a chance to join in . . . that sounds wonderful. As long as you don't distract our Miss Adair too much."

"I promise," said David.

"You know, many of our schools now prefer to use 'Ms.,'" said Pat.

"Or first names only, to foster a sense of equality," said Liz.

"Good God," said David, beating a hasty retreat.

* * *

"SEE?" HE SAID on his return. "It's all arranged. She's lovely."

"You did that on purpose," said Maggie.

"What?"

"Pretended to ask those two boots over to your school."

David's face turned serious. "No, I didn't. Why would I do that? I think it's good for the boys to be exposed to all sorts of people."

Maggie bit her tongue so she didn't say anything sharp.

"Not to worry," she said, as Claire came up to them and started to moan about being trapped by the agony of the non-French French master from Downey Boys.

"His accent, it ees *atrocious*. Like un tiny petit horse who can't stop being sick."

Maggie and David looked at each other and grinned. Great, thought Maggie. An ally.

SIMONE LAY AWAKE, listening to the waves outside crashing against the rocks below. She couldn't sleep, her heart pounding. The day had been confusing from start to finish. She didn't know what she was supposed to eat here. She didn't know what on earth the girls were talking about; St. Barts, and the South of France and eventing and dressage and how many dogs they had. She'd understood completely, though, the looks they'd given her as she'd entered each new class. English had been followed by maths, at which she shone, even though the class moved at a much faster pace here.

She liked that and the skinny, slightly odd Miss Beresford who taught it in a quick, humorless clipped style, as if the laws of mathematics were the only important thing in the universe and everything else was ephemeral. Simone would have loved to agree with her. But she couldn't. Everything else *was* important.

Having a friend. That was so important. Fliss and Alice were horrible, but she was so envious of how quickly they'd turned up and decided they liked each other. Both pretty—one dark, one blond—and both so *thin*. Why did it work like that? Why did you only get to have friends if you were thin? She'd thought maybe Imogen, the other girl in the dorm, might be easier, with her thick glasses, but she didn't want to chat at all, just get back to her books. Based on what she had on her desk—molecular biology, introduction to canine anatomy, and the hundreds of postcards of animals pinned up—Simone had asked her shyly if she wanted to be a vet. Imogen had nodded vehemently. And that had been the end of the conversation.

Another nightmare had been the afternoon. Simone had been shocked to see on her timetable that there were four periods of PE a week. Back at her old school they'd been slashed down to one, and she'd always gotten her mother to give her a note. Her and Krystal Fogerty, who was nearly sixteen stone and boasted about how when she left school she was going to get to go straight onto disability because she had obesity syndrome. They'd sit it out in the changing rooms and normally Simone would go to the vending machine for them—until they took the vending machine away.

Here, it was PE nearly every day. And half days on Saturdays girls were expected to take part in organized events of one kind or another—either sport *again*, or drama or music. Simone usually liked staying in and watching television all day on Saturdays.

So she'd gotten changed into the school PE kit: short skirts of the kind that had been outlawed at her school for years, as they made all the boys howl like dogs. They'd had to get the age sixteen size to fit her, so it came nearly to her knees at the front but stuck out over her bum at the back, displaying, she was sure, all the cellulite on the backs of her legs. The polo shirt made her breasts look absolutely massive, and her mother hadn't thought to buy her a sports bra, so she was terrified of having to do any painful running.

All the other girls looked so neat and fresh with their skinny legs bare under the skirts, their small breasts perky under the fresh white shirts as they tied numbers on their backs. Simone started to sweat with nerves. This was bound to show up on her shirt. Now she felt even more anxious. Everyone thought fat girls sweated a lot, and this would prove it. She wiped her damp hands nervously on her skirt. Oh God, please, please let them not pick teams. She couldn't bear that.

Miss James, the games mistress, walked in, stern and muscular-looking.

"Hello," she said to everyone. "Sit down." The girls perched around the changing rooms in twos and threes. Simone sat on the edge, folding her arms over her stomach to stop other people looking at it. Fliss and Alice were sitting together with their hair tied up in identical high ponytails.

"Now," she said. "Downey House has a sports tradition to be proud of. We fight hard and we fight fair. Those are the rules of the school, and I want you to work just as hard here as you do for your university entrance or anything else you do. Fulfill your potential."

She peered round fiercely for a moment.

"Because I don't like it when we get our arses kicked."

For a second there was a stunned silence at a teacher swearing. Then a murmuring at the release of tension. Miss James was obviously all right.

"OK" she said. "I've no idea whether you're a bunch of tigers or pussies. So . . ." Then she went round the room and numbered them one, two, one, two. "The ones are playing the twos," she said. "Have you all got that or do I have to run through it again for the mathematically challenged?"

Sylvie, an inordinately pretty girl with golden curly hair and round blue eyes, blinked and looked as if she was about to raise her hand, then put it down again.

"OK then. If you don't have your own stick, grab one on your way out."

Simone was a one. She made her way out as slowly as possible so nobody could walk behind her and look at her rear. The other girls had glanced at her but so far there'd been no remarks or unpleasantness. At least, not so she could hear. If there'd been boys here, they'd have already been doing whale imitations all over the floor.

"You," said Miss James. Simone was looking out on the huge playing fields. It was quite a sight. There was a running track, several netball courts, hockey fields, a lacrosse pitch, and equipment for track and field events. The grass ran on for what seemed like miles, down toward the cliff edge, where there was a wooden fence. And beyond the cliffs was just the sea, choppy waters all the way to France. It was beautiful. Simone was struck by the skyline, absolutely nothing like the single gray asphalt multipurpose pitch with weeds growing up under the stones that graced St. Cat's.

"You!" said Miss James again. Simone realized she was being spoken to.

"Good morning! Glad to have you with us!"

Some of the girls giggled. "Sorry, miss," said Simone, staring at the grass. She couldn't believe she was getting into trouble with the teachers. The one thing that never happened to her was getting into trouble with the teachers.

"I want you in goal," said Miss James. "Think you could be useful there?"

It wasn't really a question. Simone opened her mouth to say that she'd never played hockey before, then thought better of it, donned the blue vest she'd been given and marched off to the far end of the pitch.

"OK," Miss James was saying. "Any volunteers for center-forward?"

It was pretty obvious how to play, Simone realized, watching the girls attack the small, solid puck-like ball. You pretended you were going in to whack the ball, then you whacked the others' legs instead. It was clearly vicious. Simone shivered in the freshening wind coming off the sea. Fortunately most of the action was taking place up the other end of the pitch for now, but she was dreading it coming her way. She had no idea what she was doing.

Miss James was right among the throng, sizing people up, seeing who could play and had serious potential, who hated pulling their weight, and who slacked. She'd felt sorry for the bigger girl, who obviously felt horribly self-conscious. Trying not to be cruel she'd put her as far out of the way as possible, where she might even manage to get over her nerves. But really. What were parents thinking of, letting their children get so heavy? Didn't they know it was cruel?

Simone realized the play was hotting up as the girls in the green vests were coming her way, among them Alice, but not Fliss, as of course they'd been sitting next to each other. She stiffened with nerves.

"Goal! Goal!" some of the girls down the end were shouting, as the action moved closer and closer to Simone's down the line. She felt her heart in her throat. Suddenly, there was Alice, right in front of her, whacking the ball toward her with all her might. Without thinking, Simone launched herself and her stick at it— and the ball bounced off the end of her stick and back out into the field. A huge cheer went up from the girls in the blue vests as Miss James blew her whistle. Simone went pink, entirely taken by surprise, even as Alice said, "Well, of course she's going to block the goal," in a nasty tone of voice, especially as the teacher said, "Well done." Simone swallowed. She was so used to steering clear of sport. It must have been a fluke.

But, as the game progressed it became obvious that her goal-keeping skills weren't a fluke. That, ungainly and lumbering as she could be, she was good at anticipating when the ball was going to come thudding toward her, and from what angle. The blue team won by some considerable margin, largely due to her efforts. All the way back to the changing rooms the girls talked to her, asked her where she'd played before, and were friendly. Simone couldn't believe it, it felt like a totally new sensation. When she told them she'd never played before they were even more flatteringly surprised and one, a big sporty girl called Andrea whose parents lived in New Zealand, and who had scored all the goals for the blue team, announced that if they let her pick a team, Simone would be on it. Simone felt herself almost bursting with pride.

Back in the changing room, though, her heart sank as she followed the girls into the showers. They weren't communal, but the girls sashayed up to them with only small white towels and, it seemed to Simone, so much confidence. Even though they kept squeezing nonexistent bulges in the mirrors over the sinks and saying loudly, "God, I am *so* fat" whereupon the rest of the girls would chorus, "No you're not, you're *soo skinny*," and another one would take up the mantra. Simone wondered if she could take two towels in, and waited till everyone had dived off to break before she started to get dressed. There was no one to wait behind for her, even if she was not a bad goalie.

Chapter Six

The first few weeks of the new term passed in a blur. Maggie found every day her nerves at facing her classes grew less and less. It was such a refreshing change having classes filled with conscientious students, anxious to learn—often she discovered lesson plans were too short, as she had factored in her traditional disciplinary time.

In a funny way, though, she missed the boys. She missed their smart-aleck remarks, their easy laughter; the way they bounded in like mischievous puppies, clouting one another with their schoolbags. She didn't miss their aftershavey, sweaty boy smell, but she did even miss the way they teased the girls. The loud, shouty nature of it had always offended her at the time, and of course she'd had her fair share of girls in floods of tears, with late periods or worse. But now it was so much harder to get a sense for the emotional temperature of the forms. Girls' whispering was harder to monitor than boys' fighting, and whether they were sharing confidences that would make them intimate friends forever, or planning to completely exclude someone else from the lunch table could be hard to ascertain.

And that was what was difficult. She could hear it in the

elaborately elongated vowels the girls used when they were talking to her. The little remarks when she tried to introduce a contemporary poet, particularly a Scottish one. Obviously her strictness with Felicity Prosser hadn't had quite the desired effect. She was finding these girls intimidating, she couldn't help it. And on one level that was obviously showing, and they were taking advantage. Odd, how a rowdy class of forty kids shouting didn't bother her, but a silent one of fourteen was so unsettling. Plus their horrible assumptions. When reading about a character buying a lottery ticket, they'd all fixed her with large eyes.

"Have you ever bought one of those?" Sylvie Brown, her blue eyes wide and her golden hair cascading down her back, had asked her innocently.

"No," lied Maggie. She bought one every week; she and Stan used their birthdays.

"My father says they're a stupidity tax," announced Ursula confidently. Alice was watching Maggie closely.

"Would you say they're a stupidity tax, miss?" she asked slyly.

Maggie found herself slightly stuttering for words, and was sure the girls had noticed. And Stan wasn't best pleased to hear that he would have to buy the weekly lottery ticket from now on. Maggie didn't want to get caught out by someone from the school at the village store.

The weather grew colder. Now, some mornings, Maggie was waking with frost on the outside of the windowpane. She'd thought it would be milder here, but out exposed at the edge of the country there was a real chill to the wind whistling through the eaves. Also, the central heating was on as low as was possible. She wondered if this was a money-saving exercise, but Claire had assured her Veronica believed it was good for the girls not to get too stuffy, and good for the complexion too, and she'd had a cashmere throw for her bed sent over from a friend in Bruges, would Maggie like one too?

Maggie pushed her younger form on through more contemporary poetry that she thought they might like, and the compulsory Shakespeare, where she had to take the expanse of daunting-seeming blank verse and shape it; mold it into something digestible, alive, and relevant to younger minds—to all minds, she remembered a lecturer saying once. It could be a slog, but it was a highly satisfying one, as the girls finally caught the rhythm and intent behind the beautiful words. The work wasn't a problem; the girls were smart, and diligent. But their attitude to her was . . . she sighed. Her problem.

THREE WEEKS IN, Veronica summoned her to her office. Maggie swore to herself, wishing she didn't feel so nervous. Veronica had spoken to her casually a few times, of course, but Maggie usually sat at meals with Claire, who was great fun and by some disstance the youngest member of the staff, or took her lunch upstairs.

A couple of times when it had been sunny enough she'd taken her lunch out to the moor—the girls weren't allowed to leave the premises unsupervised until the fifth form, by which time they never wanted to go outside, just to hang around the common room complaining about the curfew and pretending they were desperate for a cigarette. So Maggie would take a sandwich and stroll across the lavender-scented moors and find a sheltered spot overlooking the sea where she could gaze out and try and forget her petty frustrations, her overwhelming sense of not fitting in. Sometimes great freighters rolled past on their way to Ireland, but she never saw David out walking Stephen Daedalus again. She could have gone out early in the morning, but now with lesson plans and catching up on the marking she should have done instead of watching *Lost* the night before, mornings were too fussed. Plus, she was a bit embarrassed. She didn't want it to seem as if she was out looking for him.

She was, though, she admitted to herself one day, staring out across the white-crested heads of the waves at a long vessel loaded with Maersk crates, a little lonely. She missed Stan. Their nightly phone calls were degenerating into short recountings of their days, with a lot, she felt, being left unsaid. The silences were growing longer, the calls shorter. She had promised to go and see him at half-term but wasn't really looking forward to it and was half considering, if the situation didn't improve a little, accompanying the girls staying behind to London for an outing.

And her sister's emails, while friendly, were a little short. She still hadn't been forgiven for giving up on aunt duty. "Cody and Dylan are fine," Anna would write, and Maggie could almost feel the tightness behind the words. "Dylan has been excluded from nursery and Cody has nits again." Then she would relent a little and tell her about a zoo they'd visited, or how Stan had come round and played football with them and they'd pretended to be Celtic winning the European Cup and then all gone out for KFC, then gone home and watched *Dr. Who*, which had had Dylan up all night fretting, and Maggie would feel a huge tug of longing for home; a desire to say sod it all, you stupid posh girls.

She didn't mean to tell any of this to Dr. Deveral, however, and sat rather nervously outside her office, as Miss Prenderghast smiled at her sweetly. Miss Prenderghast smiled at everyone sweetly, though, whether you were there for an award or there to get kicked out forever. Maggie was aware, somewhat uneasily, that there was a probationary period in her contract, and she was still in it. Surely Veronica couldn't be about to tell her to go home? That she wasn't suited to this school? Maybe there'd been complaints. Suddenly she felt her heart beginning to race. OK, Miss Starling didn't seem to like her, but she hadn't really given her a fair chance from the start—she thought back to the previous week when Miss Starling had stopped her in the corridor and called her into her classroom.

"I hear you and Mr. McDonald are doing a *performance*," she'd said in the same tone of voice she might have used to announce, "are planning to bring in poisonous *snakes*."

"Yes, Miss Starling," Maggie had said. "I was just coming to discuss it with you, see which classes would be best. I thought Middle School 1 . . ."

"That class," Miss Starling had said, while methodically arranging the exercise books on her desk—Miss Starling always seemed to be tidying something—". . . is best suited to total disruption, mild hysteria, and attempting to destroy the confidence of whichever mite is unlucky enough to get the leading role. I don't approve. However, as it seems you got someone else to ask me in public . . ."

"That wasn't my idea," said Maggie, instantly regretting it. Now she sounded like she was trying to weasel out of responsibility. Also, she really ought to have talked it over anyway, days ago. "I'm sorry," she'd added. "I should have . . ."

"Well, it's done now," Miss Starling had said, with a glance that made it clear that Maggie could leave. "At least don't turn it into one of those dreadful PC Winterval shows you see at other schools," she'd added disdainfully.

"No," Maggie had said, and was then cross with herself for

not standing up for her background. Although the semi-stripper dancing the fourth years had done last year at Holy Cross to the tune of "Santa Baby" and the howls and stamping of the boys probably wouldn't have done the trick.

She worried whether Miss Starling had complained to Veronica. Talked about trampling on her toes, or getting in the way? Maybe Miss Starling didn't think she was up to it. Maybe the girls had slagged her off to their parents and they'd made a complaint? Maggie steeled herself as Veronica came to the door.

"Maggie. Hello," she said, with a small smile. Maggie followed her into the room with some trepidation. Veronica sat down on the red velvet upholstered couch and indicated that Maggie should do the same. Miss Prenderghast brought in the teapot on a tray, biscuits nicely arranged. Maggie tried to ignore them; she knew Veronica would no more eat a biscuit than perm her hair.

"So, Maggie," said Veronica, leaning forward. "How are you finding things?"

Maggie swallowed. "Well . . . I mean, I really like it," she said. "I think it's a really good school. It's so nice to work with some great materials."

This was true. For example, Maggie had always had a weakness for stationery. At Holy Cross she'd always had to sign in and out of the stationery cupboard and keep to a strictly rationed budget to make sure she didn't steal any staplers from the workplace. Here, although Miss Starling had eyed her beadily, seeing her face light up with the brand-new equipment and wide range of teaching aids, pens, computers, and AV, no one tried to intimate that she was about to pillage the place and set up a secondary concern. Here, nobody had to share a book (at Holy Cross it had been one between three, sometimes) or complain about their pens running out. Oddly this had the effect of making Maggie feel guilty.

"And what about our girls?" asked Veronica. "Are they great materials too?"

Maggie felt herself color. "They're good. Most of them."

"But? I sense a but."

"Oh, nothing. I just wonder if they're perhaps a little complacent."

Veronica twisted her pearl earrings. "How so?"

Maggie thought of Felicity and Alice. Right from day one—when she had, she knew, shown a heavy hand with punishment—they had taken against her; chatted and made remarks whenever they felt themselves unobserved and in general showed a thorough lack of respect; turning up late, and usually sniggering. Felicity's work was poor too, which was strange as, according to her old school report, she was an extremely able pupil. From which Maggie could only conclude that she was doing it on purpose. To annoy her.

"I mean, they've just got such a sense of entitlement," finished Maggie crossly. "Sorry. That probably sounds really chippy."

Veronica smiled to herself. "A little." Maggie glanced down.

"Felicity Prosser probably thinks she's the unhappiest girl in this whole school," said Veronica.

"You're joking."

"No. I could tell straightaway. Her sister has done very well here. A little intense for my taste, if you know what I mean, but very much a success. I don't think Prosser minor wanted to come here at all."

"Well, that's clear enough."

"I'd keep her away from that little minx Alice Trebizon-Woods. I've had her two sisters through as well and they're all attention seekers of the highest order. Parents in the diplomatic corps, hardly notice them. But you might do all right then with Felicity—and all of your Middle School 1."

So, she had heard. Maggie felt her ears burn.

"I know you can do it," said Veronica gently. Maggie bit her lip, in case she started to cry. Veronica spotted this immediately and swiftly changed the subject. "Well, I wanted to mention two other things," she said. "Firstly, there's another girl in MS1 I want you to keep an eye on."

"Simone Pribetich," said Maggie without hesitation, glad for the change of subject.

"Yes. She's one of our scholarship girls. Very smart, but needs dragging out of herself. Miss James is doing wonders with her in sport, but it's not enough. She could do with a friend. I know you can't work miracles, but she's very bright and I'd hate for her to waste her potential."

"I'll try." Maggie was incredibly relieved. Veronica had referenced the situation, but didn't seem to think there was anything to worry about.

In fact, Veronica had expected this to happen. Downey's girls often hadn't met people from other backgrounds who weren't staff of some sort. Maggie needed to learn to cope. But she shouldn't be doing it alone.

Feeling slightly better, Maggie waited to hear what the other thing was. It must be the show. She and David had emailed a couple of times about it. She got a little surge of excitement whenever one of his emails pinged up. They were always chatty and beautifully written, and they'd narrowed the choice of extracts for the show down to four, which Mrs. Offili, the music teacher, was now looking at how to stage.

"Secondly, you, Maggie. You know this isn't prison. You are

quite welcome to get out and explore a bit, meet friends and so on. Go and visit your family."

Maggie was surprised Dr. Deveral had been so observant.

"Thank you," she said, "but they're so far away. And I have seen something of Claire and . . ."—she felt a little embarrassed saying his name out loud—". . . David."

Veronica arched an eyebrow. She'd thought as much. "Do you have . . . and forgive me for stepping outside the professional arena for a moment, but do you have a boyfriend?"

Maggie nodded, feeling obscurely embarrassed at Veronica even having to use such an adolescent word.

"Why don't you invite him down at half-term? He can't stay here, of course, but I can recommend a good B&B in the village. Teaching is a demanding job, Margaret, as you are currently finding. We all need to relax sometimes."

MAGGIE HAD RETURNED to her rooms with conflicting thoughts. After all, getting Stan down here was the right thing to do. He could see she hadn't run away from him for a life of champagne and fun and whatever else he seemed to think she was doing here.

On the other hand, she thought suddenly, would Stan fit in Downey House? Could she trust him not to make inappropriate remarks all the time and, well, *embarrass* her? She imagined Claire, with her immaculate outfits, listening to Stan discuss his latest triumphs in Championship Manager, but it was difficult to picture.

Veronica watched her walk across the forecourt. Actually, Maggie was settling in much better than she had expected. Miss Starling had reported that although a little "trendy" for her tastes (Veronica suspected anything that wasn't simply memorizing lines would be a little trendy for June Starling, particularly given they were studying poetry that didn't rhyme), but committed and hardworking, which was the most important thing in a young teacher. Finesse could come later; they were all there to help. Oh. She remembered what she'd forgotten to mention. Maggie was wearing a blue-and-white-striped shirt that looked like it was half of a pair of pajamas, and a gray skirt that wasn't quite the right length for her. She *must* have a word with her about her dress.

"I CAN'T BELIEVE they take away your phones."

Fliss was raging, and Alice was agreeing with her.

"I mean, it's completely fascist. One hour a day? That's just, like, evil and against your rights and things."

"Yeah," said Alice, whose mother could never remember the time difference and thus rarely rang.

"You know in Guildford, I'm allowed to go shopping on my own. Here you're not even blooming allowed out unless there's six of you and a teacher! Until upper fourth! It's prison."

Alice was trying to do her prep, but Fliss was deliberately ignoring hers, so Alice pushed it to one side. Egging on Fliss was more fun anyway.

"And then they fob us off with stupid common teachers." Fliss stuck out her bottom lip.

"We need to do a trick," said Alice.

"A trick?" said Fliss, as they drank Orangina in the dorm. Imogen was working quietly. Simone was nowhere to be seen.

"Yeah, you know. A good practical joke that everyone will piss themselves about."

"I know some good ones," said Fliss. "What about putting cellophane over the teachers' toilets?"

Alice sniffed. "Old hat," she said. "We need something amazing."

"Flour bombs?" ventured Fliss.

"You've got to think big," said Alice. "I shall put my brain to work. And who should be the victim?"

"Well, not Miss Beresford," said Fliss, thinking uncomfortably back to a conversation they'd had earlier that week, when the stern maths mistress had unfavorably compared the marks she was getting here with how she'd done at her old school. It was hard to make a protest about how much you hated somewhere when you actually had to get in trouble and endure the consequences. Miss Beresford had exhorted her not to let herself down. Fliss wanted to burst into tears and claim it wasn't fair, her parents were letting her down, but she thought she was unlikely to meet with much sympathy, and she'd have been right. Miss Beresford came from a poor background and, although she enjoyed teaching maths here, thought some of these little madams didn't know how good they had it.

"No, she has no sense of humor at all," agreed Alice. "Why else would you be a maths teacher?"

Fliss couldn't think. She'd seen Alice's maths books though. She'd scored 94.

"What about that horrid old bitch Miss Adair?" Fliss was still stinging from Maggie's putting her down.

"Ah, Miss What Not to Wear," said Alice thoughtfully. "You know, I think she might be just right. She's so keen for everyone to like her, she'll probably laugh it off and not get us into trouble at all. Plus she's totally green."

"Yeah," said Fliss. "Great. What shall we do?"

Alice smiled. "Leave it to me," she said.

They turned their attention to a parcel sitting on Simone's bed.

"Can you believe how much stuff she gets?" said Alice.

Fliss couldn't, especially when she was lucky to get the odd postcard. There was barely a couple of days went by without a large box arriving, with tinfoil-covered packages and cake boxes.

"Does she think that you have to pay for the food here?" said Alice. "Honestly, there's so many empty cartons in the bin. It's really starting to smell. We'll get mice. You're not even supposed to have food here." She went to her bed by the window. "God, it smells. I hate it. I'm going to tell her."

"No, Alice, don't."

"I'm serious!" Alice looked crossly out the window. "We all watch what we eat and I'm on like a total diet, and the place is a rats' nest of cakes. It's not fair. And she eats too much anyway."

"Alice, don't be mean, please." Fliss didn't mind being horrible to teachers and grown-ups, and whoever else it would take to get her out of here. But picking on another girl she didn't like.

But Alice had that glint in her eye as Simone came in. She'd been trying to use the old pay phone down the hall and couldn't get it to work. She couldn't believe that her mum had used the guideline "we discourage the middle school girls from having mobile phones" as an actual gospel law of the school. She was the only girl without one, not even for emergencies. As usual her mum's phone was engaged. She always had a million people to talk to. Just not her.

"Hi, Simone," said Alice. Simone looked up. Alice didn't usually do much more than grunt at her. Fliss was a bit better, but not much.

"Look, Simone," said Alice, getting down from the window. "Can we have a word?"

Fliss didn't like being dragged into this like it was a communal decision.

"Now, we know you're, like, a compulsive eater or whatever, and that it's like a disease and stuff and we want you to know that we're not prejudiced and we really care about you and your illness."

Alice widened her eyes in fake concern. Simone stared at her, confused and cornered.

"But we were wondering if it might be possible . . . I mean, not if it's too much trouble . . . we don't want to make things worse or anything, but if you could keep your, like, totally disgusting food out of the dorm?"

She indicated the parcel Mrs. Pribetich had stickily wound a whole rope of packing tape around.

"Is that OK?"

Simone picked up the parcel, turned around, and fled.

MAGGIE WAS HEADING for bed. It was her turn to do rounds, just to check all the girls were in bed and tucked up. It was a cold dark night outside, with rain throwing itself at the windows, and everyone seemed quite happy to be tucked up. Maggie picked up a couple of stray towels. She quite liked saying goodnight to everyone; it made her feel pastoral.

In Fliss and Alice's dorm room there was much whispering going on and no Simone. Maggie switched the overhead light on.

"Where is she?" she demanded. Fliss and Alice were both in bed, looking as though butter wouldn't melt in their mouths. Alice gave her most innocent look.

"I don't know, Miss Adair. She got a food parcel and went off . . . maybe to eat it?"

Maggie gave her a hard look. "Did she seem in a strange mood?"

It wasn't like Simone to be late for anything.

Alice propped herself up on her elbows. "You know, we're a bit worried about her. Like, she might have a problem with food or something?"

Maggie hated to admit it, but the dark-haired little minxy girl might have a point. Even in the few weeks they'd been there, she'd noticed Simone taking extra rolls at breakfast, queueing at the little snack shop. She'd put weight on, for sure. Although there was plenty of exercise prescribed on the curriculum, Simone did no extra sporting activities on offer at the weekends or after school hours; she didn't take any walks on the moors like the other girls did on their Sunday free time after church. And there was certainly plenty of hearty good fare—Mrs. Rhys, head of the catering service, was of the old school. Traditional stodge, and lots of it; toast, steamed puddings, custard, stews, and roly-poly. Maggie adored the food and was having to be very strict with herself. Simone, it appeared, was not.

"Lights out," she said sharply to the girls. "I'll bring her back myself."

Fliss lay awake in the dark. It had sounded like Alice was being interested in Simone and worried about her problem. But she knew she wasn't.

Maggie didn't have to go far. Just around the corner was an alcove, the underside of a spiral staircase. It was covered from plain view by a curtain, and the girls normally used it for confidences, or phone calls. Tonight, though, Maggie could tell by the movement of the curtain that there was someone there.

"Simone?" she said, quietly. There was no answer. "Simone?" she tried again.

A voice clearly trying to disguise its sobbing said, "I'm fine. Go away."

Maggie pulled across the curtain. Simone had obviously thought she was another pupil, as she genuinely flinched when she saw her.

"Miss Adair."

"That's right," said Maggie. "And sorry, but I'm not going away."

There was a bench in the corner of the alcove. Maggie sat down and beckoned Simone to do the same. Her face was smeared with tears and what looked like jam.

Maggie sat in silence for a couple of minutes until Simone's hiccupy sobs had slowed. "Now," she said. "What's up?"

"I don't fit in here," said Simone.

"Oh, neither do I," said Maggie, remembering Miss Starling, who that morning had mentioned that Maggie seemed to be "rushing" in the corridor, and that if she was better prepared in the mornings, perhaps she wouldn't have to. "I wouldn't worry about that."

"The other girls," sniffed Simone. "They're so confident and pretty. None of them is fat and their mothers don't send them stuff to eat and they all got to be friends really quickly and . . ."

"Ssssh," said Maggie, looking around for a handkerchief and making do with a paper napkin, presumably packed by the ever-prepared Mrs. Pribetich.

"Now look," she said. "Of course you're not going to feel right here immediately. These girls all went to primary school together. Their mothers all came here. That's just how it was."

Simone nodded.

"But that's not important, is it? Do you know how many of them could have gotten a scholarship like you did?"

Simone shook her head.

"None of them, that's how many."

In fact, Maggie had been very impressed with Simone's work, particularly her poems, which, while full of terrible angst and some horrible spelling, also had a good use of language and structure for her age.

"You're just as good as them, Simone. Better, in some instances. So you have no reason to do yourself down. And are you sure these . . ." She tilted her head toward the large pile of polenta cakes that had disgorged from the bag. "Do you think these are helping, Simone?"

Simone shook her head miserably. "But my mum sends them, and I'm just so fed up and I don't know what to do."

"Would you like me to have a word with your mum, tell her she's not allowed to send you food for, I don't know, say environmental reasons or something. Would that help?"

Simone shrugged. "I'm so fat though. It wouldn't make any difference."

"You might be amazed," said Maggie. "And I hear you're doing brilliantly at sport."

Simone twisted the corner of her pajamas and didn't say anything.

"Fewer cakes, bit more sport, you'd look better in no time, with your lovely teenage metabolism," said Maggie, adding quickly, "only if you want to change, of course."

"Of course I want to change," said Simone. "Nobody talks to me."

"Well, I'm sure once everyone settles down that will change. It's very early in the year."

"These things never change," said Simone. Maggie didn't want to tell a lie and contradict her. Sometimes they did, sometimes they didn't.

"Well, listen," she said. "How about, when you feel like you need someone to talk to, you can come over and visit me."

Simone gave a sidelong glance that indicated she didn't really believe her.

"Just pop in. I have lots of books. And not just set books either. I've got the new Sophie Kinsella *and* the new Lisa Jewell."

Maggie could tell Simone's ears were pricking up. She wasn't the first girl to take solace in reading. And it would be better for her than hiding away stuffing cake in her face, that was for sure.

"The new new one?" said Simone, sniffing. "In hardback?"

"I was saving it," said Maggie. "But I'll let you have first dibs." Simone got down from the bench. "Thanks."

"No problem. Will I take this away?" Maggie indicated the cake. Simone nodded.

"Right. Get to bed then before I have to report you and Miss Starling will have to see you."

This had the desired effect. Simone scampered away.

"And brush your teeth!" said Maggie.

"I'm REALLY GOING to get that sarky Miss Adair now," Alice hissed to Fliss the next morning as they were brushing their teeth. "Thinks she's bloody Mother McTeresa."

"This school sucks," agreed Fliss. "We need out."

Chapter Seven

The school was busy. First were auditions for the Christmas readings. The Christmas concert was a big point in the calendar. The school orchestra, jazz band, and dance troupe were all expected to perform for the parents, but as the middle school girls were so new, they were given readings to punctuate the performances. Traditionally there were lots of girls interested in this, as they were joined by the choristers from the boys' school, which meant they got a chance to meet the boys—the first two years weren't allowed to attend the mixed Christmas party; neither the parents nor Veronica liked the idea. They had a party afternoon of their own in class and there was a special Christmas dinner and that was quite enough.

"I'm sure they'll just be babies," Alice was saying, mugging heartily over "Journey of the Magi." "No use to us."

"Deffo," said Fliss. "I don't want to do it anyway."

Stand up in front of her parents and the whole school? Not bloody likely. If anything was going to prove that she'd given in and was now sucking it up it would be that, and she'd never get the chance to get back before all her friends had formed a new clique without her and started treating her like she was stuck up and horsey, the way they'd always talked about boarding-school girls. That, and the fact that their parents hated them, of course.

THERE WAS A drama teacher at the school—the rather suspiciously named Fleur Parsley—who had long hair, long skirts, and floated around the place (she also taught at Downey Boys). Lots of the girls had a crush on her. Maggie found her a tad emetic. As far as Maggie could tell, she spent a lot of time getting the girls to roll around the floor pretending to be animals. No wonder they loved drama and couldn't get their prep in on time.

Liz and Pat had loved Fleur's class, as Maggie discovered when the four found themselves sitting together at lunch.

"Then you took on the characteristics of multicultural animals from around the globe," Pat was enthusing.

Fleur smiled modestly. She was very beautiful, with long pre-Raphaelite hair and an extremely slim figure, and Pat and Liz were obviously enjoying being around her.

"Well, I believe . . ." she said—she had a very affected voice, clear as a bell, and liked to intimate that she'd given up a highly successful career as an actress because she was so dedicated to teaching—". . . that the girls here should experience influences from all over the world. They can't help being so privileged, but it's no excuse for ignorance."

Pat and Liz nodded emphatically. "Exactly," said Pat.

"It's a bit like doing the *Lion King*, isn't it?" said Maggie to make conversation.

"It's actually nothing like the *Lion King*?" said Fleur. Her voice tended to go up at the end of sentences. "It's like an opportunity for the girls to experience the consciousness of different groups of animals that exist . . . and are often persecuted . . . throughout the world?"

"Oh," said Maggie, tucking into her macaroni and cheese. "I see."

"I feel it's important to bring a spiritual dimension to my work," said Fleur. Pat, and Liz, who was on her second helping of macaroni, nodded vigorously.

"Well, I suppose I have the Christmas readings coming up," said Maggie. "I could do with your help, Fleur."

"Oh, I'm *so* busy," said Fleur, smoothing back her hair.

"What methodology are you using to action that?" asked Pat.

Maggie hesitated as she unraveled the question. "Well, I thought I'd get them all to do a reading in class, then choose two girls from that."

Pat and Liz recoiled in horror.

"You're planning to . . . humiliate the girls in front of their peers?" said Liz in horror.

"No," said Maggie. "But I think it's important that they can speak in front of other people, and I need to get an idea as to who can handle it and who will crumple in front of the audience."

"I don't really, like, believe in competition in art?" said Fleur, pushing her macaroni around her plate.

"I thought acting was very competitive," said Maggie. Fleur didn't bother replying, but let a smile play around her lips.

"I'm not sure making the children *audition* . . ."

"I'm not necessarily looking for the best," said Maggie.

"That's good, because I don't think terminology like 'best' is very helpful in an educational scenario," said Pat.

"I'm looking to see who would benefit the most."

Pat and Liz looked at each other.

"With your permission, we'd like to sit in on that class," said Pat.

"Of course," said Maggie, trying to hide her disgruntlement. Actually, two complete strangers in the class would make it much harder for the girls, surely they could see that. But she didn't want to rock the boat or make things any more difficult than they were already.

THE FIFTEEN GIRLS in Middle School Year One all felt nervous that Thursday, and resentful toward their teacher, no matter how cool they professed to be, or how much they pretended that the school concert was a complete waste of time for morons. In fact, secretly, most of them really did want the chance to stand in front of the school and get riotously applauded in front of their parents, especially if they weren't, like Astrid, so musical they'd already made it into the orchestra.

Astrid Ulverton was such a beautiful clarinet player Mrs. Offili was completely torn between wanting to keep her for school music and urging her parents to march her off to the nearest conservatoire. Astrid's parents believed a career in music was a waste of time and kept trying to get her to work hard at sciences in preparation for medical school. Poor Astrid was a dunce in other subjects, however, and couldn't look at a textbook without making a tune of the words and rapping her fingers on the spine.

Fliss had hurriedly grabbed one of the set pieces the night before, in a thorough temper that Miss Adair was going to get the chance to make her stand up again in front of all her classmates. It was the opening of *Little Women*, which started, " 'Christmas won't be Christmas without presents,' grumbled Jo, lying on the rug."

She was going to perform it in the most offhand way possible, so that she wouldn't get chosen and could stand at the back of the choir and look sulky. Alice was doing "Journey of the Magi," by T. S. Eliot, so she could be very dramatic and act out being an old man. She'd done it already for Fliss in the alcove and Fliss had been very impressed. The other option was a big long extract from *A Christmas Carol*, which was far too boring and hard to memorize, so only the complete dweebs would pick that.

MAGGIE WAS NERVOUS. She wasn't sure if this was a good idea, and talking to Pat and Liz hadn't helped matters. But no. It said in the prospectus that Downey House was about turning out confident, well-rounded young women. Jobs were all about talking to groups and it wasn't as if she was getting them to read out their own stuff, which she was thinking of doing with the year nines. It hadn't worked terribly well at Holy Cross. The boys tended to write stories about how their gang had beaten up another gang, and the class would bang on the desks and shout out at apposite moments and sometimes real fights would come out of it. She'd quickly abandoned the concept.

"OK, class," she said. It was a bright and chilly late November day. She'd noticed in the mirror that morning that her cheeks were pinker than usual, probably as a result of spending more time out of doors. Her eyes were clearer too. A lot less alcohol and some decent food were really working on her looks.

"All right, class. We're going to go for it. Nobody has to memorize anything yet, we're just going to concentrate on projection and focus."

"Miss Fleur says focus has to come from within," said blond

wide-eyed Sylvie earnestly. "She says it has to come from the heart."

Pat and Liz, who were perched on their chunky bottoms on desks at the back of the class, nodded gravely.

"Well, Miss *Fleur* is right," said Maggie, biting back a touch of irritation. "Speak from the heart. These are lovely pieces, famous for a long time. So, do your best. I'm not looking for the loudest, or the most 'acted.' I'm looking for you to try hard and show the school what an engaged class we are."

Sylvie went first, reciting from *Little Women* in a breathless chirp with slightly odd intonation. Maggie led the mandatory clapping. Next up was Astrid, who read the poem in a rhythmic monotone that rendered the scansion almost indecipherable. Third was poor shy Imogen, who was so quiet and mousy Maggie felt terrible asking her to speak up again and again. It didn't help when Pat and Liz started whispering to each other. Maggie was so furious at this rudeness she was tempted to tell them to shut up, before reminding herself that they were judging her, not Imogen, and that she really had to learn to keep her temper in check.

Just as the whole session looked like it was going to be a complete disaster, Alice, next to be called, stood up.

"A cold coming we had of it"

She started with a tragicomically grave, dramatic expression on her face. A few lines later she pointed downward to some imaginary camels.

"And the camels galled, sore-footed, refractory,
Lying down in the melting snow."

She stared out of the window, allowing her pretty face to suddenly look very sad.

> *"There were times we regretted*
> *The summer palaces on slopes, the terraces,"*

Now she shook her head wildly as if disturbed by the memories.

> *"And the silken girls bringing sherbet."*

Maggie had to bite her lip to stifle a giggle. She was a monkey, Alice, but she had spirit. Her overacting was ludicrous, but goodness, she was putting in the effort. She put a mark next to her name; if they didn't get any better, she might have to go in.

Alice came to:

> *"were we led all that way for . . ."*

Then she let a dramatic pause linger . . . and linger . . .

"BIRTH? OR DEATH?" she shouted, suddenly, making Pat jump, as she hadn't been paying attention. Could work on lazy parents, Maggie mused.

"Thank you, thank you," she said, as Alice finished the poem with *"I should be glad of another death"* before throwing herself into a great bow. The applause in the classroom was genuine and loud, and Maggie could see Alice had to work hard to stop a huge grin cracking across her face.

Next it was Simone. Maggie gave her her most encouraging look as the girl slowly got up. Alice smirked at her as she passed on her way back to her seat at the back of the class. Maggie hoped it wasn't going to be a massacre; the girls had enjoyed Alice's performance but wouldn't take too kindly to Simone stuttering along.

Suddenly, as Simone reached the front of the stage and turned to face the audience, Maggie glimpsed Pat and Liz swapping a very obvious look, Liz with an eyebrow raised like she thought she was Simon Cowell, Pat rolling her eyes to heaven. Simone could hardly not have seen it. If anyone ought to be sensitive to the girl, it should be them, with their belief in the virtues of the working classes and their supposed sensitivity to the underdog. Maggie felt the bile rising in her throat, and it was a few moments before she actually tuned in to what Simone was saying.

Simone had decided just to treat it as she did when she got called up every week by her mother to "do something clever" in front of the aunties, something which had happened on a weekly basis since the moment she could talk. She simply steeled herself and did the best she could.

Years of being forced to perform, however, had rubbed off on her, and as she launched into the Dickens extract, she couldn't help but imbue it with some feeling. It was a book she'd always loved—her parents had bought an entire set of Dickens from a book club and she'd started working her way through them at the age of eleven.

Add to this her naturally gentle, very London-sounding voice, and by the time she reached the phrase *"I have always thought of Christmas time . . . as a good time: a kind, forgiving, charitable, pleasant time . . . when men and women seem by one consent to open their shut-up hearts freely, and to think of people below them as if they really were fellow-passengers to the grave,"* Maggie was completely engrossed and marked her up for it immediately. The applause at the end was distinct and heart-felt and Simone looked surprised to hear it, as she'd tried only to focus on the meaning of the words she was saying, and not how she looked. If she stopped to think about how she looked to everyone, she'd just want to curl up in a ball. The applause was a pleasant bonus.

"Well done," said Maggie, trying to keep her tone from sounding too surprised and patronizing.

The next few girls were passable, if unremarkable, and everyone was getting bored with hearing the same three pieces regurgitated again and again. Fliss sighed with the tedium and stared out of the window. A storm looked to be coming in over the sea; the grass and scrub on the clifftops was bend-ing over. There was so much *weather* here, thought Fliss, miss-ing the gentler environs of Surrey. Apparently in London you hardly got weather at all, all the buildings protected you from it. It would be the Christmas party in the village soon. Will Hampton would probably be in town for it. She wondered if she'd see him over Christmas. God, if only her tits would grow. Then at least she might have a tiny chance of him noticing she wasn't a baby anymore. She tried to imagine herself out of this bloody itchy navy wool skirt and navy bloody ribbed tights, and into something slinky and, well, maybe even a bit sexy. Or at least that showed a shoulder or something. She would just turn up at the party and it would be like that bit in *Enchanted* when the princess enters the ballroom and everything would go a bit slow and Will would just stop whatever he was doing to stare at her, then advance toward her, with his hands out, com-pletely amazed that he'd never recognized her before . . ."

"Felicity? Felicity Prosser?"

Maggie hated daydreaming, even while she was a chronic

sufferer herself. You never knew how much they'd missed and it wasted everyone's time.

"Yes, miss?" said Fliss, as cheekily as she could manage. She was embarrassed to get picked out and even more embarrassed about what she'd been thinking. If her bad marks didn't convince her parents to take her out . . .

"It's your turn," said Maggie. "If you could grant us a moment or two of attention."

A couple of girls tittered, and Fliss felt her face flush.

"Do I really have to, miss?" she asked. "I don't want to read out at the stupid concert."

Silence fell immediately. *Nobody* questioned the concert.

Maggie weighed up what was the best way to handle it. If she let her off, she might have full-scale rebellion on her hands. Plus, all the parents were hoping their own daughters would have parts. Plus, this exercise was about reading in public anyway. And she was sick and tired of this girl, whatever Dr. Deveral said.

"Don't talk about school events that way, please," she said briskly. "I won't have rudeness in my classroom. You can discuss it with Miss Starling if you like, but while you're in my class you will try out for the concert."

Fliss pushed out her lower lip, but wasn't brave enough to continue her rebellion.

"This is like prison or something," she said, mooching to the front.

"Yes, Felicity, it's exactly like prison," said Maggie, folding her arms and waiting for Fliss to start reading.

"'Christmas isn't Christmas without presents,'" began Fliss sulkily.

Oddly, her sullen tones enlivened the reading, and Maggie

could easily see the petulant Amy, and the stubborn Jo, in the set of Fliss's jaw. By the time she got to Jo examining the heels of her shoes in a gentlemanly manner, Maggie was wondering whether it might be a combination of a good punishment and a good concert to actually put Fliss up for it.

"Can we have a word?" said Pat, as Maggie left the classroom to go and have tea, and the girls dashed off outside.

"Of course," said Maggie. She was still irritated by their distracting behavior in her classroom, but wasn't about to mention it.

"You know, when Felicity Prosser said she didn't want to be included in the concert auditioning process . . . we're a little confused as to why you still made her do it."

Maggie looked at them. "Because that was the objective of the class—to perform a piece to the rest. Whether you get picked or not isn't really the point."

"But," said Liz, "don't you think Felicity clearly demonstrated articulacy and reasoning skills when she said she didn't want to participate?"

"No," said Maggie, feeling the heat rise in her face. "She said it was stupid!"

"In the comprehensive system," said Pat, adjusting her unflattering glasses, "we don't believe in humiliating children like that."

Maggie bit back a retort about how that explained a lot.

"I didn't humiliate her. It was part of the lesson plan, and she actually did very well. How did that humiliate her?"

"Forcing children to do things against their will can destroy their self-esteem," said Pat, making a mark on a clipboard.

"Young adults," reproved Liz.

"Young adults," amended Pat immediately. "They are individuals too, with their own desires and fears."

"You don't think children should have to do what they don't want to do?" asked Maggie in amazement.

"We believe in child-centered learning," said Pat. "You should look it up sometime."

Later, Maggie wished with all her heart that she had just let it go and left then. She could have forgotten all about it. But something inside her saw red.

"I *know* about child-centered learning, thank you," she said, her voice louder than she'd intended. "I did get a first. And I also think that being pushed outside your comfort zone on occasion is what education is actually about. If you asked some of these girls to direct their own learning we'd spend the entire day kissing ponies. And while we're talking about humiliating children—sorry, *young adults*—I could have done without you two whispering, muttering, and rolling your eyes all through some of the readings. What do you think that was doing for the girls' self-esteem? You lot thinking you're Simon bloody Cowell! It was disgusting!"

Pat looked taken aback at Maggie's outburst. Liz looked rather jubilant and made some notes on her clipboard. Nobody said anything, as, just then, June Starling walked past.

JUNE STARLING HAD heard a raised voice from two classrooms over and had headed toward it as quickly as she could. Now she saw Maggie, in some disarray, red in the face, squaring up to the women from the commission. Oh, this was all she needed. Some street fighting from the outsiders.

"What's this?" she asked.

"Did you know you had a lot of dissension in the ranks?"

asked Liz in an unpleasant tone. June Starling raised her eyebrows.

"Really?"

Maggie colored up immediately. "They're trying to interfere with the way I run my classes," she spat out, before Liz could get any further.

"That's why we're examiners," went on Liz in the same patronizing way. "We're trying to help you make things better."

"But it *doesn't* . . ."

June Starling clasped Maggie firmly by the arm, as she recoiled.

"Oh, you remember when we were young teachers," she said in as blithe a tone as she could manage to Pat and Liz. "So full of passion and fire. Keep it up, you two. I can't wait to see you for the girls' cooking afternoon tea. It's entirely vegetarian, and grown on our own grounds."

"I can't believe your grounds are big enough to have orchards," sneered Pat, but June was already on the move again, Maggie clamped to her side. She didn't say a word to her until they got to her office.

Maggie sat down on the hard chair there, sure when she explained her side of things, Miss Starling would understand immediately. But then she turned round.

"What on earth were you thinking?" she said, her sharp tone not hiding the anger behind the words. "Hollering at our school examiners like a fishwife."

Maggie opened her mouth. "But . . . but they were being really unfair. Liz said . . ."

"I'm not interested in who said what," said June. "I'm interested in passing an assessment that means that parents will be interested in sending children to this school where we can teach them well. And that means, ideally, the young English teacher, who should be setting an absolute shining example of the comprehensive system, and showing that different worlds can exist and integrate side by side, not screeching her head off in full view of the girls. And I know Veronica would agree with me."

Maggie's heart felt sick. She'd been so sure that when she told her about what the women had said she'd see her side straightaway. But obviously this was not to be the case.

"I'm sorry," she said, feeling her face burn up and not feeling sorry at all.

"Let's say no more about it," said June. That girl had a very hot-tempered streak that she needed to learn to contain.

"You'll apologize to Patricia and Elizabeth."

"I *can't*," said Maggie. "I don't agree with them."

"Margaret, you're not one of my pupils. I can't order you to do anything. But you have responsibilities in being a teacher here, and one of them is handling disputes in an appropriate fashion. I don't believe you handled the assessment today in an appropriate fashion, do you?"

Maggie shook her head. "No."

"Very well then."

Miss Starling indicated that she could leave. Maggie wondered whether she'd offer a consoling word on her exit. But she didn't.

"What, no poetry today?"

Stephen Daedalus had found her first, sitting sobbing on a mossy outcrop that led far out to sea. He'd come padding up gently and licked her hand, which only made her cry more. David wasn't far behind.

"Hey, what's the matter?" he'd said gently, as Maggie had

desperately scrubbed at her face with one of the tissues she carried in her handbag.

"Nothing," she'd said fiercely.

David crouched down beside her.

"It's OK, you know. To find everything a bit overwhelming sometimes. You've come a long way."

"It's not that," said Maggie, and found herself pouring out the whole story.

"She didn't even want to hear my side! She didn't care, just sided with them straightaway."

David stared out to sea. "Didn't you ever get inspected at your last school?"

"Yes," said Maggie, defiantly. "They thought I was very good."

David smiled. "I'm sure they did. And did your school pass?"

Maggie wrinkled her nose. "Well, we didn't get put on special measures. But it was a pretty close thing."

"And did it affect the roll for the next year?" .

Maggie saw what he was getting at. "I suppose not. But. I was right and they were wrong. I thought June would back me up— or at least hear me out."

David patted Stephen Daedalus and threw him his stick of the day.

"What you have to realize about June Starling—"

"The poppet," said Maggie.

"The poppet," said David. "Now, don't get prickly. Is that she really, really cares about the school. Above everything. It's her life's work. She isn't married, she's never had children. The school is all that matters."

Maggie stuck out her bottom lip, unwilling to admit that he might have a point.

"Did you really shout at them in the corridor?" His face split into its characteristically manic grin.

"A bit. Maybe," said Maggie. She felt a smile creep on her face. "Well, they were totally asking for it."

"Were they?"

"Yes. A bit. OK, OK OK."

"What?"

"You are *very* irritating. Yes, I shouldn't have shouted at them in the corridor."

"What did I say?"

"So now I have to go and apologize, do I?"

"Would it really be the hardest thing you've ever had to do?"

"Yes," said Maggie.

"Really? Goodness, you *have* had an easy life."

Maggie's lips twitched. "You are so annoying."

"That's not me," said David, "that's your conscience."

"Well, I was right actually, so it's not."

"OK," said David. "It's the school's conscience then."

He stood up and Maggie, wiping her dirty cheek, accepted his hand to her as he pulled her up. When their fingers touched—his hand was warm and dry—she felt herself quiver, and told herself not to be so ridiculous.

"Come on, I'll walk you back."

Maggie peeked a glance at him as they headed back to the school. "You really believe all this, don't you?" she said.

"All what?"

"About loyalty to your school and all that."

David shrugged. "Why? Do you think I'm an old-fashioned weirdo?"

"No," said Maggie, though she realized as she did so that yes, she did think he was old-fashioned, and he was perhaps a little bit weird.

"You do!" said David, sounding scandalized. "You did a big pause! That means you do!"

"Well . . ."

"I'll get you for that," he said. "I'll set my very fearsome dog on you."

"If you can catch me," said Maggie suddenly, dancing away from him in the crisp autumn air.

"Oh, I can catch you."

Maggie took off with the wind at her heels, and Stephen Daedalus not far behind. David, taken by surprise, took a moment to set off after her, but when he did he caught up with her with ease. Maggie, feeling his touch on her cardigan, let the baggy garment fall off her shoulders, as she reached the gate for the girls' school.

"I'm safe, you can't come in, unless I invite you across the threshold," she panted.

"Isn't that vampires?"

"Oh, yeah." Maggie was pink-faced and giggling, and David thought how young and fresh she looked. Then he banished the thought from his head immediately.

"So, do you have your Plantagenet readers for me?" he said.

"I do," said Maggie, feeling a little foolish for teasing him as he immediately turned the conversation back to work. Her hand was still on the gatepost.

"And I have mine," he said. "We're doing the Betjeman. 'And is it true . . . and is it true.'"

"I love that," said Maggie.

"I'll try and do it well, then," he said, smiling.

"Thanks," she said, and she didn't mean for the poem.

David gave her his grin, then summoned Stephen Daedalus with a whistle. From a high turret window, Miss Starling watched them, grimly.

IN THE END, it wasn't as hard to apologize as she'd feared. Pat and Liz had been delighted to take the young teacher under their wing and give her the benefit of their wisdom, acquired through about two years in the classroom and twenty in administration, as far as Maggie could work out. Two long lectures later and they were all friends. But Maggie made a vow to herself to steer well clear of Miss Starling.

Chapter Eight

Simone was absolutely delighted to be chosen to read at the Christmas concert, although she hoped it wasn't just because Miss Adair was taking pity on her. Fliss, on the other hand, was livid. As was Alice, although for the opposite reason.

"For goodness, sake," Fliss had said when she saw her name on the list. Hattie bounced downstairs. "Well *done*, Felicity," she said in that mock-parental tone Fliss hated above all others. "Mops and Pops will be *so* proud."

"Well, I'm not doing it," said Felicity, fiercely. "I know those women said it wasn't compulsory. So there."

Hattie stopped and laughed. "You funny thing! You have to do it now! You can't let the Plantagenets down! The Tudors will think it's hysterical."

Fliss rolled her eyes. "I'll get over that."

"It's serious, Felicity."

"*It's serious, Felicity,*" mimicked Fliss.

Hattie produced a mobile phone from her blazer pocket.

"You aren't allowed those," said Fliss immediately.

"Prefects are," said Hattie, "for emergencies." She tapped some buttons and let it ring. "Daddy? Daddy? Guess what!"

Fliss started to move away, but Hattie grabbed her.

"Fliss is leading the Christmas concert!" She paused. "I know! Non-prefects can't use their phones so she couldn't tell you straightaway but she's right here."

Hattie held out the mobile to Fliss with a fearsome look, even as Fliss was backing away, shaking her hands at it. Hattie made a face and held it out farther, and with a resigned sigh, Fliss had to take it.

"Yes?" she said, nonchalantly. She couldn't deny it, though, hearing her dad's voice on the phone outside the normal Sunday hours, when her mother usually took over anyway and asked her whether she was eating too much jam roly-poly, was lovely.

"Is that my Flick-flack?"

"Hi, Daddy," she said, unable to keep the smile out of her voice.

"What's this I hear about you leading the concert?" He sounded puffed up with pride and his voice was louder than usual. She wondered if he was in a room full of people he worked with.

"I'm not *leading* the concert, Daddy," she said. "There's, like, a million people doing it. The teacher only picked me to annoy the assessment people anyway."

She could feel her dad's smile, all those miles away.

"Well, well done for being so modest," he said. "You know we'll be there with bells on."

Fliss's heart sank.

"We're so, so pleased you're doing so well. Your emails are always so negative . . . we do worry about you, you know. We don't want you to be unhappy."

Fliss felt a lump grow in her throat. She wanted to shout out that yes, she was unhappy, and they had to take her home, that she wanted to go Christmas shopping on Oxford Street with her friends and go ice-skating and she couldn't do all that because she was trapped in a horrible place with horrible food and freezing cold dorms and stupid teachers out in the middle of bloody nowhere. But right at this moment she didn't know how to tell her dad that; it sounded so petty when he was so happy.

"I miss you," she choked out eventually.

"I know, sweetheart," he said. "We miss you too."

"So why—"

But her dad knew better than to get involved in this argument again.

"That's why we can't wait to see you at the concert. And we're so pleased that you're getting on. Your marks are a bit disappointing . . . more than a bit."

Fliss gritted her teeth. At least that was working.

"But we know you're going to buck up and do just fine."

"Yes, Daddy," finished Fliss quietly, handing the phone back to Hattie, who took it triumphantly.

"See. I told you so," she said with a smug look on her face. Inwardly, Fliss decided: this was it. She was going to have to be a lot, lot worse if she had the slightest chance of ever getting home again. It wasn't fair on Ranald.

MAGGIE HAD THOUGHT about Veronica's advice, and had had a long chat with her mother, who had revealed that Stan was indeed missing her more than he'd said on the telephone; that he was still going round there for his Sunday lunch, even on his own, and that he'd been out a lot with his mates.

"Just because he misses you, of course," her mum had said. "We do too, darling. How are things?"

Jenny Colgan

Maggie didn't want to mention that she'd had a very public dressing-down from her boss and that her class had all turned against her—particularly after what was seen as vindictiveness in leaving Alice out of the school concert in favor of that fat girl, as Fliss had been saying as she'd walked in the other day. "Schemie types stick together," someone else had offered, and everyone had nodded loudly before pretending they'd just noticed her. She decided she would definitely invite Stan down, but hadn't been able to get him on the phone that Saturday, as she and Claire had gone out for tea and discussed their love lives. Or rather, she'd told Claire the whole story of Stan; Claire hadn't seemed to want to talk about her own situation too much. Romantically, Maggie wondered if she'd been involved in some terribly passionate French love affair that had gone horribly wrong and made her hide away here in the country, rather like the modern equivalent of going into a nunnery.

But all thoughts of Claire left her head when, still unable to raise Stan on his mobile, she'd gone to bed and later, much later, about two a.m., she'd received a text. The beeping woke her up.

"TX FR GRET NIGHT' it said. From Stan. She'd stared at it for a long time, her heart pounding, and a horrible sinking feeling in her stomach. This wasn't meant for her. Would it be for his mates Rugga and Dugga? But why would he text them in the middle of the night when he saw them every day at work?

With a trembling hand she called the number back, still groggy from sleep.

"Uh, yeah?" Stan sounded drunk, and a little nervous.

"Stan?"

"Wha? What time is it?"

"Did you just text me?"

There was a long pause.

 132

"Uh, did I?" said Stan. "Must have been a mistake."

Maggie felt her stomach plummet into her shoes.

"What kind of mistake?" Maggie heard the steel in her own voice.

"A daft one, knowing me," said Stan. "Uh, it was . . . I must have meant Rugga."

"Yeah?"

"Yeah. I saw Rugga. Call him tomorrow if you don't believe me." He said this in a very defensive tone.

"It's all right," said Maggie. But it wasn't, and they both knew it.

MAGGIE SPENT THE next week in a blur. What was Stan doing? Was he telling the truth? He was daft as a brush when he'd had a few, that was for sure. But he wouldn't even look at another girl, would he? I mean, surely fidelity was just taken for granted, wasn't it? That they didn't even have to discuss it. After all, if it wasn't . . . but she quickly shook away any thoughts of David from her brain. No. This was nothing to do with anyone else. It was her and Stan. Is this what being apart meant?

Anna wasn't much help.

"I haven't heard anything," she said. Normally in the hair salon Anna missed nothing that happened for miles around. "But really, Mags, if you will move so far away . . . I mean, he's a young bloke."

"Yeah, *my* young bloke," Maggie said.

"Have you asked him about it?"

"Yes. He just says it's his mates, and would I stop going on about it."

"Can you get up?"

Maggie thought about the heavy schedule of rehearsals and

marking she had on. Plus she didn't think shooting back to Glasgow at the first sign of trouble was exactly what Veronica had had in mind when she'd said she should keep in touch with her family more.

"Maybe he'll come down," she said.

"You can ask," said Anna. She hadn't been at all as sympathetic as Maggie had hoped. In fact, she'd as much as implied that if she, Maggie, was going to head off and be hoity-toity at the other end of the country, she basically deserved a boyfriend who'd cheat on her. Maggie didn't know what to think.

Feeling lonely and, for the first time since she'd arrived, really questioning whether she'd done the right thing in moving, Maggie threw herself into work. Sometimes it seemed the more she prepared her lessons for the girls, the less bothered they were. But what was the alternative?

MAGGIE WAS SHOCKED to realize she'd been at Downey House for three months as December rolled around. Three months of bells, of teaching girls who sat in rows and (usually) paid attention; of almost no male company whatsoever. Half-term had come and gone in a blur of lie-ins, marking, and wandering around the local town, where the shopping amounted to an unbelievably dated department store that sold a lot of haberdashery, bras the size of barrage balloons, and day gloves, and an outlet of Country Casuals.

Maybe she should have gone home after all. Her parents were worried about her too, no matter how much she assured them she was getting plenty of fresh air and cream teas, and she missed her sister and her little nephews, terrors though they were.

Now the school was readying itself for Christmas. Even

among the older girls, who had mocks in January, there was a palpable air of excitement running through the pupils, as great swathes of mistletoe and ivy wound their way around the banisters and the great hall. Veronica hated starting the whole Christmas folderol too early, but she did enjoy the school looking its very best.

Pat and Liz had gone away for a little while—their inspection would continue throughout the year at different points. However, Liz had gone off sick for an unspecified length of time apparently suffering from stress—Veronica had wondered whether it wasn't the set of Liz's trousers that had been suffering from all the stress, and whether the amount of chocolate biscuits Liz ate had anything to do with it—but Pat would be back at Christmas with another of her protégés. Veronica hoped they would be an improvement. The inspection was definitely not going well. It wasn't just Maggie's outburst that had had to be dealt with; Miss James in PE had insisted that if they wanted to understand her class they had to experience it, which hadn't pleased either of them—they were both very anti-competitive sports; Mlle. Crozier had the sixth form reading "that disgusting old sexist," Jean-Paul Sartre, and they had been overheard discussing how to ask for condoms in Paris, something of which Veronica had thought the inspectors would have entirely approved. She tried to put them out of her head for now as she OK'd Miss Starling's request for a shorter seniors' Christmas party this year and nothing the Downey boys could pour booze into, e.g., punch.

Veronica wandered through the hallways. Really, this year Harold the caretaker and his ground staff had excelled themselves. The greenery gathered in from the grounds gave everything a beautiful scent, and she had ordered the large wood-burning fire in the entrance hall to be lit every morning. It was comforting for the girls, coming down from their chilly dormitories, to be confronted with the fire, the Christmas cards steadily arriving in pigeonholes every day, and warm porridge with cream, honey, maple syrup, and occasionally all three, to set them up for the day ahead.

She liked hearing the laughter in the air as the girls fussed about the concert and the party to follow; to see their flushed faces as they dashed in from hockey for tea and scones by the fire. They hadn't had much trouble with the St. Thinians craze—anorexia—which was endemic in some schools. Perhaps because Downey House was known for its devotion to outdoor life and health; perhaps sensitive and prone girls just avoided it. Or maybe they'd just been lucky so far, thought Veronica, who ate like a bird herself.

"Not running, are you?" she inquired gently to one galumphing middle schooler, who immediately turned puce and slowed down. The gentle approach did seem to work the best.

Christmas was hard for her. Of course she could go to her brother's, but he was a nice simple chap, worked in a warehouse in Oldham, and his wife thought she was uppity because she didn't bring their spoiled children the latest trainers and PS3 games they wanted, even when she was told what they absolutely must have. It wasn't a prospect to relish. No, she was going to take that Greek islands tour with her friend Jane, who taught classics at a wonderful school near Oakham. A Swan Hellenic, lectures every day, walks in the winter sun, and a little learning—it would do her a world of good. Christmas was a terrible time for . . . for people like her. Veronica tried to keep her thoughts in order. After all, who knew what her son would be doing now, and where? Veronica just hoped and prayed, as she did every year, that he was happy—he would be a grown-up man now, maybe with children of his own. Best she never knew. Best nobody knew.

"I do hope you're not chewing gum, Ursula," she muttered gently to the dark-haired girl who passed her on her way to the post boxes. The girl swallowed audibly.

"No, miss," she said, eyes wide.

"Good," said Veronica. "Good."

FLISS HEADED TO Bebo to catch up on her messages. The first one that struck her eye was from Callie, her worst behaved friend from back home.

> FLISS!!! I kno you are locked to death in that school, but you have to have to have to come home for this—Will is in a band at his school and they're playing in the pub! And anyone over fourteen can get in and I think we will definitely count! It's on the 12th December!

Fliss's heart immediately started to race. The twelfth! Two days after the bloody concert, but also two days before they broke up. Would her parents let her go? Definitely not. But if Will saw her there, supporting his band—being a fan right at the beginning, before he became, like, a famous singer and everything—he'd definitely definitely talk to her. And there wouldn't be Hattie or any of the other girls around because everyone would still be at school so she'd have him all to herself, practically.

She had to be there. She had to.

"What are you thinking about?" said Alice, who'd come to find her in the computer room.

"I need to get suspended," said Fliss. "I've had enough. I really really really have to do something so awful that I get sent home."

Alice's eyes widened. "A challenge, eh?"

"Don't you want to get sent home too?"

"Don't care," said Alice. "It would only be some diplomatic nanny. I can't even remember where they are. Cairo, I think. Cairo is *so tedious*."

Fliss nodded as if she'd found Cairo very tedious every time she'd been there.

"But you really want to get chucked out?"

Fliss glanced at the frosty moors outside the window, and nodded enthusiastically. "I want to go home," she said. "I'll miss you, though."

"I'll come stay for the holidays," said Alice, philosophically. "See if this bloke you like has any mates."

Fliss wasn't sure she wanted to introduce dark gorgeous Alice to Will, but having her to stay would be great. She'd probably be grounded and stuff for a little while—for ages, after they caught her sneaking out to the gig—but then it would be Christmas and everyone would soften up and forget; Christmas was great at their house, they all got loads and loads of pressies and got to watch telly and her mum just heated up some turkey stuff from M&S but then let them eat chocolates all day and gave them a taste of champagne—and by the new year everything would be back to normal and she'd be with her friends and at a normal school again.

"OK," said Fliss. "Well, I need your help."

MAGGIE FELT NEARLY as nervous at her first rehearsal with the boys' school as her girls did. She'd drilled them after school—

having to get them to learn all the pieces off by heart was the first challenge, but they were making good progress. Fliss had suddenly become surprisingly good about it considering she hadn't wanted to be chosen in the first place. And Simone was stolidly professional, doing it the same way every time.

Simone had taken to coming over to Maggie's office occasionally, once or twice a week, to exchange a book from Maggie's large collection. They rarely spoke much, but it was a companionable silence as Maggie did her marking, or chatted with Claire, generally in Maggie's halting French so as to keep it from Simone's tender ears. When they did speak, Maggie saw further flashes of the sensitivities and humor that came through in her essays. Crippling shyness was such a terrible thing. Yet on stage she was perfectly fine. Most peculiar.

Maggie noticed that even though the girls shared a room, Felicity never included Simone in conversations with Alice or little whispered private jokes; even when heading back to the dorm together they somehow contrived to leave Simone out. Maggie hated to see it and wished she could do something about it, but didn't know how.

All the girls involved in the performance were there for the readings, plus the orchestra, and they met in the great hall that doubled as a theater. There was seating for six hundred; it was rather daunting, Maggie mused, standing on the stage and looking out. Downey House meant what it said about creating confident young ladies. She imagined the rows of parents watching her girls and applauding . . . perhaps she would be asked on to take a bow . . .

"Hello hello!" shouted a voice, startling her from her reverie. David strode into the hall on his long skinny legs, a Pied Piper leading a long line of young boys behind him. The boys looked around—they looked more confident and certainly had better skin and posture than the boys Maggie had taught, but they seemed to lack that jokey nonchalance her boys used to put on in new situations, where they would kick each other and pretend that they were twenty-five and could all drive cars. This lot probably had drivers and would be aiming for parliament by the time they were twenty-five. The girls behind her quietened down noticeably and stopped messing about.

"Right, first years all together!" said David. "We're only going to do this twice, so no messing about. Girl readers stage right, boys stage left, orchestra in the middle, dancers do your thing, and it will all be fabulous."

He stood looking up at Maggie on the stage and she was seized with a huge impulse to put out her hand and let him help her jump down. But she knew any hint of physical contact would be leaped on by the pupils and gossiped over obsessively, so she hopped down by herself. Nonetheless she could feel her heart beating, and checked again to see if the lipstick she'd surreptitiously applied earlier was still there.

"So, are your girls all ready then?" said David, giving her his grin. She felt her insides fizz.

"They're great," said Maggie, loud enough for them to hear. "It's the orchestra I'm looking forward to."

"I wish I could conduct, don't you?" said David. "It always looks like such fun. Just waving your arms about in a good coat and getting rounds of applause."

"I'm not sure that's all there is," said Maggie, laughing at his daftness.

"Yeah, course it is. Bet they earn tons of money too."

Mrs. Offili came out and shot David an affectionate look.

"Showing off your impeccable musical pedigree as ever, Mr. McDonald."

"Certainly am, Mrs O. You've seen me dance."

Mrs. Offili shook her head, although there was a smile playing on her lips, and started on the tuning up.

Watching everyone run through their parts, Maggie was impressed. But even as one of the boys, a tall, thin lad called Peregrine, was doing a spine-tingling rendition of the "Carol of the Bells," she found herself glancing at David. He was totally rapt, mouthing the verse along with the boy and, although she was sure he'd be incredibly embarrassed if it was pointed out, actually conducting the verse. Maggie looked at his long fingers and wondered . . . No. This was nonsense. She shook her head. And wildly inappropriate. She'd clearly been holed up here for too long, and was getting frustrated. It wasn't David's fault he was the only semi-nice-looking man for twenty miles. She could see the girls eyeing him up too.

Both girls did well. Fliss really would be quite beautiful when she grew up, with her pale skin and even features, thought Maggie, however overshadowed she was at the moment by the glamorous, knowing Alice.

Everything went smoothly and well until after rehearsals had finished and David and his troupe were getting ready to leave—Maggie had slightly hoped he would linger and ask if she wanted to go for coffee, or even a drink in town, but he wouldn't—and the girls went into the changing rooms at the back of the auditorium to pick up their bags. Fliss came out looking slightly upset.

"Miss? Miss?"

"Yes, Felicity?"

"I've lost my watch. I took it off to put it on the side while I was timing myself, then I definitely left it in my pocket—definitely—but it's not there now."

"What do you mean?"

"It was in my pocket before I came on stage," said Fliss, looking miserable and staring at the floor. That watch had been her grandmother's. It had been left to her, and her parents had had severe misgivings about letting her take it away to school. She'd promised to look after it. Even though this would help her case to leave the school, she was still utterly devastated. Her grandmother had loved her to bits and she'd loved her too, and her little house, full of knick-knacks, and Malinkey, her gran's little Scottie, who always tried to fight Ranald. Of course Ranald would never fight back, he was far too much of a softie. Thinking about her gran, and her dog, made the tears prick Fliss's eyes.

"It was my gran's," she said, lip starting to wobble.

"Let's go look," said Maggie. "It couldn't have fallen out?"

Fliss shook her head. "I've looked everywhere."

Simone, and Alice, who'd turned up to meet Fliss after class, were standing outside the locker room, looking dismayed. Maggie looked closely at their faces. Stealing at school was one of the most disagreeable things to deal with. It was time-consuming, unpleasant, and caused a lot of talking behind pupils' backs. With a stab of guilt she wondered if, with the amount of time she'd spent out the front talking to David, she might have been able to prevent it.

The changing room backstage was quiet, as various girls from various houses sat around, looking worried. There was a passageway to a corridor exit on the side, noted Maggie, which meant it was accessible to almost anyone in the school. Alice and Simone both looked nervous. Maggie glanced at Simone.

It couldn't be denied that she didn't own nice things like the other girls did. And that Felicity and Alice had basically ostracized her since she'd arrived. Could she do something like this to teach them a lesson?

And what about Alice? She didn't think Alice had been too thrilled about Felicity getting the part, and sharing in the glory that should have been Alice's alone. Could she be trying to get her own back? Surely she wasn't that sly?

"Hello, everyone," she announced to the silent room. All the excitement and good cheer of the rehearsals had gone; she'd also fetched in the boys from their locker room, and David stood behind her.

"We've had a report of a lost watch," she said, firmly. It wasn't time to search the children or their belongings. She wasn't sure that was the best way to go about it anyway; stolen goods could be easily hidden, and searching promoted mistrust and implied the children had no sense of moral values at all and might as well steal. And the watch probably was just lost; the kids were so careless.

"Now, I'm sure it will turn up." Behind her she could feel Felicity bristle. "However. If anyone knows anything—anything at all—about this, can I urge them to come forward to Mr. McDonald or myself, in strictest confidence, at the first opportunity, do you understand? Thanks!"

She glanced round the faces looking up at her, trying to catch a glimpse of embarrassment or guilt. Immediately she couldn't help noticing that Simone had gone brick red, and was doing her best not to catch her eye. Maggie's heart sank. The punishment for stealing could be suspension, or even worse. She really hoped Simone hadn't jeopardized her future for something as petty as this. It would be a tragedy if so.

"If for any reason this watch isn't just 'lost' you can come and see me or Mr. McDonald in our respective offices, or leave us a note. I'm sure we can clear this up without any unpleasantness being necessary. Do I make myself clear?"

There was a mumble of awkward consent.

"All right," she said. "Good rehearsal, everyone. Your parents are going to be proud. Off you go."

The children scrambled off to get a late tea the kitchen had made specially for them as Maggie and David looked at each other sadly.

"Say it isn't lost . . ." said David.

"I don't know," said Maggie. "What do you think we should do, cancel their concert?"

"They've worked so hard," groaned David. "And I hate this 'punish the many' thing. It's so overkill. Kids never rat anyway."

"I know. Bugger."

They stood in silence for a moment.

"Do you think it was stolen?" asked David.

Maggie nodded. "One of the girls went very red."

"Oh no," said David.

"I think it's my scholarship girl. Fliss isn't nice to her at all. Not bullying, but just excludes her. She just looked so horribly guilty."

"You can't jump to any conclusions," said David. "But maybe a quiet word." He sighed. "Boys just whack each other about for that kind of thing."

"I know. I think you have it easier."

"Yes," said David, moving away. "Apart from the world wars and things. Do you think your cook would have any tea left over?"

Despite her disappointment, Maggie couldn't help feeling herself perk up.

FOR ONCE, SIMONE skipped supper. Her face was flaming. She'd seen the way Miss Adair had looked at her. Accusingly. Like, "You're the poorest girl in the school. It must have been you." She'd felt the guilty blush steal over her cheeks. Fliss and Alice, too, had given her such a hard look when Fliss had realized her watch had gone. She'd wanted to shout at them that it wasn't her, that she would never do that, but she couldn't. The words wouldn't come; it was as if her throat had seized up. Now they would definitely think she'd done it; that she was jealous of Fliss just because she was pretty and popular and all of those things. Which she was.

Only Imogen was in the room, studying quietly with her back to the door. Simone undressed quickly, threw herself under the blankets, and cried herself to sleep as quietly as she could.

FLISS WAS THE center of attention at the table, as people jockeyed for position to tell her how sorry they were about her watch and try and remove themselves from suspicion.

"Who do you think it was?" asked one of the Tudor girls.

Alice looked around. "Well, don't think I mean anything by this or anything," she said. "But have you noticed the one person who's not here?"

THE CHILDREN HAD bolted their food and moved on to the television lounge by the time David and Maggie had finished clearing up and everything was dark in the cafeteria. Mrs. Rhys, the cheerful cook, had left two covered plates of sandwiches, scones, cheese, and fruit out, and the urn was still plenty hot enough for tea.

"It's still going to be a good concert," said David, his hand on her shoulder as they walked over to the deserted tables. "Don't worry about it."

Maggie stiffened instantly when she felt his hand, and nearly dropped her scones. "I know," she said. "I just want everything to be all right, you know?"

They sat down, not facing each other, but corner to corner, their heads nearly touching. She wanted to lean forward, breathe him in, but didn't dare.

"I know," he said, and for an instant, Maggie thought he was going to take her hand, in the darkened, deserted meal hall. The space between them was charged; she was sure she could see sparks leaping between their fingers. Her heart beat faster.

It was so strange. She'd gotten so used to her and Stan over the years, and had worked with so many female teachers, she hadn't really thought much about other men, apart from in an abstract, Brad Pitt kind of a way. It was strange how quickly this tall, skinny dark-eyed man with the manic grin had gotten into her head.

There was a pause, which turned into a long, loaded silence. And suddenly, she knew. Suddenly, they were staring at each other in the deserted hall. David turned his gaze on her and she returned it. For once, the noisy school had fallen completely quiet. Maggie was aware of her breathing; and of his, and she wondered, as time seemed to slow down and take on a fluid quality, if he would be rough, or smooth, or both, and, almost as if it didn't belong to her, she felt her own hand stretching out to clasp . . .

"SIR! SIR!!! LLEWELLYN'S PUSHED MIKE JUNIOR'S HEAD DOWN THE LOO AGAIN!"

"I DIDN'T! I DIDN'T! OR AT LEAST I WAS SORELY PROVOKED!"

Six boys burst into the hall like a small angry torrent of beavers. Maggie pulled her hand back immediately as if she'd been touching something hot. David gave her a quick glance—was it annoyed? regretful? she couldn't tell—and stood up.

"What? What's all this? No, on second thoughts, I DON'T want to know. Come on, you savages, back to the prison pit where you belong."

He turned to Maggie, and the look in his eyes was completely unfathomable.

"I'd better go and round up the rest of this sorry crew before they unleash the dogs of war all over your nice hall."

Maggie forced her lips into what she hoped was an unbothered smile and nodded vehemently.

"Definitely. Definitely. Of course. Right. Bye then."

Chapter Nine

The days passed, and the thief did not come forward. Although it had been the talk of the school, the chatter started to die down a little. But Simone was well aware it centered on her, and stalked the halls with her head down and her eyes red. Maggie decided she really must have a word with her, although she'd been putting it off. There had been no more cozy book swaps, either. She needed to find out what was up, she was neglecting her duty. But everyone was just so busy at this time of year.

At least nothing else had gone missing. A note had gone round the entire school, warning the pupils that there might be a thief on the loose, that valuables should be given to Matron and locked away, and that anyone with any information should come forward. No one had.

Meanwhile, Maggie had a more pressing problem on her hands. Stan was on his way. He was coming down for the week of the concert, then they could drive back up home together. The idea was he could see the Christmas show and a bit about her life, and hopefully they could spend some time together and get themselves back on track. Every time she thought about it, she felt so nervous. Partly because of what he might have been getting up to. And partly because of what had crossed her own mind. David hadn't emailed her since the rehearsal. Although disappointed, she'd realized immediately what this meant—that there was nothing going on, just her slightly feverish imagination. It must be true what they said about girls locked up in boarding schools. And it was absolutely ridiculous behavior; getting a silly crush on some teacher across the way, who probably got crushes from every child he ever met, girl or boy, she thought firmly. It was ridiculous and completely unprofessional; they were working together, and they had to stop it getting out of hand.

She and Stan had been together seven years. That was worth fighting for. And the idea of Stan cheating on her was the real issue, not distracting herself from her sadness by a dangerous flirtation.

The train from Glasgow took a long, long time to wind its way down the entire country and finally into Exeter. Maggie was standing at the barrier and saw Stan disembark a long way down the train. He was brushing a lot of pastry crumbs from his hoodie. Maggie looked at him as if through the eyes of a stranger. He looked the same as ever—long and skinny, except with an oddly protuberant pot belly that made him look a bit pregnant; spiky, gingerish hair, pale skin. He carried a large sports bag and a copy of *Top Gear* magazine—surely it couldn't have been all he'd brought to read for a ten-hour train trip. Or maybe it was.

It seemed to take forever for him to make it to the gate. All around were couples falling into each other's arms, running up and crying with happiness and relief.

"Hey," said Stan, looking nervous.

"Hey," said Maggie. She wished she was running into his

149 🐦

arms, but somehow she couldn't make herself. It would be stupid. Starting a relationship at school meant you never got overly-demonstrative.

She didn't know how to broach the subject, but she couldn't just dive in straightaway.

"How was your trip?"

"Good," said Stan. He burped. She smelled lager. "You look posh."

"Do I?" said Maggie. Veronica had very kindly mentioned that a friend of hers owned a boutique in town and offered a discount to school staff. Claire had taken her shopping, and together they'd spent rather a lot of money (Maggie was finding that without paying accommodation, food, petrol, or going-out costs she was able to save a huge amount of her salary) on some new basics for her—two beautiful wool skirts, some plain white, well-cut shirts, and a heart-stoppingly expensive cashmere jumper. The plain clothing accentuated Maggie's good legs and beautiful dark hair, which she had tied back more loosely, after Claire had insisted on pulling just a couple of fronds round her face.

Stan could see that she looked well. His heart sank. If she'd looked fat, or sad, or lonely, or any of those things. But it was patently obvious that she was doing just fine down here without him. Better, if anything. He knew it.

They stood there a tad uncomfortably for a moment, then Maggie leaned forward and kissed him awkwardly on the cheek. Stan turned his face so that the kiss could hit his mouth, but he didn't quite make it in time, so it ended up a rather awkward mishmash.

"Ehm. So. Have you crashed my car yet?" he said, as they disengaged.

"It's our car!" said Maggie. "And no, of course not."

 150

Stan heaved his bag into the boot, and climbed in the driver's seat.

"Eh," said Maggie.

"What?"

"Well, have you been drinking?"

"I had a couple of lagers on the train, but nothing . . ."

"I think I'd better drive," said Maggie. "Plus, I know the way, remember?"

Stan didn't want to get out of the car and feel like an idiot, but he supposed she did know the way.

"OK" he said, ungraciously, and moved round to the passenger seat, heaving a sigh.

They left the ring roads of Exeter behind them quickly enough, followed by the motorway, and eventually left the main roads to start the climb toward the cliffs of Downey House. Early snow had stayed on the tops of the hills and the views over the sea were quite starkly beautiful. Maggie took quick glances to her left to see if Stan was taking them in or even noticing them.

"It's scenic, isn't it?" she asked eventually.

"Hm," Stan grunted, noncommittally. "I thought you hated the country."

"So did I," said Maggie. "I'm quite surprised with myself."

"Hm," said Stan.

Maggie couldn't believe she was feeling so disloyal, but as she parked the car—at least Stan had shown a mark of surprise when he'd seen the towers emerging from behind the hills—she was wondering if he should have come at all.

"Fuck me," he'd said. "It really is a fucking castle, isn't it?"

Maggie looked at it affectionately.

"Yes," she said. "And it's starting to feel like home."

Jenny Colgan

"Thought as much," said Stan, ungraciously.

This wasn't going right at all, thought Maggie. She needed to get over the horrid panicky feeling she'd had when she'd gotten that text, and remember her priorities. She was Maggie Adair. From Govan. Who'd fallen in love with Stan when he was seventeen years old. He was her best friend. Her lover. Her Holy Cross savior.

She cast her eyes to the left. He was sitting in his Celtic top, looking so awkward and nervous. She felt her heart soften toward him. Of course it was a new environment. Of course he was nervous. Hadn't she been, the first time she'd rolled up the gravel drive in their small, unimpressive, car? The school was designed to impress, to be the best. Stan was intimidated, and she should be careful of his pride.

"Hey," she said, reaching over and grabbing his knee. "You know, they're all a bunch of English arseholes."

"Yeh," he said, glancing down at her hand on his leg. He felt bony, warm, reassuring somehow. "I know. I had to hear them shouting all the way down on the train. No wonder I drank so much lager."

Maggie nodded. The smell was noticeable in the small car.

"I really need to take a wazz," said Stan.

"We're here," said Maggie, opening the car door. Her heart suddenly skipped a beat. There, crossing the car park and looking distracted, in a tweed jacket with a long stripey scarf blowing out behind him—he couldn't have looked more like a fey English type if he tried—was David.

"MAGGIE!" he hollered, as she emerged from the car, Stan slightly crossing his legs as he levered himself out the other side. He came striding over, Stephen Daedalus bouncing excitedly when he saw Maggie there, tail wagging furiously.

152

"Thank God," said David, looking slightly breathless. "We need you. It's an emergency."

"What?" said Maggie.

"Forters Junior has put his back out doing water polo. He can't stand up for the concert."

"But it's tomorrow!"

"Yes, I know that."

Maggie thought as quickly as she could. His lovely piece, ruined. Who did she know . . .

"I think I have just the person," she said, internally rolling her eyes at how she was going to have to crawl to Alice now, and completely underscore the girl's original strongly held belief that she should have been the star all along.

"Trebizon-Woods," she said. Stan looked at her as if she was speaking a foreign language.

"Will she learn it in time?" said David. "You know what my lot are like, you have to hide the verses in porn mags and Yorkie wrappers."

"Oh, she knows it," promised Maggie. "She may be a tad reluctant to do it for me, but hopefully sheer ego and vanity should shine through. I'll flatter her a lot."

"EXCELLENT," hollered David. Then he turned his penetrating gaze on Stan, who was standing and looking increasingly awkward.

"Hello! Who are you?" David stuck out his hand. Stan didn't stick out his. David shoved his back in his pocket. "I'm David McDonald. Maggie's opposite number at the boys' school."

"I thought there were only girls here," said Stan, in a rather uncomfortably bleating tone.

"Oh, yes, yes, that's right . . . I work on the other side of the hill."

"Oh," said Stan.

"And you are?"

Maggie felt ashamed of how embarrassed she was. Of Stan, in his nylon Celtic football shirt, covered in potato chip crumbs, with his dirty jeans, pot belly, short haircut. She hated feeling like she was seeing them through David's eyes. Partly because she also suspected that David wouldn't judge people on what they wore; it wasn't his thing at all.

"I'm Stan. I really need to go to the toilet."

David's eyebrows arched temporarily. "OK. It's all girls' loos up there, but maybe Miss Starling wouldn't mind if you attacked her rhododendrons."

"David." Maggie shot a look at him. This was not the time for dry English humor. Stan looked miserable.

"Stan's my . . ."

She was scarcely conscious of the pause until it had happened.

"Boyfriend," said Stan, sullenly. It sounded strange coming from him. He'd seemed so reticent in the first place. "I'm her boyfriend."

"Ahh!" said David, looking back at Maggie and then to Stan. "Lovely!"

Maggie bit her lip. She didn't want Stan to realize that she'd known David for a while and had never mentioned him.

"Yeah," said Stan.

"There's a loo over here," said Maggie. "I'll speak to you later, David. I'll have a word with Alice and get back to you, but I'm sure it'll be fine."

David nodded and retreated, looking rather thoughtful.

Maggie showed Stan up to her rooms quickly, ignoring the sizing-up glances from the girls she passed and trying not to think about whether or not they'd gossip—of course they would. She wondered how many men in football shirts arrived here. None of their fathers or brothers, that was for sure. Stan, while moving reasonably swiftly, kept stopping on the stairs to look at things: portraits of old girls, chandeliers, paneled doors. He whistled softly to himself.

Finally they reached the little suite in the East Tower. Stan couldn't stay there, of course, not without all sorts of criminal records checks and so on, but he could have a look around. Maggie had tidied up and laid a new bedspread over the bed. It didn't make it look any more like a double than it had previously, but it cheered things up a little. She'd also added flowers, and bought some lager for the fridge.

"I'll just have a wazz," muttered Stan. Maggie stood, staring out of the window, feeling suddenly helpless.

Five minutes later Stan came back out. He'd brushed the crumbs off his shirt and eaten some toothpaste. "Hey," he said quietly. Maggie didn't turn around, just kept staring out of the window. "I didn't know there were men around here at all."

"He's just a teacher at the school across the hill," said Maggie dully. "We have to work together." She turned round to face him. She could see it in his face. He looked guilty. "Stan," she said.

With a jolt, she suddenly saw him again, as if for the first time. Seventeen and long and skinny, pretending he wasn't waiting for her outside the dinner hall. The leap in her heart as she'd seen him there; trying to hide her French jotter, which had his name scribbled all over the back page. His slow creasing smile as his mates joshed him, but he had stayed and waited for her anyway.

The bedroom felt colder than ever.

"I didn't do anything," said Stan sullenly, staring at the floor. "She wanted to, but I didn't."

"So there was a 'her,'" said Maggie, feeling her blood run cold. "And you told 'her' it was a great night."

"I didn't say I wasn't thinking about it. I said I didn't do anything. And you can believe me or not." Stan ended on a defensive flourish. Then he looked up at her to gauge her face.

"I missed you," he said simply.

Maggie felt her prejudices about him, her worry about how he came across, among her new life, her worry about whether he really cared for her or whether he was quite pleased to have the place empty for a bit . . . all of that faded away as she saw her spiky-haired Stan right there; his cocky funny side gone, and all because he loved her and missed her. She felt . . . love, mixed up with feeling a bit sorry for him.

She stepped forward. She believed him. It was as simple as that. Some woman would have come on to him, and he'd have done his best to back down from it. There might even have been some snogging, but she could deal with that. After all . . . and she banished the thought of David from her mind. She put her hand up to Stan's cheek.

"I missed you too," she said.

"Naw you didn't." He indicated all around. "Not now you're living in a fucking castle with *David*."

Maggie stepped forward. "Sssh," she said. Stan looked at her, half suspicious, half hopeful. "Want to go out and do something that is totally banned in a girls' school?"

AFTER A MOSTLY successful reunion afternoon at the local B&B, Maggie needed to get to the dorms; there was a rehearsal after supper and she had to catch Alice. She wasn't particularly looking forward to it, but there it was. Simone and Imogen were there finishing their prep. Fliss and Alice were reading about Britney Spears in a gossip magazine.

"Alice, can I see you for a minute?"

Alice heaved a sigh that was a tad too grown up for a thirteen-year-old, then brightly announced, "Of course, Miss Adair," so she couldn't get into trouble for it.

Maggie took her outside.

"Simone seems to be happier," said Alice, in that irritatingly adult way she had.

"It's not about Simone," said Maggie. "One of the Downey boys has had to drop out, and we need someone who can perform the T. S. Eliot."

Alice's eyes lit up, but she tried not to look too eager. "Yes?"

Maggie rolled her eyes. "And Mr. McDonald and I thought you might like to take it on."

Alice pretended to look as if she was thinking it over. Maggie smiled; she was pretty good.

"Well, it is a lot of extra work."

"Fine," said Maggie, "I'm sure Simone would be happy to do two."

"No! I think, I think I can fit it in."

"Good," said Maggie. Then she relented. "Well done, Alice. I'm sure you're going to be very good."

Alice nodded. "Is that your boyfriend, miss?" she asked. Not much didn't get round the school in about ten seconds, Maggie thought ruefully.

"Is that your business, Alice?" she said sharply, deeply regretting bringing Stan up the main staircase rather than sneaking him in the fire escape door.

"No, miss," said Alice, delighted she'd obviously struck a nerve and looking forward to spreading it round the class.

"Well, on you go then. And finish your prep before you pick up a gossip rag, OK?"

ALICE REENTERED THE dorm smiling broadly to herself.

"What?" said Fliss, suspiciously. She had wondered if there was any updating on the thieving. Nothing had gone missing in the last week or so and it all seemed to have settled down.

"You know we were trying to work out what you're going to do at the Christmas concert?"

Fliss felt again the big ball of anxiety in her stomach. She was horribly nervous about doing something really terrible. On the other hand, she had to get out of this school, she had to. Get back home again, go to Will's party; see Ranald, go to a proper school. She just had to steel herself and do something really bad once. It did make her feel horribly nervous and anxious, though, and was keeping her awake at night.

"Well, you just got better backup. I'm on too."

Fliss jumped up. "That's brilliant! That's great news."

Simone overheard and shrank a little inside. When it was just her and Fliss at rehearsals, Fliss wasn't that mean to her. A little quiet and distracted maybe, and friendlier to the girls from the other houses than to her, but not horrible, and sometimes she'd even walk her back to the dorm, though she never mentioned this to Alice. Fliss was someone Simone would like as a friend. She was glamorous and quite funny, nothing like as sullen as she pretended to be in class. If she could just get to know her, Simone thought she could really talk to her. If she could just get to know anyone. Simone sighed and went back to the letter she was sending her parents. They didn't have a computer, so she couldn't email and Skype like everyone else. On the other hand she did get a lot of letters in the post, which made the other girls jealous. She'd told her mother to stop sending cake, and thankfully she had.

"I am having a good time here," she wrote out carefully. "Everyone is very friendly and I get on well with everyone."

Well, she couldn't write the truth. Even isolation was better than being plucked out and sent back to her old school.

THE DRESS REHEARSAL for the concert went badly, which, as much as David said it was tradition, shook Maggie up a little. Lights didn't cue at the right time, the orchestra was all over the place, and Simone lumbered on at completely the wrong point, bursting into tears when this was pointed out to her for the second time. Alice was word perfect already, but Fliss was suddenly strangely jumpy and nervous. The weather had turned frightfully cold, and David said Stephen Daedalus could smell snow and was refusing to leave the house. Maggie wondered if he was right. It didn't snow much in Glasgow— too built up and too near the sea—and when it did it hardly lay on the ground before it got dirty and snarled up with cigarette butts and footprints.

Stan had spent his days holed up in her rooms watching television. In vain she'd tried to interest him in taking walks around the local area; visiting the beautiful, windswept beaches, or the quaint villages. He'd been happy to go to the local pub every night and eat their microwaved lasagne and drink the local beer while complaining it wasn't Eighty Shilling.

Oddly, though, Maggie was finding she didn't mind. It was just Stan, doing what he did. It was comforting. And they had fun together, taking part in the pub quiz with Claire (the English league football round stumped them all), chatting about her friends and family and what everyone was up to, then retiring to the B&B, which, perhaps through enforced intimacy and the fact that Stan couldn't eat in it, meant they were making love more often than ever.

It was only now that Maggie realized how lonely she'd been. All the silly fantasizing about David was clearly just that, the imaginings of a lonely woman who'd let her daydreams run away with her; no better than the girls she taught. This was where she belonged, sipping beer and laughing at Stan's impersonation of his boss at the distribution plant. She must just stop thinking about David, that was all. And she could tell Stan was happy too. It wasn't so unlikely that other women fancied him, after all.

IT DID SNOW, huge choking flakes through the night. The girls woke with yelps of excitement and a festive atmosphere ran through the school quicker than lightning. Mrs. Rhys took the nod from the grounds manager, and decided to make bacon and eggs rather than the weekday porridge (or gruel, as the girls referred to it). Some of the parents who were coming to the concert were staying a couple of days, to take the girls home from school in the car, though most would take the London train on which the school had a block booking. Though many girls had gone home at half-term, some hadn't seen their mum and dad for twelve weeks and were quite beside themselves. There was a flurry of nerves and packing and huge excitement as the delicious smell of cooking sausages wound its way up the stairs.

VERONICA WENT TO her office early, a heather-colored cardigan from Brora pulled tightly round her shoulders. This was not ideal at all. The snow would affect the roads, which would mean the parents would be late, the concert would overrun horribly, and everything would be out of sync. She hated disorder. Not only that but the inspectors were coming back to watch the concert. She shook her head. This wasn't *High School Musical*, the film every single girl in the school had suddenly gone mad for last year and had even gotten up a petition to go and see. It wasn't a performing arts college. The quality of the music teaching was one thing, but turning her girls into a troupe of showboats was extremely far away from her original aims.

She leafed through her paperwork. Very few girls were staying over the Christmas break; just one whose parents were diplomats in a country currently going through some upheaval, and an Australian fourth former, Noelene, who got horribly unhappy in the winter months. Veronica couldn't understand the parents sending her so very far away. Getting an English education was one thing. Getting it while your parents were sunning themselves by the pool was quite another.

There was a knock at the door, interrupting her train of thought. Miss Prenderghast popped her head round.

"It's Patricia from the inspector's commission—with a new inspector too," said Miss Prenderghast. She lowered her voice. "It's a *man*." Veronica raised her eyebrows. The men in this line of work tended toward the very pernickity, finicky types brandishing a large manual of health and safety practices. Not, frankly, ideal.

"All right, Evelyn, thank you. Send them in, please," she said.

Pat bustled in, all frenzied seriousness as usual, as if someone had just deliberately said something to upset her.

"Merry Christmas," said Veronica, conscious of the fragrant holly and mistletoe lining the fireplace. Pat raised her eyebrows.

"Do you know, many schools prefer to inclusively celebrate Winterval now? So that no child feels left out?"

"Christmas leaves no one out, Patricia," said Veronica, wondering what would constitute a safe nicety.

Her eyes moved upward to look at the man who followed her in. He appeared quiet, neat and tidy in a gray suit. Quite young for an inspector; not yet forty, she would say.

"Veronica Deveral," she said, holding out her hand. The man seemed to look at it curiously before he took it.

"Daniel Stapleton," he said. Then he shook her hand quite forcibly, staring into her face.

Veronica sighed inwardly. Were any of these inspectors quite normal? He probably learned "keep eye contact' on some money-wasting training course. "Welcome to Downey House," she said.

"Thank you," he said, his voice sounding a little trembly and nervous.

"Coffee?"

"Yes please," he said, glancing nervously at Pat. Pat nodded and said, "Miss Prenderghast, do you think we could maybe get a couple of sandwiches?"

Veronica despised anyone treating her highly organized administrator as some sort of domestic servant, but Miss Prenderghast was already heading off to the kitchen as Pat took the seat nearest the fire.

"Now, for the concert tonight, we have several quality target initiatives that we'd like to see pushing the envelope . . ."

SYLVIE RAN INTO the common room, where the girls were talking nervously about the concert and the party, in particular what they were going to wear. Everyone was asking Fliss and Alice what the boys in the orchestra were like, what the readers were like, and in particular who was the tall boy they'd seen walk in in full high-collared dress uniform?

Besides that, of course, the main topic of conversation was Miss Adair's chav boyfriend. There had been great excitement when he'd been spotted in the main halls wearing a football top! The girls were full of excited speculation as to whether he'd ever been arrested and whether or not he was a football hooligan. Ursula and Zazie, a Moroccan girl from a wealthy family who spoke perfect French and English and had a usually mischievous sense of fun, had both expressed amazement that someone as old as Miss Adair would have a boyfriend at all, rather than some ancient husband stashed somewhere.

Fliss had found her nerves all shot; she'd hardly slept the previous night. But she and Alice had talked it through; they were going to do it. She was going to do it. In front of everyone. She was going to ruin the concert and go home. Then she'd sneak out to Will's band and then . . . well, she didn't know what would happen after that, but it didn't really matter. No more stupid classes. No more stupid Miss Adair on her back all the time. No more stupid having to share a room with Imogen and fat Simone. No more having to listen to Hattie's boring stories about being a prefect, blah blah blah. She'd be back where she belonged. And once Mum and Dad got over being a bit pissed off they'd be pleased, she was sure of it. Pleased to have her back, just her on her own, no stupid sister. It would definitely be worth it. But oh my goodness, the nerves. She tried to concentrate on what the other girls were asking her—about Jake, the lanky pretty boy from the boys' school, who was reading the Betjeman. Not her type. Her type was only Will. Will. Even saying the name made her heart flutter, and steeled her resolve.

Anyway, here was Sylvie tearing in. She was meant to be dancing, but was looking as scatterbrained as usual.

"I've lost them!" she was saying.

"What?" said Alice.

"My earrings! I have special silver earrings that go with my Dickens outfit. And I can't find them! But I'm sure they were in my desk drawer."

The noisy common room went quiet. It was common knowledge that Fliss had lost her watch. Most of the girls had hoped it was a mistake or a one-off. Now it looked as though there was a serial thief among them.

Sylvie was nearly tearful. Normally nothing troubled her, so to see her upset was very unusual. She looked around.

"I know they were there because I tried them on last night for rehearsal. So it was someone who's been around the dorms since. I didn't lose them. So if it was one of you . . ." Her voice choked up. "I hope you're proud of yourselves."

Simone, crouching in the corner with one of the books Maggie had lent her, stiffened. Then Alice picked up what Sylvie was saying.

"Yes," she said. "I know not everyone has lots of money at this school. And people shouldn't be judged on how much money they have. But if you don't have much, you shouldn't take other people's things. I'm not accusing anyone. I'm just saying."

The whole room went silent. Simone felt every eye on her.

"Anyone got anything to own up?" said Alice. Nobody said anything. "Anyone?"

Simone felt herself get to her feet. Her face was flaming, a bright, bright red color she could feel. She wanted to make it clear; to show people and tell them that it wasn't her, she wasn't a thief; all the girls in her old school had gone stealing all the time and she'd thought it was disgusting. But the words wouldn't come out. Her throat was completely choked up.

"Just . . . shut up!" she half-screamed at Alice in a high-pitched tone. "SHUT UP!"

And she pushed her way through the girls and left the room.

ALL THE GIRLS were hanging out of the windows as the first cars started to pull up, snow on their roofs, into the allocated car spaces. Sixth formers were out in padded jackets to direct the traffic, along with the grounds staff. The forecourt was lit up with fairy lights, and a huge Christmas tree stood in the middle of the cobbled quad. The school looked as beautiful as it possibly could, thought Maggie, waiting for Stan to make his way up from the village. He'd taken the car, although walking would obviously have been slightly healthier for him, but she didn't want to argue.

She was wearing a new dress that she'd bought. It was a deep, Christmassy red that reflected well against her dark hair and brought out the pink in her cheeks. Pulled tight around her waist, and with a pair of Spanx on, she looked good—pretty, but not so vampy that any of the girls' families would feel uncomfortable around her.

The girls were in uniform for the concert, but were doing their best to bend the rules for the visit of the boys' school, so there were ribbons in the hair, illicit skirt turning-up, and barely traceable makeup everywhere. Yelling and running, normally completely verboten in the inner sanctum of the school, were breaking out all over. Usually very conscious of the feelings of the pupils who did not have parents coming, Veronica found this difficult, but didn't forbid it. Just because some were unhappy didn't mean you had the right to make everyone so.

Finally, quite a while after the scheduled six p.m. start, the heavy, old red curtains of the packed theater opened, and Veronica walked out.

"Welcome, everyone," she said, "particularly those of you who have come a long way. We've been very proud of our girls this term and I know that next year, as we move toward the summer, they will work harder than ever."

There were some theatrical groans at this, as the students knew they were far enough away from their austere headmistress to risk a little gentle heckling.

"But Christmas is a festival. Wherever you are from, and whatever your beliefs."

Pat's head, from where she was sitting in the audience scoffing Haribo, popped up at this.

"Northern European countries have always celebrated the depths of winter, the very nadir of the year, with celebration, dancing, warmth, food, and light. We in the Christian tradition also celebrate the birth of the infant Christ, but there are many winter traditions that surround us, and all exist to wish us peace and prosperity at this cold time of year. So on behalf of my girls, and Dr. Fitzroy, who has so kindly lent us some of his boys to make up the orchestra and some of the readings, may I wish you peace and joy from all at Downey House."

The applause was loud as Alice, looking beautiful and very meek—Maggie mentally shook her head—came out with Lars, a cellist from the upper school. The idea was to interplay the poem with a strange, eastern melody and it worked beautifully. Maggie felt a shudder go up her spine as Alice, having been told to downplay her reading, came to "This birth was hard and bitter agony for us" and the refrain was subtly echoed in the music. There was no doubt Mrs. Offili had done a wonderful job.

After that, there was dancing from the older girls, and the choir, which was nearly of professional standard, all sang except for the back-row altos, Maggie made a mental note, who were standing far too close to the boys and four of them were red-faced and sniggering about something. They weren't in her group, but she might have a word with Miss Starling.

BACKSTAGE, THE MOOD was giggly and tense among the soloists. Astrid was in a world of her own with her clarinet, tapping out melodies in the air when she was meant to be putting makeup on (the girls took this performing privilege very seriously). Clarissa Rhodes, school star, was singing a version of the "Carol of the Bells" which, it was rumored, had made Mrs. Offili cry. As usual, she didn't think she was good enough and was nervously checking the sheet music.

Alice had bounced off the stage to a mass of warm applause, and was making a terrible job of hiding her delight. Now her part was over, she could content herself by basking in how much better she'd been than everyone else. Simone was in a corner by herself. Nobody had offered to put her eyeliner on, or a bit of lip gloss. She looked terrible; her eyes were red and dark-rimmed from lack of sleep, her hair was a mess, and if anything she'd put on weight again.

Fliss was also standing alone, her heart beating at an alarming rate. She'd have been nervous about performing anyway, but this hadn't really sunk in until she'd peeked out of the red curtains and seen how many people were out there: hundreds and hundreds. She couldn't even see her own mum and dad.

"There's still time not to do it," said Alice, who was hoping very much that Fliss would. They'd cooked up the plan together in the alcove late at night. "I wouldn't tell anyone."

Fliss shook her head. "No," she said. "I have to do it. I have to get home. And this is the best way that doesn't involve hurting anyone." She glanced over at Simone. "Or stealing stuff."

At the sound of the "stealing" word, Simone had raised her head, then she buried it again. Maybe the best thing she could do would just be to tell her parents that she didn't want to go back to Downey House, that it hadn't suited her after all, that she'd been wrong. But then they'd send her back to St. Cat's. There wasn't a solution. She was trapped. She tried to focus on her piece. Her hands were shaking. She mustn't forget it. She mustn't.

The Tudor first years finished their pageant—a series of rhyming couplets they'd written themselves about Christmas down the ages. It was good, thought Maggie. She should have done something like that. It was sure to have impressed Miss Starling.

"Hello," said a voice in the wings. "Nervous?"

Maggie turned round to see David standing there, looking tall and handsome in a velvet jacket that should have looked odd and dated but actually rather suited him.

"No," she started to say. "Actually . . . yes. For them, of course."

"Of course," said David. "You look very nice."

She felt herself blush; she hadn't thought he'd pay attention to things like that.

"Thank you," she said. She'd managed, while Stan was there, to mostly wean herself off thinking about him. But she did wonder, once again: was this man gay, single, or what? It wasn't a conversation they'd ever had.

They stood in silence for a while, watching Clarissa sing the "Carol of the Bells." At first her high voice rang out accompanied only by a single bell. Then, as the choir came in on the ding-donging, Maggie felt the hairs on the back of her neck rise. Finally, the entire orchestra and choir together sang to the rafters the triumphant, "Merry merry merry merry CHRISTMAS." It was stunningly beautiful.

"Wow," Maggie said breathlessly. She realized, with a sinking heart, how aware she was of David right next to her. Maybe it hadn't gone away at all. Maybe it was just lurking, to catch her out.

"Yes," he said, turning to look straight at her. She caught her breath.

Then suddenly the quiet intimacy of the moment was lost completely as the horde of the choir pounded off through them like a flock of clumpy-shoed gazelles, to cheers from the audience. It was hard to find a quiet moment in a school. Maggie checked her program and realized she should be herding on Felicity.

"I have to go," she muttered, almost apologetically, feeling her heart pound.

"Of course; me too," said David, looking very awkward.

Maggie darted off in the direction of the dressing room. "Come on, come on," she chided Fliss, who was standing there looking slightly ill. "Don't worry, you're going to be great."

Felicity was the last act on before the interval, after which there was the senior ballet and play to get through, with Simone's monologue opening the second half. They were running late, though not ruinously so.

"Come on. You're not too nervous, are you?"

Fliss couldn't work out why Miss Adair was being so kind to her, even offering her a glass of water. Everyone at this school was horrid, except for Alice. That was why she was leaving. She was going home. That was it.

"You'll be wonderful," said Maggie, surprised Fliss was so pale and terrified. Most of the girls had reasonable poise in front of their peers; part of a class that had told them since birth they were more than good enough. But here she was, practically having to throw her on stage.

There was a silence from the auditorium now, just an expectant rustling of programs. Fliss closed her eyes.

"OK," she said. Then she walked on to the stage.

The lights were so much in Fliss's eyes at first she could scarcely see a thing. In a way that was quite good. People looked farther away; she couldn't distinguish who was who. But it did make her realize the scale of the occasion.

She stepped up to the microphone. It was set to Clarissa's height, far too tall for her, and no one had brought it down, so she had a very awkward moment fumbling for it. Maggie, watching from the wings—David had vanished—felt embarrassed that she hadn't arranged for someone to fix it for her. Oh well, sympathy would be on her side. She would deliver Jo's speech and just as it ended the orchestra would join in with some jaunty American turn-of-the-century melodies to play the audience out into the main hall, where there was exceedingly weak mulled wine for the grown-ups and sixth formers, and lemonade for the rest.

Fliss gave up her struggle with the microphone stand and decided just to hold the mike instead. She bit her lip and stepped forward. "Eh," she said. Immediately the microphone let out a howl of feedback. People were starting to sit up and take notice. There hadn't been much in the way of hopeless amateurs so far. Everyone was too good. For the bored younger brothers and sisters in the audience, as well as those members of the school not involved, a little diversionary failure couldn't come soon enough.

"There's a few things I want to say about this school before I start," said Fliss, but her voice was wobbly and not quite close enough to the mike.

"Speak up!" shouted a voice from the back.

Suddenly Fliss saw red. "This school is crap!" she yelled into the microphone. "The food is crap and the teachers are crap and you're all being ripped off!"

A thrill of delighted rebellion rushed through the younger (and some older) members of the audience.

"First of all, there's the COMPLETE unfairness of the mobile phone-locking scheme. That is a complete attack on human rights. And some of the teachers can barely speak English. Our English teacher is almost impossible to understand. Why should we have to suffer through that?"

Maggie had a quick intake of breath and moved toward the stage.

"Not to mention the horrible PE changing room where there's still communal showers like this was 1980 or something."

Some of the fathers' eyebrows were raised at this.

"SO . . ." And at that, Fliss ripped open her shirt. The entire audience gasped as the buttons popped off and, underneath it, saw she was wearing a white T-shirt, crudely scrawled with the words DOWNEY HOUSE SUCKS.

Fliss, realizing she'd captured the attention of the audience, stepped forward to continue the litany of injustice, before ending it on a chant she hoped would be taken up by the entire school—"DOWNEY HOUSE SUCKS!"—until someone ran on stage to drag her off. That English teacher most likely. That should do it.

Sure enough, Maggie, who'd hardly been listening until her name came up, so conscious was she of where David was, now made to run on stage. Mrs. Offili was already on her feet to start up the orchestra in order to drown out the noise. But right then, Fliss took one last step forward to emphasize her point . . . and dropped out of sight completely.

THE ORCHESTRA DIDN'T sit in the orchestra pit for the first half of the show; they went on the stage, so that the proud parents could pick out their daughter, the second bassoonist. They would go down there once the ballet started, but for the moment it was empty. Which could be seen as good luck, mused Veronica later, as she tried, and failed, to see an upside, as it meant Felicity Prosser broke only her own ankle and didn't injure anyone else.

The kerfuffle and yells that broke out as Felicity dropped from the stage were enormous and what had happened ran through the school at the speed of light. Most of the parents assumed the girl had been drunk, and wondered how alcohol was obtainable on the premises—and to such a young girl too. Veronica ordered the orchestra to play on and for the interval to continue as planned; of course, there was only one buzz in the air.

Maggie was third on the scene, to find David and Mrs. Offili already there ministering to a white-faced Felicity, who had tears streaming down her face from the pain.

"What the hell!" she started shouting at her, her own shock and worry about her pupil coming out too clearly in her voice. "What the HELL was that?"

David turned round from where he was looking at Felicity's

ankle. "I think we need to get her to a hospital," he said. "I can drive her if you like."

Maggie felt herself instantly reproved, and bristled. "She needs to get to a hospital because she was pulling some ridiculous stunt and it's her own fault. What on earth were you *doing*, Felicity?"

FLISS COULDN'T BREATHE for the pain. The pain in her leg and the shocking and terrible recriminations she felt raining down on her head from all the people in the hall. There was a ring of people around her as all the curious individuals came to nose about. She could hear her mother's voice saying loudly, "Where is she? What happened? What's happened to her?" and the crowd parting to let her through.

Suddenly what had seemed like such a good, rebellious idea in the dorm with Alice seemed like the worst idea ever. What had she been thinking? Making an idiot of herself in front of the whole school? And now, her ankle really, really hurt. She felt cold inside, worrying if something was really wrong with her.

The handsome English teacher from the boys' school was looking at her in a concerned way and had covered her up with his jacket, which wasn't too bad until he prodded her foot, and Miss Adair was shouting at her, but that was nothing unusual. For a second she wondered if she could make herself faint, but as her mother and outraged-looking sister pushed through the crowd she realized there was no making about it, and she dropped clean away.

The next thing she knew she was on a bed in the sanatorium. The first person she saw was Matron, who told her she was going to be fine, but she needed to go to the hospital to get her ankle seen to.

Her parents and Hattie were there too, looking confused.

"But why?" her mother was saying. "Why?"

Miss Adair was right behind her, still looking furious, as was Miss Starling. The teacher from the boys' school looked concerned. Fliss wondered if he'd carried her into the sanatorium.

She looked down at her swollen throbbing ankle.

"I just wanted to go home," she said, tears pouring down her cheeks.

The father of one of the pupils, a surgeon, came and gave his professional opinion on Felicity's ankle—that he believed it was indeed broken—and she was packed off to emergency in Truro.

Veronica was in two minds. She should perhaps call off the show. On the other hand, there were a lot of parents who'd paid a lot of money and come a long way to see their children perform, and she didn't want the antics of one to ruin the evening for the rest of them. And she disliked quitters. She came to a decision.

"Ladies and gentlemen," she announced in the grand hall, where quite a few parents were getting stuck into the mulled wine. "I do apologize for the behavior of one of our younger girls. She's very new here. But all our other wonderful girls and boys are here and ready to perform for you, so if you'd like to retake your seats . . ."

There was a general mutter of approval, particularly from parents who hadn't yet seen their own offspring, and a loud tut from Pat, who was, no doubt, Veronica reflected, judging how much she could escalate the incident in her own report, for health and safety reasons.

SIMONE, TRAPPED IN her own misery backstage, had hardly noticed the commotion, only that everyone had disappeared and left her on her own, which was hardly unusual. Now they came back in dribs and drabs, whispering excitedly—"She was drunk! She called everyone a bastard!" to one another so she gathered something had gone terribly wrong with Fliss's piece. It would probably make her more popular than ever, Simone found herself thinking meanly.

"Simone," said Maggie, somewhat wild-eyed. She was ashamed of her outburst before, shouting at a sad, injured girl in front of David. "Do you think you can go on and do your piece without managing to jeopardize the entire school?"

Simone nodded behind her owl glasses, not quite understanding.

"OK, on you go then."

The orchestra had just about calmed down enough to play a Grieg interlude, introducing the Dickens as Simone walked on. The audience was now upright and expectant, hoping that she would do something equally unexpected.

"Marley was dead, to begin with," said Simone, launching into the speech she'd rehearsed a thousand times in her head.

And she was good. Very good. Not even her mother standing up and filming in the middle of the front row, in direct contravention of instructions, as well as of the people behind who wanted to see, could stop her. She was clear and her London accent added a veracity to the words, and as she came to a close, the senior girls, who were dancing a piece based on the book, fluttered on like a clutch of Dickensian fairies, in tasteful rags and smocks, to hear her intone how "the candles were flaring in the windows of the neighboring offices, like ruddy smears upon the palpable brown air. The fog came pouring in at every chink and keyhole . . ."

The applause was massive and heartfelt, particularly from the staff and those pupils who didn't want to see the school made a laughing stock of by a pushy middle schooler. Maggie found herself grinning with relief, before she went off to check with the hospital. And Veronica couldn't help being quietly pleased and surprised at her awkward little scholarship girl. Would she yet surprise them all?

MAGGIE HAD CALLED the hospital—Felicity's parents had taken her in their car, and Matron had followed on behind. All would be fine. The corridor was empty and quiet, as the audience was entranced by the seniors' ballet (some of the fathers perhaps a little more than they ought to have been). She wondered briefly where Stan was and what he made of all this. Then out of the shadows stepped David.

Maggie felt her heart flutter. Oh, this was ridiculous, she had a huge disciplinary crisis on her hands, and, who knows, the parents could take it into their heads to sue the school, and where would they be then?

"Is she OK?" asked David. Maggie nodded; Matron had responded briskly that they were putting her in plaster and she'd be right as rain.

"Her parents will take her home while we sort out what to do."

"Just a little bit of teenage rebellion," said David.

"Just a bit," said Maggie. "Quite a big bit though."

David looked at the floor. "Look, Maggie, I think . . ."

He seemed awkward and looked up again. He was standing right underneath some mistletoe.

"Ah," he said, noticing it, but not stepping away. "The thing is, Maggie . . . God, this is bad timing. Well. Uhm. Too late now. Uh, I really like you."

Maggie stopped short and looked straight at him. Her heart

was pounding in her mouth. Surely not, with Stan here and everything. She couldn't. He couldn't. It wasn't right. It wasn't even legal on school grounds.

But suddenly she thought she wanted to kiss David McDonald more than anything else in the world, even as she could hear the orchestra play the "Coventry Carol" next door.

David tried again. "There's something I should have . . . it's very important that our relationship remain professional."

Maggie felt her heart drop like it was in an elevator shaft. Of course it was. Of course. What an idiot she was. David was looking at her, but it was hard to read his expression. Almost as if he found this painful too.

"I think it's for the best, don't you?"

Inside Maggie wanted to scream, NO! No! I want you! Instead, she just nodded her head and said, "Quite! I'm sorry, I didn't realize we'd gone beyond the normal bounds . . ."

"No," said David, shaking his head vehemently. "No, of course we haven't."

Without being able to consciously help it (or so she told herself), Maggie found herself glancing upward at the mistletoe, and then back toward David. He seemed to move toward her—was he? Did she? She found herself compelled to move forward. Her gaze was fixed on his dark eyes. Was she really going to move straight into his arms? What if they were discovered? The school really couldn't have any more scandal tonight. But to feel his lips on hers suddenly seemed more important than any rule; any job she could possibly have. She felt drunk with longing; she wanted him more than she'd ever wanted anything. Shocked by the power of her feelings, she stepped forward. It felt as though the music dropped away; the snow outside rendering everything silent and still.

"David," she breathed.

"David!" she heard.

It was a loud, friendly voice and it came from a blond woman who'd just entered the passageway. She was pretty and fresh-looking.

"Hello!" she said cheerily, putting out a hand to Maggie as she came forward. She came up to David and took his hand.

"I'm Miranda." She turned to him. "Ooh, look, mistletoe. Do you think it would be *dreadfully* naughty to kiss in school? This is where I learned after all."

"Hi! I'm David's fiancée," she added to Maggie, as if the ring on her finger and her stance of ownership could have left anyone in any doubt.

Chapter Ten

It was not the happiest of Christmases. Glasgow was covered in a gray sludge, which, Maggie felt, reflected her own state of mind. She felt so stupid, so ashamed, and so damn cross! OK, she'd never mentioned Stan, but—a *fiancée*? So, David probably had lots of girls crushing on him every year without a *teacher* embarrassing herself. Was she, a woman with a boyfriend, really going to snog another, engaged teacher, in the school when all the parents were there? Thinking about it made her shiver with horror. What on earth had she been thinking? What was wrong with her?

Stan thought she was sad because she was realizing how much she missed Glasgow and all her friends. He was being incredibly nice to her. Maggie had thought guiltily that maybe he suspected something was up, but, no, he hadn't mentioned David—he'd hardly mentioned the school at all, just arranged nights out at the pub with their friends and lots of trips round to her mum and dad's. She was grateful for the distractions and touched at Stan's kindness—long-distance relationships really were difficult. Maybe it was time to see if he'd like to come and work closer by. Stop her getting fixated on someone like a teenager who still had posters up in her bedroom.

And it was nice to get looked after by her mum and dad, and watch telly late, and play with her nephews, and come and go as she pleased without having to worry about being on show all the time. That was the thing about Downey House, and she'd never anticipated how much of a burden it could be; to eat communally, work communally, to see the same faces all day every day was quite wearing, more so than she'd realized. It was nice, after all, to slump around the house in pajamas, playing music loudly and watching television with Cody and Dylan.

"I thought we'd go out on New Year's Eve," said Stan, as she sat polishing off the a box of chocolates in front of the *Doctor Who* Christmas special they were watching for the fourth time.

"Oh yeah," said Maggie, not really paying attention. "Is Jimmy having another party?"

"Neh, thought we'd go out for dinner, something like that."

"OK," said Maggie, surprised. Going out for dinner wasn't a very Stan thing to suggest. He was improving.

New Year's Eve was, as ever, utterly freezing and bitterly wet. Maggie started regretting their plan almost immediately as they waited for a bus, having tried and failed to catch a cab into town. The restaurant was filled with large groups of noisy people shouting and bursting balloons at one another while wearing party hats, and the frazzled waiter moued apologetically as he showed them to a cramped table for two buried in the corner. Stan immediately ordered a bottle of champagne, which was very unlike him. Maggie gave him a sharp look. They were doing a little better financially as Maggie's job paid more than her old one, and she was spending a lot less. But still, this was a bit recklessly extravagant, and they should really . . .

"Maggie. Maggie!"

Stan had to say her name twice before she responded. When she looked up she saw he was kneeling on the floor.

Oh my God! Why hadn't she noticed he was wearing his only suit?

"God, I meant to do this at the end of the meal, but I'm sweating like a pig, and I don't think I can hold it in, so . . ."

Maggie stared at him. What was he doing? Oh God. This was the last thing she'd been expecting. The other, red-faced, drunken people in the restaurant had started to look round, after someone caught sight of what was going on. She shook her head in amazement. Well, David wasn't the only person who could be engaged after all.

"So, my lovely Maggie . . . you've had your time away, and I've missed you horribly and we've had our ups and downs, but I really, really want you to be mine forever, so, uh, will you marry me?"

Somebody woo-hooed in the restaurant, but everyone else had fallen suddenly, eerily silent; even the waiters had stopped scurrying around. Stan looked up from where he was kneeling, and fixed Maggie with his kind blue eyes.

"Well?"

FLISS WAS, IN the end, only rusticated. That meant, as Hattie had pushily explained, that she was suspended but without it going on her permanent record. It was only for the last three days of term. The school saw her broken ankle as quite punishment enough and had given the lightest penalty. Had she managed to deliver more of her speech, it had been made extremely clear to her in a conversation with Miss Adair, Miss Starling, and Dr. Deveral, which her parents attended—a meeting Fliss would never be able to think of again in her life without feeling the most deep and intense shame—then things could have been a lot worse.

Of course she had not made it to Will's Christmas party. Or any Christmas party. Her mother was more sympathetic, but her father's disappointment was clear to see in his face. She hated making him so miserable. Hattie, of course, was triumphant and made a show of being extra helpful by bringing her books and extra study guides to help her catch up. Only Ranald, licking her face every day like he couldn't quite believe she was home, gave her any succor.

Now, her cheek and rebelliousness felt a bit stupid and immature. Getting bad marks on purpose? Fliss thought, with a creeping sense of contrition. Did she really do that? What must the teachers think of her, even that horrid Miss Adair.

After a muted Christmas—the grounded and incapacitated Fliss opened her new clothes without much pleasure, knowing her opportunities to wear them were severely limited—and oddly stilted visits from her friends, who were full of the new shopping center, and the new boys at the school, and teachers whose names she didn't know, she was staring out of the window at the sleet driving into the orchard, while failing to take her usual comfort in rereading *What Katy Did*, when both her parents entered her room at the same time and sat down. Fliss looked up at them nervously. Being grounded was one thing. Getting another lecture on how badly she'd let everyone down and how she'd disappointed them was quite another.

So she was surprised when her mother took her hand.

"Felicity," she said. "Your dad and I have been talking. We didn't . . . we didn't realize you were so unhappy."

"I wasn't unhappy all the time," said Fliss, grudgingly. She'd had a lot of time alone in her room to think about things. She glanced at her father, but his eyes were downcast.

"We've talked about it, and we've decided," continued her mother. "We'd like you to see out the year. And then, if you still really hate it . . . well, we can talk about it then."

"I want you to give it a proper shot," said her father, his voice sounding gruffer than usual. "To see it through. None of the best things in life are easy right off the bat, Felicity."

"And we paid the fees up front," said her mum, like that was important. "I've spoken to the school. You can go back on your crutches with your plaster, they can manage that. You will apologize to everyone involved in the concert for the upset you caused. Then it will never be spoken of again. But if you as much as breathe out of line . . . I'll be furious. I want you to try, Fliss. Try your absolute hardest, OK?"

Fliss nodded, grudgingly. She'd expected a lot worse. Her book was easier to read now, after her mother had kissed her on the cheek and both parents had gone off to the charity Christmas ball. Till the summer. She could wait.

"IF I HAVE to listen to that BLOODY"—Joel, trying out the word in case it counted as swearing—"Dickens garbage one more time do you think I am going to be a) a little bit bored, b) extremely bored, or c) so bored I'm going to have to kick myself in the head?"

"You should be proud of your sister," said Mrs. Pribetich. Simone had been made to perform her extract in front of every set of relatives and friends her mother could muster to showcase her privately educated daughter.

The relief of being home, where nobody watched what she ate, or made sly remarks (apart from Joel, and she could cuff him), or accused her of being a thief, almost made her want to cry. She reveled in the very smell of home; of food cooking and her mother's perfume. Seeing her own bedroom made her sink down with relief.

But her parents' pride in her and her accomplishments was so strong.

"Shy, but with excellent imaginative and intuitive skills," Maggie had written on her report card. The fact that Simone's spelling and punctuation were behind, thanks to years of noisy undisciplined classrooms, she'd put aside with the aim of trying to boost the girl's confidence. She still didn't know how to broach the subject of stealing. She'd have to do something about that in the new year.

"A pleasure to teach," Miss Bereford the maths teacher had added. Mrs. Pribetich had brandished that report at everyone from the postman upward. So Simone swallowed her feelings and tried her best to smile and take things in good humor, even as her mother tried to get her to wear her school uniform to church.

It was only toward the end of the holiday that Simone's nerves started to bunch up again in her stomach. She was eating more, she realized. Packing her suitcase was torture. Even the thought of having to walk into that dorm again; to hear the whispers and giggles of the other girls instantly silenced as she entered. Of another lunch or supper sitting alone at the end of the table, excluded from the conversation. The thought of it made her queasy. The night before she was due to catch the train she went upstairs to finalize her packing, taking a packet of Hobnobs with her as she went.

Her father came in to find her weeping over her new chemistry textbook.

"Hey, what is it, *scumpa*?" He chucked her gently under the chin, which made her cry even more. "It's not the school, is it?" he said, sitting down on the bed. Simone wanted nothing more than to throw herself in his arms and tell him everything: about the teasing, and remarks, and the loneliness, the huge, massive, crushing loneliness.

But what for? He'd sacrificed a lot to come to this country, to see his children do well. In Romania he could be an engineer. Here he could drive a cab. He had sacrificed his own hopes and ambitions for her. She couldn't tread on his dreams, even though she knew at some level how much he hated her being away from him and thought the fancy school would carry her even further away.

And to go back to her old school. How would that be better? How would that help anything at all?

"It's nothing," she sniffed. "I'm glad to be going back. I'll just miss you all, that's all."

Her papa took her in his arms and gave her a long squeeze.

"We miss you too," he said, patting her back and rubbing his own eyes. "We miss you too. And we love you, *iubita*. You're making your mother so proud, you know? You're making all of us proud, even that *obruznicule* brother of yours. Never forget that."

VERONICA USUALLY SAW in Christmas with the minimum of fuss. She liked to keep busy. Jane was a good companion in this respect; she minded her own business and chose to discuss history rather than pry into anything personal. Veronica wondered about Jane herself, and her own preferences, never voiced, but she wouldn't dream of raising it. And the weather was clear and bright and warm in the Greek islands, where they ate moussaka and visited the ruins and in the evening put cardigans on their shoulders and strolled through villages, looking for the most authentic tavernas. It had not, flighty teenagers notwithstanding, been a bad year, on the whole. Applications were up, and the new English teacher, while hotheaded on occasion, certainly seemed enthusiastic and worked hard, two qualities, Veronica often felt, that compensated for the occasional practical deficiency, though June Starling didn't always agree. Now, she only had this wretched assessment to get through and everything would be clipping along quite nicely.

MAGGIE TOOK A deep breath. They could sort out the geography later. OK, her new job had its tough moments—and she wouldn't mind never seeing David McDonald again—but she didn't want to give it up straightaway; there was still so much to learn she could bring back later. Stan could even find something in Cornwall; he liked the pubs well enough. Anyway, it was something they could discuss. And they had plenty of time; there was nothing wrong with a long engagement.

Gosh, she also found herself thinking. Here I am. Being proposed to. How extraordinary. She was even more surprised at not having guessed it was coming. After all, they had been together a long time. But they'd had such a difficult year. She looked at Stan's scruffy, lovable face.

As the restaurant diners, almost as one, leaned closer, she let a huge smile break out.

"Of course," she said, only a tiny part of her mind wondering if this was quite right. "Of course!"

And the room let out a huge round of applause.

Chapter Eleven

The weather was sharp and cold as the cars rolled up for the spring term. Faces were solemn; this term there was sport outside in the freezing cold; mock exams for the older girls. Maggie examined the little shiny half-carat ring they'd chosen in Laings on her finger for the thousandth time and vowed that there was going to be no more nonsense of the Felicity/Alice variety—she was going to split up the troublemakers and put everyone's nose to the grindstone. She didn't care that they sniggered at her and that the girls didn't accept her. She was going to make them work. It was a broad syllabus and she wanted to prove to Veronica, to Miss Starling, to the assessors and everyone else that she was capable. No, better than capable: a good teacher.

Claire was the first to pounce when she arrived in their little suite of rooms, amazed at how pleased she was to be back there again.

"*Qu'est-ce que c'est?* What ees that on your finger!!!" she exclaimed, as soon as she heard Maggie arrive. Maggie beamed and stretched it out. They had phoned her parents, Stan's dad, and everyone they knew as soon as Stan had got up off the ground, looking as pleased with himself as if he'd just won the lottery. Everyone's happiness was so strong and palpable she'd found herself getting swept along in the champagne, and the hugs and the planning. She needed to have a conversation with Stan about maybe him moving to Cornwall for a couple of years, just while she got the experience she needed at Downey House, then they could go back to Glasgow, she'd find a school that needed her, and everything would be just fine. All the talk was of where, and when, and what it would be like, and who would come. They hadn't set a date yet, as there was too much to discuss and they only had a few days before Stan was back at work and Maggie was already making plans to go back south.

"But it won't be for long, love, will it?" Stan said hopefully, tucking into pizza on their last night together.

"Well, I think I need to be there a bit longer than three months," said Maggie, carefully folding up her new soft gray jersey dress, just like one Claire had, that she'd picked up in the January sales. "I need to get a good reference, then I can work anywhere. I should stay for at least two years."

Stan made a grumpy face. "You don't want to get married for *two years*? I thought you girls were always desperate to get down the aisle."

"Well, we could do it next summer. This summer is probably too early anyway, everything will be booked up. And it will give us longer to save up."

Stan looked at her. "Yeah? You want a big do?" He didn't seem the least bit put out by the prospect.

"I don't know," said Maggie. "We could just slip off to Vegas if you like."

"Yeah, get married by Elvis. In a cadillac," said Stan, his eyes gleaming. "Neh. It would break your mother's heart."

He was so thoughtful, she thought.

"Stan," she said. "Are you sure you couldn't look for work in Cornwall? They have newspapers there too, you know. And fish suppers."

Stan looked perturbed. "But I like it up here. All my friends are here. And my family. You're the one that wants to go down and ponce about among English folk."

"I know," said Maggie. "But I thought you'd like us to be together."

"Yuh," said Stan. "That's why I asked you to marry me. Come home. Let's get a wee house in Paisley. It'll be good."

"I know," said Maggie. And it would. It would. She just . . . "I just think I should see this job out, OK? It's a great opportunity for us. For setting up our future."

"I miss you," said Stan.

"I know," said Maggie. "I miss you too."

"And that school of yours is full of mad folk. What about that weirdo, the bloke teaching English?"

"David's not weird! He's just different."

"I didn't think they let blokes like that teach in boys' schools."

Maggie looked at him in exasperation. "I'm going to pretend I didn't hear that."

Stan smiled. He liked winding her up.

"Was EET *romantique*?" asked Claire, as they sipped tea together and watched the cars draw up.

"Well, it was in a restaurant," said Maggie. "And there were about a hundred pished folk watching. But it had its moments." She smiled to herself at the memory.

"*Bof.*" Claire had finally confided in Maggie that she was having an affair with a married man but she wouldn't tell her where. She often vanished on weekends and during the holidays, and came back slightly sad, if suntanned, and with a fabulous new pair of shoes every so often. Maggie was convinced she'd winkle it out of her sooner or later, but for the moment, Claire was content to dive on Maggie's romantic news.

"So what are you going to do?"

"Well, nothing yet," said Maggie. "I think I'd like to have a long engagement."

"Oh yes, like Monsieur McDonald."

Maggie stopped with her teacup halfway to her mouth. Claire had known? Why hadn't she mentioned it? Well, she supposed it wasn't really her business. She had never discussed David with Claire, was too afraid of a giveaway blush if she so much as thought of his name.

"Oh yes, I met his fiancée."

"She works in Exeter, I theenk," said Claire. "Does not visit very often. I sometimes think that he is lonely. The other teachers at the boys' school, they are very old, don't you think? Apart from Monsieur Graystock, *bien sûr*."

Maggie hadn't met the classics professor, but had heard Claire mention him. She'd spied him from afar at the concert; he was tall, aristocratic, and distracted-looking, and she hadn't given him much thought. But then, Maggie had never had much thought to spare for the other teachers at Downey Boys.

"So why aren't they married?" she asked.

"*Je sais pas*," said Claire, shrugging. "I heard she wanted him to move to the city, but he does not want to go and move Stephen Daedalus . . . it is true," she said, wrinkling her nose. "The English and their dogs."

Maggie would have added something about the French and their mistresses, but didn't feel it was entirely appropriate. But that was interesting about David. Pulled in different directions, just as she was. She instantly dismissed all thought of him from her head. That was pointless, and supremely silly. And she was an engaged woman now, with someone at home who loved her very much.

"We should get changed for supper," she said. "I'm sure the girls are going to be *thrilled* to see us again . . ."

"And a hardworking term too," said Claire. "I am going to be *slavedriver*. I want those *petites rosbifs* to stop just one time from mangling my beautiful language until it sounds like peedgeons fighting. Do you think it can be possible?"

"Definitely," said Maggie, as the two friends headed for the stairs.

FLISS WAS NERVOUS as they pulled into the graveled forecourt once more. She had promised her parents she'd behave, but was worried about how her teachers would be with her—particularly the hated Miss Adair, who hadn't shown the least bit of sympathy over her ankle. She'd promised faithfully to raise her marks; they could hardly get any lower. She swung her plastered ankle out of the side of the car, and waited for Dad to help her out. She was only limping slightly now, with a stick, and it didn't hurt at all, except when it was itchy. Would the other girls shun her for messing up the Christmas concert?

She needn't have worried. From the moment Alice spotted her from the dormitory window, and ran down with a scream of excitement, Fliss was enveloped in a mass of girls eagerly asking her what it had been like in the hospital, asking to sign her plaster, and, mostly, sighing over the romance of fainting and being carried to the san by dashing Mr. McDonald, just like Kate Winslet in *Sense and Sensibility*, or Keira Knightley in

Atonement. Fliss was very peeved she couldn't remember a bit of it.

"Are we really sure she hates that school?" said Fliss's father as they drove away, scarcely noticed by their popular offspring, both completely submerged in chums.

"Let's just see at the end of the year, shall we?" said her mum.

AT LEAST THERE was a heavy workload this term, thought Simone, the only person pleased at the prospect. She could bury herself in books and nobody would notice. The fuss about stealing seemed to have died down for now. Maybe those things really had just gone missing after all. She would ignore the accusatory glances, ignore everything except concentrating on work and passing exams. She was going to make her dad so proud. Even prouder than he was already. Remembering her family's love provided a small candle of warmth inside her.

"YES?" VERONICA LOOKED up at the door, as Daniel, the new assessor, knocked and slipped into the office without Pat. She was surprised, yet again, at his youth and wondered why he'd chosen this job.

"Hello," she said pleasantly. "Tea?"

"No, thank you," he said. "I think Patricia is on her way."

She nodded. Then they both spoke at the same time.

"So," she said.

"Well . . ."

They both smiled.

"You go," he said.

"I was just wondering what brought you into this line of work?" asked Veronica. "Sorry if that's a personal question."

"No, not at all," said Daniel. "I'm really a teacher, I'm just on temporary reassignment."

"Oh yes? Where do you teach?"

"I teach history in a grammar school in Kent. But this offered some travel, a chance to look at practice in independent schools. See what good ideas we can come away with."

"That's not always how assessors see it," said Veronica, smiling wryly.

"It's how I see it," said Daniel firmly. "And I was looking forward to seeing the famous Downey House . . . and meeting you. You've quite a reputation."

Veronica knew and disliked this, even though it was good for the school.

"It's not about me," she said. "It's about the girls."

Daniel smiled and nodded.

"Sorry I'm late," said Pat, breezing in without knocking, and not sounding sorry at all. "Terrible traffic."

Veronica refrained from commenting on the fact that there was never any traffic on the quiet country road that passed by the school.

"Shall we begin?" she said.

MAGGIE TOOK A deep breath. All right. So things hadn't gone brilliantly with Middle School 1 last year. But it was time for a new start for all of them. Then she winced. Oh no, she still had to deal with Felicity. She'd had her punishment, but Maggie still had absolutely no doubt that Alice Trebizon-Woods had been involved at some stage, and now she really had to split them up.

"Alice, Felicity," she said, feeling the eyes of the class on her. It hadn't escaped her notice that Felicity had been lionized for her act of defiance. "Felicity, I know you paid the price for your little prank at the Christmas concert"—a ripple ran through the room—"but nonetheless. I don't want you two sitting together anymore."

"But . . ." started Felicity, before remembering crossly that she'd promised her parents she'd behave herself and that that was her new route home.

"Uh-uh," said Maggie, stopping her. "I don't want to hear it. I want heads down this term. We have a lot of work to get through, and I want everyone applying themselves. And I mean everyone, including you, do you understand?"

"Yes, miss," said Fliss in a small voice, making a token attempt to hide the resentment in it. She picked up her books and moved to the only spare seat in the room, inevitably next to Simone, who gave her a half-smile and nothing more.

"Right. Class," said Maggie. "We're going to ease into the new year gently with 'The Crystal Set.' Here, pass copies back." She felt herself stiffen. Why did she feel like such a martinet with this class? Such a grumpy, chippy drudge?

"Miss!" said Sylvie suddenly, out of the blue. "Is that an engagement ring?"

Maggie glanced up. She'd forgotten that kids didn't miss a thing, and was still very conscious herself of the new ring on her finger.

"Yes, it is, Sylvie," she said, a half-smile crossing her lips. Their campaign of animosity forgotten, all the girls craned their necks to see it, apart from Fliss and Alice, who were sulking.

"Are you getting married, miss?" Sylvie sounded amazed that someone her age could possibly have met a chap.

"That's what being engaged means, yes, Sylvie."

"Where are you getting married, miss?"

"What's he like?"

"What is your dress going to be like?"

"Was he that skinny bloke that looked like one of the Arctic Monkeys?"

The questions came from all over the class.

"All right, all right," said Maggie, trying to hide her pleasure. "I am marrying my long-term boyfriend, who lives in Scotland, and yes, he came to the Christmas concert, which he found quite the eye-opener."

There was a little bit of laughter at this.

"We aren't marrying for a long time, so we haven't made any decisions about the wedding, and I'll be staying on for the moment. OK? But thank you for your good wishes. Now, heads down, please—Simone, will you start reading?"

" 'Just as the stars appear . . .' "

Maggie was still conscious of Felicity and Alice gazing daggers at her. But it was a chink, surely.

TERM CONTINUED TO improve. There was more snow on the ground, and it was the season for tough cross-country runs, which most of the girls despised, but it gave them pink cheeks, resistance to bugs, and a healthy appetite, so Miss James maintained the practice in the face of the annual onslaught of suggestions for figure skating, trampolining, salsa dancing, and the like.

The senior girls were taking their examinations for Oxford and Cambridge and starting to worry about boards, but for those further down the school, worries mostly centered on the sports team trials.

And Maggie found she was feeling a little happier. She enjoyed the teaching more now she was focusing fully on that. OK, so maybe she wouldn't—couldn't—ever be fully accepted here, in a world that was so different from that she knew. But if she and the girls could see past their mutual antipathy, they would find that she could teach them successfully. Perhaps, she thought, in her gloomier moments, she could be like Miss Starling. Respected, if not adored like Mrs. Offili, or even Miss James, however much they complained about her.

Stan didn't manage to get down to see her, but the weight and suspicion had lifted from their conversations; devoid of the jealousy and insecurity Stan had felt before Christmas, and the mistrust she had had, they could chat lightly about their days, without focusing too much on when and whether Maggie was going to leave.

"After all," Stan had said, "you'll be wanting a babbie after that. So, it makes sense."

"I'm only twenty-five," Maggie protested. "There's lots of time for all that. Let's put some money by first, then we'll be set up."

"Are you saying I don't make enough money?"

"No, it's not like that . . ."

So they'd move on to other topics less likely to bring sensitivities out in the other.

"Getting married, are we?" June Starling had said, without much in the way of enthusiasm. Maggie wondered if June had ever had a boyfriend. It seemed hard to imagine it; June Starling seemed to have been born forty-five years old. Perhaps, thought Maggie tragically, she'd had someone who'd been killed and it had soured her for romance ever since. Or maybe it was just because she was mean.

"Will you be leaving us, or . . .?"

"Oh no," said Maggie. "I'm staying."

She wondered whether this were true.

* * *

DANIEL TOOK TO taking tea with Veronica every time he came in for an assessment day.

"Is this because you appreciate my company, or because you're digging for dirt you can write up later?" she'd asked him, only half in jest, but he'd put his hands up and apologized and promised to stop coming.

"I didn't mean that," she'd said. In fact, he was easy company, and certainly more pleasant to spend time with than Pat and Liz. He set out his plans for teaching and changes in it, as well as showing her pictures of his family—he had a pretty teacher wife at home in Kent, two boys, and a beautiful baby girl, Eliza, whom he adored and could rarely wait to get back to. Veronica wondered if he was casting about for a job. If he was, she'd have to see what she could do.

STILL STUNG BY the memory of the way she'd behaved the previous year, Maggie wasn't consciously staying out of David's way . . . all right, perhaps she was. It was some weeks before she ran into him, down in the village shop as she was picking up, to her shame, some Maltesers (she disliked using the snack shop, and it was going to be stopped for Lent anyway) and a clutch of gossip magazines. The shop was run by a friendly couple, who sold practically everything and were good at not passing over contraband to the girls. She was putting her change away when she heard a familiar friendly voice behind her ask for six panatelas and some dog treats.

Scooping up her magazines as if they were pornography (which they probably were to him; and how could she expect to teach *Clarissa* to her fifth formers next term if she kept putting off starting it?), she wished she'd put on lipstick as she turned round, determined to seem bright and breezy.

"Hello," she said, so brightly it sounded to her ears fake and forced.

David looked a bit taken aback. So he should, she thought, crossly. She couldn't possibly have imagined all of it, could she? Mind you, could she? What had they done, really, when you thought about it? Nearly hold hands once? Have him say, "I like you, but . . ."? As the days went by, and the reality—that she was marrying Stan—fell more into place, she wondered if she'd made the whole thing up in a Cornwall/new-job-induced frenzy.

"Oh, hello," he said. Then, as if he couldn't help it, his irrepressible grin broke out. Her heart skipped, and she told it firmly to stop.

"I wasn't buying cigars."

She smiled back at him.

"I wasn't buying gossip magazines."

"You *weren't*?"

"Why are you trying to make me feel guilty? Since when do gossip magazines give you *cancer*?"

"An occasional treat," said David.

"Me too," said Maggie. She thought of her stuttered hellos to Miranda at Christmas, his pretty blond fiancée who was something high up in a shipping company in Portsmouth.

David had been warning her to back off, and she wanted to assure him that she'd gotten the message.

"Did you have a nice Christmas?" he asked now, leaning down to give Stephen Daedalus a treat. The dog was already licking Maggie's hand, delighted to see her again.

"Great," said Maggie, pleased at the opportunity to mention it. "Stan and I are getting married!"

There seemed to be a brief instant before David's grin

spread over his face again, as he held the door to let her out before him.

"That's wonderful news!" he said. "A wedding. What a wonderful thing."

"Two weddings," said Maggie. "If you count yours."

"Yes," said David. "Uh, I hadn't realized you hadn't met Miranda before. She's away a lot."

"She's great," said Maggie, determinedly light of tone.

"Yes, she is."

It was a lovely cold sunny afternoon and Maggie, wrapped up warm in a red beret and scarf, had been planning on walking back to the school. It did seem absurd for them to be heading the same way and not go together.

"Are you heading back?" asked David. Maggie nodded.

"Perhaps," he said, "we could enjoy our occasional treats on the way."

Maggie smiled. "I'd have thought a pipe was more your style."

"I did try it. Bit affected," said David. "I felt as if I should be keeping lookout for the hound of the Baskervilles."

"But cigars . . . are you celebrating something?"

David shook his head as they struck out for the cliff path, leaving the pretty pastel village behind them.

"Nope. Except for it being Saturday . . . do you mind?" He took out a book of long matches.

"Not at all," said Maggie. "I rather like it actually. My granddad used to smoke the little stubby ones. I missed the smell when he died."

"Of throat cancer," said David.

"Old age," said Maggie. "He was ninety-three."

"Excellent. Now, what about your treat?"

"Would you like a Malteser?"

"I'm not sure they go."

"Oh. Would your dog like one?"

"Definitely not. Stephen Daedalus?"

The dog came flying back in order to chase a stick David threw for him in the air. I do not fancy this man, ordered Maggie to herself, as he unfurled his long body and ran, thin as a reed and looking like an overexcited teenager, with his ridiculous cigar between two fingers. But at least they seemed to be over their awkwardness. In fact, it was as easy as ever to be with him, as he chatted about books he was reading, gave her some pointers on getting into *Clarissa,* and made her laugh telling her about the camp adult pantomime he'd unwittingly taken his nephews to, then spent two hours afterward trying to explain the double entendres. He is fun, Maggie told herself. Good company. A little peculiar, like Stan said. But fine.

EVERYTHING WENT SMOOTHLY until the middle of February, when the entire area was hit by a freezing patch. The snow came down full force and made the road impassable for two days until the plow had reached them, something that had caused much hysterical excitement among the girls, with the more impressionable genuinely believing they would be reduced to eating corpses and barricading the cellars against wolves. Once this hysteria passed, however, it was business as usual—until Astrid Ulverton's clarinet went missing.

Chapter Twelve

Maggie and June Starling had discussed the missing items before, of course. It was so sporadic and so difficult to prove—teenage girls were notorious for losing anything that wasn't nailed down—and in the end they had decided not to launch into serious further action with either Fliss's watch or Sylvie's earrings. Things did get lost, and as they weren't allowed to search lockers without good reasons for their suspicions, they had merely appealed for the culprit to come forward, without much hope of success.

This was different, however. Everyone in the school knew Astrid was married to her clarinet. It was worth a lot of money, and Astrid rarely let it out of her sight. It slept on her nightstand like a favorite teddy bear and the usually strict rules on instruments in the dorm were occasionally bent for Astrid in those difficult times when inspiration struck and she was trying to get down a new tune—her roommates, Sylvie, Ursula, and Zazie, were fairly tolerant on the issue.

But Astrid had left her clarinet on the bed and the door open while going for a shower the previous evening. The dorms were just off the common room, with plenty of girls from the first two years popping in and out. It could have been anyone. But one thing was for sure; it hadn't dropped down behind a bed or been mislaid.

Astrid was red-eyed from crying as she stood in front of Miss Starling, Maggie by her side. Veronica had been alerted but didn't want to interfere at this early stage.

"And you've looked everywhere?" said Miss Starling, sternly. "You can't possibly have lost it?"

"I couldn't have," said Astrid stoutly. "I know exactly where I put it. I never leave it alone."

"What on earth would someone want with a clarinet?" wondered Maggie. "It's not as if they can play it without giving themselves away."

"It's not about that," said Miss Starling. "It's about power, and upsetting people. Do you have any enemies, Astrid?"

Astrid looked as if she was going to burst into tears again.

"I don't *think* so," she said. In fact it was true; nearly everyone liked Astrid. Her talent was too natural and extraordinary to attract jealousy.

"We're going to have to interview them all," said Miss Starling after Astrid had been dismissed. "Scare the heebie-jeebies out of them. Threaten the police. We should be able to see after that . . . I hope. I hate stealing," she said, thumping the desk to emphasize her point. "Of all the shady, underhand, sly things to do, it's the worst. I hate to think of a Downey's girl even being capable of it."

Maggie nodded, seeing the teacher's dedication to the school. "Shall we get just the Plantagenet girls, or do we want Wessex, Tudor, and York as well?"

"Anyone who could have been through that common room," said Miss Starling. "So just the locals, I suppose. First years first, they're by far the most likely. Let me see Felicity Prosser too, and that other girl who lost something."

Maggie nodded, and went off to tell the year-group, with sinking heart.

Now THAT THE novelty of her being back and her injury had worn off, and since she couldn't join in the sports or walks or drama, Felicity was bored. And she was having to apply herself to being good, which was, as Alice kept pointing out, much duller than before. So when the investigation was announced, she was quite excited; partly because something different was happening and, because of her watch, she didn't think she was going to fall under suspicion. It was quite interesting to see trouble when she wasn't allowed to be part of it anymore. Staying on the right side of Miss Adair had been tiresome.

The girls were sent in one by one to face the inquisition. Miss Starling favored long silences that the girls could then fill, hopefully in an incriminating fashion. Even the most innocent of girls would find their conscience pricking, wondering, if only for a split second, if perhaps they *could* have done it in a moment of madness. Simone was trembling with fear as she entered.

"Hello," said Miss Starling sternly. Maggie had briefed her that Simone was a likely candidate—she'd been in the vicinity of each incident and had good reason to despise the classmates who'd done so little to welcome her, even oblivious Astrid. As she did so, Maggie felt a quick stab of guilt that she had failed in her pastoral role toward Simone, who seemed more pasty and miserable than ever. They'd had a few late-night tea and reading sessions, but Maggie had never quite found the words to get Simone to open up to her, and it had always been easier to chat about books than about how she was actually feeling. Now, seeing the miserable girl in front of her, she felt more of a misfit in this school than ever—she couldn't get on with the posh kids, but couldn't help the normal ones.

"Now you understand that we are talking to everyone?" Maggie began tentatively. Simone nodded, not trusting her voice. She had tried to work out what would be the best way to behave so that they realized she was innocent, but she didn't know how. It was like when she was being teased by Estelle Grant. It didn't matter what she said, whether she answered "yes" or "no" to the question "Are you a retard?" They were going to tease her and taunt her regardless, and talking just made everything much worse. The only way she'd found to get through those sessions was to act like a tortoise: retreat entirely into herself and try and wait it out until everyone left her alone.

"Did you take Astrid Ulverton's clarinet?" said Miss Starling, peremptorily.

Simone shook her head, still staring at her lap.

"Speak up, child," said Miss Starling. "Did you take it, yes or no?"

Simone wasn't going to get the words out and didn't even try; she shook her head again, tears forming at the corners of her eyes.

"It's all right," said Maggie, playing good cop. "Simone, if you have something to tell us, it's always best to get it off your conscience."

There was a long silence. Simone simply couldn't speak. Miss Starling looked at Maggie over the top of her spectacles.

"You can go for now," she said eventually to Simone, who scurried out.

"Well, I don't like the look of that," she said to Maggie when Simone had gone.

"She's horribly shy," said Maggie, looking worried. "I thought she might be improving, but . . . it's taking her longer to settle in here than I thought."

Miss Starling shot her a sharp look. "Yes, it can take people a while to settle in," she said, leaving Maggie wondering exactly who she was talking about. "Well, anyway, if she's stealing she won't have to worry about being here for much longer. Now who's next?"

"Alice Trebizon-Woods."

Miss Starling sniffed. "She'd tell you black was white, that one, and not bat an eye."

Maggie privately agreed, but didn't want to mark her down in front of Miss Starling, and certainly Alice, with her large brown eyes and butter-wouldn't-melt manner, made a very convincing job of knowing nothing about the thefts.

"I feel so bad for Astrid," she said sincerely. "That clarinet is her life."

Maggie wondered why, despite the fact that she agreed with Alice, she still found her manner so irritating.

"We all do, Alice," she said. "That'll be all."

THERE WAS NOTHING for it. Veronica detested these situations, but there was no way to get to the bottom of things otherwise. She would have to order a search, and if that didn't work they'd have to consider getting the police in. Parents would be furious if they didn't think absolutely everything possible was being done. They didn't encourage pupils to bring expensive items to school, but it was impossible to stop them, and most of the girls had laptops and mobiles. With a heavy heart, she gave Miss Starling the word. It was more work for the teachers too, and stress as they tried to tell who among their girls was the bad apple. She hoped fervently that it wasn't Simone, the scholarship girl, but the omens didn't look good. Which was a shame; she looked set to do very well in all her courses, with a particularly excellent showing in maths and physics; exactly the kind of girl who ended up a credit to the school.

Wednesday afternoon was put aside for the search. This was normally a time for school sport, and the fact that it was being set aside annoyed Miss James, who disliked being regarded as a second-class subject. When the girls found out, however—Miss Starling and Maggie had to pounce on the dorms shortly after making the announcement at lunch, obviously requiring an element of surprise—they didn't, on the whole, mind. They were tired of chilly lacrosse, the dreaded cross-country runs, and changing rooms that never seemed to heat up properly.

It was a terribly freezing day; unseasonably cold even for February, with icy winds blowing down from Siberia, the type of wind that found its way inside your clothes, that blew icy swirls of sleet around you and made you lean into it as you walked.

The girls were to go and sit on their beds as the search took place. Every girl's locker and wardrobe was to be taken apart, their beds and bags thoroughly rummaged through.

It was an unhappy affair; Maggie felt like a jailer, and the girls all felt under suspicion, which they were. One by one the dorms were completed until, with a heavy heart, Maggie entered Simone and Fliss's room. She was crossing names off a list and started nearest the window. Alice's clothes were much more neatly folded than her own, Maggie found herself thinking. Next was Fliss, who gave Maggie her usual pout, but none of her usual cheek.

"If you can find my watch I'd be very grateful," she said, and Maggie nodded silently.

"We're doing everything we can," she said. There had been no point in searching the bed of sad-eyed Astrid, but for the sake of propriety they'd had to do it anyway.

Finally they came to Simone's. She barely looked up as Miss Starling bent down and looked in her bedside cabinet. There were lots of books, and chocolate wrappers, which Miss Starling handled with some distaste.

"You know the rules on eating in the dorm?" she asked sternly. Simone nodded.

"It's dirty and it's dangerous," she said. "You could be encouraging rats, anything." The other girls in the dorm looked slightly nauseated. It must be secret eating still, thought Maggie. Once again she regretted bitterly being so caught up in shows, and Stan, and David, and getting along at the new school, that she'd left behind the one pupil who really really, needed someone. She had failed, it seemed, in so many ways. One student injuring herself, another . . .

Her regret deepened even further a minute later as Miss Starling, her hand under Simone's bed, made a gesture of surprise, then pulled out, one by one, Astrid's clarinet, Fliss's watch, and Sylvie's earrings.

There was silence in the room.

"Felicity," said Miss Starling. "Is this yours?"

"My watch!" shouted Felicity in delight, hobbling over. "Thank God. I hadn't told my mum yet."

She frowned, looking at Simone, whose mouth was hanging open. "Uh, maybe it could have fallen under the bed by mistake?"

"Unlikely," said Miss Starling, in a tone as cold as the weather.

207

"Someone get Astrid Ulverton and Sylvie Brown for me, please, would you?"

She made the girls identify their objects, which they did, quietly, unable to look Simone in the eye, and then sent them on their way.

"Simone," she said to the girl, who was sitting there, red in the face. "Could you come down to my office, please?"

Numbly, Simone followed the two teachers out of the door. They walked slightly ahead, glancing at each other, then admonished her to sit and wait while they went inside.

"I'LL JUST CALL Veronica," said June Starling when they got to her office.

"Yes," said Maggie. "Oh, it's such a shame. It really is. I feel so responsible. If I'd gotten more involved with her earlier . . ."

June regarded her over the tops of her spectacles. "I heard you let her come and visit you in the evenings and borrow your books."

Maggie twisted uncomfortably. "Oh, that was nothing. I should have talked to her more. It's my fault. I should have—"

"I suspect it was rather more than nothing to Simone. It was kind. Unfortunately," she continued, shuffling her papers, "in some cases, kindness is not enough."

She picked up the phone to call Veronica, who had been anticipating the call all morning and suggested with a heavy heart they come and see her. She was disappointed in her young teacher. She'd been given special responsibility to keep an eye on their new pupil, and clearly hadn't done so.

As they left the office to cross the great hall, however, Maggie noticed immediately what took June Starling a second or two to process. Simone had gone.

* * *

AT FIRST, THEY only searched around the corridors, not wanting to sound the alarm or to get anyone. But it became clear, very quickly, that Simone was not in the building, and no one had seen her.

"I'll call the police," said Miss Starling.

"I'll go after her," said Maggie immediately. "She must have run out. It's perishing out there, it's below freezing. She doesn't have a coat or anything."

June nodded. "Take Harold." She meant the head caretaker. "And make sure you wrap up too."

"I've got my phone," said Maggie. "Call me immediately."

Miss Starling got on the telephone to make the arrangements as Maggie dashed to her room to find her coat. Simone couldn't have gotten far; she wasn't sporty and the weather was cruel. And Maggie knew the crags quite well now. She also grabbed Simone's coat from her dorm, ignoring the concerned faces of the girls inside, so that the girl would have something warm to put on when they caught up with her.

Harold joined her at the doors, looking worriedly at the sky. It was cold as all hell out there, and the clouds were so low it felt as if it was getting dark already, although it was just past three o'clock.

"Reckon more snow's coming, miss."

"I'm sure we'll find her in no time," said Maggie, hurrying ahead, and hoping that was true.

Simone was nowhere to be seen around the road, and the coastal path seemed the obvious route to follow.

Once on top of the cliffs, the full force of the wind hit them in the face. Visibility was decreasing all the time, with the cold light flakes dusting them from above. For the first time Maggie felt a sense of genuine fear. Someone could seriously get into trouble out here. She moved over to the cliff's edge and peered over. Surely she couldn't . . . she wouldn't have . . . she was such a careful girl, surely she wouldn't do anything so madly impulsive?

Once again she scanned the horizon. There was no sign of another living soul . . . except one. A dark figure heading toward her. At first Maggie's heart leaped, but then she realized that it was a man's outline, not a teenage girl's. Her heart rose slightly, however, when she saw that it was David, rain or shine, out walking Stephen Daedalus. She waved her arms so he would see her through the rapidly thickening snow and walked toward him.

"I thought I would be the only person mad enough to be out on a day like today," said David. "Of course it's my dog that's mad, not me . . . what's the matter?" he said, as he saw her face.

Rapidly Maggie explained. David's face grew worried.

"She's out without a coat? In this?"

"Well, there are people searching the school, but she doesn't seem to be there."

Harold had made it as far as the headland now, and was turning back, shaking his head.

"I'll call in the teachers from our school, coordinate a wider search," said David.

"The police are on their way," said Maggie. "Is there time?"

It was a proper blizzard now. The temperature seemed to have dropped even further. David sighed as they crossed over the cliff path, checking through the gorse on the other side.

"SIMONE!" they yelled periodically, though their voices were swept away on the howling wind, which seemed to rip the very breath out of them. "SIMONE!!!!"

"I can't see any sign of her on the beach," said Harold, returning to them. Maggie felt her fingers grow cold in her pocket. "Has someone headed for the village?"

Maggie checked her phone. There was a text message from the school. No one had seen her in the village, and the police were on their way with their dogs.

"Dogs!" she exclaimed excitedly. Her fingers had felt numb as she'd tried to read the text, and she wanted desperately to plunge them back into her pockets.

"What?" said David. "Oh, what do you mean?"

"Can Stephen Daedalus do tracking? I just remembered, I've got Simone's jacket. Could he smell it and find her?"

David looked excited. "I don't know, but it's worth a shot."

He bent down. "Now. Stephen Daedalus. I have a very important job for you." He took the coat from Maggie's outstretched arm. "Can you find her? Can you, boy?"

Stephen Daedalus wagged his tail and looked at them expectantly.

"Sniff this! And go find her! You know you can do it! Good boy!"

The dog sniffed excitedly, then looked up at them again, as if to say, that was nice, but what's the next game?

"Go find her," shouted David. "Come on! You can do it!"

Stephen Daedalus took one more sniff of the jacket.

"It's not going to work," said Maggie, who was feeling that standing still was a terrible idea, for Simone, and for them in this unholy weather. "Come on, let's just keep going."

"Hang on," said David. He slowly drew the coat away and handed it back to Maggie. Then he stood up.

"On you go," he said. "On you go, good dog."

And suddenly Stephen Daedalus sat upright, sniffing the air. Then he turned tail and plunged into the undergrowth.

Maggie and David looked at each other.

"Shall we follow him?"

"His father was a hunting dog," said David. "And do you have any better ideas?"

Harold had already set off in swift pursuit.

LATER, WHEN SHE looked back, Maggie couldn't remember how long they'd spent following the dog through the moors. All the world had become white and cold, with the sky and the ground hardly demarcated at all.

Harold had a torch, their only source of light as the darkness swept across the crags like a wave. Perhaps it wasn't even that long, but it felt like days following the trail, as David took her hand and helped her up difficult inclines or across iced-over streams. They were farther and farther away from the school, its warm lights mere dots on the horizon; ahead was the Irish Sea and little else.

None of them dared to say what they thought might be true; that the dog had no idea where it was and could render them as lost as Simone. Maggie tried to check her phone—fumbling with her gloves and dropping it on the ground—but they'd gone out of range of a signal, so they had no way of knowing whether she'd been found or not. There was no sign of the police.

Finally, as the night was becoming truly black, with no moon visible behind the clouds to help light their way, and all of them terribly puffed from rushing after the dog, Stephen Daedalus stopped short of a copse, and started to bark loudly, the noise startling all three of the search party.

Maggie, who had felt her brain go dull in the everlasting whiteout and was full of horrible fears she couldn't express, suddenly got an adrenaline rush of energy as they all hurried forward.

Under the overhang, barely protected from the howling wind and snow, curled up in a ball and shivering uncontrollably, only her thin school shirt protecting her from the howling gale, was Simone.

"Good dog! Good dog!" David was shouting in a completely hoarse voice as he launched himself forward, first with Simone's coat, then his own. Maggie and David sat on either side of the girl, all of them huddling together for warmth as Harold, who knew the moors so well, dashed back for help. Even Stephen Daedalus came up and sat across them all, and his panting warmth was extremely welcome; Maggie made sure Simone's hands, frozen into claws, sank into his thick fur.

"Leave me alone. Leave me alone," was all she was saying, as she rocked back and forward.

"Don't go to sleep," David was telling her. "Don't go to sleep, Simone. Stay awake. We'll sort all of this out."

Maggie was colder than she'd ever been in her life, but took some comfort from the three of them huddling together.

"Should we try and get moving?" she said to David, who looked unsure.

"I think we should heat her up first before we start moving," he said. Maggie agreed, remembering that she'd read somewhere that they should take off their clothes to provide body heat, and reflecting dimly through her frozen brain that this was the kind of thing she'd ideally once have liked to do with David without a) Simone, b) a howling storm, or c) Stephen Daedalus. This meandering train of thought, however, was interrupted by a huge noise that rose above the storm, as a floodlight bathed the area and the copse, the snowflakes plowing through the light beam.

"We have you on our heat sensor," came a voice over the megaphone. "Please stay where you are."

Stephen Daedalus quivered and buried his nose in David's knees. But David and Maggie's hearts leaped: Harold must have gotten back in time after all. Because what they could hear was a helicopter.

Chapter Thirteen

After being briefly checked over at the hospital and declared fine, both Maggie and David were free to return to the school. From the corridor, watching David be charming to the nurses as he buttoned up his clean blue shirt, Maggie called Stan on her mobile, even though she knew it was forbidden.

"WHAT?"

Maggie squeezed her eyes tight shut. She didn't want to have to explain it again.

"What do you mean you lost one in the snow?"

"It wasn't quite like that," she implored. "And everyone's fine now. It'll be OK."

"It'll be OK when you drive to Exeter Airport and catch the next flight home to Glasgow."

"I can't, Stan. I have to stay and face the music. Simone was my responsibility. And I failed her."

"That bloody school failed you!" said Stan. "They let the pupils treat you like dirt, and now they blame you for some maniac running away!"

"It's not like that," said Maggie. "Honestly, Stan."

She caught David out of the corner of her eye looking at her inquiringly, as if asking if everything was all right. She tried to make a reassuring expression at him.

"I have to go," she said.

Stan let out an exasperated sigh. "So, I don't know when I'm seeing you, then, is that right? You've half died on a mountain but, you know, the *school* is more important."

"It's my job," said Maggie simply, and hung up the phone. She had a sneaking suspicion Stan was right. Maybe she should just go home. She was probably going to get sent home anyway, after this fiasco. But Stan couldn't, didn't understand . . .

"Are you all right?" said David, coming out of the treatment room. Maggie bit her lip in case she betrayed her feelings.

"The kids get under your skin, don't they? Can you imagine what having your own would be like?"

Once again she was grateful to him for striking the right note, even as she knew she had to face the music alone.

"Terrifying," she said, and they went outside into the freezing night, where Harold was waiting for them, in the battered old Land Rover that even a snowstorm could scarcely stop.

SIMONE WAS BEING kept in overnight as a precautionary measure. After being wrapped in silver blankets, she'd been heated up in an extremely hot bath, but so far there were no signs of hypothermia or frostbite, just a touch of exposure. The doctor did say, however, that it was lucky they'd found her when they did.

Maggie had offered to stay with her, but no one was allowed to stay overnight. Matron would be over first thing to collect her. Her parents would be driving down through the night from London.

It was well after ten by the time Harold drove them up the familiar driveway, but every light in the school was burning, and the girls were outlined at the windows.

Veronica was standing in the great hall, where the fire had been lit—outside of Christmas, an unheard-of concession. An exhausted Maggie entered, head bowed, ready to take whatever Veronica could throw at her—could it be as bad as dismissal, she wondered, to lose a vulnerable pupil? Stan would be seeing her sooner than he thought. And the girls here would hardly miss her, after all.

So Maggie wasn't expecting the round of applause that rose up from the line of girls waiting on the great stairs.

"What?" she said, looking round. David, standing just behind her, smiled to himself.

Miss Starling stepped forward. "It was very brave and clever of you to go out as you did, and to think of using Stephen Daedalus. No one could have predicted that Simone would bolt as she did."

Maggie felt her cheeks flare. Praise from Miss Starling was not something she was used to.

"I'm so sorry the situation got so out of hand," she said. "It's my fault. I should have realized she was so unhappy she was stealing . . ."

Veronica stepped forward too, shaking her head. "No, it wasn't. Simone wasn't the culprit at all."

Maggie's eyebrows shot up.

"It was Imogen Fairlie. She shared a dorm with Simone, Felicity Prosser, and Alice Trebizon-Woods. She'd felt ignored and was trying to be the center of attention, then when the searches started, lost her nerve and panicked. We've spoken to her parents. This isn't the first time, apparently. They're going to take her home."

"Oh," said Maggie, her heart suddenly going out to silent, no-trouble Imogen. What a dreadful cry for help—another one she seemed to have missed completely. "Does she have to . . . ?"

"Yes," said Veronica, firmly. "There are some things I simply can't tolerate in a Downey girl. Making a bid for attention is one thing. Cowardly letting another girl take the blame is something else altogether."

Veronica noticed David hanging back.

"And thank you," she said directly to him. "From all of us."

David looked embarrassed. "It wasn't me," he said. "It was Stephen Daedalus. And Maggie, of course."

"We were all very lucky you were there," said Veronica simply. "Now, please, both of you, come to my study. I think we all need a nightcap."

She turned round to the girls on the stairs.

"I certainly know I owe Simone Pribetich an apology. Please look in your consciences and see if you think you do too. And now, bed, everyone! It's an ordinary day tomorrow and I don't want to hear another sound out of any of you."

For once, though, Dr. Deveral's word was not taken as law, as the girls dispersed, chattering excitedly like birds.

MAGGIE HAD A long hot bath, accompanied by some of Veronica's excellent whisky, and slept in late the next morning, not even hearing the bell. Ordered by Miss Starling, the catering staff had made a large cooked breakfast for everyone. Maggie went to the san at eleven.

Simone was sitting there alone, without her parents, who had gotten trapped in the snow and had to spend the night in Devon.

"Simone," said Maggie, "I'm so sorry all this happened to

218

you. But why couldn't you just tell us it wasn't you? I was there, wasn't I?"

Simone looked down. "Nobody believed me. Everyone thought it was me."

"Well, everyone was wrong," said Maggie. "Me included."

"I'd have thought you might have understood," said Simone. Maggie knew what she meant. They came from the same world. They knew what it was like out there.

"I know," she said, feeling ashamed. "I should have. I'm sorry."

Simone shrugged.

"Do you want to come to class? I know the girls would like to see you."

Simone looked white. "Do you think?"

Maggie nodded. "Definitely. They're not all bad, you know."

Simone gave a half-smile.

"Come on," said Maggie. "I think it would do you good. Even if your parents do want to take you home."

Simone thought about it for a moment, then consented.

MISS STARLING WAS letting the Plantagenet girls watch a video of *Love's Labour's Lost*. She hated letting the girls watch DVDs, thought it morally corrupting, but you couldn't swim against the tide forever, and she had her own class to teach.

When Maggie opened the door, however, all thoughts of the video were gone. The girls stared at Simone, who instantly wondered if she'd made a mistake and that this was a really bad idea. So did Maggie. Acceptance from other children was an impossible thing to force. Maybe her running away made her even weirder in their eyes. Plus, of course, they'd have to get over their distaste for her to even say anything.

She paused the video, and for a time everyone was quiet. Then, suddenly, little Fliss Prosser, her supposedly worst pupil, stood up.

"Uhm," she said, looking at a loss for words for once. "I just wanted to say. And I don't speak for everyone or anything, but, err. Simone. I'm really, really sorry I thought you were stealing. It was a mistake, and I'm dead ashamed. Right."

And she sat down again, cheeks pink. Maggie was impressed. She didn't think Fliss had it in her.

Then Astrid stood up too.

"I'm sorry," she said. "I should have known you wouldn't take my clarinet."

All the other girls mumbled apologies in agreement after that, and Sylvie stood up and asked Simone to tell them what it was like being lost in the snow. Maggie looked at Simone and asked if she would tell the story, and then, the most surprising thing happened. To Maggie's complete astonishment, at first falteringly, but then with more of the confidence that she'd shown at the Christmas concert, and the humor Maggie'd suspected from their meetings, Simone began to tell the whole story: about how she couldn't decide whether to bolt or hide when she was waiting outside Dr. Deveral's office; how she'd run and really quickly realized she had no idea where she was because she'd missed so many of the cross-country runs; how she'd thought Stephen Daedalus was a wolf come to eat her, and the helicopter sounded like an alien spaceship, which was when she really did think she'd died and that the Scientologists were right after all.

Listening to this, Maggie realized something with amazement: Simone was funny. Hearing the girls crack up, and her good comic timing and pauses, the entire class saw a new side to the previously timid girl. At the end of her account, when she said precisely what Maggie had been thinking—that she was slightly hoping Mr. McDonald would go bare-chested with her so that at least she would know what it was like before she died, Maggie was laughing too, and there was a large spontaneous round of applause as Simone took her seat back next to Fliss, who even put her arm round her and gave her a squeeze. "Brilliant," she said audibly. "Much better than my ankle."

"I think so," said Simone. "Though the next person is really going to have to cut off a leg or something, to get Mr. McDonald's attention." The class cracked up again, except for Alice, who donated a rather wan smile. She knew, more than anyone, that she owed Simone an apology, but was finding it rather hard to choke the words out.

"OK, OK, everyone, settle down," said Maggie, but she found it hard to hide her delight. More than just Simone, she could feel a mood in the class, a relaxing, a genuine sense that they were all working together, were all on the same side.

"And more of *Love's Labour's Lost* later; I think we'll take a quick look at a poem more germane to our current situations— quickly please, Fliss and Simone, could you turn to page 271 in *Poetry Please*, and start reading 'Stopping by Woods on a Snowy Evening.'"

And without hesitation or fuss, thirteen girls immediately did so.

AMAZINGLY, SIMONE'S PARENTS, once they'd gotten over the terrible shock, were persuaded (almost entirely by Simone herself) that the whole thing had been a very minor and not at all dangerous misunderstanding. Veronica, mindful of the school's reputation, and the possibility of their suing, did not discourage them from this apprehension.

It may have helped that their first view of Simone, as she came downstairs, was of her surrounded by other girls, arm in arm with Felicity, both of them being interrogated for more details of their run-ins with Mr. McDonald. Simone, carrying her bag, said something and everyone laughed. Mrs. Pribetich looked on in pride. This was exactly how she'd always imagined Simone being: happy, pleased, surrounded by other, nice girls. She wouldn't, she reflected, have wanted to take Simone home now if she'd had a leg gnawed off by the school's own timber wolf. Simone and her father might think she didn't have a clue as to what was going through her beloved daughter's head, but she certainly did, and had been equally certain that her instinct was the correct one. Which didn't stop her screeching, "FETITZA" over the tops of everyone's heads.

Suddenly, though, Felicity thought, Simone's mum didn't look so weird. She looked just more colorful; a bit exotic. Maybe even a bit more fun than her own stodgy parents. She swallowed this thought at once; it was disloyal.

Simone didn't care and went straight up to her parents and gave them a huge hug.

"I'm so pleased to see you," she said.

"And you," said her father, gruffly. "What happened to you? Are you all right?"

"I'm fine," said Simone. In fact, she looked better than fine. She looked happy. There was a rosiness to her cheeks and a bit of a sparkle in her eye, for the first time in a long time.

"We were so worried, *fetitza*," said her mother. "Even Joel was upset."

"Where is he?"

"He wanted to go with his friends to some Warcraft thing,"

said her father, who had even less idea about Joel's hobbies than she did.

Simone had special dispensation for a sick day, but as she wasn't feeling particularly sick—the lucky effects of being fourteen, Matron had said, exhorting her to watch her chest and not go swimming—she went into Truro with her mum and dad, and they bought her a new pair of jeans at Gap and took her to Pizza Express for lunch. Simone had rarely been happier.

AND EVEN AFTER her parents returned to London, and the big thaw finally arrived, flooding the games fields in the far corner of the school grounds, and turning every trip outside into a muddy morass, things were still looking up. Both Fliss and Simone were signed off games for the foreseeable future and were spending PE sitting on the sidelines, sewing up netball vests, which was horribly dull, but gave them quite a lot of time to chat.

Fliss, to her amazement, was discovering that Simone, the kind of person she'd never have looked at twice for having as a friend, was actually funny, kind, and really good to spend time with. All the time Fliss had had her down as a shy waste of space, she was, while shy, using the time to observe people and places around the school and was, in her own way, every bit as cheeky as Alice. Sitting together in English also helped, and soon they were sharing homework, as Fliss had so far to make up her marks after her disastrous first term.

Alice didn't like the new situation at all. In fact, she hated it. It was bad enough being one of three. Being one of three to a big fat boufer was just stupid. Plus, she missed the old Fliss, whom she could coax into bad behavior. The new one was a total goody-goody. She hadn't forgotten about the trick she'd promised to play. She was just going to have to make it pretty darn spectacular. That should get the focus back in its rightful place.

STAN SEEMED FAR more worried than Simone's parents, which was touching in a way, but also slightly irritating to Maggie, who was still on a high from being treated as a heroine, rather than the disciplined disgrace she'd expected. Stan took the tortuously long train down the next weekend.

"What for?" asked Maggie, as she went to pick him up, the tip of her nose pink—the only relic from her expedition.

"What do you mean? You could have been killed. I want to have a word with that headmistress of yours."

"It wasn't her fault," said Maggie. "Simone unpredictably ran out, then I ran out. Anyway, everything ended up fine."

"Yes, by luck," said Stan. "And of course that poncey English teacher was involved."

"And we're lucky he was there," said Maggie. "Come on. I've got two free days and I don't even want to look at marking. Shall we go and visit a tin mine?"

They did so, but it wasn't an entirely comfortable experience, even though they did hold hands. Finally, they arrived, slightly chilled from the still-frosty air, in a local tea room with steam rising onto the floral-curtained windows.

"This is the best bit of sightseeing," said Maggie. "Shall we have scones?"

Stan sat down. "Thing is, Maggie, I've been thinking."

"Yes?" said Maggie, looking round for the waitress.

"I know we were talking about you staying here for another year maybe, for your career, before you come home?"

"Yes?" said Maggie, uncertainly. Two lower sixth formers, on a weekend pass, had arrived just behind them—Carla's tea shop was very popular. They had sat down self-consciously, still trying to look nonchalant in the outside world, but Maggie could tell they were craning their necks desperately to try and overhear Miss Adair and her fiancé.

"Well, after everything that's happened . . . Please. I'm sick of asking. But won't you think about coming home? Nobody would blame you for leaving now."

"They'd think I was a coward," said Maggie, ordering tea and two rounds of scones with jam and tea, hoping they could keep this light.

"You're obviously not a coward," said Stan. "You should be getting some sort of award. Anyway. If you came home, you could find a job locally and we could think about buying a new place to live. You know, before the wedding."

Maggie hated feeling so torn. Of course she wanted to go home with Stan one day; he was her partner, wasn't he? Her other half? She watched him as he piled jam on, ignoring the butter and cream as semi-nutritional by-products. At least she'd remembered not to get the raisin scones.

"But," she said, then stopped and lowered her voice. "You know." And as she said the words, she knew they were the truth. "I love this job, Stan."

There was a long pause after that, as Maggie reflected on it.

"More than you love me?" said Stan finally, stirring sugar into his tea and not looking at her.

"Of course not! We've been through this! But I made a commitment and want to follow it through; why is that so hard to understand?"

Stan stared at her. "Because we're getting married and I don't want you at the bloody dog-end of the country, getting half-frozen to death. Why is that so hard for you to understand?"

Suddenly, the atmosphere between them, which since the New Year had been so joyous and exciting, seemed to turn sour. It felt, on this issue at least, as if there was nothing more to be said. They seemed to be at something of an impasse. They ate their scones and drank their tea in silence, as quickly as possible. Maggie was acutely aware of being watched by the girls, no doubt vowing they would never be in one of those couples that sit silently in restaurants. Well, thought Maggie mutinously. They could see how they liked it when they got there.

"Shall we go?" she said, as soon as she'd swallowed her last mouthful. Stan merely nodded, but as they left, reached out to take her hand in a conciliatory fashion. She took it. They were friends again, but no closer to a resolution.

As they trudged up the wet lane, she heard a commotion from the local meadow. Glancing up, she saw David and his fiancée. They were throwing a frisbee for Stephen Daedalus, and David was laughing his head off. The weak winter sunlight reflected off Miranda's blond head.

That's what I want, Maggie found herself reflecting wistfully. When was the last time Stan and I just had a really good laugh?

"Gaw, they must be proper freezing," said Stan, who of course had refused to wear a scarf or a hat. "Nutters."

Just as he said this David caught her eye and waved. Both of them came over, leaning across the ancient stone wall that divided the field from the old cart track road.

"Hello hello," he said cheerily. "How are you, Stan? The heroine's consort."

"Hardly," said Maggie, rolling her eyes, and giving Stephen Daedalus a quick rub.

"It's amazing what you guys did," said Miranda, widening her eyes. "I couldn't believe it when I heard. It was on the radio and everything."

"Yes, you can imagine how thrilled the head is about that," said Maggie. "*Not* very. It was all Stephen Daedalus anyway."

"How's our young Simone?" asked David.

"Oh, she's good. Between her and Felicity Prosser, they're having quite the time being the ones who got most snuggle-up rescue time with you," said Maggie, realizing the light tone she'd meant to bring to the comment sounded a bit silly when she tried it out loud.

"Christ," said David. "Back to the boys for me. Or does that sound even worse?"

"It does," said Maggie grinning, and grateful to be rescued.

"Darling, let's go in, I'm freezing," said Miranda testily.

"Yeah," grunted Stan. Maggie had rather been enjoying a little sunlight, however pathetic, and David looked disappointed, but immediately deferred to Miranda's wishes.

"Absolutely. Fancy scones in the village?" he asked the whole group. Maggie found herself full of regret that they had to say no, they'd just had some, and it was all she could do not to turn her head as they waltzed off toward the village, David pontificating on something as usual.

"He's a right weirdo," said Stan as they went on. "Can't shut up."

"Some people are just like that though," said Maggie, as they came to their hotel, feeling thankful that Stan had never had a suspicious nature. "They can't help it."

"Can't bloody put a sock in it, more like," growled Stan. "What's wrong with a bit of peace and quiet anyway? Won't want to hear much from you when we're married."

"You're joking."

He took her in his arms. "Course I'm joking, you dimwit. Come here."

And his kisses tasted good, of tea and jam. But still, nothing was decided.

Chapter Fourteen

Easter was shaping up to be a much quieter term, thought Veronica, then she admonished herself firmly for thinking so: she'd made that mistake before. She looked with some pleasure at the daffodils ranging over the hills. That was spring down here; every single day something new burst into life, and the landscape changed all over again. Not at all like the dark grimy northern city where she'd grown up. She was reflecting on this when there was a knock on the door again. It would be the assessment team. They were finishing up. Liz was back, after her three months off for stress, and this would be their final session before they went to write up their report.

She hoped it would be a good one. Daniel had seemed much more sympathetic to her aims ... In fact, she was surprised to see, Daniel was standing at the door on his own, Miss Prenderghast smiling apologetically behind him—she definitely had a soft spot for the young man.

"I thought you weren't due for another twenty minutes," said Veronica, indicating the pile of applications she'd been working through. They were always oversubscribed but this year their oversubscriptions seemed a little down. She'd have to go through the figures properly with Evelyn.

"No," said Daniel. He looked nervous, as ill at ease as he had done the first time he'd arrived, now over three months ago. "I wondered if I could have a word about something?"

"Of course," she said, stepping back and welcoming him in. Perhaps he was going to finally ask her about a job. She'd be delighted; as always she was looking for good teachers, and despite the crush factor, it was good for the girls to have some men in the profession. Stopped them going into a frenzy when they hit university, and John Bart, the fiftyish physics teacher, didn't really cut it, with his head in the clouds the whole time.

"Can we sit down?" he said.

"Of course. Would you like tea?"

Daniel shook his head, although his throat was very dry. He fingered the papers in his lap. "I just want to ask you something," he said.

Veronica looked up, alerted by his tone of voice. "Yes?" she said, quite briskly.

"Was your name . . . was your name originally Vera Makepiece?"

Something happened to Veronica then. It was as if her entire self shifted a little. Her eyes went wide and she found that, despite years of rigid self-control, she seemed to have lost the ability to control her expression. She went to stand up, then sat down again . . . it was most peculiar; she, who always knew what to do, suddenly didn't know quite what to do.

Nobody knew this. Not Jane, not Evelyn. Nobody. She hadn't been Vera Makepiece for over thirty years.

"What do you mean?" she asked, realizing too late that a giveaway quaver was instantly noticeable in her voice.

"Were you born Vera Makepiece?" Daniel asked again. His voice had a tremor in it, just like her own.

Daniel looked at her with his large, gray, serious eyes, so like her own. And somehow, instantly, she just knew. She knew. All the little chats; all the early morning cups of tea. They were all for a reason. He was gathering clues about her; trying to figure her out.

She fell back in her chair, completely unable to speak. Daniel's face worked, and he looked like he was going to lose control completely.

"Who . . . who are you?" Veronica asked finally, after Daniel had managed, with a trembling hand, to pour her out a glass of water from the crystal carafe, refilled each morning, that sat on her desk.

There was a long silence, then Daniel let out a great long sigh, as if answering this question was going to take a huge load off his mind. He himself couldn't believe it. Several nights over the last few months he'd woken up bathed in sweat after dreaming of this moment; or hadn't been able to sleep at all, tossing and turning as Penny slept peacefully beside him, until the baby woke them both. He'd had a rough idea for many years but had never found the courage to do something about it before—but when the reassignment place had come up, he'd felt it was meant to be. Now, sitting here, in front of . . . her . . . he wasn't so sure.

"I was adopted in Sheffield in October 1970," said Daniel, simply. "My given name was . . ."

"James," said Veronica.

"Yes," said Daniel. "I'm James."

There. He'd said it, and got it out. Years of prevaricating, until finally he'd met this woman, this headteacher. And he could see she was quite intimidating and didn't suffer fools gladly. But he'd liked her, and been incredibly pleased when she'd seemed to like him too. How she would respond now . . . well, he hadn't thought much further than this moment. His time here was nearly up anyway; if it all went badly, he could go back to Kent and forget all about it.

He realized he was kidding himself, of course. He could never forget.

"Ohhh," said Veronica. Now she was giving up all pretense at reserve, or containment, or having any control over her emotions whatsoever. She made another attempt to stand up, and this time succeeded. "Ohhh. Are you my . . . are you my . . ."

But the word "baby" would not, of course, come out, and suddenly Veronica glanced at her hands. Tears—tears she had not shed for so long, and had sworn never to shed again—were dripping through her fingers and down onto her papers. When was the last time she had cried? She didn't have to ask herself the question. The last time she had cried was when she had held a little creature to her bosom, and the large lady had come and taken him away. After that, nothing, nothing on earth could hurt her enough to make her cry again.

Daniel didn't know if the tears were a good or a bad sign. He could feel himself wanting to cry, could feel himself as a little boy, asking his adoptive mother over and over again, "But Mummy, you wouldn't leave your big boy, would you?" and his mother, who was a kind and patient woman, had held him and said, no, but they were very lucky, because they'd got to choose him, and he was the best one there was, and that they would never leave him.

"I'm so sorry," said Daniel, "to land this on you . . ."

There were agencies he could have used to act as a go-between, but he hadn't felt comfortable with the ones he'd met—they'd been very nice, but he hadn't liked them poking their noses into his private business. He was very like his mother in that respect.

"I just got confirmation through the post this morning . . ." Daniel raised his pile of papers, uselessly, as if Veronica would want to read them and check his credentials. "And I didn't . . . I couldn't wait."

Veronica shook her head. She couldn't fall apart. She couldn't. With near superhuman effort, she managed to page through to Evelyn and tell her to cancel her engagements for that afternoon.

Then she retook her seat and stared at Daniel in tear-swept disbelief. Daniel was desperate for her to say something—anything—so he could get the least bit of a handle on what she was feeling. After all, he'd had years to plan this. His biggest fear, however—that she would simply say, "Oh yes? The baby I had? Well, jolly good, nice to meet you" and send him on his way—was thankfully not being realized.

"Please," Veronica said eventually, recovering some of her composure and making ample use of the large box of tissues she kept in the office for overemotional teenage girls. "Please. Tell me. Was the family . . ."

"My parents are great," said Daniel carefully. "They said you were very young."

Veronica swallowed hard. One of the reasons she could empathize with the girls in her care was remembering how frightened, how young she had been then.

"I was," said Veronica. "I had no choice. And then, as time went on . . . I didn't meet anyone else I could form a family with. I couldn't have gotten you anyway. And then it was too late, and it would seem cruel, and I got a grant to go to university."

She leaned across the desk, her eyes suddenly burning with intensity, and gazed straight at him. "But I never stopped thinking about you. I promise."

"Thank you," said Daniel, trying to swallow the lump in his throat. Had she really? The idea that she would have thought about him all this time was . . . well, was what he had to hear. That his mother—lovely though his adoptive mum had been—that his real mother had loved him too. He managed to swallow, and went on. "My parents said you were very young and very frightened."

"And my father was very strong-willed," murmured Veronica. "But you know. If it had only been such a very short time later, I would have kept you. Feminism came late to Sheffield, you know. It's so hard to explain to people now how much the world has changed."

"Tell me about my dad," said Daniel.

Veronica felt the knife twist in her heart.

"One day," she said. "You understand this has come as such a shock to me?"

Daniel nodded. They would have time, hopefully. There was no one named on the birth certificate.

They sat in silence, Veronica letting her gaze wander over his long nose, short gray hair—the similarities were unmistakable now that she looked at them. The thought struck her; thank goodness she had never found him attractive.

"So, you planned all this . . ."

"Actually, no," said Daniel. "It was a chance remark; Pat got your name wrong and called you Vera. And I knew from the registrar that your own mother's name was . . ."

"Deveral," nodded Veronica. "After the way my father behaved, I just wanted to get away from him . . . it was such a long time ago."

"Thirty-eight years," said Daniel. "So, then I got it, but then thought, it can't be, it just can't be, but then when the chance of the job came up, I took it, and then I saw you . . . and being in the same profession. I mean, it was just too weird."

"So you've been working with me all this time thinking I might be your mother?" mused Veronica, shaking her head. "It seems so very strange."

"It was," said Daniel. "Especially when you were so kind to me. I wanted to tell you before, but it didn't seem fair till I knew for sure."

There was a long silence.

Veronica knew she badly needed to go somewhere and cry, howl at the universe and screech at the injustice: that she should have created this person, a lovely person, but had missed it all. Every fall she could have kissed better; every sticky first day of term, with new pencil cases and trousers grown out of; making the football team; unwrapping Christmas presents; sending him off to college. It was as if a speeded-up version of the life they'd never had together flashed in front of her eyes, but she couldn't look at it; it was too painful.

And her own life hadn't been wasted, surely? Nonetheless, right now she had a fierce need to be alone.

"So what now?" said Veronica.

"I'll have to tell Mum and Dad," said Daniel. "They know I was looking for you . . . Penny will have to know too."

"Of course," said Veronica, although she had no idea what was proper protocol under the circumstances. "Please . . ." She mustn't cry. She mustn't. But why could she feel him, the sense memory so strong, feel him as a baby in her arms as if it were yesterday, before they took him away?

"Please thank them from me, for the wonderful job they have done," she managed to get out eventually.

"I will," said Daniel stiffly, holding the emotion from his voice. "And, once we've delivered the assessment, will I be able to come back and see you?"

"I would like that very much," said Veronica.

VERONICA SAT STILL at her desk for a long time. She was in no fit state to see anyone. Her head was buzzing, absolutely full of conflicting thoughts. At the fore were two: one, how wonderful, how amazing, how very much Daniel was exactly what she would have wanted for a son. Happily settled, handsome, polite, with a good job. And she wondered to herself if she could have provided him with the stable home life and good example that had obviously worked so well for him. Very possibly not.

She also felt a cold hand at her neck. This . . . well, it wouldn't be ideal. For the school. For prospective parents. Who would want to send their child to the care of a woman who had abandoned her own child, however compelling the reasons? She thought of those awful stories she'd seen in the magazines Evelyn liked to read: "I Found My Long Lost Son on the Internet" and such like.

The idea of something so private becoming common knowledge, to be gossiped about and discussed by the girls at home . . . that was an insupportable thought too. But would Daniel wish for secrecy? He could already be out, spreading the news. She clutched her teacup so hard her knuckles went white. Surely not. No, of course not.

They would discuss it sensibly. Yes. She could gradually feel her breathing ease, get back under control. She must control herself, that was it. And perhaps she could meet his adoptive parents, thank them. And . . . she hardly dared to think it, hardly dared to breathe or admit to herself how great her longing was. But if she could meet his children . . . be involved with his two little boys and the little baby girl, Eliza her name was. Being their other grandmother . . . it was a desire so strong, it frightened her. Breathing out hard, she rose to stand at the window, the view of the cliffs and the sea normally one she found infinitely calming. Today, though, the choppy April waves and gray sky, filled with fast-moving clouds, reflected her own tempestuous mind, which couldn't settle.

To look at her, though, you wouldn't suspect a thing.

Chapter Fifteen

Post-Easter, the school seemed to divide in two. For half of them there were looming exams, barriers to be surmounted; for the eldest, university interviews and coming to terms with the next phase of their lives, whether that was traveling on a gap year, or moving straight into higher education. Hanging over this for the teachers was the huge pressure on results, which meant that their desire to help the girls and not make this time too difficult for them was compounded by the need to make this year the best ever; to beat other schools in their league and show Dr. Deveral that everything was running as smoothly as ever (she had been uncharacteristically reserved lately). Clarissa Rhodes, expected to get an unprecedented six starred A's, was frequently to be found mopping her eyes in the loos, even as she was being wooed by several top universities in the UK and the United States.

"I just can't help it," she wailed to Maggie, who still felt slightly nervous teaching someone whose work was rather better than hers and whose legs certainly were. "What if I don't go to Harvard and someone else comes along and discovers a successful alternative to OPEC?"

"There, there," said Maggie encouragingly. "You are going to be just fine."

Maggie felt a little sunnier too—she and Stan had managed to get away at Easter. It was just a week in Spain, but she felt better for having a bit of color, lazy days sleeping in without bells, and wild nights drinking horrible local spirits and cutting it up a bit on the dance floor, just like they used to when they were at school. It had been fun, good straightforward fun, and all the stresses of daily life and heavy conversations had been put behind them. Maggie knew many of the other girls had spent Easter in Mustique, or Gstaad, or on safari, but sipping a ridiculous cocktail out of a coconut shell while inexplicably wearing a balloon crown, she and Stan laughing their heads off, she hadn't felt envious in the slightest.

It made such a change, at this time of year, when she had normally been in a frenzy trying to help the few children who were going to even turn up for their exams, versus those who started chafing at the bit to get outside as the days got longer and the sky clearer. It was a tricky balancing act.

Here, all the girls in her upper classes looked likely to pass, even Galina Primm, whose dyslexia was so bad it was often hard to tell what she was writing at all. But special arrangements had been put in place so that she could take longer and dictate her exam papers, which meant she shouldn't have any problem with the GCSE papers at all; it wasn't her brain that was at fault, just the wiring between her brain and her fingers.

And her lower class was, finally, falling into place. It was such a luxury to enter the classroom without worrying about Simone being in tears, again, or Alice and Fliss giggling and gossiping behind their hands. Knowing girls as she did, Maggie understood these acts of class solidarity rarely lasted for long but, in the aftermath of the stealing incident, and Simone's subsequent newfound and hard-won popularity, it was nice to see them all working well as a group.

So it was with a sunny heart she walked into class on a warm Wednesday morning in mid-May, wondering if it was time to give the girls some time off from the Ben Jonson they'd been looking at, and wondering if they'd all read Laurie Lee. If not, they'd like him.

This, and thinking about Claire, who'd become very quiet and clammed up about her love life lately, was what was going through her head as she walked into the classroom, only to find all the girls with their noses jammed in horror against the glass windows on the eastern side of the building.

ALICE HAD BEEN planning her trick for months. She needed to gain back the respect of her classmates, many of whom thought she had been unjustly hard on Simone, but were too frightened of her sharp tongue to say so to her face. She couldn't bear all this lovey-dovey atmosphere in class. The fashion was for girls to walk arm in arm. Next they'd be giving each other bead bracelets. Alice sniffed. Well, this would wake them up, and give that common Glaswegian witch something to think about too.

It wasn't normal for Alice to feel the one sidelined, particularly for someone she didn't think much of. Normally girls looked to her for guidance, but now it was all sweetness and light and everyone spending most of the day speculating romantically about that stupid English teacher from the boys' school. Well, she'd show them.

It took a while to arrive—her grandfather, and frequent partner in crime, had had some trouble digging it up from his attic, but had managed it eventually. Miss Starling had asked her what was in the large parcel, but she'd looked wide-eyed and explained her grandfather had sent her a small stool, and that had seemed to satisfy her.

Fortunately there'd been heavy rain the night before. She'd risen silently at one a.m., when the whole house was asleep, creeping over to wake Fliss, who finally had the plaster off her ankle and was back to active service.

Fliss awoke to see Alice leaning over her with a torch, and nearly screamed out loud.

"What!" she finally managed to whisper.

"Larks afoot," said Alice. "Come on. Remember I mentioned our prank?"

Fliss searched her memory. Hadn't Alice forgotten all about that ages ago?

"Uh huh," she said, slowly.

"Well, it's time," said Alice.

Fliss sat upright. "What do you mean?"

"It finally arrived. The thing I need. And it needs to be done now. So are you in or not?"

"I don't know!" said Fliss. "I'm behaving myself now, you know. Any trouble and I'm going to get into absolutely serious s-h-i-t."

"Does that include, you know, swearing to yourself?" said Alice sarcastically.

"No," said Fliss. "But I just don't want to . . . you know. Show myself up again."

"OK," said Alice. "I promise I'll take all the blame if we get caught."

"Blame for what?" came another voice. Alice rolled her eyes.

"Go back to sleep, Simone."

"But I want to know."

"Me too," said Fliss, folding her arms and looking slightly mutinous. Alice sighed. Roll on next year when she'd be able to boss around the younger pupils.

"OK," she said. "I'm going to explain. But Simone, you can't come. You just have to keep mum. Or, better still, you could be our 'Credulous Stooge.' "

"All right," said Simone. She was delighted not to have to go but to be included at the same time. Then Alice explained the prank and it was simply beyond Fliss's powers not to go along with it.

"We'll need waterproofs," she whispered.

"I've got it all sorted," said Alice. "Here, grab this mallet." Fliss's eyes widened. But she did as she was told. And with Alice clutching the heavy box, they crept silently downstairs to the unmanned fire escape.

The night was mild, and lit brightly by the moon and the stars, but evidence of the recent heavy rainfall was everywhere; the mud was thick and glutinous and it was hard going in the socks Alice had insisted on, to minimize footprints.

"I've got it all mapped out," she said. Fliss shivered; half of her wanted to collapse in hysterical laughter, half was just plain terrified.

"We'll never get away with it," she whispered.

"It is our duty to try," said Alice solemnly. "Now, be quiet, get down in the mud, and start rolling."

Two HOURS LATER they had made it back to the dorm unnoticed—Simone was lying awake, fearfully, and had thoughtfully stuffed pillows down their beds.

"In case Miss Adair came past," she said.

"Smart thinking," said Alice, surprised. They cleaned the

dirt off as well as they could in the little sink in their bathroom; the macintoshes she'd borrowed from the gardeners' shed had gone back in there—a new coating of mud hadn't made much difference. The really important thing was that their footprints didn't show—only the huge, unmistakable footprint of her grandfather's wastepaper basket, trophy of a century-old hunting trip in Africa . . .

"WHAT'S THAT?" TIMID Sylvie was saying, staring out into the mud, now lit up brightly by the spring sunshine. The light made the tops of the great marks sparkle.

Maggie could now hear an excited uproar from the other classes up and down the halls, as well as windows opening. The refectory had high windows, too high to see out of, but on this side of the building the view went all the way to sea. She could see Harold and two of the groundsmen just starting work, following something and looking puzzled. As she watched, one of them peeled off and ran up in the direction of Dr. Deveral's office.

"What is it, for goodness' sake? Girls, get down."

As she came up she could see them, right across the lawn, straight past the windows, and heading out to the pond: a huge set of hoofprints, with three large stubby toes, set in a galloping motion.

"I thought I heard something last night," said a voice behind her. She turned, and it was sensible Simone. "Kind of like a rumbling. But I didn't think much of it. But now I think of it—it could have been galloping!"

"I did too!" said Felicity Prosser, her face looking full of color suddenly. "Kind of like a rumbling, bashing noise."

Suddenly the rest of the class nodded and started loudly

agreeing that they'd heard it too, until even Maggie was wondering if she'd woken in the night—surely not.

Now Miss Starling and Claire Crozier were both outside, being given details by the groundsmen, and Maggie turned to her class.

"Calm down all of you."

"Calm down?" said Sylvie. "There's a wild animal escaped from the zoo!"

"All the better reason for you to stay indoors then," said Maggie. "Let me find out what's going on."

She stalked outside.

"This is ridiculous," Miss Starling was saying.

"I know," the gardener was saying. "But there are no footprints or anything near it, and it's definitely rhinoceros."

"That's absurd."

"I went on a safari," said the younger gardener. "We were tracking them. They were exactly like that."

"And where do the tracks go?" said Miss Starling.

"You know, there ees the safari park just at Looe," said Claire.

"That's monkeys," said Miss Starling.

"Perhaps they have expanded," said Claire.

"Ring them," said Miss Starling. She bent down to examine the marks. "I can't imagine how they got here . . . did you hear anything, Miss Adair?"

Maggie shook her head. "Though some of the girls are saying they heard rumblings in the night."

Miss Starling stalked ahead following the markings. They were set, two by two on the diagonal, and deep in the mud, as if an extremely heavy animal had indeed been running. It was entirely mysterious. The undergardener took his hat off and stared at them.

"I tell you, I've seen rhinoceros tracks, and they look just like that."

Behind them, some of the older girls had strayed into the grounds and were also following the tracks. Seeing their lead, more classes had come out to see what was going on. There was much squealing.

Miss Starling's mouth was pursed. The tracks went all the way down to the pond, where there was a broken-down wooden bridge. This area was out of bounds to pupils, and anyway dank, unpleasant, and hardly an attraction.

This morning, however, a huge part of the bridge was knocked through. It looked exactly as if a huge creature had barged through it, only to tumble into the watery depths below. The group stood there for a moment, staring into the pond.

"What a terrible thing to happen," said the undergardener. "He must have been scared out of his wits."

Maggie was busy wondering how she was going to explain to Stan that there were wild animals on the property as well as everything else. And would they have to evacuate the grounds now that they'd found its final resting place? And would they have to dredge the pond?

She glanced at Miss Starling and was surprised to see her shoulders shaking. Surely she couldn't be that upset? Maybe she was a real animal lover.

Then she looked closer. Miss Starling's shoulders were shaking . . . surely it couldn't be . . . it couldn't be with *laughter*.

"Miss Starling?" she said, moving forward. But it was true. The lady was rocking back and forth, her eyes moist, clutching her fist to her mouth.

"Are you all right?"

"I'm fine," said Miss Starling. "Tee hee hee! I mean, I'm fine."

Claire and Maggie swapped incredulous looks. Then they started laughing too.

"That," said Miss Starling, "is a new one on me. And it's not often anyone gets the chance to say that." She managed to compose herself in record time and looked around to see that they were being watched by a crowd of wide-eyed girls.

She marched up to them. "There has been some damage here," she said, sternly. "If anyone believes they can assist to repair it in any way, please come and see me. In the meantime"—and her face was so straight, Maggie could fully believe she had imagined the last five minutes—"I recommend nobody drink from the pond until we get it fully drained. Now, everyone back to class *immediately*."

ALICE, FLISS, AND Simone lay breathless on the floor of their dorm. Every time they felt they couldn't possibly laugh any more, it was too painful, someone would recall the look on Maggie's face when everyone mentioned hearing the noise, or the undergardener's scientific insights into hoofprints, and they'd all set off once more.

"I said I'd get that Miss Adair," Alice would howl again, and the hysterics would rise again.

When their sides actually hurt, there wasn't a breath left in them, and Fliss thought she was going to throw up, Alice finally rose.

"OK," she said. "Off to face the music."

"Are you going to own up?" said Fliss, impressed.

"God, yes," scoffed Alice. "Of course, who do you think I am, Imogen? My granddad said if I could pull it off he'd pay for the fence."

"I'd like to meet your granddad," said Simone, wonderingly.

"Oh, maybe you will," said Alice carelessly, and Fliss's heart leaped, recognizing in it a simple acceptance of her new friend.

"They won't send you down, though, will they?" said Fliss, suddenly worried.

"Unlikely," said Alice. "I didn't actually do anything too bad, and that bridge needed demolishing anyway. Few detentions, I think. Which will be well worth it. And I won't mention you guys, don't worry."

"Thanks," said Fliss.

As IT TURNED out, Alice was exactly right. Miss Starling was less strict than her usual self, and Alice merely received lines and a sharp telling-off. The rhinoceros-foot wastepaper bin was ordered home to its rightful owner, and although everyone in Middle School 1 knew that Alice was behind it—and treated her with reverence and incredulity because of it—it also somehow made its way into Downey House folklore that, one night, an escaped rhinoceros had run through the grounds and drowned in the pond. It was to keep generations of Downey juniors well out of reach of the water.

The other positive outcome was that Simone's willingness to support the prank cemented the girls' friendship in the dorm. Three was never an easy number, and Simone would always have a residual distrust of, and admiration for, Alice's quick wit and sharp tongue—but the three girls were now inseparable.

Chapter Sixteen

I f it hadn't been for Alice and Fliss, Simone would never have gone up for the hockey team. But they encouraged her, and it wasn't as if she was going to need too much time to study for end of term exams—she'd done so much work throughout the year, it would really just be a case of going in and writing down the answers.

All year Miss James had been putting them through their paces in various sports. Unlike most games mistresses, she wasn't keen on forcing girls into teams too early. It took some girls a while to find their feet and confidence; telling a girl she couldn't do sport too early was likely to put her off for life, and she would probably finish her career on the games field hanging around the goal chewing nonchalantly and gossiping with chums.

So she tried different sports, shook up teams, encouraged everyone to play every position. Obviously some were stronger than others, but rotating often showed unexpected skills, and some girls found, for example, some talent in trampolining where they'd failed elsewhere.

In summer term, however, there were special netball and

hockey play-offs between all the houses and that's where it got really serious. Not everyone had to try out, but there was kudos, time off other classes, and the chance to travel to other schools in later years if you made the team, so competition was fierce.

Tryouts were late in May on a Saturday morning. It was shaping up to be another lovely day. Seniors, bored with their A-level revision, glanced fondly out of their study windows, remembering past tryouts from their first year as if it were a lifetime ago.

"Right, everyone," said Miss James. She had her usual brisk manner, but no one could prevent the nerves from getting through. Fliss was sitting out this year, despite loving netball; it wasn't worth risking the ankle just yet, but she firmly hoped she'd be allowed to play next year. Alice wasn't auditioning at all, she thought sport was stupid. But Simone was there, making a feeble attempt at warming up, and her friends had gone to cheer her on.

"This is going to be super embarrassing," she said at the side-lines. "Andrea runs like the wind, and Sylvie is totally brilliant. They're all going to laugh at me."

"They're not," said Fliss. "You're great at hockey."

"I suppose I could stop the ball with my thighs," said Simone. "They're bigger than the net."

"Is that legal in hockey?" said Alice.

"Maybe I could sue them for not letting a person of unrestricted growth play," muttered Simone. Alice laughed, but Fliss didn't like Simone's habit of always putting herself down. Maybe if she got in the team she could drop a bit of weight anyway, and it wouldn't be such a problem.

"Go, Simone!" she said. "Go for it!"

Simone raised her eyes to heaven. "Will you look after my glasses? I'm much more aggressive if I can't see what I'm doing."

Miss James ran them around for a warm-up which didn't do Simone's cause much good—she was puffed out almost before they had to zigzag in among the mini traffic cones. And when it came to shooting at the goal, star shots Ursula and lanky sporty Andrea were streets ahead. But at Simone's turn in goal she stolidly and carefully blocked every shot, and Miss James made a mark on her paper anyway.

MAGGIE WAS DELIGHTED to see Simone's name up on the team list the following morning. Simone hardly ever came to see her now, only infrequently to change a book.

"I'm not reading so much now," she'd said last time. "I'm so busy." Then she'd blushed. She'd be rather pretty if she could drop a little of that weight, thought Maggie. Then she had to get on. There were final assessment sheets to be delivered off—the assessors were counter-marking the mock examinations, which had made everyone terribly nervous—end of term exams to be set for the juniors, and exam supervision to be arranged for the seniors. The end of term concert she wasn't involved in. Probably just as well. The less time she spent with David McDonald the better. And anyway, she'd managed to persuade Stan to come down for sports day, tempting him with sunny weather and the promise of walks on the beach with frequent ice cream stops. She was sure if he just spent some time in Cornwall he'd learn to love it too.

Maggie sometimes surprised herself by thinking how much she'd forgotten now her once fierce ideals about returning to the poorer areas of her homeland, though she knew somewhere in her heart that she would have to—one day. Anna kept reminding her about it, telling her how Dylan and Cody's local park had been closed down due to council cuts and how they were driving her crazy kicking about the house all day. Maggie felt guilty and vowed to get them down here too, maybe when the Scottish schools broke up, earlier than the English ones, to let them, too, run about in the fresh air, play on the crags and the beach, jump in the enormous swimming pool. It wasn't, she knew, the solution.

VERONICA WAITED FOR the final assessment meeting with some trepidation. Even the idea of being in the same room as Daniel again made her feel nervous. She was desperate just to stare at his face, even though she realized how peculiar this would be.

Pat and Liz had not been best pleased to have their previous meeting canceled and were huffy and self-important when they turned up, fussing about with unnecessary flip charts and bar charts. Present, in the small lecture auditorium, were Veronica, Miss Starling, and three representatives of the board of governors, who were normally very hands-off: Dame Lydia Johnson, a local JP; Digory Gill, a local council officer; and Majabeen Gupta, a pediatrician from London who had a holiday cottage there and had sent all three of his girls through the school. The report, once it was bound, would go to every governor, every teacher, and from then on to every parent who requested it. It had been such an eventful year, Veronica reflected ruefully. She hoped it wouldn't have a negative impact on their score.

"Now," said Liz, looking officious in a white polyester shirt that strained over her large bosoms. It was lucky she'd never attempted to button her suit jacket; it was very unlikely she'd succeed. "When we approached this task, we used the 1989 matrix inversion schedule, as popularized by McIntosh and Luther, in the Northern Schools Initiative of 1991."

Veronica glanced briefly at Digory. He was not one for jargon and tended to either complain through it or fall asleep. From the looks of him this morning, it might well be the latter.

"First we looked at how effective, efficient, and inclusive is the provision of education, integrated care, and any extended services in meeting the needs of learners," droned Liz. "We found that in many circumstances there were some problems with developmental acquisition of the proper nondiscriminatory, religion, disability, difference, and gender instruments."

Even Veronica was finding it hard to understand what she was talking about, and she had a PhD in economics. Perhaps a PhD in horrible jargon would have been more appropriate.

Over the space of the next forty minutes, however, it transpired that Pat and Liz had decided the school was not socially minded enough, did not include enough work on environmental issues, and wasn't inclusive. Veronica mentally struck this from her head. Inclusive wasn't, sadly, their business. They had girls here from every part of the world, from every race and religion, although she was well aware that the one thing they all had in common was that their parents were wealthy, and believed in educating girls. But her job was only to teach them to be tolerant and kind, not slavishly trying to right wrongs.

It didn't really matter, though, as she was hardly concentrating. She was watching Daniel. Her son, Daniel. She couldn't even believe the words as she thought them. "My son, Daniel." She'd hardly slept since he'd been to see her.

Daniel was sitting, looking grave and making notes on a piece of paper. Veronica hoped he would stay behind so they could have lunch together, and she could ask him about his parents. Daniel felt nervous too. What was expected of him now? he wondered. Maybe it would be all right if they just tried to get to know each other. What on earth were the others going to say when they found out he was Dr. Deveral's . . . he couldn't keep thinking of her like that, it was ridiculous, but so was "mother" so he'd have to keep thinking of an alternative. Anyway. What were people going to think when they found out? It was going to be strange for everyone.

"There are also some extreme safety and security issues at the school," Liz was now saying, touching as if sensitively on "breakouts" and "injuries" as if they were much more serious than she could bring herself to mention. "We have enumerated these at some length in our final report." Digory did look like he was nodding off. Just as Veronica was thinking this, she noticed June Starling give him a sharp dig in the ribs.

"However," said Pat, taking back the baton. "There are some other matters to consider."

Another sheet came up on the overhead projector. This Veronica understood immediately.

Attitude of learners
Attendance of learners
Enjoyment of learners
Involvement of learners
Attainments of learners

And lined up under those headings were the exam marks of girls from the last five years, and the projections for this year, which were higher than ever.

Everyone gazed at this slide for some time.

"So," said Pat, somewhat reluctantly. "We'll have some recommendations to make about truancy, safety procedures, and some suggestions as to how to promote inclusivity . . ."

"Yes," said Veronica, her heart beating slightly faster.

"But these aren't problems, however pressing, that are believed to be significant enough to affect the school's standing in the long run," said Liz, sounding grudging. "The girls, it seems, have spoken for you. And they like the school as it is."

There was a pause.

"Well done," said Daniel, who'd known the results in advance. He rose to his feet. "It's a top score all round."

And he came forward to shake Veronica by the hand. It was only when he did so that she realized how nervous she had been. As usual, she didn't betray herself by even a tremor. She's amazing, thought Daniel. You would never think they were more than just colleagues.

"Thank you," said Veronica. "Thank you so much everyone. And thanks for your hard work."

Pat and Liz gave thin-lipped smiles.

"You'll get the full report in the post in eight weeks," said Liz.

Eight weeks? thought Veronica, but she didn't say anything, except, "Lunch?"

DANIEL CAUGHT UP with her as they walked round the outside of the building—it was such a beautiful day. He approached her nervously; Veronica turned, equally nervous, having walked on ahead alone in the hopes that he would come and walk with her.

"Hello," she said, checking to see no one was near them. "Hello. How are you? Are you well?"

"I'm well. Yes. I'm well. You know. It's strange and everything. What about you?"

Veronica looked at the nervous young man beside her. What must he be thinking? she thought. After all, he'd been through all the work of finding her. Was he pleased? Disappointed?

"Oh, you know," she said, trying to carry off a little laugh. "Starting to come to terms with the world being a little different to how I thought of it before."

"Quite," said Daniel. He wasn't sure if it was the right thing to do, but he touched her lightly on the arm. Veronica tensed up, realizing this was the first personal contact they'd had in nearly forty years.

"Sorry," said Daniel.

"Not at all," said Veronica. He didn't remember when she'd held him, buried her face in his head and smelled his brand-new, bloodied fresh-bread smell. She'd never forgotten it.

"I, er . . . spoke to Mum and Dad."

"Oh yes?"

"They think I should go slow. You know. Take it a step at a time."

Both his parents in fact had been a little worried that he'd tracked Veronica down and confronted her, but loved him too much to tell him. Daniel swallowed.

"But I'm happy to tell the world. I don't mind."

Something in his tone made her think that suddenly he didn't sound like a thirty-eight-year-old at all, but like the little boy he must have been. She must remember that; he was not an adult when he was talking to her, not really.

Veronica smiled at him. "Well, I understand completely your parents' reticence. Of course it's too early, we don't want to go broadcasting anything until we've gotten to know each other a little."

She realized immediately by the way his face twisted that this wasn't what he'd been expecting.

"What do you mean?" said Daniel, suddenly feeling as if he'd just been snubbed. Why not? Why couldn't they be a family? Wasn't that the whole point of him telling her? His parents would be so welcoming too.

Veronica felt conflicted. For a moment she thought he was going to turn round and announce it to the others behind them, which made her shiver with horror. And she'd been looking forward so much to getting to know him slowly, on their terms, without being a topic of gossip and intrusion for the rest of the world . . . surely that was best.

"I just meant, I understand that a more cautious approach . . ."

Daniel didn't understand this at all. He'd thought she was so pleased. "You mean, you're ashamed of having an illegitimate son? In this day and age?"

"Don't be ridiculous," said Veronica, stopping short and looking straight at him. "Meeting you again has been one of the best things that has ever happened to me." She took a deep breath. "After having you."

Daniel took this in. Wow. That was . . . that was so amazing, so what he'd hoped she'd feel and say. But then why on earth would they have to keep it a secret?

"But in my position . . ." went on Veronica.

Daniel stopped short. His face looked red.

"I see," he said and started to head back to the others.

"No, no!" said Veronica, reaching out as if to hold on to him, but dropped her arms immediately. "It's not like that at all. I want to get to know you so much, Daniel. I was hoping to meet your family one day . . . even, I was thinking, you know Mrs. Sutherland retires next year from the history department, and I even thought you might be interested in coming to work here . . ."

But how could she say this and mean something else?

"But in secret?" said Daniel, rubbing the back of his head.

"Please, Daniel. I just . . . I just don't want to rush things."

"Well, you've already offered me a job, but apart from that you don't want to rush things."

Veronica looked down at her elegant hands, noticing unavoidably, as she always did, the way the veins grew uglier and more prominent every year.

"I . . . I . . . I seem to be making rather a mess of this, don't I?" she said. What could she say to him to make him realize how important he was, how important this was to her?

Daniel couldn't believe this. She really would offer him a job but not tell anyone he was her son. After everything he'd done to find her. She said she wanted him but when it came down to it, it was just like before—she didn't really want to acknowledge him at all. He felt his ears going pink, felt once more like a little boy .

"I don't . . ." he said, then decided to leave before he said something he couldn't take back. "Uh. I don't think I'll stay for lunch." And he strode off toward his car.

As Veronica watched him go, she felt a piece of herself break off, plummet into blackness. Her boy . . . her boy . . .

"Are you all right?"

It was Majabeen, come up beside her.

"It's wonderful news, isn't it?"

"What?" said Veronica, trying to wrest her brain back from where it had gone, down the road with her only son. "Oh, yes. The report. Yes, I suppose it is."

"Come on, then. I think everyone wants to celebrate. Is that young chap gone?"

"Yes," said Veronica, slowly. "Yes, he has. Let me just go and freshen up."

Chapter Seventeen

End of term! There was a heady atmosphere in the dorms as the girls were getting ready to go home, or abroad on exciting trips. Astrid was spending the summer in the special program at the Royal College of Music in London. Alice was joining her parents in Cairo. Fliss couldn't believe how much she was going to miss her friends.

"I'll only be in London," said Simone. "You can come and see me."

"No, no, come to Guildford—you can ride my pony," said Fliss. "It'll be great."

All exams were over, and all that was left was to slack off, lie tanning on the grass at lunchtime, and make plans for the summer.

"I am going to sleep till eleven o'clock every day," said Sylvie, dreamily.

"Is that the most wonderful thing you can think of to do?" said Alice, but not in as sneering a tone as she'd have used before.

"Yes, actually," said Sylvie, uncowed. "I'm very sensitive to bells."

Clarissa Rhodes was off to the Sorbonne, where she would take a vast number of high-level courses, all in French. Maggie had felt entirely embarrassed when Clarissa came by especially to thank her.

"Well done with that Rhodes girl," she now said, banging loudly on Claire's door. Hearing no answer, she popped her head round—Claire ought to be here by now.

She was lying full length on her bed, howling her eyes out.

"What's the matter?"

"Eet does not matter. *Tant pis! Je déteste les hommes.*"

"What, all of them?"

Sitting down, Maggie got from her that the affair with the married man had ended catastrophically, and that he had gone back to his wife, tragically just in time for the summer holidays.

"There, there," said Maggie, patting Claire on the back. "At least you won't have to see him anymore."

"Ah have to see him ALL THE TIME!" said Claire furiously.

"Why? What do you mean?"

Maggie had always imagined Claire's paramour to be some rich glamorous Frenchman, like Nicolas Sarkozy, only taller, who bought her jewels and had a beautiful apartment in an *arrondissement.*

"*Mais non*, it's Mr. Graystock."

Maggie shook her head. "Mr. Graystock at Downey Boys? The classics teacher?"

She dimly remembered the lanky posh chap, but had hardly given him a second glance as it was, she remembered with some embarrassment, at the height of her David mooning phase.

"Isn't he a bit of a chinless wonder?"

"'e ees BASTARD!"

Maggie stayed with her for some time, amazed at what was

going on under her nose at the school that she'd managed to completely miss.

It was still a lovely morning though. Many of the Downey boys would be coming over to see their sports day, and vice versa. She'd make excuses for Claire.

And all her girls had done well in their exams. She was so proud of them; this term they'd really got their heads down. And now all that was left was the sports day, then back to Glasgow for eight glorious weeks. Her parents were incredibly excited already and had made all sorts of plans; Stan was still here and threatening to drive the Fiat Panda all the way back to Scotland, which was fine by her. Nothing else had been said, but she knew, she just knew deep down that she wanted to come back next year. She'd had a short interview with Veronica that had confirmed what she'd hoped very much—that it was working out for her at Downey House, and they'd like to keep her. She had accepted, telling herself she'd sort it out later. But she just didn't know how long Stan would take "no" for an answer.

Frowning slightly, she wandered past the sports pitch to walk down and pick him up from the village. Lessons were canceled today as the girls all dressed up in house colors, in preparation to fight it out on the hockey pitch and athletics field. The gardeners had done an amazing job; flower beds were blazing with June flowers, reflecting the colors of the houses—rose-pink for Tudor, white for York, surrounded by green wreaths for Wessex, and fresh blue and yellow broom for the Plantagenets. Fluttering bunting had been hung up along the running track and around the stall that would be providing much-needed barley water later. It was an amazingly hot day, butterflies thronging up from the long grass beneath her feet.

She hailed the familiar figure at the foot of the driveway.

"Well met!" she shouted.

David grinned back at her, but she thought he looked a little nervous, and there was no sign of Stephen Daedalus.

"What's up? Where's Stephen Daedalus? Are you here on school business?"

David looked uncomfortable and glanced around. He was wearing long baggy khaki trousers, and a gray collarless shirt; if he hadn't seemed so awkward he would have appeared cool and fresh in the summer heat.

They couldn't be seen from the school where they were, far away from the high towers, close to the copse. She moved closer toward him.

"Uh," he said. It wasn't like David to be speechless. He couldn't be blushing, could he?

"Here's the thing." he said. "And I'm just going to say it, all right?"

Maggie found that she was holding her breath.

"I . . . I've broken up with Miranda."

Maggie squinted at him. She felt her heart start to beat faster. Why was he telling her?

"Oh, I'm so sorry."

"It doesn't matter. She didn't like having a lowly schoolmaster for a beau, and didn't really bother to hide it too much. Always pestering me to go to Portsmouth and get a job there. Like it wasn't all right to be happy in your job if you didn't make that much money . . . anyway, forget that," he said, taking a deep breath. "I . . . I. Well. I think you're . . . Anyway. Huh. This is difficult. Anyway. Listen. I'm going on holiday. I'm going to walk the Cinque Terre. In Italy. It's gorgeous, apparently, and some friends have a villa down there and I'll be staying with them, and, well, of course you can't, it's totally stupid to ask. But if you wanted to come. You could. That's all. Right. Sorry."

His dark eyes had been fixed on the ground throughout this speech, and Maggie could barely think straight. But did this mean . . . what? What did it mean?

She stood there, staring at him.

"I know. I'm sorry. I shouldn't have said anything. I'll go. Sorry. Sorry. I'm really sorry."

And he turned round. Maggie couldn't take her eyes off him. David. Her David. He was walking on now, not looking back, toward the gates of the school, his shoulders bent. She couldn't bear to watch him so . . .

"DAVID!!!" she shouted, just as he reached the entrance, even though she didn't have the faintest idea of what she was going to say to him after that. But she so wanted to say his name.

His long body stiffened, and, very slowly, he turned around. She found herself staring straight into his eyes. Very slowly, and with a faintly incredulous look on his face, he started to walk back toward her up the hill. Maggie caught her breath. Oh my. Oh . . .

"HEY!"

They both froze, still several meters apart.

"Can I come through this door, or do I get arrested as a sex pest immediately? Useful to know, like," said Stan, hovering just at the very edge of the gates. "Thought I'd come and get you, but I forgot about the pedie bit where I can't come in."

Stan was wearing odd-length shorts that seemed to stop half-way down his calves, like they'd been bought for a toddler, and his beloved Celtic top. Maggie stared at him. David was looking at her still, so intently.

"I've brought sausage sandwiches," said Stan. "Miss a meal here, you're stuffed."

David dropped his gaze, shaking his head. Then he pasted on a smile.

"Stanley," he said. "Hi there."

"Hello," said Stan, not friendly or unfriendly. "Come on, love." This to Maggie.

Maggie felt her head spin. Had she taken leave of her senses? What, was she just going to suddenly dump this man, her Stan, when she'd agreed to marry him only six months before? Had she gone crazy?

She tried out her voice experimentally. It sounded weird, like she was listening to it on tape. "Eh, hello, Stan."

Stan didn't seem to notice.

"Are they really going to let me watch all these foxy girls in sporty skirts?" he grumbled. "I'm not sure this is such a good idea."

Unable to stop herself, Maggie found herself going toward him. You do not, she told herself very firmly, confuse what is real with what is a fantasy. That is madness. Madness.

"Must go," said David. "Get the dog, you know."

"I reckon he's married to that dog," said Stan, watching him head down the lane. Then he took Maggie in his arms and kissed her. "School's nearly out, eh? Nearly finished! Yay!"

"Yay," said Maggie, slightly more quietly, then she buried her head in his shirt, taking in his familiar scent.

"Steady on," said Stan. "I don't want your terrifying Miss Starling having my guts for garters. And she would too. She'd claw them out with her bare fingernails, and smile while she did it."

"She's not that bad," said Maggie.

"Not that bad? After everything you've told me . . ."

And Stan followed a very thoughtful Maggie up the hill.

SIMONE WAS NERVOUS as she got ready in the blue and yellow polo shirt they'd had specially made up. All she had to do, she knew, was stand in the goal and do as well as she could. But it was one thing being surrounded by her own form, who supported her and had grown to like her. Girls from other classes, older girls were watching now. She bit her lip. Well, it was too late. Fliss was plaiting her hair to keep it out of the way.

"And don't let them go for your glasses," she was saying.

"No," said Simone.

Miss James got her teams together. Two ten-minute halves for six-a-side teams per game; York versus Tudor first, then Plantagenets v Wessex, followed by a play-off.

The whole school was out on the benching, in a festive mood; the senior sports coming up later. The little ones' hockey tournament was always fun, the older girls shaking their heads in disbelief that they were ever so small and immature, and laughing if things got aggressive, as they could do.

Miss James blew her whistle as the whites and pinks faced off. The game was fast and furious played with this number of players in such a short time frame, and it took a while to get a goal on the table. But at the eighth minute, Eve McGinty, a tough-faced girl from Tudor, whacked one across the goal line, followed in the second half by two more. She was clearly a formidable opponent, and York retired sulkily.

"Go, Simone," shouted Fliss, as she stood up to get on the pitch. Everyone, it seemed to Simone, was yelling.

Maggie was watching, trying to clear her bewildered head. Had David really . . . suddenly she had a vision of them both, walking through Italy, eating in simple trattorias, getting brown with the sun and healthy with the exercise; spending balmy nights with sweet pink wine in little towns where whitewashed churches rang out their bells as the stars above swelled and the velvety soft nights washed over them with the heavy scent of lilies . . .

"You all right?" said Stan, nudging her. "This fat girl's one of yours, isn't she?"

With effort, Maggie pulled herself back. And indeed, it was wonderful to see Simone out there, blocking, passing the ball back and forward, hearing the shouts from the crowd.

No one, though, it seemed, could get in to score. It looked like being sudden death in the second half when, suddenly, Andrea broke through at the last moment and hit the little ball straight into the corner of their opponents' net.

The Plantagenet girls erupted into a bouncing mass of blue and yellow from their place on the benches, jumping up and down and hugging each other.

"Well done," said Miss James, as they took five minutes before the final. "Now, watch out for Eve McGinty. She's the best in the year. Simone, do you think you can stop her?"

Simone was getting her breath back and polishing her glasses, but she nodded nervously nonetheless. She'd felt very strange out there and was thankful that the ball hadn't really come too close to her goal.

That all changed when the next match began. There was no

doubt that Eve was the star, and she went for the ball with all the aggression of a national rugby player. Simone saw the ball come straight for her, and, in a temporary loss of nerve, closed her eyes. The ball went straight between her legs and landed in the goal, glinting up at her.

There were roars from the Tudor side, and groans from the Plantagenets, even a couple of solitary boos. Maggie winced in disappointment for her, and again as Eve slammed the ball in two more times in that half alone. It was going to be a massacre.

Simone knew she was purple at half-time, partly with exhaustion, and partly with embarrassment.

"Would you like me to take you off?" said Miss James.

"She'll be all right, won't you, Simone?" said Andrea.

And at that, Simone felt her confidence rise a little. If tall, capable Andrea thought she could do it, there was no reason not to.

"I'll do my best," she said.

"Well, do better than that," said Andrea, spitting out her orange peel. "Do your job. Block these bloody goals."

And my goodness, she did! Simone was everywhere over the back of the pitch, feinting, blocking, and whacking the ball back with gusto. Even the most indifferent of pupils, who thought sport was a complete waste of everyone's time, were riveted by the chubby commando of the hockey pitch. As Eve's frustration started to show, Andrea went for her, allowing little Sylvie to slip in at the last moment and pocket one. Goal! In the ensuing kerfuffle, Andrea went headlong in again and scored almost immediately. Goal!

Almost roaring with frustration, Eve plowed down the field with the ball, heading straight, it seemed, for Simone's glasses.

Everyone waited for Simone to move. But she didn't. She held her ground, and as Eve whacked the ball with full force straight at Simone's left side, Simone merely leaned over and planted her stick on the goal line. And WHACK, the ball was off and back in the game; picked up by Ursula, passed to Sylvie, who as usual was dancing unnoticed right up at the front line, and one more was in. GOAL!

The Plantagenet girls were on their feet now, shouting and roaring like little savages. There were two minutes of the game left as Miss James threw the ball back into play. Tussling at the front was absolutely vicious, and ankles were whacked willy-nilly as both sides fought for their lives. But the ball wasn't getting anywhere up or down the field—the girls were all over it, any concept of tactical play gone completely. Finally, desperately, Eve McGinty made a huge swing at it.

The hit connected, and the ball flew through the air, as the girls all stopped to follow its parabola. Once again Simone saw it. And she did not close her eyes this time, but said to herself, "DO YOUR JOB."

Whereupon, with tremendous skill, she trapped the ball and hit it full flight across the pitch, straight to Andrea, who putted it gently into the back of the net just as the whistle blew.

The noise levels were absolutely extraordinary. Miss James was grinning like a Cheshire cat; nobody could say sport was unimportant now! Maggie, to her surprise, found herself not thinking about David for the moment, but standing up in her seat, unapologetically cheering the Plantagenet girls' victory. The team was now surrounded by the rest of their classmates, jumping up and down and screeching with excitement, a mass of color in the blazing sunshine. Miss Starling was shaking her head at the noise. Maggie rushed down to congratulate them—

she couldn't help it—and was touched and heartened by the warm welcome the girls gave her.

"ALL RIGHT," SAID Stan, when she returned to her seat in the stands—the middle school second year were about to start on their javelin throwing.

"All right what?" said Maggie, still pink with happiness.

"All right. You were right," said Stan.

"What?"

"You were right. It is good for you here. You do belong."

This was so unexpected, Maggie just stared at him.

"Lots of people have long-distance relationships for a bit— ours has been going all right, hasn't it?"

Maggie felt a surge of guilt that she squashed down as far as she could.

"Yes."

"OK. I'll stop bugging you. You stay here and . . . well, we'll see in a year or two, yeah?"

Maggie would have liked to hug him, but it was rarely advisable when surrounded by pupils. Instead she squeezed his leg, hard. Inside she was a mass of contradictions—but women were like that, weren't they? she told herself. Weren't they?

"Thank you," she said. "Thank you."

"So, ANYWAY," SAID Fliss's mum, as they drove back up the motorway. They were heading straight for Gatwick for a couple of weeks in France, even though Fliss would rather have gone back to Surrey to catch up with her old friends. Oh well, it wouldn't be for long.

"And then we never thought Simone was going to be one of us, but then it turned out she's OK really, then she helped me out a lot with my English, so I think my marks are going to be really good now, I mean, the exam was totally easy and everything, but she's all right that teacher, and I'm going to definitely try out for the team next year, my ankle's completely fine, and next year you get to travel and play other schools, and . . ."

"So," said her mother when she could get a word in edgeways. "We did say we were going to look again at whether you wanted to stay on at Downey House."

"Oh," said Fliss. She'd forgotten about that. Then she saw her dad at the wheel, smiling.

"I suppose it's OK," she said.

"I knew it!" crowed Hattie triumphantly. "I knew she'd think it was the best school in the world."

"Shut up, swotto," said Fliss.

"Shut up yourself."

"No, *you* shut up."

VERONICA TOOK A final turn around the empty classrooms before leaving the buildings in the capable hands of Harold Carruthers for the next few weeks. It was amazing how still the place felt; all the eternal noise and bustle and color of four hundred girls, bursting with life, vanished overnight.

Dust was already settling on the desks and the radiators and work peeling from the walls, and the school had a characteristic, slightly deadening smell of old ink and gym shoes, as if it knew its rightful inhabitants were missing.

She wondered, as usual these days, about Daniel. She'd written to him once or twice, hoping to hear from him, but she hadn't. She'd poured her heart out into those letters, telling him exactly what he'd always meant to her and what she hoped he could mean in the future. She could only hope it was enough.

Losing a child once had been bad enough . . . losing him again would be such a heavy burden to bear.

She went through classroom after classroom, running her hands across the desks, checking that there were no left-behind apple cores or milk bottles or anything that could cause them problems at the start of the new year. It had been an eventful time. With some good new people, and sad losses. But sometimes she felt she loved the school most of all when it was empty, with only its faint scent and her own quiet footsteps to remind her that its halls were once full of laughter and chatter and young minds being formed. And if she half-closed her eyes, she could almost hear an echo of singing, from far away and down the hall . . .

We are the girls
The Girls of Downey Hall
We stand up proud
And we hold our heads up tall
We serve the Queen
Our country, God, and home
We dare to dream
Of wider plains to roam
We are the girls
The Girls of Downey Hall.

Maggie's Poems

"The Choosing," Liz Lochhead (1970)
"My Bonnie Mary," Robert Burns (1788)
"The Journey of the Magi," T. S. Eliot (1927)
"Christmas," John Betjeman (1951)
"The Crystal Set," Kathleen Jamie (1995)
"Stopping by Woods on a Snowy Evening," Robert Frost (1922)

Acknowledgements

Thanks to Jo Dickinson, Emma Stonex, and all at Little, Brown; the National Poetry Library; W. Hickham; Kathleen Jamie; and Gunn Media Inc.

If you loved *Welcome to the School by the Sea*, read on for the first chapter of *Rules at the School by the Sea*, which details the second year at Downey House.

Rules at the School by the Sea

Jenny Colgan

For the second year at Downey House,
it's getting harder and harder to stick to the rules. . . .

It's about making them. . . .
Now that she's engaged to sweet and steady Stan,
Maggie's just got to stop thinking about David McDonald,
her opposite number at Downey Boys . . . hasn't she?

It's about breaking them. . . .
Headmistress Veronica Deveral has more
to lose than anyone. When Daniel Stapleton joins the
faculty, she's forced to confront her scandalous secret.
How long will she be able to keep it under wraps?

"Funny, page-turning and addictive."
—Sophie Kinsella

Chapter One

Maggie was dancing on a table. This was distinctly out of character, but they *had* served her cocktails earlier, in a glass so large she was surprised it didn't have a fish in it.

Plus it was a beautifully soft, warm evening, and her fiancé Stan had insisted on watching the football on a large Sky Sports screen, annoyingly situated over her head in the Spanish bar, so there wasn't much else to do—and all the other girls were dancing on tabletops.

I'm still young, Maggie had thought to herself. I'm only twenty-six years old! I can still dance all night!

And with the help of a friendly bachelorette party from Stockport on the next table, she'd found herself up there, shrugging off any self-consciousness with the help of a large margarita and grooving away to Alphabeat.

"Hey, I can't see the game," Stan complained.

"I don't care," said Maggie, suddenly feeling rather more free, happy, and determined to enjoy her holiday. She raised her arms above her head. This was definitely a good way to forget about school; to forget about David McDonald, the English teacher she'd developed a crush on last year—until she'd found out he was engaged. To just feel like herself again.

* * *

"Isn't that Miss Adair?" said Hattie.

They'd been allowed down into the town for the evening from the discreet and beautifully appointed villa they'd been staying in high on the other side of the mountain. Fliss turned round from where she'd been eyeing up fake designer hand-bags, and glanced at the tacky-looking sports pub Hattie was pointing out. Inside was a group of drunk-looking women waving their hands in the air.

"No way!" exclaimed Fliss, heading toward the door for a closer look. "I'm going in to check."

"You're not allowed in any bars!" said Hattie. "I promised Mum and Dad."

"*I promised Mum and Dad,*" mimicked Fliss. "I am fourteen, you know. That's pretty much the legal drinking age over here."

"Well, while you're with me you'll obey family rules."

Fliss stuck out her tongue and headed straight for the bar. "You're not a prefect now."

"No, but we're in a position of trust, and . . ."

Fliss stopped short in the doorway.

"Hello, senorita," said the doorman. Fliss had grown two inches over the summer, although to her huge annoyance she was still barely filling an A cup.

Maggie and the girls from Stockport were shimmying up and down to the Pussycat Dolls when she saw the girl. At first she thought it was a trick of the flashing lights. It couldn't be. After all, they'd come all this way to leave her work behind. So she could feel like a girl, not a teacher. So surely it couldn't be one of her—

"MISS ADAIR!" shrieked Fliss. "Is that you, miss?"

Maggie stopped dancing.

"Felicity Prosser," she said, feeling a resigned tone creep into her voice. She looked around, wondering what would be the most dignified way to get down from the table, under the circumstances.

NORMALLY, VERONICA DEVERAL found the Swiss Alps in summertime a cleansing balm to her soul. The clean, sharp air you could draw all the way down into your lungs; the sparkle of the grass and the glacier lakes; the cyclists and rosy-cheeked all-year skiers heading for higher ground; the freshly washed sky. She always stayed in the same hostel, and liked to take several novels—she favored the lengthy intrigues of Anthony Trollope, and was partial to a little Joanna for light relief—and luxuriate in the time to devour them, returning to Downey House rested, refreshed, and ready for the new academic year.

This year, however, had been different. After her shock at meeting her adoptive son after nearly forty years, Veronica had handled it badly and they had lost contact. And although there were budgets to be approved, a new intake to set up, and staffing to be organized, she couldn't concentrate. All she seemed to do was worry about Daniel, and wonder what he was doing.

Now back from her unsatisfying trip, she was staring out of the window of her beautiful office two days before term was due to start, when Dr. Robert Fitzroy, head of Downey Boys' School over the hill, arrived for their annual chat. The two schools did many things together, and it was useful to have some knowledge of the forthcoming agenda.

"You seem a little distracted, Veronica," Robert said, comfortably ensconced on the Chesterfield sofa, enjoying the fine view over the school grounds and to the cliffs and the sea beyond, today a perfect summer holiday blue. They weren't really getting anywhere with debating the new computer lab.

Veronica sighed and briefly considered confiding in her opposite number. He was a kind man, if a little set in his ways. She dismissed this thought immediately. She had spent years building up this school, the last thing she needed was anyone thinking she was a weak woman, prone to tears and overemotional sentimentality.

Robert droned on about new staff.

"Oh, and yes," he said, "we have a new history and classics teacher at last. Good ones are so hard to find these days."

Veronica was barely listening. She was watching the waves outside and wondering if Daniel had ever taken his children to the seaside for a holiday. So when Robert said his name it chimed with her thoughts, and at first she didn't at all understand what she'd just heard.

"Excuse me?"

"Daniel Stapleton. Our new classics teacher."

"Mom!"

Zelda was throwing ugly things in her bag. Ugly tops, ugly skirts, ugly hats. What the hell? School uniform was the stupidest idea in a country full of stupid ideas.

"Did you know I have to share, like, a bathroom? Did they tell you that?"

Zelda's mother shook her head. As if she didn't have enough to deal with, what with DuBose being so excited about the move and all. Why they all decided to run off and live in England, where she'd heard it rained all the time and everyone lived in itty-bitty houses with bathrooms the size of cupboards . . . well, it didn't bear thinking about. She doubted it would be much like Texas.

"Don' worry, darlin'," DuBose had said, in that calm drawl of his. He might get a lot of respect as a major transfered to the British Army, but it didn't cut much ice with her, nuh-huh.

"An' we'll get Zelda out of that crowd she's been runnin' with at high school. Turn her into quite the English lady."

A boarding school education was free for the daughters of senior military staff on overseas postings, and Downey House, they'd been assured, was among the very best.

As Mary-Jo looked at her daughter's heavily bitten black-painted fingernails, so strange against the stark white of her new uniform blouses, and so different from her own perfect manicure, she wondered, yet again, how they would all fit in.

SIMONE GLANCED AT Fliss's Facebook update— *Felicity is having a BLASTING time in Porto Caldo!*—and tried her best to be happy for her. The Pribetichs weren't having a holiday this year. It just wasn't practical. Which was fine by Simone: she hated struggling into her tankini and pulling a big sarong around herself, then sitting under an umbrella, hiding in case anyone saw her. So, OK, Fliss might be having great fun without her, and Alice was posting about being utterly, miserably bored learning to scuba dive with her au pair in Hurghada, and she was jealous and she did miss them—but she was doing her best to be happy for them.

Thank goodness she'd been invited to Fliss's house for the end of the holidays, so they could all travel back together. Simone had tried not to let slip to her friends just how much she was looking forward to it—and even worse, to admit how much she was looking forward to going back to school.

Jenny Colgan

It had been a long seven weeks, with not much to do but read and try to avoid Joel, her brother, who had spent the entire time indoors hunched over his game console.

She'd spent the summer dreaming of school and reading books, while eating fish finger sandwiches. Her mother had tried her best to get her involved in some local social events, but it wasn't really her thing. She winced remembering an unbelievably awkward afternoon tea with Rudi, the ugly, gangly teenage son of one of her mother's best friends. His face was covered in spots and his hair was oily and lank. They were shuffled awkwardly together onto a sofa.

Simone's misery on realizing that this was the kind of boy her mum thought she might like was compounded by the very obvious way Rudi looked her up and down and made it clear that he thought he was out of her league. She sighed again at the memory.

"You go to that posh school then," he'd muttered, when pushed by his mum.

Simone had felt a blush spread over her face, and kept her eyes tightly fixed on her hands.

"Yeah."

"Oh. Right."

And that had been that. It was pretty obvious that Rudi, overstretched as he was, would much rather be upstairs playing Grand Theft Auto with Joel.

Simone sighed. It would have been nice to go back to school with at least some adventures to tell Alice and Fliss. Still, they would share theirs with her.

"TELL ME ABOUT her thighs again," said Alice, leaning lazily on shady manicured grass, watching tiny jewel-colored lizards scrabble past and running up an enormous bill on the hotel phone.

"Jiggly," said Fliss, under an apple tree two thousand miles away in Surrey, tickling her dog Ranald on the tummy. "Honestly, you could see right up her skirt and everything."

"I never really think of teachers having legs," mused Alice. "I mean, I suppose they must and everything, but . . ."

"But what, you think they run along on wheels?" Fliss giggled.

"No, but . . . oh, it's so hot."

"FLISS!" The voice came from the next room.

"Oh god, is that the heffalump Hattie?" drawled Alice.

"I'm not going to answer," said Fliss.

"FELICITY!" Hattie huffed into the orchard garden, her tread heavy on the paving stones. "*Felicity.*"

"I'm on the *phone*," said Fliss crossly.

"Well, I have news."

"Is she pregnant?" said wicked Alice.

"Ssh," Fliss told her.

"Fine," said Hattie, turning to go. "So I guess you DON'T want to hear who's starting Downey Boys this year?"

Fliss turned and looked at her.

"What are you talking about?"

"Just that I was down in the village . . . and was talking to Will's mum . . ."

And just like that, Alice was talking to an empty telephone.

THIS BOOK BELONGS TO

. . . .

THE ANNE OF GREEN GABLES NOVELS

Anne of Green Gables
Anne of Avonlea
Anne of the Island
Anne of Windy Poplars
Anne's House of Dreams
Anne of Ingleside
Rainbow Valley
Rilla of Ingleside

THE EMILY NOVELS

Emily of New Moon
Emily Climbs
Emily's Quest

ANNE'S

HOUSE *of* DREAMS

L. M. MONTGOMERY

Our kin
Have built them temples, and therein
Pray to the gods we know; and dwell
In little houses lovable.

—RUPERT BROOKE

TUNDRA BOOKS

Published in Canada by Tundra Books,
a division of Random House of Canada Limited,
One Toronto Street, Suite 300, Toronto, Ontario M5C 2V6

LIBRARY AND ARCHIVES CANADA CATALOGUING IN PUBLICATION

Montgomery, L. M. (Lucy Maud), 1874–1942, author
Anne's house of dreams / Lucy Maud Montgomery ;
illustrated by Elly MacKay.

ISBN 978-1-77049-739-9 (pbk.)

I. MacKay, Elly, illustrator II. Title.

PS8526.O55A68 2014   JC813'.52   C2013-906960-7

This edition of *Anne's House of Dreams* is based on the version published
in Toronto in 1917 by McClelland, Goodchild and Stewart, Limited.
Some minor errors have been silently corrected.

Cover designed by Kelly Hill
Cover illustration © 2014 by Elly MacKay;
paper texture by Tomas Jasinskis/Shutterstock.com
The text was set in Fournier.

www.tundrabooks.com

Printed and bound in the United States of America

1 2 3 4 5 6   19 18 17 16 15 14

To

LAURA

in memory of the olden time

CONTENTS

ANNE'S
HOUSE *of* DREAMS

In the Garret of Green Gables

"Thanks be, I'm done with geometry, learning or teaching it," said Anne Shirley, a trifle vindictively, as she thumped a somewhat battered volume of Euclid into a big chest of books, banged the lid in triumph, and sat down upon it, looking at Diana Wright across the Green Gables garret, with gray eyes that were like a morning sky.

The garret was a shadowy, suggestive, delightful place, as all garrets should be. Through the open window, by which Anne sat, blew the sweet, scented, sun-warm air of the August afternoon; outside, poplar boughs rustled and tossed in the wind; beyond them were the woods, where Lover's Lane wound its enchanted path, and the old apple orchard which still bore its rosy harvests munificently. And, over all, was a great mountain range of snowy clouds in the blue southern sky. Through the other window was glimpsed a distant, white-capped, blue sea—the beautiful St. Lawrence Gulf, on which floats, like a jewel, Abegweit, whose softer, sweeter Indian name has long been forsaken for the more prosaic one of Prince Edward Island.

Diana Wright, three years older than when we last saw her, had grown somewhat matronly in the intervening time. But her eyes were as black and brilliant, her cheeks as rosy, and her dimples as enchanting, as in the long-ago days when she and Anne Shirley had vowed eternal friendship in the garden at Orchard Slope. In her arms she held a small, sleeping, black-curled creature, who for two happy years had been known to the world of Avonlea as "Small Anne Cordelia." Avonlea folks knew why Diana had called her Anne, of course, but Avonlea folks were puzzled by the Cordelia. There had never been a Cordelia in the Wright or Barry connections. Mrs. Harmon Andrews said she supposed Diana had found the name in some trashy novel, and wondered that Fred hadn't more sense than to allow it. But Diana and Anne smiled at each other. They knew how Small Anne Cordelia had come by her name.

"You always hated geometry," said Diana with a retrospective smile. "I should think you'd be real glad to be through with teaching, anyhow."

"Oh, I've always liked teaching, apart from geometry. These past three years in Summerside have been very pleasant ones. Mrs. Harmon Andrews told me when I came home that I wouldn't likely find married life as much better than teaching as I expected. Evidently Mrs. Harmon is of Hamlet's opinion that it may be better to bear the ills that we have than fly to others that we know not of."

Anne's laugh, as blithe and irresistible as of yore, with an added note of sweetness and maturity, rang through the garret. Marilla in the kitchen below, compounding blue plum preserve, heard it and smiled; then sighed to think how seldom that dear laugh would echo through Green Gables in the years to come. Nothing in her life had ever given Marilla so much happiness as the knowledge that Anne was going to marry Gilbert Blythe; but every joy must bring with it its little shadow of sorrow. During the three Summerside years Anne had been home often for vacations and weekends; but, after this, a bi-annual visit would be as much as could be hoped for.

"You needn't let what Mrs. Harmon says worry you," said Diana, with the calm assurance of the four-years matron. "Married life has its ups and downs, of course. You mustn't expect that everything will always go smoothly. But I can assure you, Anne, that it's a happy life, when you're married to the right man."

Anne smothered a smile. Diana's airs of vast experience always amused her a little.

"I daresay I'll be putting them on too, when I've been married four years," she thought. "Surely my sense of humour will preserve me from it, though."

"Is it settled yet where you are going to live?" asked Diana, cuddling Small Cordelia with the inimitable gesture of motherhood which always sent through Anne's heart, filled with sweet, unuttered dreams and hopes, a thrill that was half pure pleasure and half a strange, ethereal pain.

"Yes. That was what I wanted to tell you when I 'phoned to you to come down today. By the way, I can't realize that we really have telephones in Avonlea now. It sounds so preposterously up-to-date and modernish for this darling, leisurely old place."

"We can thank the A.V.I.S. for them," said Diana. "We should never have got the line if they hadn't taken the matter up and carried it through. There was enough cold water thrown to discourage any society. But they stuck to it, nevertheless. You did a splendid thing for Avonlea when you founded that society, Anne. What fun we did have at our meetings! Will you ever forget the blue hall and Judson Parker's scheme for painting medicine advertisements on his fence?"

"I don't know that I'm wholly grateful to the A.V.I.S. in the matter of the telephone," said Anne. "Oh, I know it's most convenient—even more so than our old device of signalling to each other by flashes of candlelight! And, as Mrs. Rachel says, 'Avonlea must keep up with the procession, that's what.' But somehow I feel as if I didn't want Avonlea spoiled by what Mr. Harrison, when he wants to be witty, calls 'modern inconveniences.' I should like to have it kept always just as it was in the dear old years. That's foolish—and sentimental—and impossible. So I shall immediately become wise and practical and possible. The telephone, as Mr. Harrison concedes, is 'a buster of a good thing'—even if you do know that probably half a dozen interested people are listening along the line."

"That's the worst of it," sighed Diana. "It's so annoying to hear the receivers going down whenever you ring anyone up. They say Mrs. Harmon Andrews insisted that their phone should be put in their kitchen just so that she could listen whenever it rang and keep an eye on the dinner at the same time. Today, when you called me, I distinctly heard that queer clock of the Pyes' striking. So no doubt Josie or Gertie was listening."

"Oh, so that is why you said, 'You've got a new clock at Green Gables, haven't you?' I couldn't imagine what you meant. I heard a vicious click as soon as you had spoken. I suppose it was the Pye receiver being hung up with profane energy. Well, never mind the Pyes. As Mrs. Rachel says, 'Pyes they always were and Pyes they always will be, world without end, amen.' I want to talk of pleasanter things. It's all settled as to where my new home shall be."

"Oh, Anne, where? I do hope it's near here."

"No-o-o, that's the drawback. Gilbert is going to settle at Four Winds Harbour—sixty miles from here."

"Sixty! It might as well be six hundred," sighed Diana. "I never can get further from home now than Charlottetown."

"You'll have to come to Four Winds. It's the most beautiful harbour on the Island. There's a little village called Glen St. Mary at its head, and Dr. David Blythe has been practising there for fifty years. He is Gilbert's great-uncle, you know. He is going to retire, and Gilbert is to take over his practice. Dr. Blythe is going to keep his house, though, so we shall have to find a habitation for ourselves. I don't know yet what it is, or where it will be in reality, but I have a little house o' dreams all furnished in my imagination—a tiny, delightful castle in Spain."

"Where are you going for your wedding tour?" asked Diana.

"Nowhere. Don't look horrified, Diana dearest. You suggest Mrs. Harmon Andrews. She, no doubt, will remark condescendingly that people who can't afford wedding 'towers' are real sensible not to take them; and then she'll remind me that Jane went to Europe for hers. I want to spend *my* honeymoon at Four Winds in my own dear house of dreams."

"And you've decided not to have any bridesmaid?"

"There isn't anyone to have. You and Phil and Priscilla and Jane all stole a march on me in the matter of marriage;

and Stella is teaching in Vancouver. I have no other 'kindred soul' and I won't have a bridesmaid who isn't."

"But you are going to wear a veil, aren't you?" asked Diana, anxiously.

"Yes, indeedy. I shouldn't feel like a bride without one. I remember telling Matthew, that evening when he brought me to Green Gables, that I never expected to be a bride because I was so homely no one would ever want to marry me—unless some foreign missionary did. I had an idea then that foreign missionaries couldn't afford to be finicky in the matter of looks if they wanted a girl to risk her life among cannibals. You should have seen the foreign missionary Priscilla married. He was as handsome and inscrutable as those day-dreams we once planned to marry ourselves, Diana; he was the best dressed man I ever met, and he raved over Priscilla's 'ethereal, golden beauty.' But of course there are no cannibals in Japan."

"Your wedding dress is a dream, anyhow," sighed Diana rapturously. "You'll look like a perfect queen in it—you're so tall and slender. How *do* you keep so slim, Anne? I'm fatter than ever—I'll soon have no waist at all."

"Stoutness and slimness seem to be matters of predestination," said Anne. "At all events, Mrs. Harmon Andrews can't say to you what she said to me when I came home from Summerside, 'Well, Anne, you're just about as skinny as ever.' It sounds quite romantic to be 'slender,' but 'skinny' has a very different tang."

"Mrs. Harmon has been talking about your trousseau. She admits it's as nice as Jane's, although she says Jane married a millionaire and you are only marrying a 'poor doctor without a cent to his name.'"

Anne laughed.

"My dresses *are* nice. I love pretty things. I remember the first pretty dress I ever had—the brown gloria Matthew gave me for our school concert. Before that everything I had was so ugly. It seemed to me that I stepped into a new world that night."

"That was the night Gilbert recited 'Bingen on the Rhine,' and looked at you when he said, 'There's another, *not* a sister.' And you were so furious because he put your pink tissue rose in his breast pocket! You didn't much imagine then that you would ever marry him."

"Oh, well, that's another instance of predestination," laughed Anne, as they went down the garret stairs.

The House of Dreams

There was more excitement in the air of Green Gables than there had ever been before in all its history. Even Marilla was so excited that she couldn't help showing it—which was little short of being phenomenal.

"There's never been a wedding in this house," she said, half apologetically, to Mrs. Rachel Lynde. "When I was a child I heard an old minister say that a house was not a real home until it had been consecrated by a birth, a wedding and a death. We've had deaths here—my father and mother died here as well as Matthew; and we've even had a birth here. Long ago, just after we moved into this house, we had a married hired man for a little while, and his wife had a baby here. But there's never been a wedding before. It does seem so strange to think of Anne being married. In a way she just seems to me the little girl Matthew brought home here fourteen years ago. I can't realize that she's grown up. I shall never forget what I felt when I saw Matthew bringing in a *girl*. I wonder what became of the boy we would have got if there hadn't been a mistake. I wonder what *his* fate was."

"Well, it was a fortunate mistake," said Mrs. Rachel Lynde, "though, mind you, there was a time I didn't think so—that evening I came up to see Anne and she treated us to such a scene. Many things have changed since then, that's what."

Mrs. Rachel sighed, and then brisked up again. When weddings were in order Mrs. Rachel was ready to let the dead past bury its dead.

"I'm going to give Anne two of my cotton warp spreads," she resumed. "A tobacco-stripe one and an apple-leaf one. She tells me they're getting to be real fashionable again. Well, fashion or no fashion, I don't believe there's anything prettier for a spare-room bed than a nice apple-leaf spread, that's what. I must see about getting them bleached. I've had them sewed up in cotton bags ever since Thomas died, and no doubt they're an awful colour. But there's a month yet, and dew-bleaching will work wonders."

Only a month! Marilla sighed and then said proudly:

"I'm giving Anne that half dozen braided rugs I have in the garret. I never supposed she'd want them—they're so old-fashioned, and nobody seems to want anything but hooked mats now. But she asked me for them—said she'd rather have them than anything else for her floors. They *are* pretty. I made them of the nicest rags, and braided them in stripes. It was such company these last few winters. And I'll make her enough blue plum preserve to stock her jam closet for a year. It seems real strange. Those blue plum trees hadn't even a blossom for three years, and I thought they might as well be cut down. And this last spring they were white, and such a crop of plums I never remember at Green Gables."

"Well, thank goodness that Anne and Gilbert really are going to be married after all. It's what I've always prayed for," said Mrs. Rachel, in the tone of one who is comfortably sure that her prayers have availed much. "It was a great relief to find out that she really didn't mean to take the Kingsport man. He was rich to be sure, and Gilbert is poor—at least, to begin with; but then he's an Island boy."

"He's Gilbert Blythe," said Marilla contentedly. Marilla would have died the death before she would have put into words the thought that was always in the background of her mind whenever she had looked at Gilbert from his childhood up—the thought that, had it not been for her own wilful pride long, long ago, he might have been *her* son. Marilla felt that, in some strange way, his marriage with Anne would put right that old mistake. Good had come out of the evil of the ancient bitterness.

As for Anne herself, she was so happy that she almost felt frightened. The gods, so says the old superstition, do not like to behold too happy mortals. It is certain, at least, that some human beings do not. Two of that ilk descended upon Anne one violet dusk and proceeded to do what in them lay to prick the rainbow bubble of her satisfaction. If she thought she was getting any particular prize in young Dr. Blythe, or if she imagined that he was still as infatuated with her as he might have been in his salad days, it was surely their duty to put the matter before her in another light. Yet these two worthy ladies were not enemies of Anne; on the contrary, they were really quite fond of her, and would have defended her as their own young had anyone else attacked her. Human nature is not obliged to be consistent.

Mrs. Inglis—*née* Jane Andrews, to quote from the *Daily Enterprise*—came with her mother and Mrs. Jasper Bell. But in Jane the milk of human kindness had not been curdled by years of matrimonial bickerings. Her lines had fallen in pleasant places. In spite of the fact—as Mrs. Rachel Lynde would say—that she had married a millionaire, her marriage had been happy. Wealth had not spoiled her. She was still the placid, amiable, pink-cheeked Jane of the old quartette, sympathising with her old chum's happiness and as keenly interested in all the dainty details of Anne's trousseau as if it could rival her own silken and bejewelled splendours. Jane was not brilliant, and had probably never made a remark worth listening to in her life; but she never said anything that would hurt anyone's feelings—which may be a negative talent but is likewise a rare and enviable one.

"So Gilbert didn't go back on you after all," said Mrs. Harmon Andrews, contriving to convey an expression of surprise in her tone. "Well, the Blythes generally keep their word when they've once passed it, no matter what happens. Let me see—you're twenty-five, aren't you, Anne? When I was a girl twenty-five was the first corner. But you look quite young. Red-headed people always do."

"Red hair is very fashionable now," said Anne, trying to smile, but speaking rather coldly. Life had developed in her a sense of humour which helped her over many difficulties; but as yet nothing had availed to steel her against a reference to her hair.

"So it is—so it is," conceded Mrs. Harmon. "There's no telling what queer freaks fashion will take. Well, Anne, your things are very pretty, and very suitable to your position in life, aren't they, Jane? I hope you'll be very happy. You have my best wishes, I'm sure. A long engagement doesn't often turn out well. But, of course, in your case it couldn't be helped."

"Gilbert looks very young for a doctor. I'm afraid people won't have much confidence in him," said Mrs. Jasper Bell gloomily. Then she shut her mouth tightly, as if she had said what she considered it her duty to say and held her conscience clear. She belonged to the type which always has a stringy black feather in its hat and straggling locks of hair on its neck.

Anne's surface pleasure in her pretty bridal things was temporarily shadowed; but the deeps of happiness below could not thus be disturbed; and the little stings of Mesdames Bell and Andrews were forgotten when Gilbert came later, and they wandered down to the birches of the brook, which had been saplings when Anne had come to Green Gables, but were now tall, ivory columns in a fairy palace of twilight and stars. In their shadows Anne and Gilbert talked in lover-fashion of their new home and their new life together.

"I've found a nest for us, Anne."

"Oh, where? Not right in the village, I hope. I wouldn't like that altogether."

"No. There was no house to be had in the village. This is a little white house on the harbour shore, half way between Glen St. Mary and Four Winds Point. It's a little out of the way, but when we get a 'phone in that won't matter so much. The situation is beautiful. It looks to the sunset and has the great blue harbour before it. The sand dunes aren't very far away—the sea-winds blow over them and the sea spray drenches them."

"But the house itself, Gilbert,—*our* first home? What is it like?"

"Not very large, but large enough for us. There's a splendid living room with a fireplace in it downstairs, and a dining room that looks out on the harbour, and a little room that will do for my office. It is about sixty years old—the oldest house in Four Winds. But it has been kept in pretty good repair, and was all done over about fifteen years ago—shingled, plastered and refloored. It was well built to begin with. I understand that there was some romantic story connected with its building, but the man I rented it from didn't know it. He said Captain Jim was the only one who could spin that old yarn now."

"Who is Captain Jim?"

"The keeper of the lighthouse on Four Winds Point. You'll love that Four Winds light, Anne. It's a revolving one, and it flashes like a magnificent star through the twilights. We can see it from our living room windows and our front door."

"Who owns the house?"

"Well, it's the property of the Glen St. Mary Presbyterian Church now, and I rented it from the trustees. But it belonged until lately to a very old lady, Miss Elizabeth Russell. She died last spring, and as she had no near relatives she left her property to the Glen St. Mary Church. Her furniture is still in the house, and I bought most of it—for a mere song you might say, because it was all so old-fashioned that the trustees despaired of selling it. Glen St. Mary folks prefer plush brocade and sideboards with mirrors and ornamentations, I fancy. But Miss Russell's furniture is very good and I feel sure you'll like it, Anne."

"So far, good," said Anne, nodding cautious approval. "But Gilbert, people cannot live by furniture alone. You haven't yet mentioned one very important thing. Are there *trees* about this house?"

"Heaps of them, oh, dryad! There is a big grove of fir trees behind it, two rows of Lombardy poplars down the lane, and a ring of white birches around a very delightful garden. Our front door opens right into the garden, but there is another entrance—a little gate hung between two firs. The hinges are on one trunk and the catch on the other. Their boughs form an arch overhead."

"Oh, I'm so glad! I couldn't live where there were no trees—something vital in me would starve. Well, after that, there's no use asking you if there's a brook anywhere near. *That* would be expecting too much."

"But there *is* a brook—and it actually cuts across one corner of the garden."

"Then," said Anne, with a long sigh of supreme satisfaction, "this house you have found *is* my house of dreams and none other."

The Land of Dreams Among

"Have you made up your mind who you're going to have to the wedding, Anne?" asked Mrs. Rachel Lynde, as she hemstitched table napkins industriously. "It's time your invitations were sent, even if they are to be only informal ones."

"I don't mean to have very many," said Anne. "We just want those we love best to see us married. Gilbert's people, and Mr. and Mrs. Allan, and Mr. and Mrs. Harrison."

"There was a time when you'd hardly have numbered Mr. Harrison among your dearest friends," said Marilla drily.

"Well, I wasn't *very* strongly attracted to him at our first meeting," acknowledged Anne, with a laugh over the recollection. "But Mr. Harrison has improved on acquaintance, and Mrs. Harrison is really a dear. Then, of course, there are Miss Lavendar and Paul."

"Have they decided to come to the Island this summer? I thought they were going to Europe."

"They changed their minds when I wrote them I was going to be married. I had a letter from Paul today. He says he *must* come to my wedding, no matter what happens to Europe."

"That child always idolised you," remarked Mrs. Rachel.

"That 'child' is a young man of nineteen now, Mrs. Lynde."

"How time does fly!" was Mrs. Lynde's brilliant and original response.

"Charlotta the Fourth may come with them. She sent word by Paul that she would come if her husband would let her. I wonder if she still wears those enormous blue bows, and whether her husband calls her Charlotta or Leonora. I should love to have Charlotta at my wedding. Charlotta and I were at a wedding long syne. They expect to be at Echo Lodge next week. Then there are Phil and the Reverend Jo————"

"It sounds awful to hear you speaking of a minister like that, Anne," said Mrs. Rachel severely.

"His wife calls him that."

"She should have more respect for his holy office, then," retorted Mrs. Rachel.

"I've heard you criticise ministers pretty sharply yourself," teased Anne.

"Yes, but I do it reverently," protested Mrs. Lynde. "You never heard me *nickname* a minister."

Anne smothered a smile.

"Well, there are Diana and Fred and little Fred and Small Anne Cordelia—and Jane Andrews. I wish I could have Miss Stacey and Aunt Jamesina and Priscilla and Stella. But Stella is in Vancouver, and Pris is in Japan, and Miss Stacey is married in California, and Aunt Jamesina has gone to India to explore her daughter's mission field, in spite of her horror of snakes. It's really dreadful—the way people get scattered over the globe."

"The Lord never intended it, that's what," said Mrs. Rachel authoritatively. "In my young days people grew up and married and settled down where they were born, or pretty near it. Thank goodness you've stuck to the Island, Anne. I was afraid Gilbert would insist on rushing off to the ends of the earth when he got through college, and dragging you with him."

"If everybody stayed where he was born places would soon be filled up, Mrs. Lynde."

"Oh, I'm not going to argue with you, Anne. *I* am not a B.A. What time of the day is the ceremony to be?"

"We have decided on noon—high noon, as the society reporters say. That will give us time to catch the evening train to Glen St. Mary."

"And you'll be married in the parlour?"

"No—not unless it rains. We mean to be married in the orchard—with the blue sky over us and the sunshine around us. Do you know when and where I'd like to be married, if I could? It would be at dawn—a June dawn, with a glorious sunrise, and roses blooming in the gardens; and I would slip down and meet Gilbert and we would go together to the heart of the beech woods,—and there, under the green arches that would be like a splendid cathedral, we would be married."

Marilla sniffed scornfully and Mrs. Lynde looked shocked.

"But that would be terrible queer, Anne. Why, it wouldn't really seem legal. And what would Mrs. Harmon Andrews say?"

"Ah, there's the rub," sighed Anne. "There are so many things in life we cannot do because of the fear of what Mrs. Harmon Andrews would say. ''Tis true, 'tis pity, and pity 'tis, 'tis true.' What delightful things we might do were it not for Mrs. Harmon Andrews!"

"By times, Anne, I don't feel quite sure that I understand you altogether," complained Mrs. Lynde.

"Anne was always romantic, you know," said Marilla apologetically.

"Well, married life will most likely cure her of that," Mrs. Rachel responded comfortingly.

Anne laughed and slipped away to Lover's Lane, where Gilbert found her; and neither of them seemed to entertain much fear, or hope, that their married life would cure them of romance.

The Echo Lodge people came over the next week, and Green Gables buzzed with the delight of them. Miss Lavendar had changed so little that the three years since her last Island visit might have been a watch in the night; but Anne gasped with amazement over Paul. Could this splendid six feet of manhood be the little Paul of Avonlea schooldays?

"You really make me feel old, Paul," said Anne. "Why, I have to look up to you!"

"You'll never grow old, Teacher," said Paul. "You are one of the fortunate mortals who have found and drunk from the Fountain of Youth,—you and Mother Lavendar. See here! When you're married I *won't* call you Mrs. Blythe. To me you'll always be 'Teacher'—the teacher of the best lessons I ever learned. I want to show you something."

The "something" was a pocketbook full of poems. Paul had put some of his beautiful fancies into verse, and magazine editors had not been as unappreciative as they are sometimes supposed to be. Anne read Paul's poems with real delight. They were full of charm and promise.

"You'll be famous yet, Paul. I always dreamed of having

one famous pupil. He was to be a college president—but a great poet would be even better. Someday I'll be able to boast that I whipped the distinguished Paul Irving. But then I never did whip you, did I Paul? What an opportunity lost! I think I kept you in at recess, however."

"You may be famous yourself, Teacher. I've seen a good deal of your work these last three years."

"No. I know what I can do. I can write pretty, fanciful little sketches that children love and editors send welcome cheques for. But I can do nothing big. My only chance for earthly immortality is a corner in your Memoirs."

Charlotta the Fourth had discarded the blue bows but her freckles were not noticeably less.

"I never did think I'd come down to marrying a Yankee, Miss Shirley, ma'am," she said. "But you never know what's before you, and it isn't his fault. He was born that way."

"You're a Yankee yourself, Charlotta, since you've married one."

"Miss Shirley, ma'am, I'm *not*! And I wouldn't be if I was to marry a dozen Yankees! Tom's kind of nice. And besides, I thought I'd better not be too hard to please, for I mightn't get another chance. Tom don't drink and he don't growl because he has to work between meals, and when all's said and done I'm satisfied, Miss Shirley, ma'am."

"Does he call you Leonora?" asked Anne.

"Goodness, no, Miss Shirley, ma'am. I wouldn't know who he meant if he did. Of course, when we got married he had to say, 'I take thee, Leonora,' and I declare to you, Miss Shirley, ma'am, I've had the most dreadful feeling ever since that it wasn't me he was talking to and I haven't been rightly married at all. And so you're going to be married yourself, Miss Shirley, ma'am? I always thought I'd like to marry a doctor. It would be so handy when the children had measles and croup. Tom is only a bricklayer, but he's real good-tempered. When I said to him, says I, 'Tom, can I go to Miss Shirley's wedding? I mean to go anyhow, but I'd like to have your consent,' he just says, 'Suit yourself, Charlotta, and you'll suit me.' That's a real pleasant kind of husband to have, Miss Shirley, ma'am."

Philippa and her Reverend Jo arrived at Green Gables the day before the wedding. Anne and Phil had a rapturous meeting which presently simmered down to a cosy, confidential chat over all that had been and was about to be.

"Queen Anne, you're as queenly as ever. I've got fearfully thin since the babies came. I'm not half so good-looking; but I think Jo likes it. There's not such a contrast between us, you see. And oh, it's perfectly magnificent that you're going to marry Gilbert. Roy Gardner wouldn't have done at all, at all. I can see that now, though I was horribly disappointed at the time. You know, Anne, you did treat Roy very badly."

"He has recovered, I understand," smiled Anne.

"Oh, yes. He is married and his wife is a sweet little thing and they're perfectly happy. Everything works together for good. Jo and the Bible say that, and they are pretty good authorities."

"Are Alec and Alonzo married yet?"

"Alec is, but Alonzo isn't. How those dear old days at Patty's Place come back when I'm talking to you, Anne! What fun we had!"

"Have you been to Patty's Place lately?"

"Oh, yes, I go often. Miss Patty and Miss Maria still sit by the fireplace and knit. And that reminds me—we've brought you a wedding gift from them, Anne. Guess what it is."

"I never could. How did they know I was going to be married?"

"Oh, I told them. I was there last week. And they were so interested. Two days ago Miss Patty wrote me a note asking me to call; and then she asked if I would take her gift to you. What would you wish most from Patty's Place, Anne?"

"You can't mean that Miss Patty has sent me her china dogs?"

"Go up head. They're in my trunk this very moment. And I've a letter for you. Wait a moment and I'll get it."

"Dear Miss Shirley," Miss Patty had written, "Maria and I were very much interested in hearing of your approaching nuptials. We send you our best wishes. Maria and I have never married, but we have no objection to other people doing so. We are sending you the china dogs. I intended to leave them to you in my will, because you seemed to have a sincere affection for them. But Maria and I expect to live a good while yet (D.V.), so I have decided to give you the dogs while you are young. You will not have forgotten that Gog looks to the right and Magog to the left."

"Just fancy those lovely old dogs sitting by the fireplace in my house of dreams," said Anne rapturously. "I never expected anything so delightful."

That evening Green Gables hummed with preparations for the following day; but in the twilight Anne slipped away. She had a little pilgrimage to make on this last day of her girlhood and she must make it alone. She went to Matthew's grave, in the little poplar-shaded Avonlea graveyard, and there kept a silent tryst with old memories and immortal loves.

"How glad Matthew would be tomorrow if he were here," she whispered. "But I believe he does know and is glad of it—somewhere else. I've read somewhere that 'our dead are never dead until we have forgotten them.' Matthew will never be dead to me, for I can never forget him."

She left on his grave the flowers she had brought and walked slowly down the long hill. It was a gracious evening, full of delectable lights and shadows. In the west was a sky of mackerel clouds—crimson and amber-tinted, with long strips of apple-green sky between. Beyond was the glimmering radiance of a sunset sea, and the ceaseless voice of many waters came up from the tawny shore. All around her, lying in the fine, beautiful country silence, were the hills and fields and woods she had known and loved so long.

"History repeats itself," said Gilbert, joining her as she passed the Blythe gate. "Do you remember our first walk down this hill, Anne—our first walk together anywhere, for that matter?"

"I was coming home in the twilight from Matthew's grave—and you came out of the gate; and I swallowed the pride of years and spoke to you."

"And all heaven opened before me," supplemented Gilbert. "From that moment I looked forward to tomorrow. When I left you at your gate that night and walked home I was the happiest boy in the world. Anne had forgiven me."

"I think you had the most to forgive. I was an ungrateful little wretch—and after you had really saved my life that day on the pond, too. How I loathed that load of obligation at first! I don't deserve the happiness that has come to me."

Gilbert laughed and clasped tighter the girlish hand that wore his ring. Anne's engagement ring was a circlet of pearls. She had refused to wear a diamond.

"I've never really liked diamonds since I found out they weren't the lovely purple I had dreamed. They will always suggest my old disappointment."

"But pearls are for tears, the old legend says," Gilbert had objected.

"I'm not afraid of that. And tears can be happy as well as sad. My very happiest moments have been when I had tears in my eyes—when Marilla told me I might stay at Green Gables—when Matthew gave me the first pretty dress I ever had—when I heard that you were going to recover from the fever. So give me pearls for our troth ring, Gilbert, and I'll willingly accept the sorrow of life with its joy."

But tonight our lovers thought only of joy and never of sorrow. For the morrow was their wedding day, and their house of dreams awaited them on the misty, purple shore of Four Winds Harbour.

The First Bride of Green Gables

Anne wakened on the morning of her wedding day to find the sunshine winking in at the window of the little porch gable and a September breeze frolicking with her curtains.

"I'm so glad the sun will shine on me," she thought happily.

She recalled the first morning she had wakened in that little porch room, when the sunshine had crept in on her through the blossom-drift of the old Snow Queen. That had not been a happy wakening, for it brought with it the bitter disappointment of the preceding night. But since then the little room had been endeared and consecrated by years of happy childhood dreams and maiden visions. To it she had come back joyfully after all her absences; at its window she had knelt through that night of bitter agony when she believed Gilbert dying, and by it she had sat in speechless happiness the night of her betrothal. Many vigils of joy and some of sorrow had been kept there; and today she must leave it forever. Henceforth it would be hers no more; fifteen-year-old Dora was to inherit it when she had gone. Nor did Anne wish it otherwise; the little room was sacred to youth and girlhood—to the past that was to close today before the chapter of wifehood opened.

Green Gables was a busy and joyous house that fore-noon. Diana arrived early, with little Fred and Small Anne Cordelia, to lend a hand. Davy and Dora, the Green Gables twins, whisked the babies off to the garden.

"Don't let Small Anne Cordelia spoil her clothes," warned Diana anxiously.

"You needn't be afraid to trust her with Dora," said Marilla. "That child is more sensible and careful than most of the mothers I've known. She's really a wonder in some ways. Not much like that other harum-scarum I brought up."

Marilla smiled across her chicken salad at Anne. It might even be suspected that she liked the harum-scarum best after all.

"Those twins are real nice children," said Mrs. Rachel, when she was sure they were out of earshot. "Dora is so womanly and helpful, and Davy is developing into a very smart boy. He isn't the holy terror for mischief he used to be."

"I never was so distracted in my life as I was the first six months he was here," acknowledged Marilla. "After that I sup-pose I got used to him. He's taken a great notion to farming lately, and wants me to let him try running the farm next year. I may, for Mr. Barry doesn't think he'll want to rent it much longer, and some new arrangement will have to be made."

"Well, you certainly have a lovely day for your wedding, Anne," said Diana, as she slipped a voluminous apron over her silken array. "You couldn't have had a finer one if you'd ordered it from Eaton's."

"Indeed, there's too much money going out of this Island to that same Eaton's," said Mrs. Lynde indignantly. She had strong views on the subject of octopus-like department stores, and never lost an opportunity of airing them. "And as for those catalogues of theirs, they're the Avonlea girls' Bible now, that's what. They pore over them on Sundays instead of studying the Holy Scriptures."

"Well, they're splendid to amuse children with," said Diana. "Fred and Small Anne look at the pictures by the hour."

"*I* amused ten children without the aid of Eaton's catalogue," said Mrs. Rachel severely.

"Come, you two, don't quarrel over Eaton's catalogue," said Anne gaily. "This is my day of days, you know. I'm so happy I want everyone else to be happy, too."

"I'm sure I hope your happiness will last, child," sighed Mrs. Rachel. She did hope it truly, and believed it, but she was afraid it was in the nature of a challenge to Providence to flaunt your happiness too openly. Anne, for her own good, must be toned down a trifle.

But it was a happy and beautiful bride who came down the old, homespun-carpeted stairs that September noon—the first bride of Green Gables, slender and shining-eyed, in the mist of her maiden veil, with her arms full of roses. Gilbert, waiting for her in the hall below, looked up at her with adoring eyes. She was his at last, this evasive, long-sought Anne, won after years of patient waiting. It was to him she was coming in the sweet surrender of the bride. Was he worthy of her? Could he make her as happy as he hoped? If he failed her—if he could not measure up to her standard of manhood—then, as she held out her hand, their eyes met and all doubt was swept away in a glad certainty. They belonged to each other; and, no matter what life might hold for them, it could never alter that. Their happiness was in each other's keeping and both were unafraid.

They were married in the sunshine of the old orchard, circled by the loving and kindly faces of long-familiar friends. Mr. Allan married them, and the Reverend Jo made what Mrs. Rachel Lynde afterwards pronounced to be the "most beautiful wedding prayer" she had ever heard. Birds do not often sing in September, but one sang sweetly from some hidden bough while Gilbert and Anne repeated their deathless vows. Anne heard it and thrilled to it; Gilbert heard it, and wondered only that all the birds in the world had not burst into jubilant song; Paul heard it and later wrote a lyric about it which was one of the most admired in his first volume of verse; Charlotta the Fourth heard it and was blissfully sure it meant good luck for her adored Miss Shirley. The bird sang until the ceremony was ended and then it wound up with one mad little, glad little trill. Never had the old gray-green house among its enfolding orchards known a blither, merrier afternoon. All the old jests and quips that must have done duty at weddings since Eden were served up, and seemed as new and brilliant and mirth-provoking as if they had never been uttered before. Laughter and joy had their way; and when Anne and Gilbert left to catch the Carmody train, with Paul as driver, the twins were ready with rice and old shoes, in the throwing of which Charlotta the Fourth and Mr. Harrison bore a valiant part. Marilla stood at the gate and watched the carriage out of sight down the long lane with its banks of goldenrod. Anne turned at its end to wave her last good-bye. She was gone—Green

Gables was her home no more; Marilla's face looked very gray and old as she turned to the house which Anne had filled for fourteen years, and even in her absence, with light and life.

But Diana and her small fry, the Echo Lodge people and the Allans, had stayed to help the two old ladies over the loneliness of the first evening; and they contrived to have a quietly pleasant little supper time, sitting long around the table and chatting over all the details of the day. While they were sitting there Anne and Gilbert were alighting from the train at Glen St. Mary.

The Home Coming

D r. David Blythe had sent his horse and buggy to meet them, and the urchin who had brought it slipped away with a sympathetic grin, leaving them to the delight of driving alone to their new home through the radiant evening.

Anne never forgot the loveliness of the view that broke upon them when they had driven over the hill behind the village. Her new home could not yet be seen; but before her lay Four Winds Harbour like a great, shining mirror of rose and silver. Far down, she saw its entrance between the bar of sand dunes on one side and a steep, high, grim, red-sandstone cliff on the other. Beyond the bar the sea, calm and austere, dreamed in the afterlight. The little fishing village, nestled in the cove where the sand dunes met the harbour shore, looked like a great opal in the haze. The sky over them was like a jewelled cup from which the dusk was pouring; the air was crisp with the compelling tang of the sea, and the whole landscape was infused with the subtleties of a sea evening. A few dim sails drifted along the darkening, fir-clad harbour shores.

A bell was ringing from the tower of a little white church on the far side; mellowly and dreamily sweet, the chime floated across the water blent with the moan of the sea. The great revolving light on the cliff at the channel flashed warm and golden against the clear northern sky, a trembling, quivering star of good hope. Far out along the horizon was the crinkled gray ribbon of a passing steamer's smoke.

"Oh, beautiful, beautiful," murmured Anne. "I shall love Four Winds, Gilbert. Where is our house?"

"We can't see it yet—the belt of birch running up from that little cove hides it. It's about two miles from Glen St. Mary, and there's another mile between it and the lighthouse. We won't have many neighbours, Anne. There's only one house near us and I don't know who lives in it. Shall you be lonely when I'm away?"

"Not with that light and that loveliness for company. Who lives in that house, Gilbert?"

"I don't know. It doesn't look—exactly—as if the occupants would be kindred spirits, Anne, does it?"

The house was a large, substantial affair, painted such a vivid green that the landscape seemed quite faded by contrast. There was an orchard behind it, and a nicely kept lawn before it, but, somehow, there was a certain bareness about it. Perhaps its neatness was responsible for this; the whole establishment, house, barns, orchard, garden, lawn and lane, was so starkly neat.

"It doesn't seem probable that anyone with that taste in paint could be *very* kindred," acknowledged Anne, "unless it were an accident—like our blue hall. I feel certain there are no children there, at least. It's even neater than the old Copp place on the Tory road, and I never expected to see anything neater than that."

They had not met anybody on the moist, red road that wound along the harbour shore. But just before they came to the belt of birch which hid their home, Anne saw a girl who was driving a flock of snow-white geese along the crest of a velvety green hill on the right. Great, scattered firs grew along it. Between their trunks one saw glimpses of yellow harvest fields, gleams of golden sand-hills, and bits of blue sea. The girl was tall and wore a dress of pale blue print. She walked with a certain springiness of step and erectness of bearing. She and her geese came out of the gate at the foot of the hill as Anne and Gilbert passed. She stood with her hand on the fastening of the gate, and looked steadily at them, with an expression that hardly attained to interest, but did not descend to curiosity. It seemed to Anne, for a fleeting moment, that there was even a veiled hint of hostility in it. But it was the girl's beauty which made Anne give a little gasp—a beauty so marked that it must have attracted attention anywhere. She was hatless, but heavy braids of burnished hair, the hue of ripe wheat, were twisted about her head like a coronet; her eyes were blue and star-like; her figure, in its plain print gown, was magnificent; and her lips were as crimson as the bunch of blood-red poppies she wore at her belt.

"Gilbert, who is the girl we have just passed?" asked Anne, in a low voice.

"I didn't notice any girl," said Gilbert, who had eyes only for his bride.

"She was standing by that gate—no, don't look back. She is still watching us. I never saw such a beautiful face."

"I don't remember seeing any very handsome girls while I was here. There are some pretty girls up at the Glen, but I hardly think they could be called beautiful."

"This girl is. You can't have seen her, or you would remember her. Nobody could forget her. I never saw such a face except in pictures. And her hair! It made me think of Browning's 'cord of gold' and 'gorgeous snake'!"

"Probably she's some visitor in Four Winds—likely someone from that big summer hotel over the harbour."

"She wore a white apron and she was driving geese."

"She might do that for amusement. Look, Anne—there's our house."

Anne looked and forgot for a time the girl with the splendid, resentful eyes. The first glimpse of her new home was a delight to eye and spirit—it looked so like a big, creamy seashell stranded on the harbour shore. The rows of tall Lombardy poplars down its lane stood out in stately, purple silhouette against the sky. Behind it, sheltering its garden from the too keen breath of sea winds, was a cloudy fir wood, in which the winds might make all kinds of weird and haunting music. Like all woods, it seemed to be holding and enfolding secrets in its recesses,—secrets whose charm is only to be won by entering in and patiently seeking. Outwardly, dark green arms keep them inviolate from curious or indifferent eyes.

The night winds were beginning their wild dances beyond the bar and the fishing hamlet across the harbour was gemmed with lights as Anne and Gilbert drove up the poplar lane. The door of the little house opened, and a warm glow of firelight flickered out into the dusk. Gilbert lifted Anne from the buggy and led her into the garden, through the little gate between the ruddy-tipped firs, up the trim, red path to the sandstone step.

"Welcome home," he whispered, and hand in hand they stepped over the threshold of their house of dreams.

Captain Jim

"Old Doctor Dave" and "Mrs. Doctor Dave" had come down to the little house to greet the bride and groom. Doctor Dave was a big, jolly, white-whiskered old fellow, and Mrs. Doctor was a trim, rosy-cheeked, silver-haired little lady who took Anne at once to her heart, literally and figuratively.

"I'm so glad to see you, dear. You must be real tired. We've got a bite of supper ready, and Captain Jim brought up some trout for you. Captain Jim—where are you? Oh, he's slipped out to see to the horse, I suppose. Come upstairs and take your things off."

Anne looked about her with bright, appreciative eyes as she followed Mrs. Doctor Dave upstairs. She liked the appearance of her new home very much. It seemed to have the atmosphere of Green Gables and the flavour of her old traditions.

"I think I would have found Miss Elizabeth Russell a 'kindred spirit,'" she murmured when she was alone in her room. There were two windows in it; the dormer one looked out on the lower harbour and the sandbar and the Four Winds light.

> *"A magic casement opening on the foam*
> *Of perilous seas in fairy lands forlorn,"*

quoted Anne softly. The gable window gave a view of a little harvest-hued valley through which a brook ran. Half a mile up the brook was the only house in sight—an old, rambling, gray one surrounded by huge willows through which its windows peered, like shy, seeking eyes, into the dusk. Anne wondered who lived there; they would be her nearest neighbours and she hoped they would be nice. She suddenly found herself thinking of the beautiful girl with the white geese.

"Gilbert thought she didn't belong here," mused Anne, "but I feel sure she does. There was something about her that made her part of the sea and the sky and the harbour. Four Winds is in her blood."

When Anne went downstairs Gilbert was standing before the fireplace talking to a stranger. Both turned as Anne entered.

"Anne, this is Captain Boyd. Captain Boyd, my wife."

It was the first time Gilbert had said "my wife" to anybody but Anne, and he narrowly escaped bursting with the pride of it. The old captain held out a sinewy hand to Anne; they smiled at each other and were friends from that moment. Kindred spirit flashed recognition to kindred spirit.

"I'm right down pleased to meet you, Mistress Blythe; and I hope you'll be as happy as the first bride was who came here. I can't wish you no better than *that*. But your husband doesn't introduce me jest exactly right. 'Captain Jim' is my week-a-day name and you might as well begin as you're sartain to end up—calling me that. You sartainly are a nice little bride, Mistress Blythe. Looking at you sorter makes me feel that I've jest been married myself."

Amid the laughter that followed Mrs. Doctor Dave urged Captain Jim to stay and have supper with them.

"Thank you kindly. 'Twill be a real treat, Mistress Doctor. I mostly has to eat my meals alone, with the reflection of my ugly old phiz in a looking-glass opposite for company. 'Tisn't often I have a chance to sit down with two such sweet, purty ladies."

Captain Jim's compliments may look very bald on paper, but he paid them with such a gracious, gentle deference of tone and look that the woman upon whom they were bestowed felt that she was being offered a queen's tribute in kingly fashion.

Captain Jim was a high-souled, simple-minded old man, with eternal youth in his eyes and heart. He had a tall, rather ungainly figure, somewhat stooped, yet suggestive of great strength and endurance; a clean-shaven face deeply lined and bronzed; a thick mane of iron-gray hair falling quite to his shoulders, and a pair of remarkably blue, deep-set eyes, which sometimes twinkled and sometimes dreamed, and sometimes looked out seaward with a wistful quest in them, as of one seeking something precious and lost. Anne was to learn one day what it was for which Captain Jim looked.

It could not be denied that Captain Jim was a homely man. His spare jaws, rugged mouth, and square brow were not fashioned on the lines of beauty; and he had passed through many hardships and sorrows which had marked his body as well as his soul; but though at first sight Anne thought him plain she never thought anything more about it—the spirit shining through that rugged tenement beautified it so wholly.

They gathered gaily around the supper table. The hearth fire banished the chill of the September evening, but the window of the dining room was open and sea breezes entered at their own sweet will. The view was magnificent, taking in the harbour and the sweep of low, purple hills beyond. The table was heaped with Mrs. Doctor's delicacies but the *pièce de résistance* was undoubtedly the big platter of sea-trout.

"Thought they'd be sorter tasty after travelling," said Captain Jim. "They're fresh as trout can be, Mistress Blythe. Two hours ago they were swimming in the Glen Pond."

"Who is attending to the light tonight, Captain Jim?" asked Doctor Dave.

"Nephew Alec. He understands it as well as I do. Well, now, I'm real glad you asked me to stay to supper. I'm proper hungry—didn't have much of a dinner today."

"I believe you half starve yourself most of the time down at that light," said Mrs. Doctor Dave severely. "You won't take the trouble to get up a decent meal."

"Oh, I do, Mistress Doctor, I do," protested Captain Jim. "Why, I live like a king gen'rally. Last night I was up to the Glen and took home two pounds of steak. I meant to have a spanking good dinner today."

"And what happened to the steak?" asked Mrs. Doctor Dave. "Did you lose it on the way home?"

"No." Captain Jim looked sheepish. "Just at bedtime a poor, ornery sort of dog came along and asked for a night's lodging. Guess he belonged to some of the fishermen 'long shore. I couldn't turn the poor cur out—he had a sore foot. So

I shut him in the porch, with an old bag to lie on, and went to bed. But somehow I couldn't sleep. Come to think it over, I sorter remembered that the dog looked hungry."

"And you got up and gave him that steak—*all* that steak," said Mrs. Doctor Dave, with a kind of triumphant reproof.

"Well, there wasn't anything else *to* give him," said Captain Jim deprecatingly. "Nothing a dog'd care for, that is. I reckon he *was* hungry, for he made about two bites of it. I had a fine sleep the rest of the night but my dinner had to be sorter scanty—potatoes and point, as you might say. The dog, he lit out for home this morning. I reckon *he* weren't a vegetarian."

"The idea of starving yourself for a worthless dog!" sniffed Mrs. Doctor.

"You don't know but he may be worth a lot to somebody," protested Captain Jim. "He didn't *look* of much account, but you can't go by looks in jedging a dog. Like meself, he might be a real beauty inside. The First Mate didn't approve of him, I'll allow. His language was right down forcible. But the First Mate is prejudiced. No use in taking a cat's opinion of a dog. 'Tennyrate, I lost my dinner, so this nice spread in this dee-lightful company is real pleasant. It's a great thing to have good neighbours."

"Who lives in the house among the willows up the brook?" asked Anne.

"Mrs. Dick Moore," said Captain Jim—"and her husband," he added, as if by way of an afterthought.

Anne smiled, and deduced a mental picture of Mrs. Dick Moore from Captain Jim's way of putting it; evidently a second Mrs. Rachel Lynde.

"You haven't many neighbours, Mistress Blythe," Captain Jim went on. "This side of the harbour is mighty thinly settled. Most of the land belongs to Mr. Howard up yander past the Glen, and he rents it out for pasture. The other side of the harbour, now, is thick with folks—'specially MacAllisters. There's a whole colony of MacAllisters—you can't throw a stone but you hit one. I was talking to old Leon Blacquiere the other day. He's been working on the harbour all summer. 'Dey're nearly all MacAllisters over thar,' he told me. 'Dare's Neil MacAllister and Sandy MacAllister and William MacAllister and Alec MacAllister and Angus MacAllister—and I believe dare's de Devil MacAllister.'"

"There are nearly as many Elliotts and Crawfords," said Doctor Dave, after the laughter had subsided. "You know, Gilbert, we folk on this side of Four Winds have an old saying—'From the conceit of the Elliotts, the pride of the MacAllisters, and the vain-glory of the Crawfords, good Lord deliver us.'"

"There's a plenty of fine people among them, though," said Captain Jim. "I sailed with William Crawford for many a year, and for courage and endurance and truth that man hadn't an equal. They've got brains over on that side of Four Winds. Mebbe that's why this side is sorter inclined to pick on 'em. Strange, ain't it, how folks seem to resent anyone being born a mite cleverer than they be."

Doctor Dave, who had a forty years' feud with the over-harbour people, laughed and subsided.

"Who lives in that brilliant emerald house about half a mile up the road?" asked Gilbert.

Captain Jim smiled delightedly.

"Miss Cornelia Bryant. She'll likely be over to see you soon, seeing you're Presbyterians. If you were Methodists she wouldn't come at all. Cornelia has a holy horror of Methodists."

"She's quite a character," chuckled Doctor Dave. "A most inveterate man-hater!"

"Sour grapes?" queried Gilbert, laughing.

"No, 'tisn't sour grapes," answered Captain Jim seriously. "Cornelia could have had her pick when she was young. Even yet she's only to say the word to see the old widowers jump. She jest seems to have been born with a sort of chronic spite agin men and Methodists. She's got the bitterest tongue and the kindest heart in Four Winds. Wherever there's any trouble, that woman is there, doing everything to help in the tenderest way. She never says a harsh word about another woman, and if she likes to card us poor scalawags of men down I reckon our tough old hides can stand it."

"She always speaks well of you, Captain Jim," said Mrs. Doctor.

"Yes, I'm afraid so. I don't half like it. It makes me feel as if there must be something sorter unnatural about me."

The Schoolmaster's Bride

"Who was the first bride who came to this house, Captain Jim?" Anne asked, as they sat around the fireplace after supper.

"Was she a part of the story I've heard was connected with this house?" asked Gilbert. "Somebody told me you could tell it, Captain Jim."

"Well, yes, I know it. I reckon I'm the only person living in Four Winds now that can remember the schoolmaster's bride as she was when she come to the Island. She's been dead this thirty year, but she was one of them women you never forget."

"Tell us the story," pleaded Anne. "I want to find out all about the women who have lived in this house before me."

"Well, there's jest been three—Elizabeth Russell, and Mrs. Ned Russell, and the schoolmaster's bride. Elizabeth Russell was a nice, clever little critter, and Mrs. Ned was a nice woman, too. But they weren't ever like the schoolmaster's bride.

"The schoolmaster's name was John Selwyn. He came out from the Old Country to teach school at the Glen when I was a boy of sixteen. He wasn't much like the usual run of derelicts who used to come out to P.E.I. to teach school in them days. Most of them were clever, drunken critters who taught the children the three R's when they were sober, and lambasted them when they wasn't. But John Selwyn was a fine, handsome young fellow. He boarded at my father's, and he and me were cronies, though he was ten years older'n me. We read and walked and talked a heap together. He knew about all the poetry that was ever written, I reckon, and he used to quote it to me along shore in the evenings. Dad thought it an awful waste of time, but he sorter endured it, hoping it'd put me off the notion of going to sea. Well, nothing could do *that*—mother come of a race of sea-going folk and it was born in me. But I loved to hear John read and recite. It's almost sixty years ago, but I could repeat yards of poetry I learned from him. Nearly sixty years!"

Captain Jim was silent for a space, gazing into the glowing fire in a quest of the bygones. Then, with a sigh, he resumed his story.

"I remember one spring evening I met him on the sand-hills. He looked sorter uplifted—jest like you did, Dr. Blythe, when you brought Mistress Blythe in tonight. I thought of him the minute I seen you. And he told me that he had a sweetheart back home and that she was coming out to him. I wasn't more'n half pleased, ornery young lump of selfishness that I was; I thought he wouldn't be as much my friend after she came. But I'd enough decency not to let him see it. He told me all about her. Her name was Persis Leigh, and she would have come out with him if it hadn't been for her old uncle. He was sick, and he'd looked after her when her parents died and she wouldn't leave him. And now he was dead and she was coming out to marry John Selwyn. 'Twasn't no easy journey for a woman in them days. There weren't no steamers, you must ricollect.

"'When do you expect her?' says I.

"'She sails on the *Royal William*, the 20th of June,' says he, 'and so she should be here by mid-July. I must set Carpenter Johnson to building me a home for her. Her letter come today. I knew before I opened it that it was good news for me. I saw her a few nights ago.'

"I didn't understand him, and then he explained—though I didn't understand *that* much better. He said he had a gift—or a curse. Them was his words, Mistress Blythe—a gift or a curse. He didn't know which it was. He said a great-great-grandmother of his had it, and they burned her for a witch on account of it. He said queer spells—trances, I think was the name he give 'em—come over him now and again. Are there such things, Doctor?"

"There are people who are certainly subject to trances," answered Gilbert. "The matter is more in the line of psychical research than medical. What were the trances of this John Selwyn like?"

"Like dreams," said the old doctor skeptically.

"He said he could see things in them," said Captain Jim slowly. "Mind you, I'm telling you jest what *he* said—things that were happening—things that were *going* to happen. He said they were sometimes a comfort to him and sometimes a horror. Four nights before this he'd been in one—went into it while he was sitting looking at the fire. And he saw an old room he knew well in England, and Persis Leigh in it, holding out her hands to him and looking glad and happy. So he knew he was going to hear good news of her."

"A dream—a dream," scoffed the old doctor.

"Likely—likely," conceded Captain Jim. "That's what *I* said to him at the time. It was a vast more comfortable to think so. I didn't like the idea of him seeing things like that—it was real uncanny.

"'No,' says he, 'I didn't dream it. But we won't talk of this again. You won't be so much my friend if you think much about it.'

"I told him nothing could make me any less his friend. But he jest shook his head and says, says he:

"'Lad, I know. I've lost friends before because of this. I don't blame them. There are times when I feel hardly friendly to myself because of it. Such a power has a bit of divinity in it—whether of a good or an evil divinity who shall say? And we mortals all shrink from too close contact with God or devil.'

"Them was his words. I remember them as if 'twas yesterday, though I didn't know jest what he meant. What do you s'pose he *did* mean, Doctor?"

"I doubt if he knew what he meant himself," said Doctor Dave testily.

"I think I understand," whispered Anne. She was listening in her old attitude of clasped lips and shining eyes. Captain Jim treated himself to an admiring smile before he went on with his story.

"Well, purty soon all the Glen and Four Winds people knew the schoolmaster's bride was coming, and they were all glad because they thought so much of him. And everybody took an interest in his new house—*this* house. He picked this site for it, because you could see the harbour and hear the sea from it. He made the garden out there for his bride, but he didn't plant the Lombardies. Mrs. Ned Russell planted *them*. But there's a double row of rose-bushes in the garden that the little girls who went to the Glen school set out there for the schoolmaster's bride. He said they were pink for her cheeks and white for her brow and red for her lips. He'd quoted poetry so much that he sorter got into the habit of talking it, too, I reckon.

"Almost everybody sent him some little present to help out the furnishing of the house. When the Russells came into it they were well-to-do and furnished it real handsome, as you can see; but the first furniture that went into it was plain enough. This little house was rich in love, though. The women sent in quilts and tablecloths and towels, and one man made a chest for her, and another a table and so on. Even blind old Aunt Margaret Boyd wove a little basket for her out of the sweet-scented sand-hill grass. The schoolmaster's wife used it for years to keep her handkerchiefs in.

"Well, at last everything was ready—even to the logs in the big fireplace ready for lighting. 'Twasn't exactly *this* fireplace, though 'twas in the same place. Miss Elizabeth had this put in when she made the house over fifteen years ago. It was a big, old-fashioned fireplace where you could have roasted an ox. Many's the time I've sat here and spun yarns, same's I'm doing tonight."

Again there was a silence, while Captain Jim kept a passing tryst with visitants Anne and Gilbert could not see—the folks who had sat with him around that fireplace in the vanished years, with mirth and bridal joy shining in eyes long since closed forever under churchyard sod or heaving leagues of sea. Here on olden nights children had tossed laughter lightly to and fro. Here on winter evenings friends had gathered. Dance and music and jest had been here. Here youths and maidens had dreamed. For Captain Jim the little house was tenanted with shapes entreating remembrance.

"It was the first of July when the house was finished. The schoolmaster began to count the days then. We used to see him walking along the shore, and we'd say to each other, 'She'll soon be with him now.'

"She was expected the middle of July, but she didn't come then. Nobody felt anxious. Vessels were often delayed for days and mebbe weeks. The *Royal William* was a week overdue—and then two—and then three. And at last we began to be frightened, and it got worse and worse. Fin'lly I couldn't bear to look into John Selwyn's eyes. D'ye know, Mistress Blythe"—Captain Jim lowered his voice—"I used to think that they looked just like what his old great-great-grandmother's must have been when they were burning her to death. He never said much but he taught school like a man in a dream and then hurried to the shore. Many a night he walked there from dark to dawn. People said he was losing his mind. Everybody had given up hope—the *Royal William* was eight weeks overdue. It was the middle of September and the schoolmaster's bride hadn't come—never would come, we thought.

"There was a big storm then that lasted three days, and on the evening after it died away I went to the shore. I found the schoolmaster there, leaning with his arms folded against a big rock, gazing out to sea.

"I spoke to him but he didn't answer. His eyes seemed to be looking at something I couldn't see. His face was set, like a dead man's.

"'John—John,' I called out—jest like that—jest like a frightened child, 'wake up—wake up.'

"That strange, awful look seemed to sorter fade out of his eyes. He turned his head and looked at me. I've never forgot his face—never will forget it till I ships for my last voyage.

"'All is well, lad,' he says. 'I've seen the *Royal William* coming around East Point. She will be here by dawn. Tomorrow night I shall sit with my bride by my own hearth fire.'

"Do you think he did see it?" demanded Captain Jim abruptly.

"God knows," said Gilbert softly. "Great love and great pain might compass we know not what marvels."

"I am sure he did see it," said Anne earnestly.

"Fol-de-rol," said Doctor Dave, but he spoke with less conviction than usual.

"Because, you know," said Captain Jim solemnly, "the *Royal William* came into Four Winds Harbour at daylight the next morning. Every soul in the Glen and along the shore was at the old wharf to meet her. The schoolmaster had been watching there all night. How we cheered as she sailed up the channel."

Captain Jim's eyes were shining. They were looking at the Four Winds Harbour of sixty years agone, with a battered old ship sailing through the sunrise splendour.

"And Persis Leigh was on board?" asked Anne.

"Yes—her and the captain's wife. They'd had an awful passage—storm after storm—and their provisions give out, too. But there they were at last. When Persis Leigh stepped onto the old wharf John Selwyn took her in his arms—and folks stopped cheering and begun to cry. I cried myself, though 'twas years, mind you, afore I'd admit it. Ain't it funny how ashamed boys are of tears?"

"Was Persis Leigh beautiful?" asked Anne.

"Well, I don't know that you'd call her beautiful exactly— I—don't—know," said Captain Jim slowly. "Somehow, you never got so far along as to wonder if she was handsome or not. It jest didn't matter. There was something so sweet and winsome about her that you had to love her, that was all. But she was pleasant to look at—big, clear, hazel eyes and heaps of glossy brown hair, and an English skin. John and her were married at our house that night at early candle-lighting; everybody from far and near was there to see it and we all brought them down here afterwards. Mistress Selwyn lighted the fire, and we went away and left them sitting here, jest as John had seen in that vision of his. A strange thing—a strange thing! But I've seen a turrible lot of strange things in my time."

Captain Jim shook his head sagely.

"It's a dear story," said Anne, feeling that for once she had got enough romance to satisfy her. "How long did they live here?"

"Fifteen years. I ran off to sea soon after they were married, like the young scalawag I was. But every time I come back from a voyage I'd head for here, even before I went home, and tell Mistress Selwyn all about it. Fifteen happy years! They had a sort of talent for happiness, them two. Some folks are like that, if you've noticed. They *couldn't* be unhappy for long, no matter what happened. They quarrelled once or twice, for they was both high-sperrited. But Mistress Selwyn says to me once, says she, laughing in that pretty way of hers, 'I felt dreadful when John and I quarrelled, but underneath it all I was very happy because I had such a nice husband to quarrel with and make it up with.' Then they moved to Charlottetown, and Ned Russell bought this house and brought his bride here. They were a gay young pair, as I remember them. Miss Elizabeth Russell was Alec's sister. She came to live with them a year or so later, and she was a creature of mirth, too. The walls of this house must be sorter *soaked* with laughing and good times. You're the third bride I've seen come here, Mistress Blythe— and the handsomest."

Captain Jim contrived to give his sunflower compliment the delicacy of a violet, and Anne wore it proudly. She was looking her best that night, with the bridal rose on her cheeks and the love-light in her eyes; even gruff old Doctor Dave gave her an approving glance, and told his wife, as they drove home together, that that red-headed wife of the boy's was something of a beauty.

"I must be getting back to the light," announced Captain Jim. "I've enj'yed this evening something tremenjus."

"You must come often to see us," said Anne.

"I wonder if you'd give that invitation if you knew how likely I'll be to accept it," Captain Jim remarked whimsically.

"Which is another way of saying you wonder if I mean it," smiled Anne. "I do, 'cross my heart,' as we used to say at school."

"Then I'll come. You're likely to be pestered with me at any hour. And I'll be proud to have you drop down and visit me now and then, too. Gin'rally I haven't anyone to talk to but the First Mate, bless his sociable heart. He's a mighty good

listener, and has forgot more'n any MacAllister of them all
ever knew, but he isn't much of a conversationalist. You're
young and I'm old, but our souls are about the same age, I
reckon. We both belong to the race that knows Joseph, as
Cornelia Bryant would say."

"'The race that knows Joseph?'" puzzled Anne.

"Yes. Cornelia divides all the folks in the world into two
kinds—the race that knows Joseph and the race that don't. If
a person sorter sees eye to eye with you, and has pretty much
the same ideas about things, and the same taste in jokes—
why, then he belongs to the race that knows Joseph."

"Oh, I understand," exclaimed Anne, light breaking in
upon her. "It's what I used to call—and still call in quotation
marks—'kindred spirits.'"

"Jest so—jest so," agreed Captain Jim. "We're *it*, whatever it is. When you come in tonight, Mistress Blythe, I says to
myself, says I, 'Yes, she's of the race that knows Joseph.' And
mighty glad I was, for if it wasn't so we couldn't have had any
real satisfaction in each other's company. The race that knows
Joseph is the salt of the airth, I reckon."

The moon had just risen when Anne and Gilbert went to
the door with their guests. Four Winds Harbour was beginning to be a thing of dream and glamour and enchantment—a
spellbound haven where no tempest might ever ravin. The
Lombardies down the lane, tall and sombre as the priestly
forms of some mystic band, were tipped with silver.

"Always liked Lombardies," said Captain Jim, waving a
long arm at them. "They're the trees of princesses. They're out
of fashion now. Folks complain that they die at the top and get
ragged-looking. So they do—so they do, if you don't risk

your neck every spring climbing up a light ladder to trim them out. I always did it for Miss Elizabeth, so her Lombardies never got out-at-elbows. She was especially fond of them. She liked their dignity and stand-offishness. *They* don't hobnob with every Tom, Dick and Harry. If it's maples for company, Mistress Blythe, it's Lombardies for society."

"What a beautiful night," said Mrs. Doctor Dave, as she climbed into the Doctor's buggy.

"Most nights are beautiful," said Captain Jim. "But I 'low that moonlight over Four Winds makes me sorter wonder what's left for heaven. The moon's a great friend of mine, Mistress Blythe. I've loved her ever since I can remember. When I was a little chap of eight I fell asleep in the garden one evening and wasn't missed. I woke up along in the night and I was most scared to death. What shadows and queer noises there was! I dursn't move. Jest crouched there quaking, poor small mite. Seemed 'sif there wasn't anyone in the world but meself and it was mighty big. Then all at once I saw the moon looking down to me through the apple boughs, jest like an old friend. I was comforted right off. Got up and walked to the house as brave as a lion, looking at her. Many's the night I've watched her from the deck of my vessel, on seas far away from here. Why don't you folks tell me to take in the slack of my jaw and go home?"

The laughter of the goodnights died away. Anne and Gilbert walked hand in hand around their garden. The brook that ran across the corner dimpled pellucidly in the shadows of the birches. The poppies along its banks were like shallow cups of moonlight. Flowers that had been planted by the hands of the schoolmaster's bride flung their sweetness on the shadowy air, like the beauty and blessing of sacred yesterdays. Anne paused in the gloom to gather a spray.

"I love to smell flowers in the dark," she said. "You get hold of their soul then. Oh, Gilbert, this little house is all I've dreamed it. And I'm so glad that we are not the first who have kept bridal tryst here!"

Miss Cornelia Bryant Comes to Call

That September was a month of golden mists and purple hazes at Four Winds Harbour—a month of sunsteeped days and of nights that were swimming in moonlight, or pulsating with stars. No storm marred it, no rough wind blew. Anne and Gilbert put their nest in order, rambled on the shores, sailed on the harbour, drove about Four Winds and the Glen, or through the ferny, sequestered roads of the woods around the harbour head; in short, had such a honeymoon as any lovers in the world might have envied them.

"If life were to stop short just now it would still have been richly worthwhile, just for the sake of these past four weeks, wouldn't it?" said Anne. "I don't suppose we will ever have four such perfect weeks again—but we've *had* them. Everything— wind, weather, folks, house of dreams—has conspired to make our honeymoon delightful. There hasn't even been a rainy day since we came here."

"And we haven't quarrelled once," teased Gilbert.

"Well, 'that's a pleasure all the greater for being deferred,'" quoted Anne. "I'm so glad we decided to spend our honeymoon here. Our memories of it will always belong here, in our house of dreams, instead of being scattered about in strange places."

There was a certain tang of romance and adventure in the atmosphere of their new home which Anne had never found in Avonlea. There, although she had lived in sight of the sea, it had not entered intimately into her life. In Four Winds it surrounded her and called to her constantly. From every window of her new home she saw some varying aspect of it. Its haunting murmur was ever in her ears. Vessels sailed up the harbour every day to the wharf at the Glen, or sailed out again through the sunset, bound for ports that might be half way round the globe. Fishing boats went white-winged down the channel in the mornings, and returned laden in the evenings. Sailors and fisher-folk travelled the red, winding harbour roads, light-hearted and content. There was always a certain sense of things going to happen—of adventures and farings-forth. The ways of Four Winds were less staid and settled and grooved than those of Avonlea; winds of change blew over them; the sea called ever to the dwellers on shore, and even those who might not answer its call felt the thrill and unrest and mystery and possibilities of it.

"I understand now why some men must go to sea," said Anne. "That desire which comes to us all at times—'to sail beyond the bourne of sunset'—must be very imperious when it is born in you. I don't wonder Captain Jim ran away because of it. I never see a ship sailing out of the channel, or a gull soaring over the sandbar, without wishing I were on board the ship or had wings, not like a dove 'to fly away and be at rest,' but like a gull, to sweep out into the very heart of a storm."

"You'll stay right here with me, Anne-girl," said Gilbert lazily. "I won't have you flying away from me into the hearts of storms."

They were sitting on their red sandstone doorstep in the late afternoon. Great tranquillities were all about them in land and sea and sky. Silvery gulls were soaring over them. The horizons were laced with long trails of frail, pinkish clouds. The hushed air was threaded with a murmurous refrain of minstrel winds and waves. Pale asters were blowing in the sere and misty meadows between them and the harbour.

"Doctors who have to be up all night waiting on sick folk don't feel very adventurous, I suppose," Anne said indulgently. "If you had had a good sleep last night, Gilbert, you'd be as ready as I am for a flight of imagination."

"I did good work last night, Anne," said Gilbert quietly. "Under God, I saved a life. This is the first time I could ever really claim that. In other cases I may have helped; but Anne, if I had not stayed at Allonby's last night and fought death hand to hand, that woman would have died before morning. I tried an experiment that was certainly never tried in Four Winds before. I doubt if it was ever tried anywhere before outside of a hospital. It was a new thing in Kingston hospital last winter. I could never have dared try it here if I had not been absolutely certain that there was no other chance. I risked it—and it succeeded. As a result, a good wife and mother is saved for long years of happiness and usefulness. As I drove home this morning, while the sun was rising over the harbour, I thanked God that I had chosen the profession I did. I had fought a good fight and won—think of it, Anne, *won*, against the Great Destroyer. It's what I dreamed of doing long ago when we talked together of what we wanted to do in life. That dream of mine came true this morning."

"Was that the only one of your dreams that has come true?" asked Anne, who knew perfectly well what the substance of his answer would be, but wanted to hear it again.

"*You* know, Anne-girl," said Gilbert, smiling into her eyes. At that moment there were certainly two perfectly happy people sitting on the doorstep of a little white house on the Four Winds Harbour shore.

Presently Gilbert said, with a change of tone, "Do I or do I not see a full-rigged ship sailing up our lane?"

Anne looked and sprang up.

"That must be either Miss Cornelia Bryant or Mrs. Moore coming to call," she said.

"I'm going into the office, and if it is Miss Cornelia I warn you that I'll eavesdrop," said Gilbert. "From all I've heard regarding Miss Cornelia I conclude that her conversation will not be dull, to say the least."

"It may be Mrs. Moore."

"I don't think Mrs. Moore is built on those lines. I saw her working in her garden the other day, and, though I was too far away to see clearly, I thought she was rather slender. She doesn't seem very socially inclined when she has never called on you yet, although she's your nearest neighbour."

"She can't be like Mrs. Lynde, after all, or curiosity would have brought her," said Anne. "This caller is, I think, Miss Cornelia."

Miss Cornelia it was; moreover, Miss Cornelia had not come to make any brief and fashionable wedding call. She had her work under her arm in a substantial parcel, and when Anne asked her to stay she promptly took off her capacious sun-hat, which had been held on her head, despite irreverent September breezes, by a tight elastic band under her hard little knob of fair hair. No hat pins for Miss Cornelia, an it please ye! Elastic bands had been good enough for her mother and they were good enough for *her*. She had a fresh, round, pink-and-white face, and jolly brown eyes. She did not look in the least like the traditional old maid, and there was something in her expression which won Anne instantly. With her old instinctive quickness to discern kindred spirits she knew she was going to like Miss Cornelia, in spite of uncertain oddities of opinion, and certain oddities of attire.

Nobody but Miss Cornelia would have come to make a call arrayed in a striped blue-and-white apron and a wrapper of chocolate print, with a design of huge, pink roses scattered over it. And nobody but Miss Cornelia could have looked dignified and suitably garbed in it. Had Miss Cornelia been entering a palace to call on a prince's bride, she would have been just as dignified and just as wholly mistress of the situation. She would have trailed her rose-spattered flounce over the marble floors just as unconcernedly, and she would have proceeded just as calmly to disabuse the mind of the princess of any idea that the possession of a mere man, be he prince or peasant, was anything to brag of.

"I've brought my work, Mrs. Blythe, dearie," she remarked, unrolling some dainty material. "I'm in a hurry to get this done, and there isn't any time to lose."

Anne looked in some surprise at the white garment spread over Miss Cornelia's ample lap. It was certainly a baby's dress, and it was most beautifully made, with tiny frills and tucks.

Miss Cornelia adjusted her glasses and fell to embroidering with exquisite stitches.

"This is for Mrs. Fred Proctor up at the Glen," she announced. "She's expecting her eighth baby any day now, and not a stitch has she ready for it. The other seven have wore out all she made for the first, and she's never had time or strength or spirit to make any more. That woman is a martyr, Mrs. Blythe, believe *me*. When she married Fred Proctor *I* knew how it would turn out. He was one of your wicked, fascinating men. After he got married he left off being fascinating and just kept on being wicked. He drinks and he neglects his family. Isn't that like a man? I don't know how Mrs. Proctor would ever keep her children decently clothed if her neighbours didn't help her out."

As Anne was afterwards to learn, Miss Cornelia was the only neighbour who troubled herself much about the decency of the young Proctors.

"When I heard this eighth baby was coming I decided to make some things for it," Miss Cornelia went on. "This is the last and I want to finish it today."

"It's certainly very pretty," said Anne. "I'll get my sewing and we'll have a little thimble party of two. You are a beautiful sewer, Miss Bryant."

"Yes, I'm the best sewer in these parts," said Miss Cornelia in a matter-of-fact tone. "I ought to be! Lord, I've done more of it than if I'd had a hundred children of my own, believe *me*! I s'pose I'm a fool, to be putting hand embroidery on this dress for an eighth baby. But, Lord, Mrs. Blythe, dearie, it isn't to blame for being the eighth, and I kind of wished it to have one real pretty dress, just as if it *was* wanted. Nobody's wanting the poor mite—so I put some extra fuss on its little things just on that account."

"Any baby might be proud of that dress," said Anne, feeling still more strongly that she was going to like Miss Cornelia.

"I s'pose you've been thinking I was never coming to call on you," resumed Miss Cornelia. "But this is harvest month, you know, and I've been busy—and a lot of extra hands hanging round, eating more'n they work, just like the men. I'd have come yesterday, but I went to Mrs. Roderick MacAllister's funeral. At first I thought my head was aching so badly I couldn't enjoy myself if I did go. But she was a hundred years old, and I'd always promised myself that I'd go to her funeral."

"Was it a successful function?" asked Anne, noticing that the office door was ajar.

"What's that? Oh, yes, it was a tremendous funeral. She had a very large connection. There was over one hundred and twenty carriages in the procession. There was one or two funny things happened. I thought that die I would to see old Joe Bradshaw, who is an infidel and never darkens the door of a church, singing 'Safe in the Arms of Jesus' with great gusto and fervour. He glories in singing—that's why he never misses a funeral. Poor Mrs. Bradshaw didn't look much like singing—all wore out slaving. Old Joe starts out once in a while to buy her a present and brings home some new kind of farm machinery. Isn't that like a man? But what else would you expect of a man who never goes to church, even a Methodist one? I was real thankful to see you and the young doctor in the Presbyterian church your first Sunday. No doctor for me who isn't a Presbyterian."

"We were in the Methodist church last Sunday evening," said Anne wickedly.

"Oh, I s'pose Dr. Blythe has to go to the Methodist church once in a while or he wouldn't get the Methodist practice."

"We liked the sermon very much," declared Anne boldly. "And I thought the Methodist minister's prayer was one of the most beautiful I ever heard."

"Oh, I've no doubt he can pray. I never heard anyone make more beautiful prayers than old Simon Bentley, who was always drunk, or hoping to be, and the drunker he was the better he prayed."

"The Methodist minister is very fine looking," said Anne, for the benefit of the office door.

"Yes, he's quite ornamental," agreed Miss Cornelia. "Oh, and very ladylike. And he thinks that every girl who looks at him falls in love with him! If you and the young doctor take *my* advice, you won't have much to do with the Methodists. My motto is—if you *are* a Presbyterian, *be* a Presbyterian."

"Don't you think that Methodists go to heaven as well as Presbyterians?" asked Anne smilelessly.

"That isn't for *us* to decide. It's in higher hands than ours," said Miss Cornelia solemnly. "But I ain't going to associate with them on earth whatever I may have to do in heaven. *This* Methodist minister isn't married. The last one they had was, and his wife was the silliest, flightiest little thing I ever saw. I told her husband once that he should have waited till she was grown up before he married her. He said he wanted to have the training of her. Wasn't that like a man?"

"It's rather hard to decide just when people *are* grown up," laughed Anne.

"That's a true word, dearie. Some are grown up when they're born, and others ain't grown up when they're eighty, believe *me*. That same Mrs. Roderick I was speaking of never grew up. She was as foolish when she was a hundred as when she was ten."

"Perhaps that was why she lived so long," suggested Anne.

"Maybe 'twas. *I*'d rather live fifty sensible years than a hundred foolish ones."

"But just think what a dull world it would be if everyone was sensible," pleaded Anne.

Miss Cornelia disdained any skirmish of flippant epigram.

"Mrs. Roderick was a Milgrave, and the Milgraves never had much sense. Her nephew, Ebenezer Milgrave, used to be insane for years. He believed he was dead and used to rage at his wife because she wouldn't bury him. *I*'d a-done it."

Miss Cornelia looked so grimly determined that Anne could almost see her with a spade in her hand.

"Don't you know *any* good husbands, Miss Bryant?"

"Oh, yes, lots of them—over yonder," said Miss Cornelia, waving her hand through the open window towards the little graveyard of the church across the harbour.

"But living—going about in the flesh?" persisted Anne.

"Oh, there's a few, just to show that with God all things are possible," acknowledged Miss Cornelia reluctantly. "I don't deny that an odd man here and there, if he's caught young and trained up proper, and if his mother has spanked him well beforehand, may turn out a decent being. *Your* husband, now, isn't so bad, as men go, from all I hear. I s'pose"—Miss Cornelia looked sharply at Anne over her glasses—"you think there's nobody like him in the world."

"There isn't," said Anne promptly.

"Ah, well, I heard another bride say that once," sighed Miss Cornelia. "Jennie Dean thought when she married that there wasn't anybody like *her* husband in the world. And she was right—there wasn't! And a good thing, too, believe *me*! He led her an awful life—and he was courting his second wife while Jennie was dying. Wasn't that like a man? However, I hope *your* confidence will be better justified, dearie. The young doctor is taking real well. I was afraid at first he mightn't, for folks hereabouts have always thought old Doctor Dave the only doctor in the world. Doctor Dave hadn't much tact, to be sure—he was always talking of ropes in houses where someone had hanged himself. But folks forgot their hurt feelings when they had a pain in their stomachs. If he'd been a minister instead of a doctor they'd never have forgiven him. Soul-ache doesn't worry folks near as much as stomach-ache. Seeing as we're both Presbyterians and no Methodists around, will you tell me your candid opinion of *our* minister?"

"Why—really—I—well," hesitated Anne.

Miss Cornelia nodded.

"Exactly. I agree with you, dearie. We made a mistake when we called *him*. His face just looks like one of those long, narrow stones in the graveyard, doesn't it? 'Sacred to the memory' ought to be written on his forehead. I shall never forget the first sermon he preached after he came. It was on the subject of everyone doing what they were best fitted for—a very good subject, of course; but such illustrations as he used! He said, 'If you had a cow and an apple tree, and if you tied the apple tree in your stable and planted the cow in your orchard, with her legs up, how much milk would you get from the apple tree, or how many apples from the cow?' Did you ever hear the like in your born days, dearie? I was so thankful there were no Methodists there that day—they'd never have been done hooting over it. But what I dislike most in him is his habit of agreeing with everybody, no matter what is said. If you said to him, 'You're a scoundrel,' he'd say, with that smooth smile of his, 'Yes, that's so.' A minister should have more backbone. The long and the short of it is, I consider him a reverend jackass. But, of course, this is just between you and me. When there are Methodists in hearing I praise him to the skies. Some folks think his wife dresses too gay, but *I* say when she has to live with a face like that she needs something to cheer her up. You'll never hear *me* condemning a woman for her dress. I'm only too thankful when her husband isn't too mean and miserly to allow it. Not that I bother much with dress myself. Women just dress to please the men, and I'd never stoop to *that*. I have had a real placid, comfortable life, dearie, and it's just because I never cared a cent what the men thought."

"Why do you hate the men so, Miss Bryant?"

"Lord, dearie, I don't hate them. They aren't worth it. I just sort of despise them. I think I'll like *your* husband if he keeps on as he has begun. But apart from him, about the only men in the world I've much use for are the old doctor and Captain Jim."

"Captain Jim is certainly splendid," agreed Anne cordially.

"Captain Jim is a good man, but he's kind of vexing in one way. You *can't* make him mad. I've tried for twenty years and he just keeps on being placid. It does sort of rile me. And I s'pose the woman he should have married got a man who went into tantrums twice a day."

"Who was she?"

"Oh, I don't know, dearie. I never remember of Captain Jim making up to anybody. He was edging on old as far as my memory goes. He's seventy-six, you know. I never heard any reason for his staying a bachelor, but there must be one, believe *me*. He sailed all his life till five years ago, and there's no corner of the earth he hasn't poked his nose into. He and Elizabeth Russell were great cronies, all their lives, but they never had any notion of sweet-hearting. Elizabeth never married, though she had plenty of chances. She was a great beauty when she was young. The year the Prince of Wales came to the Island she was visiting her uncle in Charlottetown and he was a Government official, and so she got invited to the great ball. She was the prettiest girl there, and the Prince danced with her, and all the other women he didn't dance with were furious about it, because their social standing was higher than hers and they said he shouldn't have passed them over. Elizabeth was always very proud of that dance. Mean folks said that was why she never married—she shouldn't put up with an ordinary man after dancing with a prince. But that wasn't so. She told me the reason once—it was because she had such a temper that she was afraid she couldn't live peaceably with any man. She *had* an awful temper—she used to have to go upstairs and bite pieces out of her bureau to keep it down by times. But I told her that wasn't any reason for not marrying if she wanted to. There's no reason why we should let the men have a monopoly of temper, is there, Mrs. Blythe, dearie?"

"I've a bit of temper myself," sighed Anne.

"It's well you have, dearie. You won't be half so likely to

be trodden on, believe *me*! My, how that golden glow of yours is blooming! Your garden looks fine. Poor Elizabeth always took such care of it."

"I love it," said Anne. "I'm glad it's so full of old-fashioned flowers. Speaking of gardening, we want to get a man to dig up that little lot beyond the fir grove and set it out with strawberry plants for us. Gilbert is so busy he will never get time for it this fall. Do you know anyone we can get?"

"Well, Henry Hammond up at the Glen goes out doing jobs like that. He'll do, maybe. He's always a heap more interested in his wages than in his work, just like a man, and he's so slow in the uptake that he stands still for five minutes before it dawns on him that he's stopped. His father threw a stump at him when he was small. Nice gentle missile, wasn't it? So like a man! Course, the boy never got over it. But he's the only one I can recommend at all. He painted my house for me last spring. It looks real nice now, don't you think?"

Anne was saved by the clock striking five.

"Lord, is it that late?" exclaimed Miss Cornelia. "How time does slip by when you're enjoying yourself! Well, I must betake myself home."

"No indeed! You are going to stay and have tea with us," said Anne eagerly.

"Are you asking me because you think you ought to, or because you really want to?" demanded Miss Cornelia.

"Because I really want to."

"Then I'll stay. *You* belong to the race that knows Joseph."

"I know we are going to be friends," said Anne, with the smile that only they of the household of faith ever saw.

"Yes, we are, dearie. Thank goodness, we can choose our friends. We have to take our relatives as they are, and be thankful if there are no penitentiary birds among them. Not that I've many—none nearer than second cousins. I'm a kind of lonely soul, Mrs. Blythe."

There was a wistful note in Miss Cornelia's voice.

"I wish you would call me Anne," exclaimed Anne impulsively. "It would seem more *homey*. Everyone in Four Winds, except my husband, calls me Mrs. Blythe, and it makes me feel like a stranger. Do you know that your name is very near being the one I yearned after when I was a child. I hated 'Anne' and I called myself 'Cordelia' in imagination."

"I like Anne. It was my mother's name. Old-fashioned names are the best and sweetest in my opinion. If you're going to get tea you might send the young doctor to talk to me. He's been lying on the sofa in that office ever since I came, laughing fit to kill over what I've been saying."

"How did you know?" cried Anne, too aghast at this instance of Miss Cornelia's uncanny prescience to make a polite denial.

"I saw him sitting beside you when I came up the lane, and I know men's tricks," retorted Miss Cornelia. "There, I've finished my little dress, dearie, and the eighth baby can come as soon as it pleases."

An Evening at Four Winds Point

It was late September when Anne and Gilbert were able to pay Four Winds light their promised visit. They had often planned to go, but something always occurred to prevent them. Captain Jim had "dropped in" several times at the little house.

"I don't stand on ceremony, Mistress Blythe," he told Anne. "It's a real pleasure to me to come here, and I'm not going to deny myself jest because you havan't got down to see me. There oughtn't to be no bargaining like that among the race that knows Joseph. I'll come when I can, and you come when you can, and so long's we have our pleasant little chat it don't matter a mite what roof's over us."

Captain Jim took a great fancy to Gog and Magog, who were presiding over the destinies of the hearth in the little house with as much dignity and aplomb as they had done at Patty's Place.

"Aren't they the cutest little cusses?" he would say delightedly; and he bade them greeting and farewell as gravely and invariably as he did his host and hostess. Captain Jim was not going to offend household deities by any lack of reverence and ceremony.

"You've made this little house just about perfect," he told Anne. "It never was so nice before. Mistress Selwyn had your taste and she did wonders; but folks in those days didn't have the pretty little curtains and pictures and nicknacks you have. As for Elizabeth, she lived in the past. You've kinder brought the future into it, so to speak. I'd be real happy even if we couldn't talk at all, when I come here—jest to sit and look at you and your pictures and your flowers would be enough of a treat. It's beautiful—beautiful."

Captain Jim was a passionate worshipper of beauty. Every lovely thing heard or seen gave him a deep, subtle, inner joy that irradiated his life. He was quite keenly aware of his own lack of outward comeliness and lamented it.

"Folks say I'm good," he remarked whimsically upon one occasion, "but I sometimes wish the Lord had made me only half as good and put the rest of it into looks. But there, I reckon He knew what He was about, as a good Captain should. Some of us have to be homely, or the purty ones—like Mistress Blythe here—wouldn't show up so well."

One evening Anne and Gilbert finally walked down to the Four Winds light. The day had begun sombrely in gray cloud and mist, but it had ended in a pomp of scarlet and gold. Over the western hills beyond the harbour were amber deeps and crystalline shallows, with the fire of sunset below. The north was a mackerel sky of little, fiery golden clouds. The red light flamed on the white sails of a vessel gliding down the channel, bound to a southern port in a land of palms. Beyond her, it smote upon and incarnadined the shining, white, grassless faces of the sand dunes. To the right, it fell on the old house among the willows up the brook, and gave it for a fleeting space casements more splendid than those of an old cathedral. They glowed out of its quiet and grayness like the throbbing, blood-red thoughts of a vivid soul imprisoned in a dull husk of environment.

"That old house up the brook always seems so lonely," said Anne. "I never see visitors there. Of course, its lane opens on the upper road—but I don't think there's much coming and going. It seems odd we've never met the Moores yet, when they live within fifteen minutes' walk of us. I may have seen them in church, of course, but if so I didn't know them. I'm sorry they are so unsociable, when they are our only near neighbours."

"Evidently they don't belong to the race that knows Joseph," laughed Gilbert. "Have you ever found out who that girl was whom you thought so beautiful?"

"No. Somehow I have never remembered to ask about her. But I've never seen her anywhere, so I suppose she must have been a stranger. Oh, the sun has just vanished—and there's the light."

As the dusk deepened, the great beacon cut swathes of light through it, sweeping in a circle over the fields and the harbour, the sandbar and the gulf.

"I feel as if it might catch me and whisk me leagues out to sea," said Anne, as one drenched them with radiance; and she felt rather relieved when they got so near the Point that they were inside the range of those dazzling, recurrent flashes.

As they turned into the little lane that led across the fields to the Point they met a man coming out of it—a man of such extraordinary appearance that for a moment they both frankly stared. He was a decidedly fine-looking person—tall, broad-shouldered, well-featured, with a Roman nose and frank gray eyes; he was dressed in a prosperous farmer's Sunday best; in so far he might have been any inhabitant of Four Winds or the Glen. But, flowing over his breast nearly to his knees, was a river of crinkly brown beard; and adown his back, beneath his commonplace felt hat, was a corresponding cascade of thick, wavy, brown hair.

"Anne," murmured Gilbert, when they were out of ear-shot, "you didn't put what Uncle Dave calls 'a little of the Scott Act' in that lemonade you gave me just before we left home, did you?"

"No, I didn't," said Anne, stifling her laughter, lest the retreating enigma should hear her. "Who in the world can he be?"

"I don't know; but if Captain Jim keeps apparitions like that down at this Point I'm going to carry cold iron in my pocket when I come here. He wasn't a sailor, or one might pardon his eccentricity of appearance; he must belong to the over-harbour clans. Uncle Dave says they have several freaks over there."

"Uncle Dave is a little prejudiced, I think. You know all the over-harbour people who come to the Glen Church seem very nice. Oh, Gilbert, isn't this beautiful?"

The Four Winds light was built on a spur of red sandstone cliff jutting out into the gulf. On one side, across the channel, stretched the silvery sandshore of the bar; on the other, extended a long, curving beach of red cliffs, rising steeply from the pebbled coves. It was a shore that knew the magic and mystery of storm and star. There is a great solitude about such a shore. The woods are never solitary—they are full of whispering, beckoning, friendly life. But the sea is a mighty soul, forever moaning of some great, unshareable sorrow, which shuts it up into itself for all eternity. We can never pierce its infinite mystery—we may only wander, awed and spellbound, on the outer fringe of it. The woods call to us with a hundred voices, but the sea has one only—a mighty voice that drowns our souls in its majestic music. The woods are human, but the sea is of the company of the archangels.

Anne and Gilbert found Uncle Jim sitting on a bench outside the lighthouse, putting the finishing touches to a wonderful, full-rigged, toy schooner. He rose and welcomed them to his abode with the gentle, unconscious courtesy that became him so well.

"This has been a purty nice day all through, Mistress Blythe, and now, right at the last, it's brought its best. Would you like to sit down here outside a bit, while the light lasts? I've just finished this bit of a plaything for my little grand-nephew, Joe, up at the Glen. After I promised to make it for him I was kinder sorry, for his mother was vexed. She's afraid he'll be wanting to go to sea later on and she doesn't want the notion encouraged in him. But what could I do, Mistress Blythe? I'd *promised* him, and I think it's sorter real dastardly to break a promise you make to a child. Come, sit down. It won't take long to stay an hour."

The wind was off shore, and only broke the sea's surface into long, silvery ripples, and sent sheeny shadows flying out across it, from every point and headland, like transparent wings. The dusk was hanging a curtain of violet gloom over the sand dunes and the headlands where gulls were huddling. The sky was faintly filmed over with scarfs of silken vapour. Cloud fleets rode at anchor along the horizons. An evening star was watching over the bar.

"Isn't that a view worth looking at?" said Captain Jim, with a loving, proprietary pride. "Nice and far from the marketplace, ain't it? No buying and selling and getting gain. You don't have to pay anything—all that sea and sky free—'without money and without price.' There's going to be a moonrise purty soon, too—I'm never tired of finding out what a moonrise can be over them rocks and sea and harbour. There's a surprise in it every time."

They had their moonrise, and watched its marvel and magic in a silence that asked nothing of the world or each other. Then they went up into the tower, and Captain Jim showed and explained the mechanism of the great light. Finally they found themselves in the dining room, where a fire of driftwood was weaving flames of wavering, elusive, sea-born hues in the open fireplace.

"I put this fireplace in myself," remarked Captain Jim. "The Government don't give lighthouse keepers such luxuries. Look at the colours that wood makes. If you'd like some drift-wood for your fire, Mistress Blythe, I'll bring you up a load someday. Sit down. I'm going to make you a cup of tea."

Captain Jim placed a chair for Anne, having first removed therefrom a huge, orange-coloured cat and a newspaper.

"Get down, Matey. The sofa is your place. I must put this paper away safe till I can find time to finish the story in it. It's called *A Mad Love*. 'Tisn't my favourite brand of fiction, but I'm reading it jest to see how long she can spin it out. It's at the sixty-second chapter now, and the wedding ain't any nearer than when it begun, far's I can see. When little Joe comes I have to read him pirate yarns. Ain't it strange how innocent little creatures like children like the blood-thirstiest stories?"

"Like my lad Davy at home," said Anne. "He wants tales that reek with gore."

Captain Jim's tea proved to be nectar. He was pleased as a child with Anne's compliments, but he affected a fine indifference.

"The secret is I don't skimp the cream," he remarked airily. Captain Jim had never heard of Oliver Wendell Holmes, but he evidently agreed with that writer's dictum that "big heart never liked little cream pot."

"We met an odd-looking personage coming out of your lane," said Gilbert as they sipped. "Who was he?"

Captain Jim grinned.

"That's Marshall Elliott—a mighty fine man with jest one streak of foolishness in him. I s'pose you wondered what his object was in turning himself into a sort of dime museum freak."

"Is he a modern Nazarite or a Hebrew prophet left over from olden times?" asked Anne.

"Neither of them. It's politics that's at the bottom of his freak. All those Elliotts and Crawfords and MacAllisters are dyed-in-the-wool politicians. They're born Grit or Tory, as the case may be, and they live Grit or Tory, and they die Grit or Tory; and what they're going to do in heaven, where there's probably no politics, is more than I can fathom. This Marshall Elliott was born a Grit. I'm a Grit myself in moderation, but there's no moderation about Marshall. Fifteen years ago there was a specially bitter general election. Marshall fought for his party tooth and nail. He was dead sure the Liberals would win—so sure that he got up at a public meeting and vowed that he wouldn't shave his face or cut his hair until the Grits were in power. Well, they didn't go in—and they've never got in yet—and you saw the result tonight for yourselves. Marshall stuck to his word."

"What does his wife think of it?" asked Anne.

"He's a bachelor. But if he had a wife I reckon she couldn't make him break that vow. That family of Elliotts has always been more stubborn than nateral. Marshall's brother Alexander had a dog he set great store by, and when it died the man actilly wanted to have it buried in the graveyard, 'along with the other Christians,' he said. Course, he wasn't allowed to; so he buried it just outside the graveyard fence, and never darkened the church door again. But Sundays he'd drive his family to church and sit by that dog's grave and read his Bible all the time service was going on. They say when he was dying he asked his wife to bury him beside the dog; she was a meek little soul but she fired up at *that*. She said *she* wasn't going to be buried beside no dog, and if he'd rather have his last resting place beside the dog than beside her, jest to say so. Alexander Elliott was a stubborn mule, but he was fond of his wife, so he give in and said, 'Well, durn it, bury me where you please. But when Gabriel's trump blows I expect my dog to rise with the rest of us, for he had as much soul as any durned Elliott or Crawford or MacAllister that ever strutted.' Them was *his* parting words. As for Marshall, we're all used to him, but he must strike strangers as right down peculiar-looking. I've known him ever since he was ten—he's about fifty now—and

I like him. Him and me was out cod-fishing today. That's about all I'm good for now—catching trout and cod occasional. But 'tweren't always so—not by no manner of means. I used to do other things, as you'd admit if you saw my life-book."

Anne was just going to ask what his life-book was when the First Mate created a diversion by springing upon Captain Jim's knee. He was a gorgeous beastie, with a face as round as a full moon, vivid green eyes, and immense, white, double paws. Captain Jim stroked his velvet back gently.

"I never fancied cats much till I found the First Mate," he remarked, to the accompaniment of the Mate's tremendous purrs. "I saved his life, and when you've saved a creature's life you're bound to love it. It's next thing to giving life. There's some turrible thoughtless people in the world, Mistress Blythe. Some of them city folks who have summer homes over the harbour are so thoughtless that they're cruel. It's the worst kind of cruelty—the thoughtless kind. You can't cope with it. They keep cats there in the summer, and feed and pet 'em, and doll 'em up with ribbons and collars. And then in the fall they go off and leave 'em to starve or freeze. It makes my blood boil, Mistress Blythe. One day last winter I found a poor old mother cat dead on the shore, lying against the skin-and-bone bodies of her three little kittens. She'd died trying to shelter 'em. She had her poor stiff paws around 'em. Master, I cried. Then I swore. Then I carried them poor little kittens home and fed 'em up and found good homes for 'em. I knew the woman who left the cat and when she come back this summer I jest went over the harbour and told her my opinion of her. It was rank meddling, but I do love meddling in a good cause."

"How did she take it?" asked Gilbert.

"Cried and said she 'didn't think.' I says to her, says I, 'Do you s'pose that'll be held for a good excuse in the day of Jedgment, when you'll have to account for that poor old mother's life? The Lord'll ask you what He give you your brains for if it wasn't to think, I reckon.' I don't fancy she'll leave cats to starve another time."

"Was the First Mate one of the forsaken?" asked Anne, making advances to him which were responded to graciously, if condescendingly.

"Yes. I found *him* one bitter cold day in winter, caught in the branches of a tree by his durn-fool ribbon collar. He was almost starving. If you could have seen his eyes, Mistress Blythe! He was nothing but a kitten, and he'd got his living somehow since he'd been left until he got hung up. When I loosed him he give my hand a pitiful swipe with his little red tongue. He wasn't the able seaman you see now. He was meek as Moses. That was nine years ago. His life has been long in the land for a cat. He's a good old pal, the First Mate is."

"I should have expected you to have a dog," said Gilbert. Captain Jim shook his head.

"I had a dog once. I thought so much of him that when he died I couldn't bear the thought of getting another in his place. He was a *friend*—you understand, Mistress Blythe? Matey's only a pal. I'm fond of Matey—all the fonder on account of the spice of devilment that's in him—like there is in all cats. But I *loved* my dog. I always had a sneaking sympathy for Alexander Elliott about *his* dog. There isn't any devil in a good dog. That's why they're more lovable than cats, I reckon. But I'm darned if they're as interesting. Here I am, talking too much. Why don't you check me? When I do get a chance to talk to anyone I run on turrible. If you've done your tea I've a few little things you might like to look at—picked 'em up in the queer corners I used to be poking my nose into."

Captain Jim's "few little things" turned out to be a most interesting collection of curios, hideous, quaint and beautiful. And almost every one had some striking story attached to it.

Anne never forgot the delight with which she listened to those old tales that moonlit evening by that enchanted driftwood fire, while the silver sea called to them through the open window and sobbed against the rocks below them.

Captain Jim never said a boastful word, but it was impossible to help seeing what a hero the man had been—brave, true, resourceful, unselfish. He sat there in his little room and made those things live again for his hearers. By a lift of the eyebrow, a twist of the lip, a gesture, a word, he painted a whole scene or character so that they saw it as it was.

Some of Captain Jim's adventures had such a marvelous edge that Anne and Gilbert secretly wondered if he were not drawing a rather long bow at their credulous expense. But in this, as they found later, they did him injustice. His tales were all literally true. Captain Jim had the gift of the born storyteller, whereby "unhappy, far-off things" can be brought vividly before the hearer in all their pristine poignancy.

Anne and Gilbert laughed and shivered over his tales, and once Anne found herself crying. Captain Jim surveyed her tears with pleasure shining from his face.

"I like to see folks cry that way," he remarked. "It's a compliment. But I can't do justice to the things I've seen or helped to do. I've 'em all jotted down in my life-book, but I haven't got the knack of writing them out properly. If I could hit on jest the right words and string 'em together proper on paper I could make a great book. It would beat *A Mad Love* holler, and I believe Joe'd like it as well as the pirate yarns. Yes, I've had some adventures in my time; and, do you know, Mistress Blythe, I still lust after 'em. Yes, old and useless as I be, there's an awful longing sweeps over me at times to sail out—out—out there—forever and ever."

"Like Ulysses, you would

> *Sail beyond the sunset and the baths*
> *Of all the western stars until you die,*

said Anne dreamily.

"Ulysses? I've read of him. Yes, that's jest how I feel— jest how all us old sailors feel, I reckon. I'll die on land after all, I s'pose. Well, what is to be will be. There was old William Ford at the Glen who never went on the water in his life, 'cause he was afraid of being drowned. A fortune-teller had predicted he would be. And one day he fainted and fell with his face in the barn trough and was drowned. Must you go? Well, come soon and come often. The doctor is to do the talking next time. He knows a heap of things I want to find out. I'm sorter lonesome here by times. It's been worse since Elizabeth Russell died. Her and me was such cronies."

Captain Jim spoke with the pathos of the aged, who see their old friends slipping from them one by one—friends whose place can never be quite filled by those of a younger generation, even of the race that knows Joseph. Anne and Gilbert promised to come soon and often.

"He's a rare old fellow, isn't he?" said Gilbert, as they walked home.

"Somehow, I can't reconcile his simple, kindly personality with the wild, adventurous life he has lived," mused Anne.

"You wouldn't find it so hard if you had seen him the other day down at the fishing village. One of the men of Peter Gautier's boat made a nasty remark about some girl along the shore. Captain Jim fairly scorched the wretched fellow with the lightning of his eyes. He seemed a man transformed. He didn't say much—but the way he said it! You'd have thought it would strip the flesh from the fellow's bones. I understand that Captain Jim will never allow a word against any woman to be said in his presence."

"I wonder why he never married," said Anne. "He should have sons with their ships at sea now, and grandchildren climbing over him to hear his stories—he's that kind of a man. Instead, he has nothing but a magnificent cat."

But Anne was mistaken. Captain Jim had more than that. He had a memory.

Leslie Moore

"I'm going for a walk to the outside shore tonight," Anne told Gog and Magog one October evening. There was no one else to tell, for Gilbert had gone over the harbour. Anne had her little domain in the speckless order one would expect of anyone brought up by Marilla Cuthbert, and felt that she could gad shoreward with a clear conscience. Many and delightful had been her shore rambles, sometimes with Gilbert, sometimes with Captain Jim, sometimes alone with her own thoughts and new, poignantly-sweet dreams that were beginning to span life with their rainbows. She loved the gentle, misty harbour shore and the silvery, wind-haunted sandshore, but best of all she loved the rock shore, with its cliffs and caves and piles of surf-worn boulders, and its coves where the pebbles glittered under the pools; and it was to this shore she hied herself tonight.

There had been an autumn storm of wind and rain, lasting for three days. Thunderous had been the crash of billows on the rocks, wild the white spray and spume that blew over the bar, troubled and misty and tempest-torn the erstwhile blue peace of Four Winds Harbour. Now it was over, and the shore lay clean-washed after the storm; not a wind stirred, but there was still a fine surf on, dashing on sand and rock in a splendid white turmoil—the only restless thing in the great, pervading stillness and peace.

"Oh, this is a moment worth living through weeks of storm and stress for," Anne exclaimed, delightedly sending her far gaze across the tossing waters from the top of the cliff where she stood. Presently she scrambled down the steep path to the little cove below, where she seemed shut in with rocks and sea and sky.

"I'm going to dance and sing," she said. "There's no one here to see me—the sea-gulls won't carry tales of the matter. I may be as crazy as I like."

She caught up her skirt and pirouetted along the hard strip of sand just out of reach of the waves that almost lapped her feet with their spent foam. Whirling round and round, laughing like a child, she reached the little headland that ran out to the east of the cove; then she stopped suddenly, blushing crimson; she was not alone; there had been a witness to her dance and laughter.

The girl of the golden hair and sea-blue eyes was sitting on a boulder of the headland, half-hidden by a jutting rock. She was looking straight at Anne with a strange expression— part wonder, part sympathy, part—could it be?—envy. She was bareheaded, and her splendid hair, more than ever like Browning's "gorgeous snake," was bound about her head with a crimson ribbon. She wore a dress of some dark material, very plainly made; but swathed about her waist, outlining its fine curves, was a vivid girdle of red silk. Her hands, clasped over her knee, were brown and somewhat work-hardened; but the skin of her throat and cheeks was as white as cream. A flying gleam of sunset broke through a low-lying western cloud and fell across her hair. For a moment she seemed the spirit of the sea personified—all its mystery, all its passion, all its elusive charm.

"You—you must think me crazy," stammered Anne, trying to recover her self-possession. To be seen by this stately girl in such an abandon of childishness she, Mrs. Dr. Blythe, with all the dignity of the matron to keep up—it was too bad!

"No," said the girl, "I don't."

She said nothing more; her voice was expressionless; her manner slightly repellent; but there was something in her eyes—eager yet shy, defiant yet pleading—which turned Anne from her purpose of walking away. Instead, she sat down on the boulder beside the girl.

"Let's introduce ourselves," she said, with the smile that had never yet failed to win confidence and friendliness. "I am Mrs. Blythe—and I live in that little white house up the harbour shore."

"Yes, I know," said the girl. "I am Leslie Moore—Mrs. Dick Moore," she added stiffly.

Anne was silent for a moment from sheer amazement. It had not occurred to her that this girl was married—there seemed nothing of the wife about her. And that she should be the neighbour whom Anne had pictured as a commonplace Four Winds housewife! Anne could not quickly adjust her mental focus to this astonishing change.

"Then—then you live in that gray house up the brook," she stammered.

"Yes. I should have gone over to call on you long ago," said the other. She did not offer any explanation or excuse for not having gone.

"I wish you *would* come," said Anne, recovering herself somewhat. "We're such near neighbours we ought to be friends. That is the sole fault of Four Winds—there aren't quite enough neighbours. Otherwise it is perfection."

"You like it?"

"*Like* it! I love it. It is the most beautiful place I ever saw."

"I've never seen many places," said Leslie Moore, slowly, "but I've always thought it was very lovely here. I   I love it, too."

She spoke, as she looked, shyly, yet eagerly. Anne had an odd impression that this strange girl—the word "girl" would persist—could say a good deal if she chose.

"I often come to the shore," she added.

"So do I," said Anne. "It's a wonder we haven't met here before."

"Probably you come earlier in the evening than I do. It is generally late—almost dark—when I come. And I love to come just after a storm—like this. I don't like the sea so well when it's calm and quiet. I like the struggle—and the crash—and the noise."

"I love it in all its moods," declared Anne. "The sea at Four Winds is to me what Lover's Lane was at home. Tonight it seemed so free—so untamed—something broke loose in me, too, out of sympathy. That was why I danced along the shore in that wild way. I didn't suppose anybody was looking, of course. If Miss Cornelia Bryant had seen me she would have foreboded a gloomy prospect for poor young Dr. Blythe."

"You know Miss Cornelia?" said Leslie, laughing. She had an exquisite laugh; it bubbled up suddenly and unexpectedly with something of the delicious quality of a baby's. Anne laughed, too.

"Oh, yes. She has been down to my house of dreams several times."

"Your house of dreams?"

"Oh, that's a dear, foolish little name Gilbert and I have for our home. We just call it that between ourselves. It slipped out before I thought."

"So Miss Russell's little white house is *your* house of dreams," said Leslie wonderingly. "*I* had a house of dreams once—but it was a palace," she added, with a laugh, the sweetness of which was marred by a little note of derision.

"Oh, I once dreamed of a palace, too," said Anne. "I suppose all girls do. And then we settle down contentedly in eight-room houses that seem to fulfil all the desires of our hearts—because our prince is there. *You* should have had your palace really, though—you are so beautiful. You *must* let me say it—it *has* to be said—I'm nearly bursting with admiration. You are the loveliest thing I ever saw, Mrs. Moore."

"If we are to be friends you must call me Leslie," said the other with an odd passion.

"Of course I will. And *my* friends call me Anne."

"I suppose I am beautiful," Leslie went on, looking stormily out to sea. "I hate my beauty. I wish I had always been as brown and plain as the brownest and plainest girl at the fishing village over there. Well, what do you think of Miss Cornelia?"

The abrupt change of subject shut the door on any further confidences.

"Miss Cornelia is a darling, isn't she?" said Anne. "Gilbert and I were invited to her house to a state tea last week. You've heard of groaning tables."

"I seem to recall seeing the expression in the newspaper reports of weddings," said Leslie, smiling.

"Well, Miss Cornelia's groaned—at least, it creaked—positively. You couldn't have believed she would have cooked so much for two ordinary people. She had every kind of pie you could name, I think,—except lemon pie. She said she had taken the prize for lemon pies at the Charlottetown Exhibition ten years ago and had never made any since for fear of losing her reputation for them."

"Were you able to eat enough pie to please her?"

"*I* wasn't. Gilbert won her heart by eating—I won't tell you how much. She said she never knew a man who didn't like pie better than his Bible. Do you know, I love Miss Cornelia."

"So do I," said Leslie. "She is the best friend I have in the world."

Anne wondered secretly why, if this were so, Miss Cornelia had never mentioned Mrs. Dick Moore to her. Miss Cornelia had certainly talked freely about every other individual in or near Four Winds.

"Isn't that beautiful?" said Leslie, after a brief silence, pointing to the exquisite effect of a shaft of light falling through a cleft in the rock behind them, across a dark green pool at its base. "If I had come here—and seen nothing but just that—I would go home satisfied."

"The effects of light and shadow all along these shores are wonderful," agreed Anne. "My little sewing room looks out on the harbour, and I sit at its window and feast my eyes.

The colours and shadows are never the same two minutes together."

"And you are never lonely?" asked Leslie abruptly. "Never—when you are alone?"

"No. I don't think I've ever been lonely in my life," answered Anne. "Even when I'm alone I have real good company—dreams and imaginations and pretendings. I *like* to be alone now and then, just to think over things and *taste* them. But I love friendship—and nice, jolly little times with people. Oh, *won't* you come to see me—often? Please do. I believe," Anne added, laughing, "that you'd like me if you knew me."

"I wonder if *you* would like *me*," said Leslie seriously. She was not fishing for a compliment. She looked out across the waves that were beginning to be garlanded with blossoms of moonlit foam, and her eyes filled with shadows.

"I'm sure I would," said Anne. "And please don't think I'm utterly irresponsible because you saw me dancing on the shore at sunset. No doubt I shall be dignified after a time. You see, I haven't been married very long. I feel like a girl, and sometimes like a child, yet."

"I have been married twelve years," said Leslie.

Here was another unbelievable thing.

"Why, you can't be as old as I am!" exclaimed Anne. "You must have been a child when you were married."

"I was sixteen," said Leslie, rising, and picking up the cap and jacket lying beside her. "I am twenty-eight now. Well, I must go back."

"So must I. Gilbert will probably be home. But I'm so glad we both came to the shore tonight and met each other."

Leslie said nothing, and Anne was a little chilled. She had

offered friendship frankly but it had not been accepted very graciously, if it had not been absolutely repelled. In silence they climbed the cliffs and walked across a pasture-field of which the feathery, bleached, wild grasses were like a carpet of creamy velvet in the moonlight. When they reached the shore lane Leslie turned.

"I go this way, Mrs. Blythe. You will come over and see me sometime, won't you?"

Anne felt as if the invitation had been thrown at her. She got the impression that Leslie Moore gave it reluctantly.

"I will come if you really want me to," she said a little coldly.

"Oh, I do—I do," exclaimed Leslie, with an eagerness which seemed to burst forth and beat down some restraint that had been imposed on it.

"Then I'll come. Good-night—Leslie."

"Good-night, Mrs. Blythe."

Anne walked home in a brown study and poured out her tale to Gilbert.

"So Mrs. Dick Moore isn't one of the race that knows Joseph?" said Gilbert teasingly.

"No—o—o, not exactly. And yet—I think she *was* one of them once, but has gone or got into exile," said Anne musingly. "She is certainly very different from the other women about here. You can't talk about eggs and butter to her. To think I've been imagining her a second Mrs. Rachel Lynde! Have you ever seen Dick Moore, Gilbert?"

"No. I've seen several men working about the fields of the farm, but I don't know which was Moore."

"She never mentioned him. I *know* she isn't happy."

"From what you tell me I suppose she was married before she was old enough to know her own mind or heart, and found out too late that she had made a mistake. It's a common tragedy enough, Anne. A fine woman would have made the best of it. Mrs. Moore has evidently let it make her bitter and resentful."

"Don't let us judge her till we know," pleaded Anne. "I don't believe her case is so ordinary. You will understand her fascination when you meet her, Gilbert. It is a thing quite apart from her beauty. I feel that she possesses a rich nature, into which a friend might enter as into a kingdom; but for some reason she bars everyone out and shuts all her possibilities up in herself, so that they cannot develop and blossom. There, I've been struggling to define her to myself ever since I left her, and that is the nearest I can get to it. I'm going to ask Miss Cornelia about her."

The Story of Leslie Moore

"Yes, the eighth baby arrived a fortnight ago," said Miss Cornelia, from a rocker before the fire of the little house one chilly October afternoon. "It's a girl. Fred was ranting mad said he wanted a boy when the truth is he didn't want it at all. If it had been a boy he'd have ranted because it wasn't a girl. They had four girls and three boys before, so I can't see that it made much difference what this one was, but of course he'd have to be cantankerous, just like a man. The baby is real pretty, dressed up in its nice little clothes. It has black eyes and the dearest, tiny hands."

"I must go and see it. I just love babies," said Anne, smiling to herself over a thought too dear and sacred to be put into words.

"I don't say but what they're nice," admitted Miss Cornelia. "But some folks seem to have more than they really need, believe *me*. My poor cousin Flora up at the Glen had eleven, and such a slave as she is! Her husband suicided three years ago. Just like a man!"

"What made him do that?" asked Anne, rather shocked.

"Couldn't get his way over something, so he jumped into the well. A good riddance! He was a born tyrant. But of course it spoiled the well. Flora could never abide the thought of using it again, poor thing! So she had another dug and a frightful expense it was, and the water as hard as nails. If he *had* to drown himself there was plenty of water in the harbour, wasn't there? I've no patience with a man like that. We've only had two suicides in Four Winds in my recollection. The other was Frank West—Leslie Moore's father. By the way, has Leslie ever been over to call on you yet?"

"No, but I met her on the shore a few nights ago and we scraped an acquaintance," said Anne, pricking up her ears.

Miss Cornelia nodded.

"I'm glad, dearie. I was hoping you'd foregather with her. What do you think of her?"

"I thought her very beautiful."

"Oh, of course. There was never anybody about Four Winds could touch her for looks. Did you ever see her hair? It reaches to her feet when she lets it down. But I meant how did you like her?"

"I think I could like her very much if she'd let me," said Anne slowly.

"But she wouldn't let you—she pushed you off and kept you at arm's length. Poor Leslie! You wouldn't be much surprised if you knew what her life has been. It's been a tragedy— a tragedy!" repeated Miss Cornelia emphatically.

"I wish you would tell me all about her—that is, if you can do so without betraying any confidence."

"Lord, dearie, everybody in Four Winds knows poor

Leslie's story. It's no secret—the *outside*, that is. Nobody knows the *inside* but Leslie herself, and she doesn't take folks into her confidence. I'm about the best friend she has on earth, I reckon, and she's never uttered a word of complaint to me. Have you ever seen Dick Moore?"

"No."

"Well, I may as well begin at the beginning and tell you everything straight through, so you'll understand it. As I said, Leslie's father was Frank West. He was clever and shiftless—just like a man. Oh, he had heaps of brains—and much good they did him! He started to go to college, and he went for two years, and then his health broke down. The Wests were all inclined to be consumptive. So Frank came home and started farming. He married Rose Elliott from over harbour. Rose was reckoned the beauty of Four Winds— Leslie takes her looks from her mother, but she has ten times the spirit and go that Rose had, and a far better figure. Now you know, Anne, I always take the ground that us women ought to stand by each other. We've got enough to endure at the hands of the men, the Lord knows, so I hold we hadn't ought to clapper-claw one another, and it isn't often you'll find me running down another woman. But I never had much use for Rose Elliott. She was spoiled to begin with, believe *me*, and she was nothing but a lazy, selfish, whining creature. Frank was no hand to work, so they were poor as Job's turkey. Poor! They lived on potatoes and point, believe *me*. They had two children—Leslie and Kenneth. Leslie had her mother's looks and her father's brains, and something she didn't get from either of them. She took after her Grandmother West—a splendid old lady. She was the brightest, friendliest, merriest thing when she was a child, Anne. Everybody liked her. She was her father's favourite and she was awful fond of him. They were 'chums,' as she used to say. She couldn't see any of his faults—and he *was* a taking sort of man in some ways.

"Well, when Leslie was twelve years old, the first dreadful thing happened. She worshipped little Kenneth—he was four years younger than her, and he *was* a dear little chap. And he was killed one day—fell off a big load of hay just as it was going into the barn, and the wheel went right over his little body and crushed the life out of it. And mind you, Anne, Leslie saw it. She was looking down from the loft. She gave one screech—the hired man said he never heard such a sound in all his life—he said it would ring in his ears till Gabriel's trump drove it out. But she never screeched or cried again about it. She jumped from the loft onto the load and from the load to the floor, and caught up the little bleeding, warm, dead body, Anne—they had to tear it from her before she would let it go. They sent for me—I can't talk of it."

Miss Cornelia wiped the tears from her kindly brown eyes and sewed in bitter silence for a few minutes.

"Well," she resumed, "it was all over—they buried little Kenneth in that graveyard over the harbour, and after a while Leslie went back to her school and her studies. She never mentioned Kenneth's name—I've never heard it cross her lips from that day to this. I reckon that old hurt still aches and burns at times; but she was only a child and time is real kind to children, Anne, dearie. After a while she began to laugh again—she had the prettiest laugh. You don't often hear it now."

"I heard it once the other night," said Anne. "It *is* a beautiful laugh."

"Frank West began to go down after Kenneth's death. He wasn't strong and it was a shock to him, because he was real fond of the child, though, as I've said, Leslie was his favourite. He got mopey and melancholy, and couldn't or wouldn't work. And one day, when Leslie was fourteen years of age, he hanged himself—and in the parlour, too, mind you, Anne, right in the middle of the parlour from the lamp hook in the ceiling. Wasn't that like a man? It was the anniversary of his wedding day, too. Nice, tasty time to pick for it, wasn't it? And, of course, that poor Leslie had to be the one to find him. She went into the parlour that morning, singing, with some fresh flowers for the vases, and there she saw her father hanging from the ceiling, his face as black as a coal. It was something awful, believe me!"

"Oh, how horrible!" said Anne, shuddering. "The poor, poor child!"

"Leslie didn't cry at her father's funeral any more than she had cried at Kenneth's. Rose whooped and howled for two, however, and Leslie had all she could do trying to calm and comfort her mother. I was disgusted with Rose and so was everyone else, but Leslie never got out of patience. She loved her mother. Leslie is clannish—her own could never do wrong in her eyes. Well, they buried Frank West beside Kenneth, and Rose put up a great big monument to him. It was bigger than his character, believe *me*! Anyhow, it was bigger than Rose could afford, for the farm was mortgaged for more than its value. But not long after Leslie's old grandmother West died and she left Leslie a little money—enough to give her a year at Queen's Academy. Leslie had made up her mind to pass for a teacher if she could, and then earn enough to put herself through Redmond College. That had been her father's pet scheme—he wanted her to have what he had lost. Leslie was full of ambition and her head was chock full of brains. She went to Queen's, and she took two years' work in one year and got her First; and when she came home she got the Glen school. She was so happy and hopeful and full of life and eagerness. When I think of what she was then and what she is now, I say—drat the men!"

Miss Cornelia snipped her thread off as viciously as if, Nero-like, she was severing the neck of mankind by the stroke.

"Dick Moore came into her life that summer. His father, Abner Moore, kept store at the Glen, but Dick had a sea-going streak in him from his mother; he used to sail in summer and clerk in his father's store in winter. He was a big, handsome fellow, with a little ugly soul. He was always wanting something till he got it, and then he stopped wanting it—just like a man. Oh, he didn't growl at the weather when it was fine, and he was mostly real pleasant and agreeable when everything went right. But he drank a good deal, and there were some nasty stories told of him and a girl down at the fishing village. He wasn't fit for Leslie to wipe her feet on, that's the long and short of it. And he was a Methodist! But he was clean mad about her—because of her good looks in the first place, and because she wouldn't have anything to say to him in the second. He vowed he'd have her—and he got her!"

"How did he bring it about?"

"Oh, it was an iniquitous thing! I'll never forgive Rose West. You see, dearie, Abner Moore held the mortgage on the West farm, and the interest was overdue some years, and Dick just went and told Mrs. West that if Leslie wouldn't marry him he'd get his father to foreclose the mortgage. Rose carried on terrible—fainted and wept, and pleaded with Leslie not to let her be turned out of her home. She said it would break her heart to leave the home she'd come to as a bride. I wouldn't have blamed her for feeling dreadful bad over it—but you wouldn't have thought she'd be so selfish as to sacrifice her own flesh and blood because of it, would you? Well, she was. And Leslie gave in—she loved her mother so much she would have done anything to save her pain. She married Dick Moore. None of us knew why at the time. It wasn't till long afterward that I found out how her mother had worried her into it. I was sure there was something wrong, though, because I knew how she had snubbed him time and again, and it wasn't like Leslie to turn face-about like that. Besides, I knew that Dick Moore wasn't the kind of man Leslie could ever fancy, in spite of his good looks and dashing ways. Of course, there was no wedding, but Rose asked me to go and see them married. I went, but I was sorry I did. I'd seen Leslie's face at her brother's funeral and at her father's funeral—and now it seemed to me I was seeing it at her own funeral. But Rose was smiling as a basket of chips, believe *me*!

"Leslie and Dick settled down on the West place—Rose couldn't bear to part with her dear daughter!—and lived there for the winter. In the spring Rose took pneumonia and died—a year too late! Leslie was heartbroken enough over it. Isn't it terrible the way some unworthy folks are loved, while others that deserve it far more, you'd think, never get much affection? As for Dick, he'd had enough of quiet married life—just like a man. He was for up and off. He went over to Nova Scotia to visit his relations—his father had come from

Nova Scotia—and he wrote back to Leslie that his cousin, George Moore, was going on a voyage to Havana and he was going too. The name of the vessel was the *Four Sisters* and they were to be gone about nine weeks.

"It must have been a relief to Leslie. But she never said anything. From the day of her marriage she was just what she is now—cold and proud, and keeping everyone but me at a distance. I won't *be* kept at a distance, believe *me*! I've just stuck to Leslie as close as I knew how in spite of everything."

"She told me you were the best friend she had," said Anne.

"Did she?" exclaimed Miss Cornelia delightedly. "Well, I'm real thankful to hear it. Sometimes I've wondered if she really did want me around at all—she never let me think so. You must have thawed her out more than you think, or she wouldn't have said that much itself to you. Oh, that poor, heart-broken girl! I never see Dick Moore but I want to run a knife clean through him."

Miss Cornelia wiped her eyes again and having relieved her feelings by her blood-thirsty wish, took up her tale.

"Well, Leslie was left over there alone. Dick had put in the crop before he went, and old Abner looked after it. The summer went by and the *Four Sisters* didn't come back. The Nova Scotia Moores investigated, and found she had got to Havana and discharged her cargo and took on another and left for home; and that was all they ever found out about her. By degrees people began to talk of Dick Moore as one that was dead. Almost everyone believed that he was, though no one felt certain, for men have turned up here at the harbour after they'd been gone for years. Leslie never thought he was dead—and she was right. A thousand pities too! The next summer Captain

Jim was in Havana—that was before he gave up the sea, of course. He thought he'd poke round a bit—Captain Jim was always meddlesome, just like a man—and he went to inquiring round among the sailors' boarding houses and places like that, to see if he could find out anything about the crew of the *Four Sisters*. He'd better have let sleeping dogs lie, in my opinion! Well, he went to one out-of-the-way place, and there he found a man and he knew at first sight it was Dick Moore, though he had a big beard. Captain Jim got it shaved off and then there was no doubt—Dick Moore it was—his body at least. His mind wasn't there—as for his soul, in my opinion he never had one!"

"What had happened to him?"

"Nobody knows the rights of it. All the folks who kept the boarding house could tell was that about a year before they had found him lying on their doorstep one morning in an awful condition—his head battered to a jelly almost. They supposed he'd got hurt in some drunken row, and likely that's the truth of it. They took him in, never thinking he could live. But he did—and he was just like a child when he got well. He hadn't memory or intellect or reason. They tried to find out who he was but they never could. He couldn't even tell them his name—he could only say a few simple words. He had a letter on him beginning 'Dear Dick' and signed 'Leslie,' but there was no address on it and the envelope was gone. They let him stay on—he learned to do a few odd jobs about the place—and there Captain Jim found him. He brought him home—and I've always said it was a bad day's work, though I s'pose there was nothing else he could do. He thought maybe when Dick got home and saw his old surroundings and familiar faces his memory would wake up. But it hadn't any effect. There he's been at the house up the brook ever since. He's just like a child, no more nor less. Takes fractious spells occasionally, but mostly he's just vacant and good humoured and harmless. He's apt to run away if he isn't watched. That's the burden Leslie has had to carry for eleven years—and all alone. Old Abner Moore died soon after Dick was brought home and it was found he was almost bankrupt. When things were settled up there was nothing for Leslie and Dick but the old West farm. Leslie rented it to John Ward, and the rent is all she has to live on. Sometimes in summer she takes a boarder to help out. But most visitors prefer the other side of the harbour where the hotels and summer cottages are. Leslie's house is too far from the bathing shore. She's taken care of Dick and she's never been away from him for eleven years—she's tied to that imbecile for life. And after all the dreams and hopes she once had! You can imagine what it has been like for her, Anne, dearie—with her beauty and spirit and pride and cleverness. It's just been a living death."

"Poor, poor girl!" said Anne again. Her own happiness seemed to reproach her. What right had she to be so happy when another human soul must be so miserable?

"Will you tell me just what Leslie said and how she acted the night you met her on the shore?" asked Miss Cornelia.

She listened intently and nodded her satisfaction.

"*You* thought she was stiff and cold, Anne dearie, but I can tell you she thawed out wonderful for her. She must have taken to you real strong. I'm so glad. You may be able to help her a good deal. I was thankful when I heard that a young couple was coming to this house, for I hoped it would mean some friends for Leslie; especially if you belonged to the race that knows Joseph. You *will* be her friend, won't you, Anne, dearie?"

"Indeed I will, if she'll let me," said Anne, with all her own sweet, impulsive earnestness.

"No, you must be her friend, whether she'll let you or not," said Miss Cornelia resolutely. "Don't you mind if she's stiff by times—don't notice it. Remember what her life has been—and is—and must always be, I suppose, for creatures like Dick Moore live forever, I understand. You should see how fat he's got since he came home. He used to be lean enough. Just *make* her be friends—you can do it—you're one of those who have the knack. Only you mustn't be sensitive. And don't mind if she doesn't seem to want you to go over there much. She knows that some women don't like to be where Dick is—they complain he gives them the creeps. Just get her to come over here as often as she can. She can't get away so very much—she can't leave Dick long, for the Lord knows what he'd do—burn the house down most likely. At nights, after he's in bed and asleep, is about the only time she's free. He always goes to bed early and sleeps like the dead till next morning. That is how you came to meet her at the shore likely. She wanders there considerable."

"I will do everything I can for her," said Anne. Her interest in Leslie Moore, which had been vivid ever since she had seen her driving her geese down the hill, was intensified a thousand fold by Miss Cornelia's narration. The girl's beauty and sorrow and loneliness drew her with an irresistible fascination. She had never known anyone like her; her friends had hitherto been wholesome, normal, merry girls like herself, with only the average trials of human care and bereavement to shadow their girlish dreams. Leslie Moore stood apart, a tragic appealing figure of thwarted womanhood. Anne resolved that she would win entrance into the kingdom of that lonely soul and find there the comradeship it could so richly give, were it not for the cruel fetters that held it in a prison not of its own making.

"And mind you this, Anne, dearie," said Miss Cornelia, who had not yet wholly relieved her mind. "You mustn't think Leslie is an infidel because she hardly ever goes to church—or even that she's a Methodist. She can't take Dick to church, of course—not that he ever troubled church much in his best days. But you just remember that she's a real strong Presbyterian at heart, Anne, dearie."

Leslie Comes Over

L eslie came over to the house of dreams one frosty October night, when moonlit mists were hanging over the harbour and curling like silver ribbons along the seaward glens. She looked as if she repented coming when Gilbert answered her knock; but Anne flew past him, pounced on her, and drew her in.

"I'm so glad you picked tonight for a call," she said gaily. "I made up a lot of extra good fudge this afternoon and we want someone to help us eat it—before the fire—while we tell stories. Perhaps Captain Jim will drop in, too. This is his night."

"No. Captain Jim is over home," said Leslie. "He—he made me come here," she added, half defiantly.

"I'll say a thank-you to him for that when I see him," said Anne, pulling easy chairs before the fire.

"Oh, I don't mean that I didn't want to come," protested Leslie, flushing a little. "I—I've been thinking of coming— but it isn't always easy for me to get away."

"Of course it must be hard for you to leave Mr. Moore," said Anne, in a matter-of-fact tone. She had decided that it would be best to mention Dick Moore occasionally as an accepted fact, and not give undue morbidness to the subject by avoiding it. She was right, for Leslie's air of constraint suddenly vanished. Evidently she had been wondering how much Anne knew of the conditions of her life and was relieved that no explanations were needed. She allowed her cap and jacket to be taken, and sat down with a girlish snuggle in the big armchair by Magog. She was dressed prettily and carefully, with the customary touch of colour in the scarlet geranium at her white throat. Her beautiful hair gleamed like molten gold in the warm firelight. Her sea-blue eyes were full of soft laughter and allurement. For the moment, under the influence of the little house of dreams, she was a girl again—a girl forgetful of the past and its bitterness. The atmosphere of the many loves that had sanctified the little house was all about her; the companionship of two healthy, happy, young folks of her own generation encircled her; she felt and yielded to the magic of her surroundings—Miss Cornelia and Captain Jim would scarcely have recognized her; Anne found it hard to believe that this was the cold, unresponsive woman she had met on the shore—this animated girl who talked and listened with the eagerness of a starved soul. And how hungrily Leslie's eyes looked at the bookcases between the windows!

"Our library isn't very extensive," said Anne, "but every book in it is a *friend*. We've picked our books up through the years, here and there, never buying one until we had first read it and knew that it belonged to the race of Joseph."

Leslie laughed—beautiful laughter that seemed akin to all the mirth that had echoed through the little house in the vanished years.

"I have a few books of father's—not many," she said. "I've read them until I know them almost by heart. I don't get many books. There's a circulating library at the Glen store—but I don't think the committee who pick the books for Mr. Parker know what books are of Joseph's race—or perhaps they don't care. It was so seldom I got one I really liked that I gave up getting any."

"I hope you'll look on our bookshelves as your own," said Anne. "You are entirely and wholeheartedly welcome to the loan of any book on them."

"You are setting a feast of fat things before me," said Leslie, joyously. Then, as the clock struck ten, she rose, half unwillingly.

"I must go. I didn't realize it was so late. Captain Jim is always saying it doesn't take long to stay an hour. But I stayed two—and oh, but I've enjoyed them," she added frankly.

"Come often," said Anne and Gilbert. They had risen and stood together in the firelight's glow. Leslie looked at them—youthful, hopeful, happy, typifying all she had missed and must forever miss. The light went out of her face and eyes; the girl vanished; it was the sorrowful, cheated woman who answered the invitation almost coldly and got herself away with a pitiful haste.

Anne watched her until she was lost in the shadows of the chill and misty night. Then she turned slowly back to the glow of her own radiant hearthstone.

"Isn't she lovely, Gilbert? Her hair fascinates me. Miss Cornelia says it reaches to her feet. Ruby Gillis had beautiful hair—but Leslie's is *alive*—every thread of it is living gold."

"She is very beautiful," agreed Gilbert, so heartily that Anne almost wished he was a *little* less enthusiastic.

"Gilbert, would you like my hair better if it were like Leslie's?" she asked wistfully.

"I wouldn't have your hair any colour but just what it is for the world," said Gilbert, with one or two convincing accompaniments. "You wouldn't be *Anne* if you had golden hair—or hair of any colour but"—

"Red," said Anne, with gloomy satisfaction.

"Yes, red—to give warmth to that milk-white skin and those shining gray-green eyes of yours. Golden hair wouldn't suit you at all, Queen Anne—*my* Queen Anne—queen of my heart and life and home."

"Then you may admire Leslie's all you like," said Anne magnanimously.

XIII

A Ghostly Evening

One evening, a week later, Anne decided to run over the fields to the house up the brook for an informal call. It was an evening of gray fog that had crept in from the gulf, swathed the harbour, filled the glens and valleys, and clung heavily to the autumnal meadows. Through it the sea sobbed and shuddered. Anne saw Four Winds in a new aspect, and found it weird and mysterious and fascinating; but it also gave her a little feeling of loneliness. Gilbert was away and would be away until the morrow, attending a medical pow-wow in Charlottetown. Anne longed for an hour of fellowship with some girlfriend. Captain Jim and Miss Cornelia were "good fellows" each, in their own way; but youth yearned to youth.

"If only Diana or Phil or Pris or Stella could drop in for a chat," she said to herself, "how delightful it would be! This is such a *ghostly* night. I'm sure all the ships that ever sailed out of Four Winds to their doom could be seen tonight sailing up the harbour with their drowned crews on their decks, if that shrouding fog could suddenly be drawn aside. I feel as

if it concealed innumerable mysteries—as if I were surrounded by the wraiths of old generations of Four Winds
people peering at me through that gray veil. If ever the dear
dead ladies of this little house came back to revisit it they
would come on just such a night as this. If I sit here any longer
I'll see one of them there opposite me in Gilbert's chair. This
place isn't exactly canny tonight. Even Gog and Magog have
an air of pricking up their ears to hear the footsteps of unseen
guests. I'll run over to see Leslie before I frighten myself with
my own fancies, as I did long ago in the matter of the Haunted
Wood. I'll leave my house of dreams to welcome back its old
inhabitants. My fire will give them my good-will and greeting—they will be gone before I come back, and my house
will be mine once more. Tonight I am sure it is keeping a tryst
with the past."

Laughing a little over her fancy, yet with something of a
creepy sensation in the region of her spine, Anne kissed her
hand to Gog and Magog and slipped out into the fog, with
some of the new magazines under her arm for Leslie.

"Leslie's wild for books and magazines," Miss Cornelia
had told her, "and she hardly ever sees one. She can't afford
to buy them or subscribe for them. She's really pitifully poor,
Anne. I don't see how she makes out to live at all on the little
rent the farm brings in. She never even hints a complaint on
the score of poverty, but I know what it must be. She's been
handicapped by it all her life. She didn't mind it when she was
free and ambitious, but it must gall now, believe *me*. I'm glad
she seemed so bright and merry the evening she spent with
you. Captain Jim told me he had fairly to put her cap and coat
on and push her out of the door. Don't be too long going to

see her either. If you are she'll think it's because you don't like
the sight of Dick, and she'll crawl into her shell again. Dick's
a great, big, harmless baby, but that silly grin and chuckle of
his do get on some people's nerves. Thank goodness, I've no
nerves myself. I like Dick Moore better now than I ever did
when he was in his right senses—though the Lord knows
that isn't saying much. I was down there one day in house-
cleaning time helping Leslie a bit, and I was frying doughnuts. Dick was hanging round to get one, as usual, and all at
once he picked up a scalding hot one I'd just fished out and
dropped it on the back of my neck when I was bending over.
Then he laughed and laughed. Believe *me*, Anne, it took all
the grace of God in my heart to keep me from just whisking
up that stew-pan of boiling fat and pouring it over his head."

Anne laughed over Miss Cornelia's wrath as she sped
through the darkness. But laughter accorded ill with that
night. She was sober enough when she reached the house
among the willows. Everything was very silent. The front
part of the house seemed dark and deserted, so Anne slipped
round the side door, which opened from the veranda into a
little sitting room. There she halted noiselessly.

The door was open. Beyond, in the dimly lighted room,
sat Leslie Moore, with her arms flung out on the table and her
head bent upon them. She was weeping horribly—with low,
fierce, choking sobs, as if some agony in her soul were trying
to tear itself out. An old black dog was sitting by her, his nose
resting on her lap, his big doggish eyes full of mute, imploring sympathy and devotion. Anne drew back in dismay. She
felt that she could not intermeddle with this bitterness. Her
heart ached with a sympathy she might not utter. To go in

now would be to shut the door forever on any possible help or friendship. Some instinct warned Anne that the proud, bitter girl would never forgive the one who thus surprised her in her abandonment of despair.

Anne slipped noiselessly from the veranda and found her way across the yard. Beyond, she heard voices in the gloom and saw the dim glow of a light. At the gate she met two men—Captain Jim with a lantern, and another who she knew must be Dick Moore—a big man, badly gone to fat, with a broad, round, red face, and vacant eyes. Even in the dull light Anne got the impression that there was something unusual about his eyes.

"Is this you, Mistress Blythe?" said Captain Jim. "Now, now, you hadn't oughter be roaming about alone on a night like this. You could get lost in this fog easier than not. Jest you wait till I see Dick safe inside the door and I'll come back and light you over the fields. I ain't going to have Dr. Blythe coming home and finding that you walked clean over Cape Leforce in the fog. A woman did that once, forty years ago."

"So you've been over to see Leslie," he said, when he rejoined her.

"I didn't go in," said Anne, and told what she had seen. Captain Jim sighed.

"Poor, poor, little girl! She don't cry often, Mistress Blythe—she's too brave for that. She must feel terrible when she does cry. A night like this is hard on poor women who have sorrows. There's something about it that kinder brings up all we've suffered—or feared."

"It's full of ghosts," said Anne, with a shiver. "That was why I came over—I wanted to clasp a human hand and hear

a human voice. There seem to be so many *inhuman* presences
about tonight. Even my own dear house was full of them.
They fairly elbowed me out. So I fled over here for companionship of my kind."

"You were right not to go in, though, Mistress Blythe.
Leslie wouldn't have liked it. She wouldn't have liked me going
in with Dick, as I'd have done if I hadn't met you. I had Dick
down with me all day. I keep him with me as much as I can to
help Leslie a bit."

"Isn't there something odd about his eyes?" asked Anne.

"You noticed that? Yes, one is blue and t'other is hazel—
his father had the same. It's a Moore peculiarity. That was what
told me he was Dick Moore when I saw him first down in
Cuby. If it hadn't a-bin for his eyes I mightn't a-known him,
what with his beard and fat. You know, I reckon, that it was me
found him and brought him home. Miss Cornelia always says I
shouldn't have done it, but I can't agree with her. It was the
right thing to do—and so 'twas the only thing. There ain't no
question in my mind about *that*. But my old heart aches for
Leslie. She's only twenty-eight and she's eaten more bread
with sorrow than most women do in eighty years."

They walked on in silence for a little while. Presently Anne
said, "Do you know, Captain Jim, I never like walking with a
lantern. I have always the strangest feeling that just outside the
circle of light, just over its edge in the darkness, I am surrounded by a ring of furtive, sinister things, watching me from
the shadows with hostile eyes. I've had that feeling from childhood. What is the reason? I never feel like that when I'm really
in the darkness—when it is close all around me—I'm not the
least frightened."

"I've something of that feeling myself," admitted Captain Jim. "I reckon when the darkness is close to us it is a friend. But when we sorter push it away from us—divorce ourselves from it, so to speak, with lantern light—it becomes an enemy. But the fog is lifting. There's a smart west wind rising, if you notice. The stars will be out when you get home."

They were out; and when Anne re-entered her house of dreams the red embers were still glowing on the hearth, and all the haunting presences were gone.

November Days

The splendour of colour which had glowed for weeks along the shores of Four Winds Harbour had faded out into the soft gray-blue of late autumnal hills. There came many days when fields and shores were dim with misty rain, or shivering before the breath of a melancholy sea-wind—nights, too, of storm and tempest, when Anne sometimes wakened to pray that no ship might be beating up the grim north shore, for if it were so not even the great, faithful light, whirling through the darkness unafraid, could avail to guide it into safe haven.

"In November I sometimes feel as if spring could never come again," she sighed, grieving over the hopeless unsightliness of her frosted and bedraggled flower-plots. The gay little garden of the schoolmaster's bride was rather a forlorn place now, and the Lombardies and birches were under bare poles, as Captain Jim said. But the fir-wood behind the little house was forever green and staunch; and even in November and December there came gracious days of sunshine and purple hazes, when the harbour danced and sparkled as blithely as in midsummer, and the gulf was so softly blue and tender that the storm and the wild wind seemed only things of a long-past dream.

Anne and Gilbert spent many an autumn evening at the lighthouse. It was always a cheery place. Even when the east wind sang in minor and the sea was dead and gray, hints of sunshine seemed to be lurking all about it. Perhaps this was because the First Mate always paraded it in panoply of gold. He was so large and effulgent that one hardly missed the sun, and his resounding purrs formed a pleasant accompaniment to the laughter and conversation which went on around Captain Jim's fireplace. Captain Jim and Gilbert had many long discussions and high converse on matters beyond the ken of cat or king.

"I like to ponder on all kinds of problems, though I can't solve 'em," said Captain Jim. "My father held that we should never talk of things we couldn't understand, but if we didn't, Doctor, the subjects for conversation would be mighty few. I reckon the gods laugh many a time to hear us, but what matters so long as we remember that we're only men and don't take to fancying that we're gods ourselves, really, knowing good and evil. I reckon our pow-pows won't do us or anyone much harm, so let's have another whack at the whence, why and whither this evening, Doctor."

While they "whacked," Anne listened or dreamed. Sometimes Leslie went to the lighthouse with them, and she and Anne wandered along the shore in the eerie twilight, or sat on the rocks below the lighthouse until the darkness drove them back to the cheer of the driftwood fire. Then Captain Jim would brew them tea and tell them

> *"tales of land and sea*
> *And whatsoever might betide*
> *The great forgotten world outside."*

Leslie seemed always to enjoy those lighthouse carousals very much, and bloomed out for the time being into ready wit and beautiful laughter, or glowing-eyed silence. There was a certain tang and savour in the conversation when Leslie was present which they missed when she was absent. Even when she did not talk she seemed to inspire others to brilliancy. Captain Jim told his stories better, Gilbert was quicker in argument and repartee, Anne felt little gushes and trickles of fancy and imagination bubbling to her lips under the influence of Leslie's personality.

"That girl was born to be a leader in social and intellectual circles, far away from Four Winds," she said to Gilbert as they walked home one night. "She's just wasted here—wasted."

"Weren't you listening to Captain Jim and yours truly the other night when we discussed that subject generally? We came to the comforting conclusion that the Creator probably knew how to run His universe quite as well as we do, and that, after all, there are no such things as 'wasted' lives, saving and except when an individual wilfully squanders and wastes his own life—which Leslie Moore certainly hasn't done. And some people might think that a Redmond B.A., whom editors were beginning to honour, was 'wasted' as the wife of a struggling country doctor in the rural community of Four Winds."

"Gilbert!"

"If you had married Roy Gardner, now," continued Gilbert mercilessly, "*you* could have been 'a leader in social and intellectual circles far away from Four Winds.'"

"Gilbert *Blythe!*"

"You *know* you were in love with him at one time, Anne."

"Gilbert, that's mean—'p'isen mean, just like all the men,' as Miss Cornelia says. I *never* was in love with him. I only imagined I was. *You* know that. You *know* I'd rather be your wife in our house of dreams and fulfilment than a queen in a palace."

Gilbert's answer was not in words; but I am afraid that both of them forgot poor Leslie speeding her lonely way across the fields to a house that was neither a palace nor the fulfilment of a dream.

The moon was rising over the sad, dark sea behind them and transfiguring it. Her light had not yet reached the harbour, the further side of which was shadowy and suggestive, with dim coves and rich glooms and jewelling lights.

"How the homelights shine out tonight through the dark!" said Anne. "That string of them over the harbour looks like a necklace. And what a coruscation there is up at the Glen! Oh, look, Gilbert, there is ours. I'm so glad we left it burning. I hate to come home to a dark house. *Our* homelight, Gilbert! Isn't it lovely to see?"

"Just one of earth's many millions of homes, Anne-girl—but ours—*ours*—our beacon in 'a naughty world.' When a fellow has a home and a dear, little, red-haired wife in it what more need he ask of life?"

"Well, he might ask *one* thing more," whispered Anne happily. "Oh, Gilbert, it seems as if I just *couldn't* wait for the spring."

Christmas at Four Winds

At first Anne and Gilbert talked of going home to Avonlea for Christmas; but eventually they decided to stay in Four Winds. "I want to spend the first Christmas of our life together in our own home," decreed Anne.

So it fell out that Marilla and Mrs. Rachel Lynde and the twins came to Four Winds for Christmas. Marilla had the face of a woman who had circumnavigated the globe. She had never been sixty miles away from home before; and had never eaten a Christmas dinner anywhere save at Green Gables.

Mrs. Rachel had made and brought with her an enormous plum pudding. Nothing could have convinced Mrs. Rachel that a college graduate of the younger generation could make a Christmas plum pudding properly; but she bestowed approval on Anne's house.

"Anne's a good housekeeper," she said to Marilla in the spare room the night of their arrival. "I've looked into her bread box and her scrap pail. I always judge a housekeeper by those, that's what. There's nothing in the pail that shouldn't have been thrown away, and no stale pieces in the bread box.

Of course, she was trained up with you—but, then, she went to college afterwards. I notice she's got my tobacco stripe quilt on the bed here, and that big round braided mat of yours before her living-room fire. It makes me feel right at home."

Anne's first Christmas in her own house was as delightful as she could have wished. The day was fine and bright; the first skim of snow had fallen on Christmas Eve and made the world beautiful; the harbour was still open and glittering.

Captain Jim and Miss Cornelia came to dinner. Leslie and Dick had been invited, but Leslie made excuse; they always went to her Uncle Isaac West's for Christmas, she said.

"She'd rather have it so," Miss Cornelia told Anne. "She can't bear taking Dick where there are strangers. Christmas is always a hard time for Leslie. She and her father used to make a lot of it."

Miss Cornelia and Mrs. Rachel did not take a very violent fancy to each other. "Two suns hold not their courses in one sphere." But they did not clash at all, for Mrs. Rachel was in the kitchen helping Anne and Marilla with the dinner, and it fell to Gilbert to entertain Captain Jim and Miss Cornelia,—or rather to be entertained by them, for a dialogue between those two old friends and antagonists was assuredly never dull.

"It's many a year since there was a Christmas dinner here, Mistress Blythe," said Captain Jim. "Miss Russell always went to her friends in town for Christmas. But I was here to the first Christmas dinner that was ever eaten in this house— and the schoolmaster's bride cooked it. That was sixty years ago today, Mistress Blythe—and a day very like this—just enough snow to make the hills white, and the harbour as blue as June. I was only a lad, and I'd never been invited out to dinner before, and I was too shy to eat enough. I've got all over *that*."

"Most men do," said Miss Cornelia, sewing furiously. Miss Cornelia was not going to sit with idle hands, even on Christmas. Babies come without any consideration for holidays, and there was some expected in a poverty-stricken household at Glen St. Mary. Miss Cornelia had sent that household a substantial dinner for its little swarm, and so meant to eat her own with a comfortable conscience.

"Well, you know, the way to a man's heart is through his stomach, Cornelia," explained Captain Jim.

"I believe you—when he *has* a heart," retorted Miss Cornelia. "I suppose that's why so many women kill themselves cooking—just as poor Amelia Baxter did. She died last Christmas morning, and she said it was the first Christmas since she was married that she didn't have to cook a big, twenty-plate dinner. It must have been a real pleasant change for her. Well, she's been dead a year, so you'll soon hear of Horace Baxter taking notice."

"I heard he was taking notice already," said Captain Jim, winking at Gilbert. "Wasn't he up to your place one Sunday lately, with his funeral blacks on, and a boiled collar?"

"No, he wasn't. And he needn't come neither. I could have had him long ago when he was fresh. I don't want any second-hand goods, believe *me*. As for Horace Baxter, he was in financial difficulties a year ago last summer, and he prayed to the Lord for help; and when his wife died and he got her life insurance he said he believed it was the answer to his prayer. Wasn't that like a man?"

"Have you really proof that he said that, Cornelia?"

"I have the Methodist minister's word for it—if you call that proof. Robert Baxter told me the same thing too, but I admit *that* isn't evidence. Robert Baxter isn't often known to tell the truth."

"Come, come, Cornelia, I think he generally tells the truth, but he changes his opinion so often it sometimes sounds as if he didn't."

"It sounds like it mighty often, believe *me*. But trust one man to excuse another. I have no use for Robert Baxter. He turned Methodist just because the Presbyterian choir happened to be singing 'Behold the bridegroom cometh' for a collection piece when him and Margaret walked up the aisle the Sunday after they were married. Served him right for being late! He always insisted the choir did it on purpose to insult him, as if he was of that much importance. But that family always thought they were much bigger potatoes than they really were. His brother Eliphalet imagined the devil was always at his elbow—but *I* never believed the devil wasted that much time on him."

"I—don't—know," said Captain Jim thoughtfully. "Eliphalet Baxter lived too much alone—hadn't even a cat or dog to keep him human. When a man is alone he's mighty apt to be with the devil—if he ain't with God. He has to choose which company he'll keep, I reckon. If the devil always was at Life Baxter's elbow it must have been because Life liked to have him there."

"Man-like," said Miss Cornelia, and subsided into silence over a complicated arrangement of tucks until Captain Jim deliberately stirred her up again by remarking in a casual way:

"I was up to the Methodist church last Sunday morning."

"You'd better have been home reading your Bible," was Miss Cornelia's retort.

"Come now, Cornelia, *I* can't see any harm in going to the Methodist church when there's no preaching in your own. I've been a Presbyterian for seventy-six years, and it isn't likely my theology will hoist anchor at this late day."

"It's setting a bad example," said Miss Cornelia grimly.

"Besides," continued wicked Captain Jim, "I wanted to hear some good singing. The Methodists have a good choir; and you can't deny, Cornelia, that the singing in our church is awful since the split in the choir."

"What if the singing isn't good? They're doing their best, and God sees no difference between the voice of a crow and the voice of a nightingale."

"Come, come, Cornelia," said Captain Jim mildly, "I've a better opinion of the Almighty's ear for music than *that*."

"What caused the trouble in our choir?" asked Gilbert, who was suffering from suppressed laughter.

"It dates back to the new church, three years ago," answered Captain Jim. "We had a fearful time over the building of that church—fell out over the question of a new site. The two sites wasn't more'n two hundred yards apart, but you'd have thought they was a thousand by the bitterness of that fight. We was split up into three factions—one wanted the east site and one the south, and one held to the old. It was fought out in bed and at board, and in church and at market. All the old scandals of three generations were dragged out of their graves and aired. Three matches was broken up by it. And the meetings we had to try to settle the question! Cornelia, will you ever forget the one when old Luther Burns got up and made a speech? *He* stated his opinions forcibly."

"Call a spade a spade, Captain. You mean he got red-mad and raked them all, fore and aft. They deserved it too—a pack of incapables. But what would you expect of a committee of men? That building committee held twenty-seven meetings, and at the end of the twenty-seventh weren't no nearer having a church than when they begun—not so near, for a fact, for in one fit of hurrying things along they'd gone to work and tore the old church down, so there we were, without a church, and no place but the hall to worship in."

"The Methodists offered us their church, Cornelia."

"The Glen St. Mary church wouldn't have been built to this day," went on Miss Cornelia, ignoring Captain Jim, "if we women hadn't just started in and took charge. We said *we* meant to have a church, if the men meant to quarrel till doomsday, and we were tired of being a laughing-stock for the Methodists. We held *one* meeting and elected a committee and canvassed for subscriptions. We got them, too. When any of the men tried to sass us we told them they'd tried for two years to build a church and it was our turn now. We shut them up close, believe *me*, and in six months we had our church. Of course when the men saw we were determined they stopped fighting and went to work, man-like, as soon as they saw they had to, or quit bossing. Oh, women can't preach or be elders; but they can build churches and scare up the money for them."

"The Methodists allow women to preach," said Captain Jim.

Miss Cornelia glared at him.

"I never said the Methodists hadn't common sense, Captain. What I say is, I doubt if they have much religion."

"I suppose you are in favour of votes for women, Miss Cornelia," said Gilbert.

"I'm not hankering after the vote, believe *me*," said Miss Cornelia scornfully, "*I* know what it is to clean up after the men. But some of these days, when the men realize they've got the world into a mess they can't get it out of, they'll be glad to give us the vote, and shoulder their troubles over on us. That's *their* scheme. Oh, it's well that women are patient, believe *me*!"

"What about Job?" suggested Captain Jim.

"Job! It was such a rare thing to find a patient man that when one was really discovered they were determined he shouldn't be forgotten," retorted Miss Cornelia triumphantly. "Anyhow, the virtue doesn't go with the name. There never was such an impatient man born as old Job Taylor over harbour."

"Well, you know, he had a good deal to try him, Cornelia. Even you can't defend his wife. I always remember what old William MacAllister said of her at her funeral, 'There's nae doot she was a Chreestian wumman, but she had the de'il's own temper.'"

"I suppose she *was* trying," admitted Miss Cornelia reluctantly, "but that didn't justify what Job said when she died. He rode home from the graveyard the day of the funeral with my father. He never said a word till they got near home. Then he heaved a big sigh and said, 'You may not believe it, Stephen, but this is the happiest day of my life!' Wasn't that like a man?"

"I s'pose poor old Mrs. Job did make life kinder uneasy for him," reflected Captain Jim.

"Well, there's such a thing as decency, isn't there? Even if a man is rejoicing in his heart over his wife being dead, he needn't proclaim it to the four winds of heaven. And happy day or not, Job Taylor wasn't long in marrying again, you might notice. His second wife could manage him. She made him walk Spanish, believe me! The first thing she did was to make him hustle round and put up a tombstone to the first Mrs. Job—and she had a place left on it for her own name. She said there'd be nobody to make Job put up a monument to *her*."

"Speaking of Taylors, how is Mrs. Lewis Taylor up at the Glen, Doctor?" asked Captain Jim.

"She's getting better slowly—but she has to work too hard," replied Gilbert.

"Her husband works hard too—raising prize pigs," said Miss Cornelia. "He's noted for his beautiful pigs. He's a heap prouder of his pigs than of his children. But then, to be sure, his pigs are the best pigs possible, while his children don't amount to much. He picked a poor mother for them, and starved her while she was bearing and rearing them. His pigs got the cream and his children got the skim milk."

"There are times, Cornelia, when I have to agree with you, though it hurts me," said Captain Jim. "That's just exactly the truth about Lewis Taylor. When I see those poor, miserable children of his, robbed of all children ought to have, it p'isens my own bite and sup for days afterwards."

Gilbert went out to the kitchen in response to Anne's beckoning. Anne shut the door and gave him a connubial lecture.

"Gilbert, you and Captain Jim must stop baiting Miss Cornelia. Oh, I've been listening to you—and I just won't allow it."

"Anne, Miss Cornelia is enjoying herself hugely. You know she is."

"Well, never mind. You two needn't egg her on like that. Dinner is ready now, and Gilbert, *don't* let Mrs. Rachel carve the geese. I know she means to offer to do it because she doesn't think you can do it properly. Show her you can."

"I ought to be able to. I've been studying A-B-C-D diagrams of carving for the past month," said Gilbert. "Only don't talk to me while I'm doing it, Anne, for if you drive the letters out of my head I'll be in a worse predicament than you were in old geometry days when the teacher changed them."

Gilbert carved the geese beautifully. Even Mrs. Rachel had to admit that. And everybody ate of them and enjoyed them. Anne's first Christmas dinner was a great success and she beamed with housewifely pride. Merry was the feast and long; and when it was over they gathered around the cheer of the red hearth flame and Captain Jim told them stories until the red sun swung low over Four Winds Harbour, and the long shadows of the Lombardies fell across the snow in the lane.

"I must be getting back to the light," he said finally. "I'll jest have time to walk home before sun-down. Thank you for a beautiful Christmas, Mistress Blythe. Bring Master Davy down to the light some night before he goes home."

"I want to see those stone gods," said Davy with a relish.

New Year's Eve at the Light

The Green Gables folk went home after Christmas, Marilla under solemn covenant to return for a month in the spring. More snow came before New Year's, and the harbour froze over, but the gulf still was free, beyond the white, imprisoned fields. The last day of the old year was one of those bright, cold dazzling winter days, which bombard us with their brilliancy, and command our admiration but never our love. The sky was sharp and blue; the snow diamonds sparkled insistently; the stark trees were bare and shameless, with a kind of brazen beauty; the hills shot assaulting lances of crystal. Even the shadows were sharp and stiff and clear-cut, as no proper shadows should be. Everything that was handsome seemed ten times handsomer and less attractive in the glaring splendour; and everything that was ugly seemed ten times uglier, and everything was either handsome or ugly. There was no soft blending, or kind obscurity, or elusive mistiness in that searching glitter. The only things that held their own individuality were the firs—for the fir is the tree of mystery and shadows, and yields never to the encroachments of crude radiance.

But finally the day began to realize that she was growing old. Then a certain pensiveness fell over her beauty which dimmed yet intensified it; sharp angles, glittering points, melted away into curves and enticing gleams. The white harbour put on soft grays and pinks; the far-away hills turned amethyst.

"The old year is going away beautifully," said Anne. She and Leslie and Gilbert were on their way to the Four Winds Point, having plotted with Captain Jim to watch the New Year in at the light. The sun had set and in the southwestern sky hung Venus, glorious and golden, having drawn as near to her earth-sister as is possible for her. For the first time Anne and Gilbert saw the shadow cast by that brilliant star of evening, that faint, mysterious shadow, never seen save when there is white snow to reveal it, and then only with averted vision, vanishing when you gaze at it directly.

"It's like the spirit of a shadow, isn't it?" whispered Anne. "You can see it so plainly haunting your side when you look ahead; but when you turn and look at it—it's gone."

"I have heard that you can see the shadow of Venus only once in a lifetime, and that within a year of seeing it your life's most wonderful gift will come to you," said Leslie. But she spoke rather hardly; perhaps she thought that even the shadow of Venus could bring her no gift of life. Anne smiled in the soft twilight; she felt quite sure what the mystic shadow promised her.

They found Marshall Elliott at the lighthouse. At first Anne felt inclined to resent the intrusion of this long-haired, long-bearded eccentric into the familiar little circle. But Marshall Elliott soon proved his legitimate claim to membership in the household of Joseph. He was a witty, intelligent, well-read man, rivalling Captain Jim himself in the knack of telling a good story. They were all glad when he agreed to watch the old year out with them.

Captain Jim's small nephew Joe had come down to spend New Year's with his great-uncle, and had fallen asleep on the sofa with the First Mate curled up in a huge golden ball at his feet.

"Ain't he a dear little man?" said Captain Jim gloatingly. "I do love to watch a little child asleep, Mistress Blythe. It's the most beautiful sight in the world, I reckon. Joe does love to get down here for a night, because I have him sleep with me. At home he has to sleep with the other two boys, and he doesn't like it. 'Why can't I sleep with father, Uncle Jim?' say he. 'Everybody in the Bible sleep with their fathers.' As for the questions he asks, the minister himself couldn't answer them. They fair swamp me. 'Uncle Jim, if I wasn't *me* who'd I be?' and, 'Uncle Jim, what would happen if God died?' He fired them two off at me tonight, afore he went to sleep. As for his imagination, it sails away from everything. He makes up the most remarkable yarns—and then his mother shuts him up in the closet for telling stories. And he sits down and makes up another one, and has it ready to relate to her when she lets him out. He had one for me when he come down tonight. 'Uncle Jim,' says he, solemn as a tombstone, 'I had a 'venture in the Glen today.' 'Yes, what was it?' says I, expecting something quite startling, but nowise prepared for what I really got. 'I met a wolf in the street,' says he, 'a normous wolf with a big, red mouf and *awful* long teeth, Uncle Jim.' 'I didn't know there was any wolves up at the Glen,' says I. 'Oh, he comed there from far, far away,' says Joe, 'and I fought he was going to eat me up, Uncle Jim.' 'Were you scared?' says I. 'No, 'cause I had a big gun,' says Joe, 'and I shot the wolf dead, Uncle Jim,—solid dead—and then he went up to heaven and bit God,' says he. Well, I was fair staggered, Mistress Blythe."

The hours bloomed into mirth around the driftwood fire. Captain Jim told tales, and Marshall Elliott sang old Scotch ballads in a fine tenor voice; finally Captain Jim took down his old brown fiddle from the wall and began to play. He had a tolerable knack of fiddling, which all appreciated save the First Mate, who sprang from the sofa as if he had been shot, emitted a shriek of protest, and fled wildly up the stairs.

"Can't cultivate an ear for music in that cat nohow," said Captain Jim. "He won't stay long enough to learn to like it. When we got the organ up at the Glen church old Elder Richards bounced up from his seat the minute the organist began to play and scuttled down the aisle and out of the church at the rate of no-man's-business. It reminded me so strong of the First Mate tearing loose as soon as I begin to fiddle that I come nearer to laughing out loud in church than I ever did before or since."

There was something so infectious in the rollicking tunes which Captain Jim played that very soon Marshall Elliott's feet began to twitch. He had been a noted dancer in his youth. Presently he started up and held out his hands to Leslie. Instantly she responded. Round and round the firelit room they circled with a rhythmic grace that was wonderful. Leslie danced like one inspired; the wild, sweet abandon of the music seemed to have entered into and possessed her. Anne watched her in fascinated admiration. She had never seen her like this. All the innate richness and colour and charm of her nature seemed to have broken loose and overflowed in crimson cheek and glowing eye and grace of motion. Even the aspect of Marshall Elliott, with his long beard and hair, could not spoil the picture. On the contrary, it seemed to enhance it. Marshall Elliott looked like a Viking of elder days, dancing with one of the blue-eyed golden-haired daughters of the Northland.

"The purtiest dancing I ever saw, and I've seen some in my time," declared Captain Jim, when at last the bow fell from his tired hand. Leslie dropped into her chair, laughing, breathless.

"I love dancing," she said apart to Anne. "I haven't danced since I was sixteen—but I love it. The music seems to run through my veins like quicksilver and I forget everything— everything—except the delight of keeping time to it. There isn't any floor beneath me, or roof over me—I'm floating amid the stars."

Captain Jim hung his fiddle up in its place, beside a large frame enclosing several banknotes.

"Is there anybody else of your acquaintance who can afford to hang his walls with banknotes for pictures?" he asked. "There's twenty ten-dollar notes there, not worth the glass over them. They're old Bank of P. E. Island notes. Had them by me when the bank failed, and I had 'em framed and hung up, partly as a reminder not to put your trust in banks, and partly to give me a real luxurious, millionairy feeling. Hullo, Matey, don't be scared. You can come back now. The music and revelry is over for tonight. The old year has just another hour to stay with us. I've seen seventy-six New Years come in over that gulf yonder, Mistress Blythe."

"You'll see a hundred," said Marshall Elliott.

Captain Jim shook his head.

"No; and I don't want to—at least, I think I don't. Death

grows friendlier as we grow older. Not that one of us really wants to die though, Marshall. Tennyson spoke truth when he said that. There's old Mrs. Wallace up at the Glen. She's had heaps of trouble all her life, poor soul, and she's lost almost everyone she cared about. She's always saying that she'll be glad when her time comes, and she doesn't want to sojourn any longer in this vale of tears. But when she takes a sick spell there's a fuss! Doctors from town, and a trained nurse, and enough medicine to kill a dog. Life may be a vale of tears, all right, but there are some folks who enjoy weeping, I reckon."

They spent the old year's last hour quietly around the fire. A few minutes before twelve Captain Jim rose and opened the door.

"We must let the New Year in," he said.

Outside was a fine blue night. A sparkling ribbon of moonlight garlanded the gulf. Inside the bar the harbour shone like a pavement of pearl. They stood before the door and waited— Captain Jim with his ripe, full experience, Marshall Elliott in his vigorous but empty middle life, Gilbert and Anne with their precious memories and exquisite hopes, Leslie with her record of starved years and her hopeless future. The clock on the little shelf above the fireplace struck twelve.

"Welcome, New Year," said Captain Jim, bowing low as the last stroke died away. "I wish you all the best year of your lives, mates. I reckon that whatever the New Year brings us will be the best the Great Captain has for us—and somehow or other we'll all make port in a good harbour."

A Four Winds Winter

Winter set in vigorously after New Year's. Big, white drifts heaped themselves about the little house, and palms of frost covered its windows. The harbour ice grew harder and thicker, until the Four Winds people began their usual winter travelling over it. The safe ways were "bushed" by a benevolent Government, and night and day the gay tinkle of the sleigh bells sounded on it. On moonlit nights Anne heard them in her house of dreams like fairy chimes. The gulf froze over, and the Four Winds light flashed no more. During the months when navigation was closed Captain Jim's office was a sinecure.

"The First Mate and I will have nothing to do till spring except keep warm and amuse ourselves. The last lighthouse keeper used always to move up to the Glen in winter; but I'd rather stay at the Point. The First Mate might get poisoned or chewed up by dogs at the Glen. It's a mite lonely, to be sure, with neither the light nor the water for company, but if our friends come to see us often we'll weather it through."

Captain Jim had an ice boat, and many a wild, glorious

spin Gilbert and Anne and Leslie had over the glib harbour ice with him. Anne and Leslie took long snowshoe tramps together, too, over the fields, or across the harbour after storms, or through the woods beyond the Glen. They were very good comrades in their rambles and their fireside communings. Each had something to give the other—each felt life the richer for friendly exchange of thought and friendly silence; each looked across the white fields between their homes with a pleasant consciousness of a friend beyond. But, in spite of all this, Anne felt that there was always a barrier between Leslie and herself—a constraint that never wholly vanished.

"I don't know why I can't get closer to her," Anne said one evening to Captain Jim. "I like her so much—I admire her so much—I *want* to take her right into my heart and creep right into hers. But I can never cross the barrier."

"You've been too happy all your life, Mistress Blythe," said Captain Jim thoughtfully. "I reckon that's why you and Leslie can't get real close together in your souls. The barrier between you is her experience of sorrow and trouble. She ain't responsible for it and you ain't; but it's there and neither of you can cross it."

"My childhood wasn't very happy before I came to Green Gables," said Anne, gazing soberly out of the window at the still, sad, dead beauty of the leafless tree-shadows on the moonlit snow.

"Mebbe not—but it was just the usual unhappiness of a child who hasn't anyone to look after it properly. There hasn't been any *tragedy* in your life, Mistress Blythe. And poor Leslie's has been almost *all* tragedy. She feels, I reckon, though mebbe she hardly knows she feels it, that there's a vast deal in her life you can't enter nor understand—and so she has to keep you back from it—hold you off, so to speak, from hurting her. You know if we've got anything about us that hurts we shrink from anyone's touch on or near it. It holds good with our souls as well as our bodies, I reckon. Leslie's soul must be near raw—it's no wonder she hides it away."

"If that were really all, I wouldn't mind, Captain Jim. I would understand. But there are times—not always, but now and again—when I almost have to believe that Leslie doesn't—doesn't like me. Sometimes I surprise a look in her eyes that seems to show resentment and dislike—it goes so quickly—but I've seen it, I'm sure of that. And it hurts me, Captain Jim. I'm not used to being disliked—and I've tried so hard to win Leslie's friendship."

"You have won it, Mistress Blythe. Don't you go cherishing any foolish notion that Leslie don't like you. If she didn't she wouldn't have anything to do with you, much less chumming with you as she does. I know Leslie Moore too well not to be sure of that."

"The first time I ever saw her, driving her geese down the hill on the day I came to Four Winds, she looked at me with the same expression," persisted Anne. "I felt it, even in the midst of my admiration of her beauty. She looked at me resentfully—she did, indeed, Captain Jim."

"The resentment must have been about something else, Mistress Blythe, and you jest come in for a share of it because you happened past. Leslie *does* take sullen spells now and again, poor girl. I can't blame her, when I know what she has to put up with. I don't know why it's permitted. The doctor and I have talked a lot about the origin of evil, but we haven't quite found out all about it yet. There's a vast of onunderstandable things in life, ain't there, Mistress Blythe? Sometimes things seem to work out real proper-like, same as with you and the doctor. And then again they all seem to go catawampus. There's Leslie, so clever and beautiful you'd think she was meant for a queen, and instead she's cooped up over there, robbed of almost everything a woman'd value, with no prospect except waiting on Dick Moore all her life. Though, mind you, Mistress Blythe, I daresay she'd choose her life now, such as it is, rather than the life she lived with Dick before he went away. *That's* something a clumsy old sailor's tongue mustn't meddle with. But you've helped Leslie a lot— she's a different creature since you come to Four Winds. Us old friends see the difference in her, as you can't. Miss Cornelia and me was talking it over the other day, and it's one of the mighty few p'ints that we see eye to eye on. So jest you throw overboard any idea of her not liking you."

Anne could hardly discard it completely, for there were undoubtedly times when she felt, with an instinct that was not to be combatted by reason, that Leslie harboured a queer, indefinable resentment towards her. At times, this secret consciousness marred the delight of their comradeship; at others it was almost forgotten; but Anne always felt the hidden thorn was there, and might prick her at any moment. She felt a cruel sting from it on the day when she told Leslie of what she hoped the spring would bring to the little house of dreams. Leslie looked at her with hard, bitter, unfriendly eyes.

"So you are to have *that*, too," she said in a choked voice. And without another word she had turned and gone across the fields homeward. Anne was deeply hurt; for the moment she felt as if she could never like Leslie again. But when Leslie came over a few evenings later she was so pleasant, so friendly, so frank, and witty, and winsome, that Anne was charmed into forgiveness and forgetfulness. Only, she never mentioned her darling hope to Leslie again; nor did Leslie ever refer to it.

But one evening, when late winter was listening for the word of spring, she came over to the little house for a twilight chat; and when she went away she left a small, white box on the table. Anne found it after she was gone and opened it wonderingly. In it was a tiny white dress of exquisite workmanship— delicate embroidery, wonderful tucking, sheer loveliness. Every stitch in it was handwork; and the little frills of lace at neck and sleeves were of real Valençiennes. Lying on it was a card—"with Leslie's love."

"What hours of work she must have put on it," said Anne. "And the material must have cost more than she could really afford. It is very sweet of her."

But Leslie was brusque and curt when Anne thanked her, and again the latter felt thrown back upon herself.

Leslie's gift was not alone in the little house. Miss Cornelia had, for the time being, given up sewing for unwanted, unwelcome eighth babies, and fallen to sewing for a very much wanted first one, whose welcome would leave nothing to be desired. Philippa Blake and Diana Wright each sent a marvellous garment; and Mrs. Rachel Lynde sent several, in which good material and honest stitches took the place of embroidery and frills. Anne herself made many, desecrated by no touch of machinery, spending over them the happiest hours of that happy winter.

Captain Jim was the most frequent guest of the little house, and none was more welcome. Everyday Anne loved the simple-souled, true-hearted old sailor more and more. He was as refreshing as a sea-breeze, as interesting as some ancient chronicle. She was never tired of listening to his stories, and his quaint remarks and comments were a continual delight to her. Captain Jim was one of those rare and interesting people who "never speak but they say something." The milk of human kindness and the wisdom of the serpent were mingled in his composition in delightful proportions. Nothing ever seemed to put Captain Jim out or depress him in any way.

"I've kind of contracted a habit of enj'ying things," he remarked once, when Anne had commented on his invariable cheerfulness. "It's got so chronic that I believe I even enj'y the disagreeable things. It's great fun thinking they can't last. 'Old rheumatiz,' says I, when it grips me hard, 'you've *got* to stop aching sometime. The worse you are the sooner you'll stop, mebbe. I'm bound to get the better of you in the long run whether in the body or out of the body.'"

One night, by the fireside at the light Anne saw Captain Jim's "life-book." He needed no coaxing to show it and proudly gave it to her to read.

"I writ it to leave to little Joe," he said. "I don't like the idea of everything I've done and seen being clean forgot after I've shipped for my last v'yage. Joe, he'll remember it, and tell the yarns to his children."

It was an old leather-bound book filled with the record of his voyages and adventures. Anne thought what a treasure trove it would be to a writer. Every sentence was a nugget. In itself the book had no literary merit; Captain Jim's charm of story-telling failed him when he came to pen and ink; he could only jot down the outline of his famous tales, and both spelling and grammar were sadly askew. But Anne felt that if anyone possessed of the gift could take that simple record of a brave, adventurous life, reading between the bald lines the tales of dangers staunchly faced and duty manfully done, a wonderful story might be made from it. Rich comedy and thrilling tragedy were both lying hidden in Captain Jim's "life-book," waiting for the touch of the master hand to waken the laughter and grief and horror of thousands.

Anne said something of this to Gilbert as they walked home.

"Why don't you try your hand at it yourself, Anne?"

Anne shook her head.

"No. I only wish I could. But it's not in the power of my gift. You know what my forte is, Gilbert—the fanciful, the fairylike, the pretty. To write Captain Jim's life-book as it should be written one should be a master of vigorous yet subtle style, a keen psychologist, a born humourist and a born tragedian. A rare combination of gifts is needed. Paul might do it if he were older. Anyhow, I'm going to ask him to come down next summer and meet Captain Jim."

"Come to this shore," wrote Anne to Paul. "I'm afraid you cannot find here Nora or the Golden Lady or the Twin Sailors; but you will find one old sailor who can tell you wonderful stories."

Paul, however, wrote back, saying regretfully that he could not come that year. He was going abroad for two years' study.

"When I return I'll come to Four Winds, dear Teacher," he wrote.

"But meanwhile, Captain Jim is growing old," said Anne, sorrowfully, "and there is nobody to write his life-book."

XVIII

Spring Days

The ice in the harbour grew black and rotten in the March suns; in April there were blue waters and a windy, white-capped gulf and again the Four Winds light begemmed the twilights.

"I'm so glad to see it once more," said Anne, on the first evening of its reappearance. "I've missed it so all winter. The north-western sky has seemed blank and lonely without it."

The land was tender with brand-new, golden-green, baby leaves. There was an emerald mist on the woods beyond the Glen. The seaward valleys were full of fairy mists at dawn.

Vibrant winds came and went with salt foam in their breath. The sea laughed and flashed and preened and allured, like a beautiful, coquettish woman. The herring schooled and the fishing village woke to life. The harbour was alive with white sails making for the channel. The ships began to sail outward and inward again.

"On a spring day like this," said Anne, "I know exactly what my soul will feel like on the resurrection morning."

"There are times in spring when I sorter feel that I might

have been a poet if I'd been caught young," remarked Captain Jim. "I catch myself conning over old lines and verses I heard the schoolmaster reciting sixty years ago. They don't trouble me at other times. Now I feel as if I had to get out on the rocks or the fields or the water and spout them."

Captain Jim had come up that afternoon to bring Anne a load of shells for the garden, and a little bunch of sweet-grass which he had found in a ramble over the sand dunes.

"It's getting real scarce along this shore now," he said. "When I was a boy there was a-plenty of it. But now it's only once in a while you'll find a plot—and never when you're looking for it. You jest have to stumble on it—you're walking along on the sand-hills, never thinking of sweet-grass—and all at once the air is full of sweetness—and there's the grass under your feet. I favour the smell of sweet-grass. It always makes me think of my mother."

"She was fond of it?" asked Anne.

"Not that I knows on. Dunno's she ever saw any sweet-grass. No, it's because it has a kind of motherly perfume—not too young, you understand—something kind of seasoned and wholesome and dependable—jest like a mother. The schoolmaster's bride always kept it among her handkerchiefs. You might put that little bunch among yours, Mistress Blythe. I don't like these boughten scents—but a whiff of sweet-grass belongs anywhere a lady does."

Anne had not been especially enthusiastic over the idea of surrounding her flower beds with quahog shells; as a decoration they did not appeal to her on first thought. But she would not have hurt Captain Jim's feelings for anything; so she assumed a virtue she did not at first feel, and thanked him heartily. And when Captain Jim had proudly encircled every bed with a rim of the big, milk-white shells, Anne found to her surprise that she liked the effect. On a town lawn, or even up at the Glen, they would not have been in keeping, but here, in the old-fashioned, seabound garden of the little house of dreams, they *belonged*.

"They *do* look nice," she said sincerely.

"The schoolmaster's bride always had cow-hawks round her beds," said Captain Jim. "She was a master hand with flowers. She *looked* at 'em—and touched 'em—and touched 'em—*so*—and they grew like mad. Some folks have that knack—I reckon you have it, too, Mistress Blythe."

"Oh, I don't know—but I love my garden, and I love working in it. To potter with green, growing things, watching each day to see the dear, new sprouts come up, is like taking a hand in creation, I think. Just now my garden is like faith—the substance of things hoped for. But bide a wee."

"It always amazes me to look at the little, wrinkled brown seeds and think of the rainbows in 'em," said Captain Jim. "When I ponder on them seeds I don't find it nowise hard to believe that we've got souls that'll live in other worlds. You couldn't hardly believe there was life in them tiny things, some no bigger than grains of dust, let alone colour and scent, if you hadn't seen the miracle, could you?"

Anne, who was counting her days like silver beads on a rosary, could not now take the long walk to the lighthouse or up the Glen road. But Miss Cornelia and Captain Jim came very often to the little house. Miss Cornelia was the joy of Anne's and Gilbert's existence. They laughed side-splittingly over her speeches after every visit. When Captain Jim and she happened to visit the little house at the same time there was much sport for the listening. They waged wordy warfare, she attacking, he defending. Anne once reproached the Captain for his baiting of Miss Cornelia.

"Oh, I do love to set her going, Mistress Blythe," chuckled the unrepentant sinner. "It's the greatest amusement I have in life. That tongue of hers would blister a stone. And you and that young dog of a doctor enj'y listening to her as much as I do."

Captain Jim came along another evening to bring Anne some mayflowers. The garden was full of the moist, scented air of a maritime spring evening. There was a milk-white mist on the edge of the sea, with a young moon kissing it, and a silver gladness of stars over the Glen. The bell of the church across the harbour was ringing dreamily sweet. The mellow chime drifted through the dusk to mingle with the soft spring-moan of the sea. Captain Jim's mayflowers added the last completing touch to the charm of the night.

"I haven't seen any this spring, and I've missed them," said Anne, burying her face in them.

"They ain't to be found around Four Winds, only in the barrens away behind the Glen up yander. I took a little trip today to the Land-of-nothing to-do, and hunted these up for you. I reckon they're the last you'll see this spring, for they're nearly done."

"How kind and thoughtful you are, Captain Jim. Nobody else—not even Gilbert"—with a shake of her head at him—"remembered that I always long for mayflowers in spring."

"Well, I had another errand, too—I wanted to take Mr. Howard back yander a mess of trout. He likes one occasional, and it's all I can do for a kindness he did me once. I stayed all the afternoon and talked to him. He likes to talk to me, though he's a highly eddicated man and I'm only an ignorant old sailor, because he's one of the folks that's *got* to talk or they're miserable, and he finds listeners scarce around here. The Glen folks fight shy of him because they think he's an infidel. He ain't that far gone exactly—few men is, I reckon—but he's what you might call a heretic. Heretics are wicked, but they're mighty interesting. It's jest that they've got sorter lost looking for God, being under the impression that He's hard to find— which He ain't never. Most of 'em blunder to Him after awhile, I guess. I don't think listening to Mr. Howard's arguments is likely to do *me* much harm. Mind you, I believe what I was brought up to believe. It saves a vast of bother—and back of it all, God is good. The trouble with Mr. Howard is that he's a leetle too clever. He thinks that he's bound to live up to his cleverness, and that it's smarter to thrash out some new way of getting to heaven than to go by the old track the common, ignorant folks is travelling. But he'll get there sometime all right, and then he'll laugh at himself."

"Mr. Howard was a Methodist to begin with," said Miss Cornelia, as if she thought he had not far to go from that to heresy.

"Do you know, Cornelia," said Captain Jim gravely, "I've often thought that if I wasn't a Presbyterian I'd be a Methodist."

"Oh, well," conceded Miss Cornelia, "if you weren't a Presbyterian it wouldn't matter much what you were. Speaking of heresy, reminds me, Doctor—I've brought back that book you lent me—that *Natural Law in the Spiritual World*—I didn't read more'n a third of it. I can read sense, and I can read nonsense, but that book is neither the one nor the other."

"It *is* considered rather heretical in some quarters," admitted Gilbert, "but I told you that before you took it, Miss Cornelia."

"Oh, I wouldn't have minded its being heretical. I can stand wickedness, but I can't stand foolishness," said Miss Cornelia calmly, and with the air of having said the last thing there was to say about *Natural Law.*

"Speaking of books, *A Mad Love* come to an end at last two weeks ago," remarked Captain Jim musingly. "It run to one hundred and three chapters. When they got married the book stopped right off, so I reckon their troubles were all over. It's real nice that that's the way in books anyhow, isn't it, even if 'tisn't so anywhere else?"

"I never read novels," said Miss Cornelia. "Did you hear how Geordie Russell was today, Captain Jim?"

"Yes, I called in on my way home to see him. He's getting round all right—but stewing in a broth of trouble, as usual, poor man. 'Course he brews up most of it for himself, but I reckon that don't make it any easier to bear."

"He's an awful pessimist," said Miss Cornelia.

"Well, no he ain't a pessimist exactly, Cornelia. He only jest never finds anything that suits him."

"And isn't that a pessimist?"

"No, no. A pessimist is one who never expects to find anything to suit him. Geordie hain't got *that* far yet."

"You'd find something good to say of the devil himself, Jim Boyd."

"Well, you've heard the story of the old lady who said he was persevering. But no, Cornelia, I've nothing good to say of the devil."

"Do you believe in him at all?" asked Miss Cornelia seriously.

"How can you ask that when you know what a good Presbyterian I am, Cornelia? How could a Presbyterian get along without a devil?"

"*Do* you?" persisted Miss Cornelia.

Captain Jim suddenly became grave.

"I believe in what I heard a minister once call 'a mighty and malignant and *intelligent* power of evil working in the universe,'" he said solemnly. "I do *that*, Cornelia. You can call it the devil, or the 'principle of evil,' or the Old Scratch, or any name you like. It's *there*, and all the infidels and heretics in the world can't argue it away, any more'n they can argue God away. It's there, and it's working. But, mind you, Cornelia, I believe it's going to get the worst of it in the long run."

"I am sure I hope so," said Miss Cornelia, none too hopefully. "But speaking of the devil, I am positive that Billy Booth is possessed by him now. Have you heard of Billy's latest performance?"

"No, what was that?"

"He's gone and burned up his wife's new, brown broadcloth suit, that she paid twenty-five dollars for in Charlottetown, because he declares the men looked too admiring at her when she wore it to church the first time. Wasn't that like a man?"

"Mistress Booth *is* mighty pretty, and brown's her colour," said Captain Jim reflectively.

"Is that any good reason why he should poke her new suit into the kitchen stove? Billy Booth is a jealous fool, and he makes his wife's life miserable. She's cried all the week about her suit. Oh, Anne, I wish I could write like you, believe *me*. Wouldn't I score some of the men round here!"

"Those Booths are all a mite queer," said Captain Jim. "Billy seemed the sanest of the lot till he got married and then this queer jealous streak cropped out in him. His brother Daniel, now, was always odd."

"Took tantrums every few days or so and wouldn't get out of bed," said Miss Cornelia with a relish. "His wife would have to do all the barn work till he got over his spell. When he died people wrote her letters of condolence; if I'd written anything it would have been one of congratulation. Their father, old Abram Booth, was a disgusting old sot. He was drunk at his wife's funeral, and kept reeling round and hiccuping 'I didn't dri—i—i—nk much but I feel a—a—awfully que— e—e—r.' I gave him a good jab in the back with my umbrella when he came near me, and it sobered him up until they got the casket out of the house. Young Johnny Booth was to have been married yesterday, but he couldn't be because he's gone and got the mumps. Wasn't that like a man?"

"How could he help getting the mumps, poor fellow?"

"I'd poor fellow him, believe *me*, if I was Kate Sterns. I don't know how he could help getting the mumps, but I *do* know the wedding supper was all prepared and everything will be spoiled before he's well again. Such a waste! He should have had the mumps when he was a boy."

"Come, come, Cornelia, don't you think you're a mite unreasonable?"

Miss Cornelia disdained to reply and turned instead to Susan Baker, a grim-faced, kind-hearted elderly spinster of the Glen, who had been installed as maid-of-all-work at the little house for some weeks. Susan had been up to the Glen to make a sick call, and had just returned.

"How is poor old Aunt Mandy tonight?" asked Miss Cornelia.

Susan sighed.

"Very poorly—very poorly, Cornelia. I am afraid she will soon be in heaven, poor thing!"

"Oh, surely, it's not so bad as that!" exclaimed Miss Cornelia, sympathetically.

Captain Jim and Gilbert looked at each other. Then they suddenly rose and went out.

"There are times," said Captain Jim, between spasms, "when it would be a sin *not* to laugh. Them two excellent women!"

XIX

Dawn and Dusk

I n early June, when the sand-hills were a great glory of pink wild roses, and the Glen was smothered in apple-blossoms, Marilla arrived at the little house, accompanied by a black horse-hair trunk, patterned with brass nails, which had reposed undisturbed in the Green Gables garret for half a century. Susan Baker, who, during her few weeks' sojourn in the little house, had come to worship "young Mrs. Doctor," as she called Anne, with blind fervour, looked rather jealously askance at Marilla at first. But as Marilla did not try to interfere in kitchen matters, and showed no desire to interrupt Susan's ministrations to young Mrs. Doctor, the good handmaiden became reconciled to her presence, and told her cronies at the Glen that Miss Cuthbert was a fine old lady and knew her place.

One evening, when the sky's limpid bowl was filled with a red glory, and the robins were thrilling the golden twilight with jubilant hymns to the stars of evening, there was a sudden commotion in the little house of dreams. Telephone messages were sent up to the Glen, Doctor Dave and a white-capped nurse came hastily down, Marilla paced the garden walks between the quahog shells, murmuring prayers between her set lips, and Susan sat in the kitchen with cotton wool in her ears and her apron over her head.

Leslie, looking out from the house up the brook, saw that every window of the little house was alight, and did not sleep that night.

The June night was short; but it seemed an eternity to those who waited and watched.

"Oh, will it *never* end?" said Marilla; then she saw how grave the nurse and Doctor Dave looked, and she dared ask no more questions. Suppose Anne—but Marilla could not suppose it.

"Do not tell me," said Susan fiercely, answering the anguish in Marilla's eyes, "that God could be so cruel as to take that darling lamb from us when we all love her so much."

"He has taken others as well beloved," said Marilla hoarsely.

But at dawn, when the rising sun rent apart the mists hanging over the sandbar, and made rainbows of them, joy came to the little house. Anne was safe, and a wee, white lady, with her mother's big eyes, was lying beside her. Gilbert, his face gray and haggard from his night's agony, came down to tell Marilla and Susan.

"Thank God," shuddered Marilla.

Susan got up and took the cotton wool out of her ears.

"Now for breakfast," she said briskly. "I am of the opinion that we will all be glad of a bite and sup. You tell young Mrs. Doctor not to worry about a single thing—Susan is at the helm. You tell her just to think of her baby."

Gilbert smiled sadly as he went away. Anne, her pale face blanched with its baptism of pain, her eyes aglow with the holy passion of motherhood, did not need to be told to think of her baby. She thought of nothing else. For a few hours she tasted of happiness so rare and exquisite that she wondered if the angels in heaven did not envy her.

"Little Joyce," she murmured, when Marilla came in to see the baby. "We planned to call her that if she were a girlie. There were so many we would have liked to name her for; we couldn't choose between them, so we decided on Joyce —we can call her Joy for short—Joy it suits so well. Oh, Marilla, I thought I was happy before. Now I know that I just dreamed a pleasant dream of happiness. *This* is the reality."

"You mustn't talk, Anne—wait till you're stronger," said Marilla warningly.

"You know how hard it is for me *not* to talk," smiled Anne.

At first she was too weak and too happy to notice that Gilbert and the nurse looked grave and Marilla sorrowful. Then, as subtly, and coldly, and remorselessly as a sea-fog stealing landward, fear crept into her heart. Why was not Gilbert gladder? Why would he not talk about the baby? Why would they not let her have it with her after that first heavenly-happy hour? Was—was there anything wrong?

"Gilbert," whispered Anne imploringly, "the baby—is all right—isn't she? Tell me—tell me."

Gilbert was a long while in turning round; then he bent over Anne and looked in her eyes. Marilla, listening fearfully outside the door, heard a pitiful, heartbroken moan, and fled to the kitchen where Susan was weeping.

"Oh, the poor lamb—the poor lamb! How can she bear it, Miss Cuthbert? I am afraid it will kill her. She has been that built up and happy, longing for that baby, and planning for it. Cannot anything be done nohow, Miss Cuthbert?"

"I'm afraid not, Susan. Gilbert says there is no hope. He knew from the first the little thing couldn't live."

"And it is such a sweet baby," sobbed Susan. "I never saw one so white—they are mostly red or yallow. And it opened its big eyes as if it was months old. The little, little thing! Oh, the poor, young Mrs. Doctor!"

At sunset the little soul that had come with the dawning went away, leaving heartbreak behind it. Miss Cornelia took the wee, white lady from the kindly but stranger hands of the nurse, and dressed the tiny waxen form in the beautiful dress Leslie had made for it. Leslie had asked her to do that. Then she took it back and laid it beside the poor, broken, tear-blinded little mother.

"The Lord has given and the Lord has taken away, dearie," she said through her own tears. "Blessed be the name of the Lord."

Then she went away, leaving Anne and Gilbert alone together with their dead.

The next day, the small white Joy was laid in a velvet casket which Leslie had lined with apple-blossoms, and taken to the graveyard of the church across the harbour. Miss Cornelia and Marilla put all the little love-made garments away, together with the ruffled basket which had been befrilled and belaced for dimpled limbs and downy head. Little Joy was never to sleep there; she had found a colder, narrower bed.

"This has been an awful disappointment to me," sighed

Miss Cornelia. "I've looked forward to this baby—and I did want it to be a girl, too."

"I can only be thankful that Anne's life was spared," said Marilla, with a shiver, recalling those hours of darkness when the girl she loved was passing through the valley of the shadow.

"Poor, poor lamb! Her heart is broken," said Susan.

"I *envy* Anne," said Leslie suddenly and fiercely, "and I'd envy her even if she had died! She was a mother for one beautiful day. I'd gladly give my life for *that*!"

"I wouldn't talk like that, Leslie, dearie," said Miss Cornelia deprecatingly. She was afraid that the dignified Miss Cuthbert would think Leslie quite terrible.

Anne's convalescence was long, and made bitter for her by many things. The bloom and sunshine of the Four Winds world grated harshly on her; and yet, when the rain fell heavily, she pictured it beating so mercilessly down on that little grave across the harbour; and when the wind blew around the eaves she heard sad voices in it she had never heard before.

Kindly callers hurt her, too, with the well-meant platitudes with which they strove to cover the nakedness of bereavement. A letter from Phil Blake was an added sting. Phil had heard of the baby's birth, but not of its death, and she wrote Anne a congratulatory letter of sweet mirth which hurt her horribly.

"I would have laughed over it so happily if I had my baby," she sobbed to Marilla. "But when I haven't it just seems like wanton cruelty—though I know Phil wouldn't hurt me for the world. Oh, Marilla, I don't see how I can *ever* be happy again—*everything* will hurt me all the rest of my life."

"Time will help you," said Marilla, who was racked with sympathy but could never learn to express it in other than age-worn formulas.

"It doesn't seem *fair*," said Anne rebelliously. "Babies are born and live where they are not wanted—where they will be neglected—where they will have no chance. I would have loved my baby so—and cared for it so tenderly—and tried to give her every chance for good. And yet I wasn't allowed to keep her."

"It was God's will, Anne," said Marilla, helpless before the riddle of the universe—the *why* of undeserved pain. "And little Joy is better off."

"I can't believe *that*," cried Anne bitterly. Then, seeing that Marilla looked shocked, she added passionately, "Why should she be born at all—why should anyone be born at all—if she's better off dead? I *don't* believe it is better for a child to die at birth than to live its life out—and love and be loved—and enjoy and suffer—and do its work—and develop a character that would give it a personality in eternity. And how do you know it was God's will? Perhaps it was just a thwarting of His purpose by the Power of Evil. We can't be expected to be resigned to *that*."

"Oh, Anne, don't talk so," said Marilla, genuinely alarmed lest Anne were drifting into deep and dangerous waters. "We can't understand—but we must have faith—we *must* believe that all is for the best. I know you find it hard to think so, just now. But try to be brave—for Gilbert's sake. He's so worried about you. You aren't getting strong as fast as you should."

"Oh, I know I've been very selfish," sighed Anne. "I love Gilbert more than ever—and I want to live for his sake.

But it seems as if part of me was buried over there in that little harbour graveyard—and it hurts so much that I'm afraid of life."

"It won't hurt so much always, Anne."

"The thought that it may stop hurting sometimes hurts me worse than all else, Marilla."

"Yes, I know, I've felt that too, about other things. But we all love you, Anne. Captain Jim has been up every day to ask for you—and Mrs. Moore haunts the place—and Miss Bryant spends most of her time, I think, cooking up nice things for you. Susan doesn't like it very well. She thinks she can cook as well as Miss Bryant."

"Dear Susan! Oh, everybody has been so dear and good and lovely to me, Marilla. I'm not ungrateful—and perhaps—when this horrible ache grows a little less—I'll find that I can go on living."

Lost Margaret

Anne found that she could go on living; the day came when she even smiled again over one of Miss Cornelia's speeches. But there was something in the smile that had never been in Anne's smile before and would never be absent from it again.

On the first day she was able to go for a drive Gilbert took her down to Four Winds Point, and left her there while he rowed over the channel to see a patient at the fishing village. A rollicking wind was scudding across the harbour and the dunes, whipping the water into white-caps and washing the sandshore with long lines of silvery breakers.

"I'm real proud to see you here again, Mistress Blythe," said Captain Jim. "Sit down—sit down. I'm afeared it's mighty dusty here today—but there's no need of looking at dust when you can look at such scenery, is there?"

"I don't mind the dust," said Anne, "but Gilbert says I must keep in the open air. I think I'll go and sit on the rocks down there."

"Would you like company or would you rather be alone?"

"If by company you mean yours I'd much rather have it than be alone," said Anne, smiling. Then she sighed. She had never before minded being alone. Now she dreaded it. When she was alone now she felt so dreadfully alone.

"Here's a nice little spot where the wind can't get at you," said Captain Jim, when they reached the rocks. "I often sit here. It's a great place jest to sit and dream."

"Oh—dreams," sighed Anne. "I can't dream now, Captain Jim—I'm done with dreams."

"Oh, no, you're not, Mistress Blythe—oh, no, you're not," said Captain Jim meditatively. "I know how you feel jest now—but if you keep on living you'll get glad again and the first thing you know you'll be dreaming again—thank the good Lord for it! If it wasn't for our dreams they might as well bury us. How'd we stand living if it wasn't for our dream of immortality? And that's a dream that's *bound* to come true, Mistress Blythe. You'll see your little Joyce again someday."

"But she won't be my baby," said Anne, with trembling lips. "Oh, she may be, as Longfellow says, 'a fair maiden clothed with celestial grace'—but she'll be a stranger to me."

"God will manage better'n *that*, I believe," said Captain Jim.

They were both silent for a little time. Then Captain Jim said very softly:

"Mistress Blythe, may I tell you about lost Margaret?"

"Of course," said Anne gently. She did not know who "lost Margaret" was, but she felt that she was going to hear the romance of Captain Jim's life.

"I've often wanted to tell you about her," Captain Jim went on. "Do you know why, Mistress Blythe? It's because I want somebody to remember and think of her sometime after I'm gone. I can't bear that her name should be forgotten by all living souls. And now nobody remembers lost Margaret but me."

Then Captain Jim told the story—an old, old forgotten story, for it was over fifty years since Margaret had fallen asleep one day in her father's dory and drifted—or so it was supposed, for nothing was ever certainly known as to her fate—out of the channel, beyond the bar, to perish in the black thunder-squall which had come up so suddenly that long-ago summer afternoon. But to Captain Jim those fifty years were but as yesterday when it is past.

"I walked the shore for months after that," he said sadly, "Looking to find her dear, sweet little body; but the sea never give her back to me. But I'll find her sometime. Mistress Blythe—I'll find her sometime. She's waiting for me. I wish I could tell you jest how she looked, but I can't. I've seen a fine, silvery mist hanging over the bar at sunrise that seemed like her—and then again I've seen a white birch in the woods back yander that made me think of her. She had pale, brown hair and a little white, sweet face, and long slender fingers like yours, Mistress Blythe, only browner, for she was a shore girl. Sometimes I wake up in the night and hear the sea calling to me in the old way, and it seems as if lost Margaret called in it. And when there's a storm and the waves are sobbing and moaning I hear her lamenting among them. And when they laugh on a gay day it's *her* laugh—lost Margaret's sweet, roguish, little laugh. The sea took her from me, but someday I'll find her, Mistress Blythe. It can't keep us apart forever."

"I am glad you have told me about her," said Anne. "I have often wondered why you had lived all your life alone."

"I couldn't ever care for anyone else. Lost Margaret took my heart with her—out there," said the old lover, who had been faithful for fifty years to his drowned sweetheart. "You won't mind if I talk a good deal about her, will you, Mistress Blythe? It's a pleasure to me—for all the pain went out of her memory years ago and jest left its blessing. I know you'll never forget her, Mistress Blythe. And if the years, as I hope, bring other little folks to your home, I want you to promise me that you'll tell *them* the story of lost Margaret, so that her name won't be forgotten among humankind."

XXI

Barriers Swept Away

"Anne," said Leslie, breaking abruptly a short silence, "you don't know how *good* it is to be sitting here with you again—working—and talking—and being silent together."

They were sitting among the blue-eyed grasses on the bank of the brook in Anne's garden. The water sparkled and crooned past them; the birches threw dappled shadows over them; roses bloomed along the walks. The sun was beginning to be low, and the air was full of woven music. There was one music of the wind in the firs behind the house, and another of the waves on the bar, and still another from the distant bell of the church near which the wee, white lady slept. Anne loved that bell, though it brought sorrowful thoughts now.

She looked curiously at Leslie, who had thrown down her sewing and spoken with a lack of restraint that was very unusual with her.

"On that horrible night when you were so ill," Leslie went on, "I kept thinking that perhaps we'd have no more talks and walks and *works* together. And I realized just what your

friendship had come to mean to me—just what *you* meant—
and just what a hateful little beast I had been."

"Leslie! Leslie! I never allow anyone to call my friends
names."

"It's true. That's exactly what I am—a hateful little beast.
There's something I've *got* to tell you, Anne. I suppose it will
make you despise me, but I *must* confess it. Anne, there have
been times this past winter and spring when I have *hated* you."

"I knew it," said Anne calmly.

"You *knew* it?"

"Yes, I saw it in your eyes."

"And yet you went on liking me and being my friend."

"Well, it was only now and then you hated me, Leslie.
Between times you loved me, I think."

"I certainly did. But that other horrid feeling was always
there, spoiling it, back in my heart. I kept it down—sometimes I forgot it—but sometimes it would surge up and take
possession of me. I hated you because I *envied* you—oh, I was
sick with envy of you at times. You had a dear little home—
and love—and happiness—and glad dreams—everything I
wanted—and never had—and never could have. Oh, never
could have! *That* was what stung. I wouldn't have envied you,
if I had had any *hope* that life would ever be different for me.
But I hadn't—I hadn't—and it didn't seem *fair*. It made me
rebellious—and it hurt me—and so I hated you at times. Oh,
I was so ashamed of it—I'm dying of shame now—but I
couldn't conquer it. That night, when I was afraid you mightn't
live—I thought I was going to be punished for my wickedness—and I loved you so then. Anne, Anne, I never had anything to love since my mother died, except Dick's old dog—and

it's so dreadful to have nothing to love—life is so *empty*—and there's *nothing* worse than emptiness—and I might have loved you so much—and that horrible thing had spoiled it—"

Leslie was trembling and growing almost incoherent with the violence of her emotion.

"Don't, Leslie," implored Anne, "oh, don't. I understand—don't talk of it any more."

"I must—I must. When I knew you were going to live I vowed that I would tell you as soon as you were well—that I wouldn't go on accepting your friendship and companionship without telling you how unworthy I was of it. And I've been so afraid—it would turn you against me."

"You needn't fear that, Leslie."

"Oh, I'm so glad—so glad, Anne." Leslie clasped her brown, work-hardened hands tightly together to still their shaking. "But I want to tell you everything, now I've begun. You don't remember the first time I saw you, I suppose—it wasn't that night on the shore—"

"No, it was the night Gilbert and I came home. You were driving your geese down the hill. I should think I *do* remember it! I thought you were so beautiful—I longed for weeks after to find out who you were."

"I knew who *you* were, although I had never seen either of you before. I had heard of the new doctor and his bride who were coming to live in Miss Russell's little house. I—I hated you that very moment, Anne."

"I felt the resentment in your eyes—then I doubted—I thought I must be mistaken—because *why* should it be?"

"It was because you looked so happy. Oh, you'll agree with me now that I *am* a hateful beast—to hate another woman just because she was happy,—and when her happiness didn't take anything from me! That was why I never went to see you. I knew quite well I ought to go—even our simple Four Winds customs demanded that. But I couldn't. I used to watch you from my window—I could see you and your husband strolling about your garden in the evening—or you running down the poplar lane to meet him. And it hurt me. And yet in another way I wanted to go over. I felt that, if I were not so miserable, I could have liked you and found in you what I've never had in my life—an intimate, *real* friend of my own age. And then you remember that night at the shore? You were afraid I would think you crazy. You must have thought *I* was."

"No, but I couldn't understand you, Leslie. One moment you drew me to you—the next you pushed me back."

"I was very unhappy that evening. I had had a hard day. Dick had been very—very hard to manage that day. Generally he is quite good-natured and easily controlled, you know, Anne. But some days he is very different. I was so heartsick—I ran away to the shore as soon as he went to sleep. It was my only refuge. I sat there thinking of how my poor father had ended his life, and wondering if I wouldn't be driven to it someday. Oh, my heart was full of black thoughts! And then you came dancing along the cove like a glad, light-hearted child. I—I hated you more then than I've ever done since. And yet I craved your friendship. The one feeling swayed me one moment; the other feeling the next. When I got home that night I cried for shame of what you must think of me. But it's always been just the same when I came over here. Sometimes I'd be happy and enjoy my visit. And at other times that hideous feeling would mar it all. There were times when everything about you and your house hurt me. You had so many dear little things I couldn't have. Do you know—it's ridiculous—but I had an especial spite at those china dogs of yours. There were times when I wanted to catch up Gog and Magog and bang their pert black noses together! Oh, you smile, Anne—but it was never funny to me. I would come here and see you and Gilbert with your books and your flowers, and your household gods, and your little family jokes—and your love for each other showing in every look and word, even when you didn't know it—and I would go home to—you know what I went home to! Oh, Anne, I don't believe I'm jealous and envious by nature. When I was a girl I lacked many things my schoolmates had, but I never cared—I never disliked them for it. But I seem to have grown so hateful—"

"Leslie, dearest, stop blaming yourself. You are *not* hateful or jealous or envious. The life you have to live has warped you a little, perhaps—but it would have ruined a nature less fine and noble than yours. I'm letting you tell me all this because I believe it's better for you to talk it out and rid your soul of it. But don't blame yourself anymore."

"Well, I won't. I just wanted you to know me as I am. That time you told me of your darling hope for the spring was the worst of all, Anne. I shall never forgive myself for the way I behaved then. I repented it with tears. And I *did* put many a tender and loving thought of you into the little dress I made. But I might have known that anything I made could only be a shroud in the end."

"Now, Leslie, that *is* bitter and morbid—put such thoughts away. I was so glad when you brought the little dress; and since

I had to lose little Joyce I like to think that the dress she wore was the one you made for her when you let yourself love me."

"Anne, do you know, I believe I shall always love you after this. I don't think I'll ever feel that dreadful way about you again. Talking it all out seems to have done away with it, somehow. It's very strange—and I thought it so real and bitter. It's like opening the door of a dark room to show some hideous creature you've believed to be there—and when the light streams in your monster turns out to have been just a shadow, vanishing when the light comes. It will never come between us again."

"No, we are real friends now, Leslie, and I am very glad."

"I hope you won't misunderstand me if I say something else. Anne, I was grieved to the core of my heart when you lost your baby; and if I could have saved her for you by cutting off one of my hands I would have done it. But your sorrow has brought us closer together. Your perfect happiness isn't a barrier any longer. Oh, don't misunderstand, dearest—I'm *not* glad that your happiness isn't perfect any longer—I can say that sincerely; but since it isn't, there isn't such a gulf between us."

"I *do* understand that, too, Leslie. Now, we'll just shut up the past and forget what was unpleasant in it. It's all going to be different. We're both of the race of Joseph now. I think you've been wonderful—wonderful. And, Leslie, I can't help believing that life has something good and beautiful for you yet."

Leslie shook her head.

"No," she said dully. "There isn't any hope. Dick will never be better—and even if his memory were to come back—oh, Anne, it would be worse, even worse, than it is now. *This* is something you can't understand, you happy bride. Anne, did Miss Cornelia ever tell you how I came to marry Dick?"

"Yes."

"I'm glad—I wanted you to know—but I couldn't bring myself to talk of it if you hadn't known. Anne, it seems to me that ever since I was twelve years old life has been bitter. Before that I had a happy childhood. We were very poor—but we didn't mind. Father was so splendid—so clever and loving and sympathetic. We were chums as far back as I can remember. And mother was so sweet. She was very, very beautiful. I look like her, but I am not so beautiful as she was."

"Miss Cornelia says you are far more beautiful."

"She is mistaken—or prejudiced. I think my figure *is* better—mother was slight and bent by hard work—but she had the face of an angel. I used just to look up at her in worship. We all worshipped her,—father and Kenneth and I."

Anne remembered that Miss Cornelia had given her a very different impression of Leslie's mother. But had not love the truer vision? Still, it *was* selfish of Rose West to make her daughter marry Dick Moore.

"Kenneth was my brother," went on Leslie. "Oh, I can't tell you how I loved him. And he was cruelly killed. Do you know how?"

"Yes."

"Anne, I saw his little face as the wheel went over him. He fell on his back. Anne—Anne—I can see it now. I shall always see it. Anne, all I ask of heaven is that that recollection shall be blotted out of my memory. O my God!"

"Leslie, don't speak of it. I know the story—don't go into

details that only harrow your soul up unavailingly. It *will* be blotted out."

After a moment's struggle, Leslie regained a measure of self-control.

"Then father's health got worse and he grew despondent—his mind became unbalanced—you've heard all that, too?"

"Yes."

"After that I had just mother to live for. But I was very ambitious. I meant to teach and earn my way through college. I meant to climb to the very top—oh, I won't talk of that either. It's no use. You know what happened. I couldn't see my dear little heart-broken mother, who had been such a slave all her life, turned out of her home. Of course, I could have earned enough for us to live on. But mother *couldn't* leave her home. She had come there as a bride—and she had loved father so—and all her memories were there. Even yet, Anne, when I think that I made her last year happy I'm not sorry for what I did. As for Dick—I didn't hate him when I married him—I just felt for him the indifferent, friendly feeling I had for most of my schoolmates. I knew he drank some—but I had never heard the story of the girl down at the fishing cove. If I had, I *couldn't* have married him, even for mother's sake. Afterwards—I *did* hate him—but mother never knew. She died—and then I was alone. I was only seventeen and I was alone. Dick had gone off in the *Four Sisters*. I hoped he wouldn't be home very much more. The sea had always been in his blood. I had no other hope. Well, Captain Jim brought him home, as you know—and that's all there is to say. You know me now, Anne—the worst of me—the barriers are all down. And you still want to be my friend?"

Anne looked up through the birches, at the white paper-lantern of a half moon drifting downwards to the gulf of sunset. Her face was very sweet.

"I am your friend and you are mine, for always," she said. "Such a friend as I never had before. I have had many dear and beloved friends—but there is a something in you, Leslie, that I never found in anyone else. You have more to offer me in that rich nature of yours, and I have more to give you than I had in my careless girlhood. We are both women—and friends forever."

They clasped hands and smiled at each other through the tears that filled the gray eyes and the blue.

XXII

Miss Cornelia Arranges Matters

Gilbert insisted that Susan should be kept on at the little house for the summer. Anne protested at first.

"Life here with just the two of us is so sweet, Gilbert. It spoils it a little to have anyone else. Susan is a dear soul, but she is an outsider. It won't hurt me to do the work here."

"You must take your doctor's advice," said Gilbert. "There's an old proverb to the effect that shoemakers' wives go barefoot and doctors' wives die young. I don't mean that it shall be true in my household. You will keep Susan until the old spring comes back into your step, and those little hollows on your cheeks fill out."

"You just take it easy, Mrs. Doctor, dear," said Susan, coming abruptly in. "Have a good time and do not worry about the pantry. Susan is at the helm. There is no use in keeping a dog and doing your own barking. I am going to take your breakfast up to you every morning."

"Indeed you are not," laughed Anne. "I agree with Miss Cornelia that it's a scandal for a woman who isn't sick to eat her breakfast in bed, and almost justifies the men in any enormities."

"Oh, Cornelia!" said Susan, with ineffable contempt. "I think you have better sense, Mrs. Doctor, dear, than to heed what Cornelia Bryant says. I cannot see why she must be always running down the men, even if she is an old maid. *I* am an old maid, but you never hear *me* abusing the men. I like 'em. I would have married one if I could. Is it not funny nobody ever asked me to marry him, Mrs. Doctor, dear? I am no beauty, but I am as good-looking as most of the married women you see. But I never had a beau. What do you suppose is the reason?"

"It may be predestination," suggested Anne, with unearthly solemnity.

Susan nodded.

"That is what I have often thought, Mrs. Doctor, dear, and a great comfort it is. I do not mind nobody wanting me if the Almighty decreed it so for His own wise purposes. But sometimes doubt creeps in, Mrs. Doctor, dear, and I wonder if maybe the Old Scratch has not more to do with it than anyone else. I cannot feel resigned *then*. But maybe," added Susan, brightening up, "I will have a chance to get married yet. I often and often think of the old verse my aunt used to repeat:

> *There never was a goose so gray but sometime*
> *   soon or late*
> *Some honest gander came her way and took her*
> *   for his mate!*

A woman cannot ever be sure of not being married till she is buried, Mrs. Doctor, dear, and meanwhile I will make a batch of cherry pies. I notice the doctor favours 'em, and I *do* like cooking for a man who appreciates his victuals."

Miss Cornelia dropped in that afternoon, puffing a little.

"I don't mind the world or the devil much, but the flesh *does* rather bother me," she admitted. "You always look as cool as a cucumber, Anne, dearie. Do I smell cherry pie? If I do, ask me to stay for tea. Haven't tasted a cherry pie this summer. My cherries have all been stolen by those scamps of Gilman boys from the Glen."

"Now, now, Cornelia," remonstrated Captain Jim, who had been reading a sea novel in a corner of the living room, "you shouldn't say that about those two poor, motherless little Gilman boys, unless you've got certain proof. Jest because their father ain't none too honest isn't any reason for calling them thieves. It's more likely it's been the robins took your cherries. They're turrible thick this year."

"Robins!" said Miss Cornelia disdainfully. "Humph! Two-legged robins, believe *me*!"

"Well, most of the Four Winds robins *are* constructed on that principle," said Captain Jim gravely.

Miss Cornelia stared at him for a moment. Then she leaned back in her rocker and laughed long and ungrudgingly.

"Well, you *have* got one on me at last, Jim Boyd, I'll admit. Just look how pleased he is, Anne, dearie, grinning like a Chessy-cat. As for the robins' legs, if robins have great, big, bare, sunburned legs, with ragged trousers hanging on 'em, such as I saw up in my cherry tree one morning at sunrise last week, I'll beg the Gilman boys' pardon. By the time I got down they were gone. I couldn't understand how they had disappeared so quick, but Captain Jim has enlightened me. They flew away, of course."

Captain Jim laughed and went away, regretfully declining an invitation to stay to supper and partake of cherry pie.

"I'm on my way to see Leslie and ask her if she'll take a boarder," Miss Cornelia resumed. "I'd a letter yesterday from a Mrs. Daly in Toronto, who boarded a spell with me two years ago. She wanted me to take a friend of hers for the summer. His name is Owen Ford, and he's a newspaper man, and it seems he's a grandson of the schoolmaster who built this house. John Selwyn's oldest daughter married an Ontario man named Ford, and this is her son. He wants to see the old place his grandparents lived in. He had a bad spell of typhoid in the spring and hasn't got rightly over it, so his doctor has ordered him to the sea. He doesn't want to go to the hotel— he just wants a quiet home place. I can't take him, for I have to be away in August. I've been appointed a delegate to the W.F.M.S. convention in Kingsport and I'm going. I don't know whether Leslie'll want to be bothered with him, either, but there's no one else. If she can't take him he'll have to go over the harbour."

"When you've seen her come back and help us eat our cherry pies," said Anne. "Bring Leslie and Dick, too, if they can come. And so you're going to Kingsport? What a nice time you will have. I must give you a letter to a friend of mine there—Mrs. Jonas Blake."

"I've prevailed on Mrs. Thomas Holt to go with me," said Miss Cornelia complacently. "It's time she had a little holiday, believe *me*. She has just about worked herself to death. Tom Holt can crochet beautifully, but he can't make a living for his family. He never seems to be able to get up early enough to do any work, but I notice he can always get up early to go fishing. Isn't that like a man?"

Anne smiled. She had learned to discount largely Miss Cornelia's opinions of the Four Winds men. Otherwise she must have believed them the most hopeless assortment of reprobates and ne'er-do-wells in the world, with veritable slaves and martyrs for wives. This particular Tom Holt, for example, she knew to be a kind husband, a much loved father, and an excellent neighbour. If he were rather inclined to be lazy, liking better the fishing he had been born for than the farming he had not, and if he had a harmless eccentricity for doing fancy work, nobody save Miss Cornelia seemed to hold it against him. His wife was a "hustler," who gloried in hustling; his family got a comfortable living off the farm; and his strapping sons and daughters, inheriting their mother's energy, were all in a fair way to do well in the world. There was not a happier household in Glen St. Mary than the Holts'.

Miss Cornelia returned satisfied from the house up the brook.

"Leslie's going to take him," she announced. "She jumped at the chance. She wants to make a little money to shingle the roof of her house this fall, and she didn't know how she was going to manage it. I expect Captain Jim'll be more than interested when he hears that a grandson of the Selwyns is coming here. Leslie said to tell you she hankered after cherry pie, but she couldn't come to tea because she has to go and hunt up her turkeys. They've strayed away. But she said, if there was a piece left, for you to put it in the pantry and she'd run over in the cat's light, when prowling's in order, to get it. You don't know, Anne, dearie, what good it did my heart to hear Leslie send you a message like that, laughing like she used to long ago. There's a great change come over her lately. She laughs and jokes like a girl, and from her talk I gather she's here real often."

"Every day—or else I'm over there," said Anne. "I don't know what I'd do without Leslie, especially just now when Gilbert is so busy. He's hardly ever home except for a few hours in the wee sma's. He's really working himself to death. So many of the over-harbour people send for him now."

"They might better be content with their own doctor," said Miss Cornelia. "Though to be sure I can't blame them, for he's a Methodist. Ever since Dr. Blythe brought Mrs. Allonby round folks think he can raise the dead. I believe Dr. Dave is a mite jealous—just like a man. He thinks Dr. Blythe has too many new-fangled notions! 'Well,' I says to him, 'it was a new-fangled notion saved Rhoda Allonby. If *you'd* been attending her she'd have died, and had a tombstone saying it had pleased God to take her away.' Oh, I *do* like to speak my mind to Dr. Dave! He's bossed the Glen for years, and he thinks he's forgotten more than other people ever knew. Speaking of doctors, I wish Dr. Blythe'd run over and see to that boil on Dick Moore's neck. It's getting past Leslie's skill. I'm sure I don't know what Dick Moore wants to start in having boils for—as if he wasn't enough trouble without that!"

"Do you know, Dick has taken quite a fancy to me," said Anne. "He follows me round like a dog, and smiles like a pleased child when I notice him."

"Does it make you creepy?"

"Not at all. I rather like poor Dick Moore. He seems so pitiful and appealing, somehow."

"You wouldn't think him very appealing if you'd see him on his cantankerous days, believe *me*. But I'm glad you don't mind him—it's all the nicer for Leslie. She'll have more to do when her boarder comes. I hope he'll be a decent creature. You'll probably like him—he's a writer."

"I wonder why people so commonly suppose that if two individuals are both writers they must therefore be hugely congenial," said Anne, rather scornfully. "Nobody would expect two blacksmiths to be violently attracted towards each other merely because they were both blacksmiths."

Nevertheless, she looked forward to the advent of Owen Ford with a pleasant sense of expectation. If he were young and likeable he might prove a very pleasant addition to society in Four Winds. The latch-string of the little house was always out for the race of Joseph.

XXIII

Owen Ford Comes

One evening Miss Cornelia telephoned down to Anne. "The writer man has just arrived here. I'm going to drive him down to your place, and you can show him the way to Leslie's. It's shorter than driving round by the other road, and I'm in a mortal hurry. The Reese baby has gone and fallen into a pail of hot water at the Glen, and got nearly scalded to death and they want me right off—to put a new skin on the child, I presume. Mrs. Reese is always so careless, and then expects other people to mend her mistakes. You won't mind, will you, dearie? His trunk can go down tomorrow."

"Very well," said Anne. "What is he like, Miss Cornelia?"

"You'll see what he's like outside when I take him down. As for what he's like inside only the Lord who made him knows *that*. I'm not going to say another word, for every receiver in the Glen is down."

"Miss Cornelia evidently can't find much fault with Mr. Ford's looks, or she would find it in spite of the receivers," said Anne. "I conclude therefore, Susan, that Mr. Ford is rather handsome than otherwise."

"Well, Mrs. Doctor, dear, I *do* enjoy seeing a well-looking man," said Susan candidly. "Had I not better get up a snack for him? There is a strawberry pie that would melt in your mouth."

"No, Leslie is expecting him and has his supper ready. Besides, I want that strawberry pie for my own poor man. He won't be home till late, so leave the pie and a glass of milk for him, Susan."

"That I will, Mrs. Doctor, dear. Susan is at the helm. After all, it is better to give pie to your own men than to strangers, who may be only seeking to devour, and the doctor himself is as well-looking a man as you often come across."

When Owen Ford came Anne secretly admitted, as Miss Cornelia towed him in, that he was very "well-looking" indeed. He was tall and broad-shouldered, with thick, brown hair, finely-cut nose and chin, large and brilliant dark-gray eyes.

"And did you notice his ears and his teeth, Mrs. Doctor, dear?" queried Susan later on. "He has got the nicest-shaped ears I ever saw on a man's head. I am choice about ears. When I was young I was scared that I might have to marry a man with ears like flaps. But I need not have worried, for never a chance did I have with any kind of ears."

Anne had not noticed Owen Ford's ears, but she did see his teeth, as his lips parted over them in a frank and friendly smile. Unsmiling, his face was rather sad and absent in expression, not unlike the melancholy, inscrutable hero of Anne's own early dreams; but mirth and humour and charm lighted it up when he smiled. Certainly, on the outside, as Miss Cornelia said, Owen Ford was a very presentable fellow.

"You cannot realise how delighted I am to be here, Mrs. Blythe," he said, looking around him with eager, interested eyes. "I have an odd feeling of coming home. My mother was born and spent her childhood here, you know. She used to talk a great deal to me of her old home. I know the geography of it as well as of the one I lived in, and of course, she told me the story of the building of the house, and of my grandfather's agonized watch for the *Royal William*. I had thought that so old a house must have vanished years ago, or I should have come to see it before this."

"Old houses don't vanish easily on this enchanted coast," smiled Anne. "This is a 'land where all things always seem the same'—nearly always, at least. John Selwyn's house hasn't even been much changed, and outside the rose-bushes your grandfather planted for his bride are blooming this very minute."

"How the thought links me with them! With your leave I must explore the whole place soon."

"Our latch-string will always be out for you," promised Anne. "And do you know that the old sea captain who keeps the Four Winds light knew John Selwyn and his bride well in his boyhood? He told me their story the night I came here— the third bride of the old house."

"Can it be possible? This *is* a discovery. I must hunt him up."

"It won't be difficult; we are all cronies of Captain Jim. He will be as eager to see you as you could be to see him. Your grandmother shines like a star in his memory. But I think Mrs. Moore is expecting you. I'll show you our 'cross-lots' road."

Anne walked with him to the house up the brook, over a field that was as white as snow with daisies. A boat-load of people were singing far across the harbour. The sound drifted over the water like faint, unearthly music, wind-blown across a starlit sea. The big light flashed and beaconed. Owen Ford looked around him with satisfaction.

"And so this is Four Winds," he said. "I wasn't prepared to find it quite so beautiful, in spite of all mother's praises. What colours—what scenery—what charm! I shall get as strong as a horse in no time. And if inspiration comes from beauty, I should certainly be able to begin my great Canadian novel here."

"You haven't begun it yet?" asked Anne.

"Alack-a-day, no. I've never been able to get the right central idea for it. It lurks beyond me—it allures—and beckons—and recedes—I almost grasp it and it is gone. Perhaps amid this peace and loveliness, I shall be able to capture it. Miss Bryant tells me that you write."

"Oh, I do little things for children. I haven't done much since I was married. And I have no designs on a great Canadian novel," laughed Anne. "That is quite beyond me."

Owen Ford laughed too.

"I dare say it is beyond me as well. All the same I mean to have a try at it someday, if I can ever get time. A newspaper man doesn't have much chance for that sort of thing. I've done a good deal of short story writing for the magazines, but I've never had the leisure that seems to be necessary for the writing of a book. With three months of liberty I ought to make a start, though—if I could only get the necessary *motif* for it— the *soul* of the book."

An idea whisked through Anne's brain with a suddenness that made her jump. But she did not utter it, for they had reached the Moore house. As they entered the yard Leslie came out on the veranda from the side door, peering through the gloom for some sign of her expected guest. She stood just where the warm yellow light flooded her from the open door. She wore a plain dress of cheap, cream-tinted cotton voile, with the usual girdle of crimson. Leslie was never without her touch of crimson. She had told Anne that she never felt satisfied without a gleam of red somewhere about her, if it were only a flower. To Anne, it always seemed to symbolize Leslie's glowing, pent-up personality, denied all expression save in that flaming glint. Leslie's dress was cut a little away at the neck and had short sleeves. Her arms gleamed like ivory-tinted marble. Every exquisite curve of her form was outlined in soft darkness against the light. Her hair shone in it like flame. Beyond her was a purple sky, flowering with stars over the harbour.

Anne heard her companion give a gasp. Even in the dusk she could see the amazement and admiration on his face.

"Who is that beautiful creature?" he asked.

"That is Mrs. Moore," said Anne. "She is very lovely, isn't she?"

"I—I never saw anything like her," he answered, rather dazedly. "I wasn't prepared—I didn't expect—good heavens, one *doesn't* expect a goddess for a landlady! Why, if she were clothed in a gown of sea-purple, with a rope of amethysts in her hair, she would be a veritable sea-queen. And she takes in boarders!"

"Even goddesses must live," said Anne. "And Leslie isn't a goddess. She's just a very beautiful woman, as human as the rest of us. Did Miss Bryant tell you about Mr. Moore?"

"Yes,—he's mentally deficient, or something of the sort, isn't he? But she said nothing about Mrs. Moore, and I supposed she'd be the usual hustling country housewife who takes in boarders to earn an honest penny."

"Well, that's just what Leslie is doing," said Anne crisply. "And it isn't altogether pleasant for her, either. I hope you won't mind Dick. If you do, please don't let Leslie see it. It would hurt her horribly. He's just a big baby, and sometimes a rather annoying one."

"Oh, I won't mind him. I don't suppose I'll be much in the house anyhow, except for meals. But what a shame it all is! Her life must be a hard one."

"It is. But she doesn't like to be pitied."

Leslie had gone back into the house and now met them at the front door. She greeted Owen Ford with cold civility, and told him in a business-like tone that his room and his supper were ready for him. Dick, with a pleased grin, shambled upstairs with the valise, and Owen Ford was installed as an inmate of the old house among the willows.

XXIV

The Life-Book of Captain Jim

"**I** have a little brown cocoon of an idea that may possibly expand into a magnificent moth of fulfillment," Anne told Gilbert when she reached home. He had returned earlier than she had expected, and was enjoying Susan's strawberry pie. Susan herself hovered in the background, like a rather grim but beneficent guardian spirit, and found as much pleasure in watching Gilbert eat pie as he did in eating it.

"What is your idea?" he asked.

"I sha'n't tell you just yet—not till I see if I can bring the thing about."

"What sort of a chap is Ford?"

"Oh, very nice, and quite good-looking."

"Such beautiful ears, Doctor, dear," interjected Susan with a relish.

"He is about thirty or thirty-five, I think, and he meditates writing a novel. His voice is pleasant and his smile delightful, and he knows how to dress. He looks as if life hadn't been altogether easy for him, somehow."

Owen Ford came over the next evening with a note to Anne from Leslie; they spent the sunset-time in the garden and then went for a moonlit sail on the harbour, in the little boat Gilbert had set up for summer outings. They liked Owen immensely and had that feeling of having known him for many years which distinguishes the freemasonry of the house of Joseph. "He is as nice as his ears, Mrs. Doctor, dear," said Susan, when he had gone. He had told Susan that he had never tasted anything like her strawberry shortcake and Susan's susceptible heart was his forever.

"He has got a way with him," she reflected, as she cleared up the relics of the supper. "It is real queer he is not married, for a man like that could have anybody for the asking. Well, maybe he is like me, and has not met the right one yet."

Susan really grew quite romantic in her musings as she washed the supper dishes.

Two nights later Anne took Owen Ford down to Four Winds Point to introduce him to Captain Jim. The clover fields along the harbour shore were whitening in the western wind, and Captain Jim had one of his finest sunsets on exhibition. He himself had just returned from a trip over the harbour.

"I had to go over and tell Henry Pollock he was dying. Everybody else was afraid to tell him. They expected he'd take on turrible, for he's been dreadful determined to live, and been making no end of plans for the fall. His wife thought he oughter be told and that I'd be the best one to break it to him that he couldn't get better. Henry and me are old cronies—we sailed in the *Gray Gull* for years together. Well, I went over and sat down by Henry's bed and I says to him, says I, jest right out plain and simple, for if a thing's got to be told it may as well be told first as last, says I, 'Mate, I reckon you've got your sailing orders this time.' I was sorter quaking inside, for it's an awful thing to have to tell a man who hain't any idea he's dying that he is. But lo and behold, Mistress Blythe, Henry looks up at me, with those bright old black eyes of his in his wizened face and says, says he, 'Tell me something I don't know, Jim Boyd, if you want to give me information. I've known *that* for a week.' I was too astonished to speak, and Henry, he chuckled. 'To see you coming in here,' says he, 'with your face as solemn as a tombstone and sitting down there with your hands clasped over your stomach, and passing me out a blue-mouldy old item of news like that! It'd make a cat laugh, Jim Boyd,' says he. 'Who told you?' says I, stupid like. 'Nobody,' says he. 'A week ago Tuesday night I was lying here awake—and I jest knew. I'd suspicioned it before, but then I *knew*. I've been keeping up for the wife's sake. And I'd *like* to have got that barn built, for Eben'll never get it right. But anyhow, now that you've eased your mind, Jim, put on a smile and tell me something interesting.' Well, there it was. They'd been so scared to tell him and he knew it all the time. Strange how nature looks out for us, ain't it, and lets us know what we should know when the time comes? Did I never tell you the yarn about Henry getting the fish hook in his nose, Mistress Blythe?"

"No."

"Well, him and me had a laugh over it today. It happened nigh unto thirty years ago. Him and me and several more was out mackerel fishing one day. It was a great day—never saw such a school of mackerel in the gulf—and in the general excitement Henry got quite wild and contrived to stick a fish hook clean through one side of his nose. Well, there he was; there was barb on one end and a big piece of lead on the other, so it couldn't be pulled out. We wanted to take him ashore at once, but Henry was game; he said he'd be jiggered if he'd leave a school like that for anything short of lockjaw; then he kept fishing away, hauling in hand over fist and groaning between times. Fin'lly the school passed and we come in with a load; I got a file and begun to try to file through that hook. I tried to be as easy as I could, but you should have heard Henry no, you shouldn't either. It was well no ladies were around. Henry wasn't a swearing man, but he'd heard some few matters of that sort along shore in his time, and he fished 'em all out of his recollection and hurled 'em at me. Fin'lly he declared he couldn't stand it and I had no bowels of compassion. So we hitched up and I drove him to a doctor in Charlottetown, thirty-five miles—there weren't none nearer in them days—with that blessed hook still hanging from his nose. When we got there old Dr. Crabb jest took a file and filed that hook jest the same as I'd tried to do, only he weren't a mite particular about doing it easy!"

Captain Jim's visit to his old friend had revived many recollections and he was now in the full tide of reminiscences.

"Henry was asking me today if I remembered the time old Father Chiniquy blessed Alexander MacAllister's boat. Another odd yarn—and true as gospel. I was in the boat myself. We went out, him and me, in Alexander MacAllister's boat one morning at sunrise. Besides, there was a French boy in the boat—Catholic of course. You know old Father Chiniquy had turned Protestant, so the Catholics hadn't much use for him. Well, we sat out in the gulf in the broiling sun till noon, and not a bite did we get. When we went ashore old Father Chiniquy had to go, so he said in that polite way of his, 'I'm very sorry I cannot go out with you dis afternoon, Mr. MacAllister, but I leave you my blessing. You will catch a t'ousand dis afternoon.' Well, we did not catch a thousand, but we caught exactly nine hundred and ninety-nine—the biggest catch for a small boat on the whole north shore that summer. Curious, wasn't it? Alexander MacAllister, he says to Andrew Peters, 'Well, and what do you think of Father Chiniquy now?' 'Vell,' growled Andrew, 'I t'ink de old devil has got a blessing left yet.' Laws, how Henry did laugh over that today!"

"Do you know who Mr. Ford is, Captain Jim?" asked Anne, seeing that Captain Jim's fountain of reminiscence had run out for the present. "I want you to guess."

Captain Jim shook his head.

"I never was any hand at guessing, Mistress Blythe, and yet I seen them eyes before?—for I *have* seen 'em."

"Think of a September morning many years ago," said Anne, softly. "Think of a ship sailing up the harbour—a ship long waited for and despaired of. Think of the day the *Royal William* came in and the first look you had at the schoolmaster's bride."

Captain Jim sprang up.

"They're Persis Selwyn's eyes," he almost shouted. "You can't be her son—you must be her—"

"Grandson; yes, I am Alice Selwyn's son."

Captain Jim swooped down on Owen Ford and shook his hand over again.

"Alice Selwyn's son! Lord, but you're welcome! Many's the time I've wondered where the descendants of the schoolmaster were living. I knew there was none on the Island. Alice— Alice—the first baby ever born in that little house. No baby ever brought more joy! I've dandled her a hundred times. It was from my knee she took her first steps alone. Can't I see her mother's face watching her—and it was near sixty years ago. Is she living yet?"

"No, she died when I was only a boy."

"Oh, it doesn't seem right that I should be living to hear that," sighed Captain Jim. "But I'm heart glad to see you. It's brought back my youth for a little while. You won't know yet what boon *that* is. Mistress Blythe here has the trick—she does it quite often for me."

Captain Jim was still more excited when he discovered that Owen Ford was what he called a "real writing man." He gazed at him as at a superior being. Captain Jim knew that Anne wrote, but he had never taken that fact very seriously. Captain Jim thought women were delightful creatures, who ought to have the vote, and everything else they wanted, bless their hearts; but he did not believe they could write.

"Jest look at *A Mad Love*," he would protest. "A woman wrote that and jest look at it—one hundred and three chapters when it could all have been told in ten. A writing woman never knows when to stop; that's the trouble. The p'int of good writing is to know when to stop."

"Mr. Ford wants to hear some of your stories, Captain Jim," said Anne. "Tell him the one about the captain who went crazy and imagined he was the Flying Dutchman."

This was Captain Jim's best story. It was a compound of horror and humour, and though Anne had heard it several times she laughed as heartily and shivered as fearsomely over it as Mr. Ford did. Other tales followed, for Captain Jim had an audience after his own heart. He told how his vessel had been run down by a steamer; how he had been boarded by Malay pirates; how his ship had caught fire; how he helped a political prisoner escape from a South African republic; how he had been wrecked one fall on the Magdalens and stranded there for the winter; how a tiger had broken loose on board ship; how his crew had mutinied and marooned him on a barren island—these and many other tales, tragic or humorous or grotesque, did Captain Jim relate. The mystery of the sea, the fascination of far lands, the lure of adventure, the laughter of the world—his hearers felt and realized them all. Owen Ford listened, with his head on his hand, and the First Mate purring on his knee, his brilliant eyes fastened on Captain Jim's rugged, eloquent face.

"Won't you let Mr. Ford see your life-book, Captain Jim?" asked Anne, when Captain Jim finally declared that yarn-spinning must end for the time.

"Oh, he won't want to be bothered with *that*," protested Captain Jim, who was secretly dying to show it.

"I should like nothing better than to see it, Captain Boyd," said Owen. "If it is half as wonderful as your tales it will be worth seeing."

With pretended reluctance Captain Jim dug his life-book out of his old chest and handed it to Owen.

"I reckon you won't care to wrastle long with my old hand o' write. I never had much schooling," he observed carelessly. "Just wrote that there to amuse my nephew Joe. He's always wanting stories. Comes here yesterday and says to me, reproachful-like, as I was lifting a twenty-pound codfish out of my boat, 'Uncle Jim, ain't a codfish a dumb animal?' I'd been a-telling him, you see, that he must be real kind to dumb animals, and never hurt 'em in any way. I got out of the scrape by saying a codfish was dumb enough but it wasn't an animal, but Joe didn't look satisfied, and I wasn't satisfied myself. You've got to be mighty careful what you tell them little critters. *They* can see through you."

While talking, Captain Jim watched Owen Ford from the corner of his eyes as the latter examined the life-book; and presently observing that his guest was lost in its pages, he turned smilingly to his cupboard and proceeded to make a pot of tea. Owen Ford separated himself from the life-book, with as much reluctance as a miser wrenches himself from his gold, long enough to drink his tea, and then returned to it hungrily.

"Oh, you can take that thing home with you if you want to," said Captain Jim, as if the "thing" were not his most treasured possession. "I must go down and pull my boat up a bit on the skids. There's a wind coming. Did you notice the sky tonight?

> *Mackerel skies and mares' tails*
> *Make tall ships carry short sails.*"

Owen Ford accepted the offer of the life-book gladly. On their way home Anne told him the story of lost Margaret.

"That old captain is a wonderful old fellow," he said. "What a life he has led! Why, the man had more adventures in one week of his life than most of us have in a lifetime. Do you really think his tales are all true?"

"I certainly do. I am sure Captain Jim could not tell a lie; and besides, all the people about here say that everything happened as he relates it. There used to be plenty of his old shipmates alive to corroborate him. He's one of the last of the old type of P. E. Island sea-captains. They are almost extinct now."

XXV

The Writing of the Book

O wen Ford came over to the little house the next morning in a state of great excitement.

"Mrs. Blythe, this is a wonderful book—absolutely wonderful. If I could take it and use the material for a book I feel certain I could make the novel of the year out of it. Do you suppose Captain Jim would let me do it?"

"Let you! I'm sure he would be delighted," cried Anne. "I admit that it was what was in my head when I took you down last night. Captain Jim has always been wishing he could get somebody to write his life-book properly for him."

"Will you go down to the Point with me this evening, Mrs. Blythe? I'll ask him about the life-book myself, but I want you to tell him that you told me the story of lost Margaret and ask him if he will let me use it as a thread of romance with which to weave the stories of the life-book into a harmonious whole."

Captain Jim was more excited than ever when Owen Ford told him of his plan. At last his cherished dream was to be realized and his "life-book" given to the world. He was also pleased that the story of lost Margaret should be woven into it.

"It will keep her name from being forgotten," he said wistfully. "That's why I want it put in."

"We'll collaborate," cried Owen delightedly. "You will give the soul and I the body. Oh, we'll write a famous book between us, Captain Jim. And we'll get right to work."

"And to think my book is to be writ by the schoolmaster's grandson!" exclaimed Captain Jim. "Lad, your grandfather was my dearest friend. I thought there was nobody like him. I see now why I had to wait so long. It couldn't be writ till the right man come. You *belong* here—you've got the soul of this old north shore in you—you're the only one who *could* write it."

It was arranged that the tiny room off the living room at the lighthouse should be given over to Owen for a workshop. It was necessary that Captain Jim should be near him as he wrote, for consultation upon many matters of sea-faring and gulf lore of which Owen was quite ignorant.

He began work on the book the very next morning, and flung himself into it heart and soul. As for Captain Jim, he was a happy man that summer. He looked upon the little room where Owen worked as a sacred shrine. Owen talked everything over with Captain Jim, but he would not let him see the manuscript.

"You must wait until it is published," he said. "Then you'll get it all at once in its best shape."

He delved into the treasures of the life-book and used them freely. He dreamed and brooded over lost Margaret until she became a vivid reality to him and lived in his pages.

As the book progressed it took possession of him and he worked at it with feverish eagerness. He let Anne and Leslie read the manuscript and criticize it; and the concluding chapter of the book, which the critics, later on, were pleased to call idyllic, was modelled upon a suggestion of Leslie's.

Anne fairly hugged herself with delight over the success of her idea.

"I knew when I looked at Owen Ford that he was the very man for it," she told Gilbert. "Both humour and passion were in his face, and that, together with the art of expression, was just what was necessary for the writing of such a book. As Mrs. Rachel would say, he was predestined for the part."

Owen Ford wrote in the mornings. The afternoons were generally spent in some merry outing with the Blythes. Leslie often went, too, for Captain Jim took charge of Dick frequently, in order to set her free. They went boating on the harbour and up the three pretty rivers that flowed into it; they had clam-bakes on the bar and mussel-bakes on the rocks; they picked strawberries on the sand dunes; they went out cod-fishing with Captain Jim; they shot plover in the shore fields and wild ducks in the cove—at least, the men did. In the evenings they rambled in the low-lying, daisied shore fields under a golden moon, or they sat in the living room at the little house where often the coolness of the sea breeze justified a drift-wood fire, and talked of the thousand and one things which happy, eager, clever young people can find to talk about.

Ever since the day on which she had made her confession to Anne, Leslie had been a changed creature. There was no trace of her old coldness and reserve, no shadow of her old bitterness. The girlhood of which she had been cheated seemed to come back to her with the ripeness of womanhood; she expanded like a flower of flame and perfume; no laugh was readier than hers, no wit quicker, in the twilight circles of that enchanted summer. When she could not be with them, all felt that some exquisite savour was lacking in their intercourse. Her beauty was illumined by the awakened soul within, as some rosy lamp might shine through a flawless vase of alabaster. There were hours when Anne's eyes seemed to ache with the splendour of her. As for Owen Ford, the "Margaret" of his book, although she had the soft brown hair and elfin face of the real girl who had vanished so long ago, "pillowed where lost Atlantis sleeps," had the personality of Leslie Moore, as it was revealed to him in those halcyon days at Four Winds Harbour.

All in all, it was a never-to-be-forgotten summer—one of those summers which come seldom into any life, but leave a rich heritage of beautiful memories in their going—one of those summers which, in a fortunate combination of delightful weather, delightful friends and delightful doings, come as near to perfection as anything can come in this world.

"Too good to last," Anne told herself with a little sigh, on the September day when a certain nip in the wind and a certain shade of intense blue on the gulf water said that autumn was hard by.

That evening Owen Ford told them that he had finished his book and that his vacation must come to an end.

"I have a good deal to do to it yet—revising and pruning and so forth," he said, "but in the main it's done. I wrote the last sentence this morning. If I can find a publisher for it, it will probably be out next summer or fall."

Owen had not much doubt that he would find a publisher. He knew that he had written a great book—a book that would score a wonderful success—a book that would *live*. He knew that it would bring him both fame and fortune; but when he had written the last line of it he had bowed his head on the manuscript and so sat for a long time. And his thoughts were not of the good work he had done.

XXVI

Owen Ford's Confession

"I'm so sorry Gilbert is away," said Anne. "He had to go—Allan Lyons at the Glen has met with a serious accident. He will not likely be home till very late. But he told me to tell you he'd be up and over early enough in the morning to see you before you left. It's too provoking. Susan and I had planned such a nice little jamboree for your last night here."

She was sitting beside the garden brook on the little rustic seat Gilbert had built. Owen Ford stood before her, leaning against the bronze column of a yellow birch. He was very pale and his face bore the marks of the preceding sleepless night. Anne glancing up at him, wondered if, after all, his summer had brought him the strength it should. Had he worked too hard over his book? She remembered that for a week he had not been looking well.

"I'm rather glad the doctor is away," said Owen slowly. "I wanted to see you alone, Mrs. Blythe. There is something I must tell somebody, or I think it will drive me mad. I've been trying for a week to look it in the face—and I can't. I know I can trust you—and, besides, you will understand. A woman with eyes like yours always understands. You are one of the folks people instinctively tell things to. Mrs. Blythe, I love Leslie. *Love* her! That seems too weak a word!"

His voice suddenly broke with the suppressed passion of his utterance. He turned his head away and hid his face on his arm. His whole form shook. Anne sat looking at him, pale and aghast. She had never thought of this! And yet—how was it she had never thought of it? It now seemed a natural and inevitable thing. She wondered at her own blindness. But—but things like this did not happen in Four Winds. Elsewhere in the world human passions might set at defiance human conventions and laws—but not *here*, surely. Leslie had kept summer boarders off and on for ten years, and nothing like this had happened. But perhaps they had not been like Owen Ford; and the vivid, *living* Leslie of this summer was not the cold, sullen girl of other years. Oh, *somebody* should have thought of this! Why hadn't Miss Cornelia thought of it? Miss Cornelia was always ready enough to sound the alarm where men were concerned. Anne felt an unreasonable resentment against Miss Cornelia. Then she gave a little inward groan. No matter who was to blame the mischief was done. And Leslie— what of Leslie? It was for Leslie Anne felt most concerned.

"Does Leslie know this, Mr. Ford?" she asked quietly.

"No—no,—unless she has guessed it. You surely don't think I'd be cad and scoundrel enough to tell her, Mrs. Blythe. I couldn't help loving her—that's all—and my misery is greater than I can bear."

"Does *she* care?" asked Anne. The moment the question crossed her lips she felt that she should not have asked it.

Owen Ford answered it with over-eager protest. "No—no, of course not. But I could make her care if she were free—I know I could."

"She does care—and he knows it," thought Anne. Aloud she said, sympathetically but decidedly:

"But she is not free, Mr. Ford. And the only thing you can do is to go away in silence and leave her to her own life."

"I know—I know," groaned Owen. He sat down on the grassy bank and stared moodily into the amber water beneath him. "I know there's nothing to do—nothing but to say conventionally, 'Good-bye, Mrs. Moore. Thank you for all your kindness to me this summer,' just as I would have said it to the sonsy, bustling, keen-eyed housewife I expected her to be when I came. Then I'll pay my board money like any honest boarder and go! Oh, it's very simple. No doubt—no perplexity—a straight road to the end of the world! And I'll walk it—you needn't fear that I won't, Mrs. Blythe. But it would be easier to walk over red-hot ploughshares."

Anne flinched with the pain of his voice. And there was so little she could say that would be adequate to the situation. Blame was out of the question—advice was not needed—sympathy was mocked by the man's stark agony. She could only feel with him in a maze of compassion and regret. Her heart ached for Leslie! Had not that poor girl suffered enough without this?

"It wouldn't be so hard to go and leave her if she were only happy," resumed Owen passionately. "But to think of her living death—to realize what it is to which I do leave her! *That* is the worst of all. I would give my life to make her happy—and I can do nothing even to help her—nothing. She is bound forever to that poor wretch—with nothing to look forward to but growing old in a succession of empty, meaningless, barren years. It drives me mad to think of it. But I must go through my life, never seeing her, but always knowing what she is enduring. It's hideous—hideous!"

"It is very hard," said Anne sorrowfully. "We—her friends here—all know how hard it is for her."

"And she is so richly fitted for life," said Owen rebelliously. "Her beauty is the least of her dower—and she is the most beautiful woman I've ever known. That laugh of hers! I've angled all summer to evoke that laugh, just for the delight of hearing it. And her eyes—they are as deep and blue as the gulf out there. I never saw such blueness—and gold! Did you ever see her hair down, Mrs. Blythe?"

"No."

"I did—once. I had gone down to the Point to go fishing with Captain Jim but it was too rough to go out, so I came back. She had taken the opportunity of what she expected to be an afternoon alone to wash her hair, and she was standing on the veranda in the sunshine to dry it. It fell all about her to her feet in a fountain of living gold. When she saw me she hurried in, and the wind caught her hair and swirled it all around her—Danae in her cloud. Somehow, just then the knowledge that I loved her came home to me—and I realized that I had loved her from the moment I first saw her standing against the darkness in that glow of light. And she must live on here—petting and soothing Dick, pinching and saving for a mere existence, while I spend my life longing vainly for her, and debarred, by that very fact, from even giving her the little help a friend might. I walked the shore last night, almost till dawn, and thrashed it all out over and over again. And yet, in spite of everything, I can't find it in my heart to be sorry that I came to Four Winds. It seems to me that, bad as everything is, it would be still worse never to have known Leslie. It's burning, searing pain to love her and leave her—but not to have loved her is unthinkable. I suppose all this sounds very crazy—all these terrible emotions always do sound foolish when we put them into our inadequate words. They are not meant to be spoken—only felt and endured. I shouldn't have spoken—but it has helped—some. At least, it has given me strength to go away respectably tomorrow morning, without making a scene. You'll write me now and then, won't you, Mrs. Blythe, and give me what news there is to give of her?"

"Yes," said Anne. "Oh, I'm so sorry you are going— we'll miss you so—we've all been such friends! If it were not for this you could come back other summers. Perhaps, even yet—by-and-by—when you've forgotten, perhaps—"

"I shall never forget—and I shall never come back to Four Winds," said Owen briefly.

Silence and twilight fell over the garden. Far away the sea was lapping gently and monotonously on the bar. The wind of evening in the poplars sounded like some sad, weird, old rune—some broken dream of old memories. A slender shapely young aspen rose up before them against the fine maize and emerald and paling rose of the western sky, which brought out every leaf and twig in dark, tremulous, elfin loveliness.

"Isn't that beautiful?" said Owen, pointing to it with the air of a man who puts a certain conversation behind him.

"It's so beautiful that it hurts me," said Anne softly. "Perfect things like that always did hurt me—I remember I called it 'the queer ache' when I was a child. What is the reason that pain like this seems inseparable from perfection? Is it the pain of finality—when we realize that there can be nothing beyond but retrogression?"

"Perhaps," said Owen dreamily, "it is the prisoned infinite in us calling out to its kindred infinite as expressed in that visible perfection."

"You seem to have a cold in the head. Better rub some tallow on your nose when you go to bed," said Miss Cornelia, who had come in through the little gate between the firs in time to catch Owen's last remark. Miss Cornelia liked Owen; but it was a matter of principle with her to visit any "high-falutin" language from a man with a snub.

Miss Cornelia personated the comedy that ever peeps around the corner at the tragedy of life. Anne, whose nerves had been rather strained, laughed hysterically, and even Owen smiled. Certainly, sentiment and passion had a way of shrinking out of sight in Miss Cornelia's presence. And yet to Anne nothing seemed quite as hopeless and dark and painful as it had seemed a few moments before. But sleep was far from her eyes that night.

XXVII

On the Sandbar

Owen Ford left Four Winds the next morning. In the evening Anne went over to see Leslie, but found nobody. The house was locked and there was no light in any window. It looked like a home left soulless. Leslie did not run over on the following day—which Anne thought a bad sign.

Gilbert having occasion to go in the evening to the fishing cove, Anne drove with him to the Point, intending to stay awhile with Captain Jim. But the great light, cutting its swathes through the fog of the autumn evening, was in care of Alec Boyd and Captain Jim was away.

"What will you do?" asked Gilbert. "Come with me?"

"I don't want to go to the cove—but I'll go over the channel with you, and roam about on the sandshore till you come back. The rock shore is too slippery and grim tonight."

Alone on the sands of the bar Anne gave herself up to the eerie charm of the night. It was warm for September, and the late afternoon had been very foggy; but a full moon had in part lessened the fog and transformed the harbour and the gulf and the surrounding shores into a strange, fantastic, unreal world of pale silver mist, through which everything loomed phantom-like. Captain Josiah Crawford's black schooner sailing down the channel, laden with potatoes for Bluenose ports, was a spectral ship bound for a far uncharted land, ever receding, never to be reached. The calls of unseen gulls overhead were the cries of the souls of doomed seamen. The little curls of foam that blew across the sand were elfin things stealing up from the sea-caves. The big, round-shouldered sand dunes were the sleeping giants of some old northern tale. The lights that glimmered palely across the harbour were the delusive beacons on some coast of fairyland. Anne pleased herself with a hundred fancies as she wandered through the mist. It was delightful—romantic—mysterious to be roaming here alone on this enchanted shore.

But was she alone? Something loomed in the mist before her—took shape and form—suddenly moved towards her across the wave-rippled sand.

"Leslie!" exclaimed Anne in amazement. "Whatever are you doing—*here*—tonight?"

"If it comes to that, whatever are *you* doing here?" said Leslie, trying to laugh. The effort was a failure. She looked very pale and tired; but the love locks under her scarlet cap were curling about her face and eyes like little sparkling rings of gold.

"I'm waiting for Gilbert—he's over at the cove. I intended to stay at the light, but Captain Jim is away."

"Well, *I* came here because I wanted to walk—and walk—and *walk*," said Leslie restlessly. "I couldn't on the rock shore—the tide was too high and the rocks prisoned me. I had to come here—or I should have gone mad, I think. I rowed myself over the channel in Captain Jim's flat. I've been here for an hour. Come—come—let us walk. I can't stand still. Oh, Anne!"

"Leslie, dearest, what is the trouble?" asked Anne, though she knew too well already.

"I can't tell you—don't ask me. I wouldn't mind your knowing—I wish you did know—but I can't tell you—I can't tell anyone. I've been such a fool, Anne—and oh, it hurts so terribly to be a fool. There's nothing so painful in the world."

She laughed bitterly. Anne slipped her arm around her.

"Leslie, is it that you have learned to care for Mr. Ford?"

Leslie turned herself about passionately.

"How did you know?" she cried. "Anne, how did you know? Oh, is it written in my face for everyone to see? Is it as plain as that?"

"No, no. I—I can't tell you how I knew. It just came into my mind, somehow. Leslie, don't look at me like that!"

"Do you despise me?" demanded Leslie in a fierce, low tone. "Do you think I'm wicked—unwomanly? Or do you think I'm just plain fool?"

"I don't think you any of those things. Come, dear, let's just talk it over sensibly, as we might talk over any other of the great crises of life. You've been brooding over it and let yourself drift into a morbid view of it. You know you have a little tendency to do that about everything that goes wrong, and you promised me that you would fight against it."

"But—oh, it's so—so shameful," murmured Leslie. "To love him—unsought—and when I'm not free to love anybody."

"There's nothing shameful about it. But I'm very sorry that you have learned to care for Owen, because, as things are, it will only make you more unhappy."

"I didn't *learn* to care," said Leslie, walking on and speaking passionately. "If it had been like that I could have prevented it. I never dreamed of such a thing until that day, a week ago, when he told me he had finished his book and must soon go away. Then—then I knew. I felt as if someone had struck me a terrible blow. I didn't say anything—I couldn't speak—but I don't know what I looked like. I'm so afraid my face betrayed me. Oh, I would die of shame if I thought he knew—or suspected."

Anne was miserably silent, hampered by her deductions from her conversation with Owen. Leslie went on feverishly, as if she found relief in speech.

"I was so happy all this summer, Anne—happier than I ever was in my life. I thought it was because everything had been made clear between you and me, and that it was our friendship which made life seem so beautiful and full once more. And it *was*, in part—but not all—oh, not nearly all. I know now why everything was so different. And now it's all over—and he has gone. How can I live, Anne? When I turned back into the house this morning after he had gone the solitude struck me like a blow in the face."

"It won't seem so hard by-and-by, dear," said Anne, who always felt the pain of her friends so keenly that she could not speak easy, fluent words of comforting. Besides, she remembered how well-meant speeches had hurt her in her own sorrow and was afraid.

"Oh, it seems to me it will grow harder all the time," said Leslie miserably. "I've nothing to look forward to. Morning will come after morning—and he will not come back—he will never come back. Oh, when I think that I will never see him again I feel as if a great brutal hand had twisted itself among my heartstrings, and was wrenching them. Once, long ago, I dreamed of love—and I thought it must be beautiful—and *now*—it's like *this*. When he went away yesterday morning he was so cold and indifferent. He said 'Good-bye, Mrs. Moore' in the coldest tone in the world—as if we had not even been friends—as if I meant absolutely nothing to him. I know I don't—I didn't want him to care—but he *might* have been a little kinder."

"Oh, I wish Gilbert would come," thought Anne. She was racked between her sympathy for Leslie and the necessity of avoiding anything that would betray Owen's confidence. She knew why his good-bye had been so cold—why it could not have the cordiality that their good-comradeship demanded—but she could not tell Leslie.

"I couldn't help it, Anne—I couldn't help it," said poor Leslie.

"I know that."

"Do you blame me so very much?"

"I don't blame you at all."

"And you won't—you won't tell Gilbert?"

"Leslie! Do you think I would do such a thing?"

"Oh, I don't know—you and Gilbert are such *chums*. I don't see how you could help telling him everything."

"Everything about my own concerns—yes. But not my friends' secrets."

"I couldn't have *him* know. But I'm glad *you* know. I would feel guilty if there were anything I was ashamed to tell you. I hope Miss Cornelia won't find out. Sometimes I feel as if those terrible, kind brown eyes of hers read my very soul. Oh, I wish this mist would never lift—I wish I could just stay in it forever, hidden away from every living being. I don't see how I can go on with life. This summer has been so full. I never was lonely for a moment. Before Owen came there used to be horrible moments—when I had been with you and Gilbert—and then had to leave you. You two would walk away together and I would walk away *alone*. After Owen came he was always there to walk home with me—we would laugh and talk as you and Gilbert were doing—there were no more lonely, envious moments for me. And *now*! Oh, yes, I've been a fool. Let's have done talking about my folly. I'll never bore you with it again."

"Here is Gilbert, and you are coming back with us," said Anne, who had no intention of leaving Leslie to wander alone on the sandbar on such a night and in such a mood. "There's plenty of room in our boat for three, and we'll tie the flat on behind."

"Oh, I suppose, I must reconcile myself to being the odd one again," said poor Leslie with another bitter laugh. "Forgive me, Anne—that was hateful. I ought to be thankful—and I *am*—that I have two good friends who are glad to count me in as a third. Don't mind my hateful speeches. I just seem to be one great pain all over and everything hurts me."

"Leslie seemed very quiet tonight, didn't she?" said Gilbert, when he and Anne reached home. "What in the world was she doing over there on the bar alone?"

"Oh, she was tired—and you know she likes to go to the shore after one of Dick's bad days."

"What a pity she hadn't met and married a fellow like Ford long ago," ruminated Gilbert. "They'd have made an ideal couple, wouldn't they?"

"For pity's sake, Gilbert, don't develop into a matchmaker. It's an abominable profession for a man," cried Anne rather sharply, afraid that Gilbert might blunder on the truth if he kept on in this strain.

"Bless us, Anne-girl, I'm not matchmaking," protested Gilbert, rather surprised at her tone. "I was only thinking of one of the might-have-beens."

"Well, don't. It's a waste of time," said Anne. Then she added suddenly:

"Oh, Gilbert, I wish everybody could be as happy as we are."

XXVIII

Odds and Ends

"I've been reading obituary notices," said Miss Cornelia, laying down the *Daily Enterprise* and taking up her sewing.

The harbour was lying black and sullen under a dour November sky; the wet, dead leaves clung drenched and sodden to the window sills; but the little house was gay with firelight and spring-like with Anne's ferns and geraniums.

"It's always summer here, Anne," Leslie had said one day; and all who were the guests of that house of dreams felt the same.

"The *Enterprise* seems to run to obituaries these days," quoth Miss Cornelia. "It always has a couple of columns of them, and I read every line. It's one of my forms of recreation, especially when there's some original poetry attached to them. Here's a choice sample for you:

> *She's gone to be with her Maker,*
> *Never more to roam.*
> *She used to play and sing with joy*
> *The song of Home, Sweet Home.*

Who says we haven't any poetical talent on the Island! Have you ever noticed what heaps of good people die, Anne, dearie? It's kind of pitiful. Here's ten obituaries, and every one of them saints and models, even the men. Here's old Peter Stimson, who has 'left a large circle of friends to mourn his untimely loss.' Lord, Anne, dearie, that man was eighty, and everybody who knew him had been wishing him dead these thirty years. Read obituaries when you're blue, Anne, dearie—especially the ones of folks you know. If you've any sense of humour at all they'll cheer you up, believe *me*. I just wish *I* had the writing of the obituaries of some people. Isn't 'obituary' an awful ugly word? This very Peter I've been speaking of had a face exactly like one. I never saw it but I thought of the word *obituary* then and there. There's only one uglier word that I know of, and that's *relict*. Lord, Anne, dearie, I may be an old maid, but there's this comfort in it—I'll never be any man's 'relict.'"

"It *is* an ugly word," said Anne, laughing. "Avonlea graveyard was full of old tombstones 'sacred to the memory of So-and-So, *relict* of the late So-and-So.' It always made me think of something worn out and moth-eaten. Why is it that so many of the words connected with death are so disagreeable? I do wish that the custom of calling a dead body 'the remains' could be abolished. I positively shiver when I hear the undertaker say at a funeral, 'All who wish to see the remains please step this way.' It always gives me the horrible impression that I am about to view the scene of a cannibal feast."

"Well, all I hope," said Miss Cornelia calmly, "is that when I'm dead nobody will call me 'our departed sister.' I took a scunner at this sistering-and-brothering business five years ago when there was a travelling evangelist holding meetings at the Glen. I hadn't any use for him from the start. I felt in my bones that there was something wrong with him. And there was. Mind you, he was pretending to be a Presbyterian— Presby*tar*ian, *he* called it—and all the time he was a Methodist. He brothered and sistered everybody. He had a large circle of relations, that man had. He clutched my hand fervently one night, and said imploringly, 'My *dear* sister Bryant, are you a Christian?' I just looked him over a bit, and then I said calmly, 'The only brother I ever had, Mr. Fiske, was buried fifteen years ago, I haven't adopted any since. As for being a Christian, I was that, I hope and believe, when you were crawling about the floor in petticoats.' *That* squelched him, believe *me*. Mind you, Anne, dearie, I'm not down on all evangelists. We've had some real fine, earnest men, who did a lot of good and made the old sinners squirm. But this Fiske-man wasn't one of them. I had a good laugh all to myself one evening. Fiske had asked all who were Christians to stand up. *I* didn't, believe *me*! I never had any use for that sort of thing. But most of them did, and then he asked all who wanted to be Christians to stand up. Nobody stirred for a spell, so Fiske started up a hymn at the top of his voice. Just in front of me poor little Ikey Baker was sitting in the Millison pew. He was a home boy, ten years old, and Millison just about worked him to death. The poor little creature was always so tired he fell asleep right off whenever he went to church or anywhere he could sit still for a few minutes. He'd been sleeping all through the meeting, and I was thankful to see the poor child getting a rest, believe *me*. Well, when Fiske's voice went soaring skyward and the rest joined in, poor Ikey wakened with a start. He thought it was just an ordinary singing and that everybody ought to stand up, so he

scrambled to his feet mighty quick knowing he'd get a combing down from Maria Millison for sleeping in meeting. Fiske
saw him, stopped and shouted, 'Another soul saved! Glory
Hallelujah!' And there was poor, frightened Ikey, only half
awake and yawning, never thinking about his soul at all. Poor
child, he never had time to think of anything but his tired,
overworked little body.

"Leslie went one night and the Fiske-man got right after
her—oh, he was especially anxious about the souls of the
nice-looking girls, believe me!—and he hurt her feelings so
she never went again. And then he prayed every night after
that, right in public that the Lord would soften her hard heart.
Finally I went to Mr. Leavitt, our minister then, and told him
if he didn't make Fiske stop that I'd just rise up the next night
and throw my hymn book at him when he mentioned that
'beautiful but unrepentant young woman.' I'd have done it
too, believe *me*. Mr. Leavitt did put a stop to it, but Fiske kept
on with his meetings until Charley Douglas put an end to his
career in the Glen. Mrs. Charley had been out in California
all winter. She'd been real melancholy in the fall—religious
melancholy—it ran in her family. Her father worried so much
over believing that he had committed the unpardonable sin
that he died in the asylum. So when Rose Douglas got that
way Charley packed her off to visit her sister in Los Angeles.
She got perfectly well and came home just when the Fiske
revival was in full swing. She stepped off the train at the Glen,
real smiling and chipper, and the first thing she saw staring
her in the face on the black, gable-end of the freight shed, was
the question, in big white letters, two feet high, 'Wither goest
thou—to heaven or hell?' That had been one of Fiske's ideas,

and he had got Henry Hammond to paint it. Rose just gave a shriek and fainted; and when they got her home she was worse than ever. Charley Douglas went to Mr. Leavitt and told him that every Douglas would leave the church if Fiske was kept there any longer. Mr. Leavitt had to give in, for the Douglases paid half his salary, so Fiske departed, and we had to depend on our Bibles once more for instructions on how to get to heaven. After he was gone Mr. Leavitt found out he was just a masquerading Methodist, and he felt pretty sick, believe *me*. Mr. Leavitt fell short in some ways, but he was a good, sound Presbyterian."

"By the way, I had a letter from Mr. Ford yesterday," said Anne. "He asked me to remember him kindly to you."

"I don't want his remembrances," said Miss Cornelia, curtly.

"Why?" said Anne, in astonishment. "I thought you liked him."

"Well, so I did, in a kind of way. But I'll never forgive him for what he done to Leslie. There's that poor child eating her heart out about him—as if she hadn't had trouble enough—and him ranting round Toronto, I've no doubt, enjoying himself same as ever. Just like a man."

"Oh, Miss Cornelia, how did you find out?"

"Lord, Anne, dearie, I've got eyes, haven't I? And I've known Leslie since she was a baby. There's been a new kind of heartbreak in her eyes all the fall, and I know that writer-man was behind it somehow. I'll never forgive myself for being the means of bringing him here. But I never expected he'd be like he was. I thought he'd just be like the other men Leslie had boarded—conceited young asses, every one of them, that she never had any use for. One of them did try to flirt with her once and she froze him out—so bad, I feel sure he's never got himself thawed since. So I never thought of any danger."

"Don't let Leslie suspect you know her secret," said Anne hurriedly. "I think it would hurt her."

"Trust me, Anne, dearie. *I* wasn't born yesterday. Oh, a plague on all the men! One of them ruined Leslie's life to begin with, and now another of the tribe comes and makes her still more wretched. Anne, this world is an awful place, believe *me*."

> *"There's something in the world amiss*
> *Will be unriddled by and by."*

quoted Anne dreamily.

"If it is, it'll be in a world where there aren't any men," said Miss Cornelia gloomily.

"What have the men been doing now?" asked Gilbert entering.

"Mischief—mischief! What else did they ever do?"

"It was Eve ate the apple, Miss Cornelia."

"'Twas a he-creature tempted her," retorted Miss Cornelia triumphantly.

Leslie, after her first anguish was over, found it possible to go on with life after all, as most of us do, no matter what our particular form of torment has been. It is even possible that she enjoyed moments of it, when she was one of the gay circle in the little house of dreams. But if Anne ever hoped that she was forgetting Owen Ford she would have been undeceived by the furtive hunger in Leslie's eyes whenever his name was mentioned. Pitiful to that hunger, Anne always contrived to tell Captain Jim or Gilbert bits of news from

Owen's letters when Leslie was with them. The girl's flush and pallor at such moments spoke all too eloquently of the emotion that filled her being. But she never spoke of him to Anne, or mentioned that night on the sandbar.

One day her old dog died and she grieved bitterly over him.

"He's been my friend so long," she said sorrowfully to Anne. "He was Dick's old dog, you know—Dick had him for a year or so before we were married. He left him with me when he sailed on the *Four Sisters*. Carlo got very fond of me—and his dog-love helped me through that first dreadful year after mother died, when I was all alone. When I heard that Dick was coming back I was afraid Carlo wouldn't be so much mine. But he never seemed to care for Dick, though he had been so fond of him once. He would snap and growl at him as if he were a stranger. I was glad. It was nice to have one thing whose love was all mine. That old dog has been such a comfort to me, Anne. He got so feeble in the fall that I was afraid he couldn't live long—but I hoped I could nurse him through the winter. He seemed pretty well this morning. He was lying on the rug before the fire; then, all at once, he got up and crept over to me; he put his head on my lap and gave me one loving look out of his big, soft, dog eyes—and then he just shivered and died. I shall miss him so."

"Let me give you another dog, Leslie," said Anne. "I'm getting a lovely Gordon setter for a Christmas present for Gilbert. Let me give you one too."

Leslie shook her head.

"Not just now, thank you, Anne. I don't feel like having another dog yet. I don't seem to have any affection left for another. Perhaps—in time—I'll let you give me one. I really need one as a kind of protection. But there was something almost human about Carlo—it wouldn't be *decent* to fill his place too hurriedly, dear old fellow."

Anne went to Avonlea a week before Christmas and stayed until after the holidays. Gilbert came up for her, and there was a glad New Year celebration at Green Gables, when Barrys and Blythes and Wrights assembled to devour a dinner which had cost Mrs. Rachel and Marilla much careful thought and preparation. When they went back to Four Winds the little house was almost drifted over, for the third storm of a winter that was to prove phenomenally stormy had whirled up the harbour and heaped huge snow mountains about everything it encountered. But Captain Jim had shovelled out doors and paths, and Miss Cornelia had come down and kindled the hearth-fire.

"It's good to see you back Anne, dearie! But did you ever see such drifts? You can't see the Moore place at all unless you go upstairs. Leslie'll be so glad you're back. She's almost buried alive over there. Fortunately Dick can shovel snow, and thinks it's great fun. Susan sent me word to tell you she would be on hand tomorrow. Where are you off to now, Captain?"

"I reckon I'll plough up to the Glen and sit a bit with old Martin Strong. He's not far from his end and he's lonesome. He hasn't many friends—been too busy all his life to make any. He's made heaps of money, though."

"Well, he thought that since he couldn't serve God and Mammon he'd better stick to Mammon," said Miss Cornelia crisply. "So he shouldn't complain if he doesn't find Mammon very good company now."

Captain Jim went out, but remembered something in the yard and turned back for a moment.

"I'd a letter from Mr. Ford, Mistress Blythe, and he says the life-book is accepted and is going to be published next fall. I felt fair uplifted when I got the news. To think that I'm to see it in print at last."

"That man is clean crazy on the subject of his life-book," said Miss Cornelia compassionately. "For my part, I think there's far too many books in the world now."

XXIX

Gilbert and Anne Disagree

G ilbert laid down the ponderous medical tome over which he had been poring until the increasing dusk of the March evening made him desist. He leaned back in his chair and gazed meditatively out of the window. It was early spring—probably the ugliest time of the year. Not even the sunset could redeem the dead, sodden landscape and rotten-black harbour ice upon which he looked. No sign of life was visible, save a big black crow winging his solitary way across a leaden field. Gilbert speculated idly concerning that crow. Was he a family crow, with a black but comely crow wife awaiting him in the woods beyond the Glen? Or was he a glossy young buck of a crow on courting thoughts intent? Or was he a cynical bachelor crow, believing that he travels the fastest who travels alone? Whatever he was, he soon disappeared in congenial gloom and Gilbert turned to the cheerier view indoors.

The firelight flickered from point to point, gleaming on the white and green coats of Gog and Magog, on the sleek, brown head of the beautiful setter basking on the rug, on the picture frames on the walls, on the vaseful of daffodils from the window garden, on Anne herself, sitting by her little table, with her sewing beside her and her hands clasped over her knee while she traced out pictures in the fire—Castles in Spain whose airy turrets pierced moonlit cloud and sunset bar-ships sailing from the Haven of Good Hopes straight to Four Winds Harbour with precious burthen. For Anne was again a dreamer of dreams, albeit a grim shape of fear went with her night and day to shadow and darken her visions.

Gilbert was accustomed to refer to himself as "an old married man." But he still looked upon Anne with the incredulous eyes of a lover. He couldn't wholly believe yet that she was really his. It *might* be only a dream after all, part and parcel of this magic house of dreams. His soul still went on tip-toe before her, lest the charm be shattered and the dream dispelled.

"Anne," he said slowly, "lend me your ears. I want to talk with you about something."

Anne looked across at him through the fire-lit gloom.

"What is it?" she asked, gaily. "You look fearfully solemn, Gilbert. I really haven't done anything naughty today. Ask Susan."

"It's not of you—or ourselves—I want to talk. It's about Dick Moore."

"Dick Moore?" echoed Anne, sitting up alertly. "Why, what in the world have you to say about Dick Moore?"

"I've been thinking a great deal about him lately. Do you remember that time last summer I treated him for those carbuncles on his neck?"

"Yes—yes."

"I took the opportunity to examine the scars on his head thoroughly. I've always thought Dick was a very interesting case from a medical point of view. Lately I've been studying the history of trephining and the cases where it has been employed. Anne, I have come to the conclusion that if Dick Moore were taken to a good hospital and the operation of trephining performed on several places in his skull, his memory and faculties might be restored."

"Gilbert!" Anne's voice was full of protest. "Surely you don't mean it!"

"I do, indeed. And I have decided that it is my duty to broach the subject to Leslie."

"Gilbert Blythe, you shall *not* do any such thing," cried Anne vehemently. "Oh, Gilbert, you won't—you won't. You couldn't be so cruel. Promise me you won't."

"Why, Anne-girl, I didn't suppose you would take it like this. Be reasonable—"

"I won't be reasonable—I can't be reasonable—I *am* reasonable. It is you who are unreasonable. Gilbert, have you ever once thought what it would mean for Leslie if Dick Moore were to be restored to his right senses? Just stop and think! She's unhappy enough now; but life as Dick's nurse and attendant is a thousand times easier for her than life as Dick's wife. I know—I *know*! It's unthinkable. Don't you meddle with the matter. Leave well enough alone."

"I *have* thought over that aspect of the case thoroughly, Anne. But I believe that a doctor is bound to set the sanctity of a patient's mind and body above all other considerations, no matter what the consequences may be. I believe it his duty to endeavour to restore health and sanity, if there is any hope whatever of it."

"But Dick isn't your patient in that respect," cried Anne, taking another tack. "If Leslie had asked you if anything could be done for him, *then* it might be your duty to tell her what you really thought. But you've no right to meddle."

"I don't call it meddling. Uncle Dave told Leslie twelve years ago that nothing could be done for Dick. She believes that, of course."

"And why did Uncle Dave tell her that, if it wasn't true?" cried Anne, triumphantly. "Doesn't he know as much about it as you?"

"I think not—though it may sound conceited and presumptuous to say it. And you know as well as I that he is rather prejudiced against what he calls 'these newfangled notions of cutting and carving.' He's even opposed to operating for appendicitis."

"He's right," exclaimed Anne, with a complete change of front. "I believe myself that you modern doctors are entirely too fond of making experiments with human flesh and blood."

"Rhoda Allonby would not be a living woman today if I had been afraid of making a certain experiment," argued Gilbert. "I took the risk—and saved her life."

"I'm sick and tired of hearing about Rhoda Allonby," cried Anne—most unjustly, for Gilbert had never mentioned Mrs. Allonby's name since the day he had told Anne of his success in regard to her. And he could not be blamed for other people's discussion of it.

Gilbert felt rather hurt.

"I had not expected you to look at the matter as you do, Anne," he said a little stiffly, getting up and moving towards the office door. It was their first approach to a quarrel.

But Anne flew after him and dragged him back.

"Now Gilbert, you are not 'going off mad.' Sit down here and I'll apologise bee-*yew*-ti-fully. I shouldn't have said that. But—oh, if you knew—"

Anne checked herself just in time. She had been on the very verge of betraying Leslie's secret.

"Knew what a woman feels about it," she concluded lamely.

"I think I do know. I've looked at the matter from every point of view—and I've been driven to the conclusion that it is my duty to tell Leslie that I believe it is possible that Dick can be restored to himself; there my responsibility ends. It will be for her to decide what she will do."

"I don't think you've any right to put such a responsibility on her. She has enough to bear. She is poor—how could she afford such an operation?"

"That is for her to decide," persisted Gilbert stubbornly.

"You say you think that Dick can be cured. But are you *sure* of it?"

"Certainly not. Nobody could be sure of such a thing. There may have been lesions of the brain itself, the effect of which can never be removed. But if, as I believe, his loss of memory and other faculties is due merely to the pressure on the brain centres of certain depressed areas of bone, then he can be cured."

"But it's only a possibility!" insisted Anne. "Now, suppose you tell Leslie and she decides to have the operation. It will cost a great deal. She will have to borrow the money, or sell her little property. And suppose the operation is a failure and Dick remains the same. How will she be able to pay back the money she borrows, or make a living for herself and that big helpless creature if she sells the farm?"

"Oh, I know—I know. But it is my duty to tell her. I can't get away from that conviction."

"Oh, I know the Blythe stubbornness," groaned Anne. "But don't do this solely on your own responsibility. Consult Doctor Dave."

"I *have* done so," said Gilbert reluctantly.

"And what did he say?"

"In brief—as you say—leave well enough alone. Apart from his prejudice against newfangled surgery, I'm afraid he looks at the case from your point of view—don't do it, for Leslie's sake."

"There now," cried Anne triumphantly. "I do think, Gilbert, that you ought to abide by the judgment of a man nearly eighty, who has seen a great deal and saved scores of lives himself—surely his opinion ought to weight more than a mere boy's."

"Thank you."

"Don't laugh. It's too serious."

"That's just my point. It *is* serious. Here is a man who is a helpless burden. He may be restored to reason and usefulness—"

"He was so very useful before," interjected Anne witheringly.

"He may be given a chance to make good and redeem the past. His wife doesn't know this. I do. It is therefore my duty to tell her that there is such a possibility. That, boiled down, is my decision."

"Don't say 'decision' yet, Gilbert. Consult somebody else. Ask Captain Jim what he thinks about it."

"Very well. But I'll not promise to abide by his opinion, Anne. This is something a man must decide for himself. My conscience would never be easy if I kept silent on the subject."

"Oh, your conscience!" moaned Anne. "I suppose that Uncle Dave has a conscience too, hasn't he?"

"Yes. But I am not the keeper of his conscience. Come Anne, if this affair did not concern Leslie—if it were a purely abstract case, you would agree with me,—you know you would."

"I wouldn't," vowed Anne, trying to believe it herself. "Oh, you can argue all night, Gilbert, but you won't convince me. Just you ask Miss Cornelia what she thinks of it."

"You're driven to the last ditch, Anne, when you bring up Miss Cornelia as a reinforcement. She will say, 'Just like a man,' and rage furiously. No matter. This is no affair for Miss Cornelia to settle. Leslie alone must decide it."

"You know very well how she will decide it," said Anne, almost in tears. "She has ideals of duty, too. I don't see how you can take such a responsibility on your shoulders. *I* couldn't."

> *"Because right is right to follow right*
> *Were wisdom in the scorn of consequence,"*

quoted Gilbert.

"Oh, you think a couplet of poetry a convincing argument" scoffed Anne. "That is so like a man."

And then she laughed in spite of herself. It sounded so like an echo of Miss Cornelia.

"Well, if you won't accept Tennyson as an authority,

perhaps you will believe the words of a Greater than he," said Gilbert seriously. "'Ye shall know the truth and the truth shall make you free.' I believe that, Anne, with all my heart. It's the greatest and grandest verse in the Bible—or in any literature—and the *truest*, if there are comparative degrees of trueness. And it's the first duty of a man to tell the truth, as he sees it and believes it."

"In this case the truth won't make poor Leslie free," sighed Anne. "It will probably end in still more bitter bondage for her. Oh, Gilbert, I *can't* think you are right."

XXX

Leslie Decides

A sudden outbreak of a virulent type of influenza at the Glen and down at the fishing village kept Gilbert so busy for the next fortnight that he had no time to pay the promised visit to Captain Jim. Anne hoped against hope that he had abandoned the idea about Dick Moore, and, resolving to let sleeping dogs lie, she said no more about the subject. But she thought of it incessantly.

"I wonder if it would be right for me to tell him that Leslie cares for Owen," she thought. "He would never let her suspect that he knew, so her pride would not suffer, and it *might* convince him that he should let Dick Moore alone. Shall I— shall I? No, after all, I cannot. A promise is sacred, and I've no right to betray Leslie's secret. But oh, I never felt so worried over anything in my life as I do over this. It's spoiling the spring—it's spoiling everything."

One evening Gilbert abruptly proposed that they go down and see Captain Jim. With a sinking heart Anne agreed, and they set forth. Two weeks of kind sunshine had wrought a miracle in the bleak landscape over which

Gilbert's crow had flown. The hills and fields were dry and brown and warm, ready to break into bud and blossom; the harbour was laughter-shaken again; the long harbour road was like a gleaming red ribbon; down on the dunes a crowd of boys, who were out smelt fishing, were burning the thick, dry sand-hill grass of the preceding summer. The flames swept over the dunes rosily, flinging their cardinal banners against the dark gulf beyond, and illuminating the channel and the fishing village. It was a picturesque scene which would at other times have delighted Anne's eyes; but she was not enjoying this walk. Neither was Gilbert. Their usual good-comradeship and Josephian community of taste and viewpoint were sadly lacking. Anne's disapproval of the whole project showed itself in the haughty uplift of her head and the studied politeness of her remarks. Gilbert's mouth was set in all the Blythe obstinacy, but his eyes were troubled. He meant to do what he believed to be his duty; but to be at outs with Anne was a high price to pay. Altogether, both were glad when they reached the light— and remorseful that they should be glad.

Captain Jim put away the fishing net upon which he was working, and welcomed them joyfully. In the searching light of the spring evening he looked older than Anne had ever seen him. His hair had grown much grayer, and the strong old hand shook a little. But his blue eyes were clear and steady, and the staunch soul looked out through them gallant and unafraid.

Captain Jim listened in amazed silence while Gilbert said what he had come to say. Anne, who knew how the old man worshipped Leslie, felt quite sure that he would side with her, although she had not much hope that this would influence Gilbert. She was therefore surprised beyond measure when Captain Jim, slowly and sorrowfully, but unhesitatingly, gave it as his opinion that Leslie should be told.

"Oh, Captain Jim, I didn't think you'd say that," she exclaimed reproachfully. "I thought you wouldn't want to make more trouble for her."

Captain Jim shook his head.

"I don't want to. I know how you feel about it, Mistress Blythe—just as I feel meself. But it ain't our feelings we have to steer by through life—no, no we'd make shipwreck mighty often if we did that. There's only the one safe compass and we've got to set our course by that—what it's right to do. I agree with the doctor. If there's a chance for Dick, Leslie should be told of it. There's no two sides to that, in my opinion."

"Well," said Anne, giving up in despair, "wait until Miss Cornelia gets after you two men."

"Cornelia'll rake us fore and aft, no doubt," assented Captain Jim. "You women are lovely critters, Mistress Blythe, but you're just a mite illogical. You're a highly eddicated lady and Cornelia isn't, but you're like as two peas when it comes to that. I dunno's you're any the worse for it. Logic is a sort of hard, merciless thing, I reckon. Now, I'll brew a cup of tea and we'll drink it and talk of pleasant things, jest to calm our minds a bit."

At least, Captain Jim's tea and conversation calmed Anne's mind to such an extent that she did not make Gilbert suffer so acutely on the way home as she had deliberately intended to do. She did not refer to the burning question at all, but she chatted amiably of other matters, and Gilbert understood that he was forgiven under protest.

"Captain Jim seems very frail and bent this spring. The winter has aged him," said Anne sadly. "I am afraid that he will soon be going to seek lost Margaret. I can't bear to think of it."

"Four Winds won't be the same place when Captain Jim 'sets out to sea,'" agreed Gilbert.

The following evening he went to the house up the brook. Anne wandered dismally around until his return.

"Well, what did Leslie say?" she demanded when he came in.

"Very little. I think she felt rather dazed."

"And is she going to have the operation?"

"She is going to think it over and decide very soon."

Gilbert flung himself wearily into the easy chair before the fire. He looked tired. It had not been an easy thing for him to tell Leslie. And the terror that had sprung into her eyes when the meaning of what he told her came home to her was not a pleasant thing to remember. Now, when the die was cast, he was beset with doubts of his own wisdom.

Anne looked at him remorsefully; then she slipped down on the rug beside him and laid her glossy red head on his arm.

"Gilbert, I've been rather hateful over this. I won't be any more. Please just call me red-headed and forgive me."

By which Gilbert understood that, no matter what came of it, there would be no I-told-you-so's. But he was not wholly comforted. Duty in the abstract is one thing; duty in the concrete is quite another, especially when the doer is confronted by a woman's stricken eyes.

Some instinct made Anne keep away from Leslie for the next three days. On the third evening Leslie came down to the little house and told Gilbert that she had made up her mind; she would take Dick to Montreal and have the operation.

She was very pale and seemed to have wrapped herself in her old mantle of aloofness. But her eyes had lost the look which had haunted Gilbert; they were cold and bright; and she proceeded to discuss details with him in a crisp, business-like way. There were plans to be made and many things to be thought over. When Leslie had got the information she wanted she went home. Anne wanted to walk part of the way with her.

"Better not," said Leslie curtly. "Today's rain has made the ground damp. Good-night."

"Have I lost my friend?" said Anne with a sigh. "If the operation is successful and Dick Moore finds himself again Leslie will retreat into some remote fastness of her soul where none of us can ever find her."

"Perhaps she will leave him," said Gilbert.

"Leslie would never do that, Gilbert. Her sense of duty is very strong. She told me once that her Grandmother West always impressed upon her the fact that when she assumed any responsibility she must never shirk it, no matter what the consequences might be. That is one of her cardinal rules. I suppose it's very old-fashioned."

"Don't be bitter, Anne-girl. You know you don't think it old-fashioned—you know you have the very same idea of the sacredness of assumed responsibilities yourself. And you are right. Shirking responsibilities is the curse of our modern life—the secret of all the unrest and discontent that is seething in the world."

"Thus saith the preacher," mocked Anne. But under the mockery she felt that he was right; and she was very sick at heart for Leslie.

A week later Miss Cornelia descended like an avalanche upon the little house. Gilbert was away and Anne was compelled to bear the shock of the impact alone.

Miss Cornelia hardly waited to get her hat off before she began.

"Anne, do you mean to tell me it's true what I've heard—that Dr. Blythe has told Leslie Dick can be cured, and that she is going to take him to Montreal to have him operated on?"

"Yes, it is quite true, Miss Cornelia," said Anne bravely.

"Well, it's inhuman cruelty, that's what it is," said Miss Cornelia, violently agitated. "I did think Dr. Blythe was a decent man. I didn't think he could have been guilty of this."

"Dr. Blythe thought it was his duty to tell Leslie that there was a chance for Dick," said Anne with spirit, "and," she added, loyalty to Gilbert getting the better of her, "I agree with him."

"Oh, no, you don't, dearie," said Miss Cornelia. "No person with any bowels of compassion could."

"Captain Jim does."

"Don't quote that old ninny to me," cried Miss Cornelia. "And I don't care who agrees with him. Think—*think* what it means to that poor hunted, harried girl."

"We *do* think of it. But Gilbert believes that a doctor should put the welfare of a patient's mind and body before all other considerations."

"That's just like a man. But I expected better things of you, Anne," said Miss Cornelia, more in sorrow than in wrath;

then she proceeded to bombard Anne with precisely the same arguments with which the latter had attacked Gilbert; and Anne valiantly defended her husband with the weapons he had used for his own protection. Long was the fray, but Miss Cornelia made an end at last.

"It's an iniquitous shame," she declared, almost in tears. "That's just what it is—an iniquitous shame. Poor, poor Leslie!"

"Don't you think Dick should be considered a little, too?" pleaded Anne.

"Dick! Dick Moore! *He's* happy enough. He's a better-behaved and more reputable member of society now than he ever was before. Why, he was a drunkard and perhaps worse. Are you going to set him loose again to roar and to devour?"

"He may reform," said poor Anne, beset by foe without and traitor within.

"Reform your grandmother!" retorted Miss Cornelia. "Dick Moore got the injuries that left him as he is in a drunken brawl. He *deserves* his fate. It was sent on him for a punishment. I don't believe the doctor has any business to tamper with the visitations of God."

"Nobody knows how Dick was hurt, Miss Cornelia. It may not been in a drunken brawl at all. He may have been waylaid and robbed."

"Pigs *may* whistle, but they've poor mouths for it," said Miss Cornelia. "Well, the gist of what you tell me is that the thing is settled and there's no use in talking. If that's so I'll hold my tongue. I don't propose to wear *my* teeth out gnawing files. When a thing has to be I give in to it. But I like to make mighty sure first that it *has* to be. Now, I'll devote *my* energies to comforting and sustaining Leslie. And after all," added Miss Cornelia, brightening up hopefully, "perhaps nothing can be done for Dick."

XXXI

The Truth Makes Free

Leslie, having once made up her mind what to do, proceeded to do it with characteristic resolution and speed. House-cleaning must be finished with first, whatever issues of life and death might await beyond. The gray house up the brook was put into flawless order and cleanliness, with Miss Cornelia's ready assistance. Miss Cornelia, having said her say to Anne, and later on to Gilbert and Captain Jim—sparing neither of them, let it be assured—never spoke of the matter to Leslie. She accepted the fact of Dick's operation, referred to it when necessary in a businesslike way, and ignored it when it was not. Leslie never attempted to discuss it. She was very cold and quiet during these beautiful spring days. She seldom visited Anne, and though she was invariably courteous and friendly, that very courtesy was as an icy barrier between her and the people of the little house. The old jokes and laughter and chumminess of common things could not reach her over it. Anne refused to feel hurt. She knew that Leslie was in the grip of a hideous dread—a dread that wrapped her away from all little glimpses of happiness and hours of pleasure. When one great passion seizes possession of the soul all other feelings are crowded aside. Never in all her life had Leslie Moore shuddered away from the future with more intolerable terror. But she went forward as unswervingly in the path she had elected as the martyrs of old walked their chosen way, knowing the end of it to be the fiery agony of the stake.

The financial question was settled with greater ease than Anne had feared. Leslie borrowed the necessary money from Captain Jim, and, at her insistence, he took a mortgage on the little farm.

"So that is one thing off the poor girl's mind," Miss Cornelia told Anne, "and off mine too. Now, if Dick gets well enough to work again he'll be able to earn enough to pay the interest on it; and if he doesn't I know Captain Jim'll manage someway that Leslie won't have to. He said as much to me. 'I'm getting old, Cornelia,' he said, 'and I've no chick or child of my own. Leslie won't take a gift from a living man, but mebbe she will from a dead one.' So it will be all right as far as *that* goes. I wish everything else might be settled as satisfactorily. As for that wretch of a Dick, he's been awful these last few days. The devil was in him, believe *me*! Leslie and I couldn't get on with our work for the tricks he'd play. He chased all her ducks one day around the yard till most of them died. And not one thing would he do for us. Sometimes, you know, he'll make himself quite handy, bringing in pails of water and wood. But this week if we sent him to the well he'd try to climb down into it. I thought once, 'If you'd only shoot down there head-first everything would be nicely settled.'"

"Oh, Miss Cornelia!"

"Now, you needn't Miss Cornelia me, Anne, dearie. *Anybody* would have thought the same. If the Montreal doctors can make a rational creature out of Dick Moore they're wonders."

Leslie took Dick to Montreal early in May. Gilbert went with her, to help her, and make the necessary arrangements for her. He came home with the report that the Montreal surgeon whom they had consulted agreed with him that there was a good chance of Dick's restoration.

"Very comforting," was Miss Cornelia's sarcastic comment.

Anne only sighed. Leslie had been very distant at their parting. But she had promised to write. Ten days after Gilbert's return the letter came. Leslie wrote that the operation had been successfully performed and that Dick was making a good recovery.

"What does she mean by 'successfully'?" asked Anne. "Does she mean that Dick's memory is really restored?"

"Not likely—since she says nothing of it," said Gilbert. "She uses the word 'successfully' from the surgeon's point of view. The operation has been performed and followed by normal results. But it is too soon to know whether Dick's faculties will be eventually restored, wholly or in part. His memory would not be likely to return to him all at once. The process will be gradual, if it occurs at all. Is that all she says?"

"Yes—there's her letter. It's very short. Poor girl, she must be under a terrible strain. Gilbert Blythe, there are heaps of things I long to say to you, only it would be mean."

"Miss Cornelia says them for you," said Gilbert with a rueful smile. "She combs me down every time I encounter her. She makes it plain to me that she regards me as little better than a murderer, and that she thinks it a great pity that Dr. Dave ever let me step into his shoes. She even told me that the Methodist doctor over the harbour was to be preferred before me. With Miss Cornelia the force of condemnation can no further go."

"If Cornelia Bryant was sick, it would not be Doctor Dave or the Methodist doctor she would send for," sniffed Susan. "She would have you out of your hard-earned bed in the middle of the night, Doctor, dear, if she took a spell of misery, that she would. And then she would likely say your bill was past all reason. But do not you mind her, Doctor, dear. It takes all kinds of people to make a world."

No further word came from Leslie for some time. The May days crept away in a sweet succession and the shores of Four Winds Harbour greened and bloomed and purpled. One day in late May Gilbert came home to be met by Susan in the stable yard.

"I am afraid something has upset Mrs. Doctor, Doctor, dear," she said mysteriously. "She got a letter this afternoon and since then she has just been walking round the garden and talking to herself. You know it is not good for her to be on her feet so much, Doctor, dear. She did not see fit to tell me what her news was, and I am no pry, Doctor, dear, and never was, but it is plain something has upset her. And it is not good for her to be upset."

Gilbert hurried rather anxiously to the garden. Had anything happened at Green Gables? But Anne, sitting on the rustic seat by the brook, did not look troubled, though she was certainly much excited. Her eyes were their grayest, and scarlet spots burned on her cheeks.

"What has happened, Anne?"

Anne gave a queer little laugh.

"I think you'll hardly believe it when I tell you, Gilbert. *I* can't believe it yet. As Susan said the other day, 'I feel like a fly coming to life in the sun—dazed-like.' It's all so incredible. I've read the letter a score of times and every time it's just the same—I can't believe my own eyes. Oh, Gilbert, you were right—so right. I can see that clearly enough now—and I'm so ashamed of myself—and will you ever really forgive me?"

"Anne, I'll shake you if you don't grow coherent. Redmond would be ashamed of you. *What* has happened?"

"You won't believe it—you won't believe it—"

"I'm going in to 'phone for Uncle Dave," said Gilbert, pretending to start for the house.

"Sit down, Gilbert. I'll try to tell you. I've had a letter, and oh, Gilbert, it's all so amazing—so incredibly amazing—we never thought—not one of us ever dreamed—"

"I suppose," said Gilbert, sitting down with a resigned air, "the only thing to do in a case of this kind is to have patience and go at the matter categorically. Whom is your letter from?"

"Leslie—and, oh, Gilbert—"

"Leslie! Whew! What has she to say? What's the news about Dick?"

Anne lifted the letter and held it out, calmly dramatic in a moment.

"There is *no* Dick! The man we have thought Dick Moore—whom everybody in Four Winds has believed for twelve years to be Dick Moore—is his cousin, George Moore, of Nova Scotia, who, it seems, always resembled him very strikingly. Dick Moore died of yellow fever thirteen years ago in Cuba."

XXXII

Miss Cornelia Discusses the Affair

"And do you mean to tell me, Anne, dearie, that Dick Moore has turned out not to be Dick Moore at all but somebody else? Is *that* what you 'phoned up to me today?"

"Yes, Miss Cornelia. It is very amazing, isn't it?"

"It's—it's—just like a man," said Miss Cornelia helplessly. She took off her hat with trembling fingers. For once in her life Miss Cornelia was undeniably staggered.

"I can't seem to sense it, Anne," she said. "I've heard you say it—and I believe you—but I can't take it in. Dick Moore is dead—has been dead all these years—and Leslie is free?"

"Yes. The truth has made her free. Gilbert was right when he said that verse was the grandest in the Bible."

"Tell me everything, Anne, dearie. Since I got your 'phone I've been in a regular muddle, believe *me*. Cornelia Bryant was never so kerflummuxed before."

"There isn't a very great deal to tell. Leslie's letter was short. She didn't go into particulars. This man—George Moore—has recovered his memory and knows who he is. He says Dick took yellow fever in Cuba, and the *Four Sisters* had to sail without him. George stayed behind to nurse him. But he died very shortly afterwards. George did not write Leslie because he intended to come right home and tell her himself."

"And why didn't he?"

"I suppose his accident must have intervened. Gilbert says it is quite likely that George Moore remembers nothing of his accident, or what led to it, and may never remember it. It probably happened very soon after Dick's death. We may find out more particulars when Leslie writes again."

"Does she say what she is going to do? When is she coming home?"

"She says she will stay with George Moore until he can leave the hospital. She has written to his people in Nova Scotia. It seems that George's only near relative is a married sister much older than himself. She was living when George sailed on the *Four Sisters*, but of course we do not know what may have happened since. Did you ever see George Moore, Miss Cornelia?"

"I did. It is all coming back to me. He was here visiting his Uncle Abner eighteen years ago, when he and Dick would be about seventeen. They were double cousins, you see. Their fathers were brothers and their mothers were twin sisters, and they did look a terrible lot alike. Of course," added Miss Cornelia scornfully, "it wasn't one of those freak resemblances you read of in novels where two people are so much alike that they can fill each other's places and their nearest and dearest can't tell between them. In those days you could tell easy enough which was George and which was Dick, if you saw them together and near at hand. Apart, or some distance away, it wasn't so easy. They played lots of tricks on people and thought it great fun, the two scamps. George Moore was a little taller and a good deal fatter than Dick—though neither of them was what you would call fat—they were both of the lean kind. Dick had higher colour than George, and his hair was a shade lighter. But their features were just alike, and they both had that queer freak of eyes—one blue and one hazel. They weren't much alike in any other way, though. George was a real nice fellow, though he was a scalawag for mischief, and some said he had a liking for a glass even then. But everybody liked him better than Dick. He spent about a month here. Leslie never saw him; she was only about eight or nine then and I remember now that she spent that whole winter over harbour with her grandmother West. Captain Jim was away, too—that was the winter he was wrecked on the Magdalens. I don't suppose either he or Leslie had ever heard about the Nova Scotia cousin looking so much like Dick. Nobody ever thought of him when Captain Jim brought Dick—George, I should say—home. Of course, we all thought Dick had changed considerable—he'd got so lumpish and fat. But we put that down to what had happened to him, and no doubt that was the reason, for, as I've said, George wasn't fat to begin with either. And there was no other way we could have guessed, for the man's senses were clean gone. I can't see that it is any wonder we were all deceived. But it's a staggering thing. And Leslie has sacrificed the best years of her life to nursing a man who hadn't any claim on her! Oh, drat the men! No matter what they do, it's the wrong thing. And no matter who they are, it's somebody they shouldn't be. They do exasperate me."

"Gilbert and Captain Jim are men, and it is through them that the truth has been discovered at last," said Anne.

"Well, I admit that," conceded Miss Cornelia reluctantly. "I'm sorry I raked the doctor off so. It's the first time in my life I've ever felt ashamed of anything I said to a man. I don't know as I shall tell him so, though. He'll just have to take it for granted. Well, Anne, dearie, it's a mercy the Lord doesn't answer all our prayers. I've been praying hard right along that the operation wouldn't cure Dick. Of course I didn't put it just quite so plain. But that was what was in the back of my mind, and I have no doubt the Lord knew it."

"Well, He has answered the spirit of your prayer. You really wished that things shouldn't be made any harder for Leslie. I'm afraid that in my secret heart I've been hoping the operation wouldn't succeed, and I am wholesomely ashamed of it."

"How does Leslie seem to take it?"

"She writes like one dazed. I think that, like ourselves, she hardly realizes it yet. She says, 'It all seems like a strange dream to me, Anne.' That is the only reference she makes to herself."

"Poor child! I suppose when the chains are struck off a prisoner he'd feel queer and lost without them for a while. Anne, dearie, there's a thought keeps coming into my mind. What about Owen Ford? We both know Leslie was fond of him. Did it ever occur to you that he was fond of her?"

"It—did—once," admitted Anne, feeling that she might say so much.

"Well, I hadn't any reason to think he was, but it just appeared to me he *must* be. Now, Anne, dearie, the Lord knows

I'm not a match-maker, and I scorn all such doings. But if I were you and writing to that Ford man I'd just mention, casual-like, what has happened. That is what *I'd* do."

"Of course I will mention it when I write him," said Anne, a trifle distantly. Somehow, this was a thing she could not discuss with Miss Cornelia. And yet, she had to admit that the same thought had been lurking in her mind ever since she had heard of Leslie's freedom. But she would not desecrate it by free speech.

"Of course there is no great rush, dearie. But Dick Moore's been dead for thirteen years and Leslie has wasted enough of her life for him. We'll just see what comes of it. As for this George Moore, who's gone and come back to life when everyone thought he was dead and done for, just like a man, I'm real sorry for him. He won't seem to fit in anywhere."

"He is still a young man, and if he recovers completely, as seems likely, he will be able to make a place for himself again. It must be very strange for him, poor fellow. I suppose all these years since his accident will not exist for him."

XXXIII

Leslie Returns

A fortnight later Leslie Moore came home alone to the old house where she had spent so many bitter years. In the June twilight she went over the fields to Anne's, and appeared with ghost-like suddenness in the scented garden.

"Leslie!" cried Anne in amazement. "Where have you sprung from? We never knew you were coming. Why didn't you write? We would have met you."

"I couldn't write somehow, Anne. It seemed so futile to try to say anything with pen and ink. And I wanted to get back quietly and unobserved."

Anne put her arms about Leslie and kissed her. Leslie returned the kiss warmly. She looked pale and tired, and she gave a little sigh as she dropped down on the grasses beside a great bed of daffodils that were gleaming through the pale, silvery twilight like golden stars.

"And you have come home alone, Leslie?"

"Yes. George Moore's sister came to Montreal and took him home with her. Poor fellow, he was sorry to part with me—though I was a stranger to him when his memory first came back. He clung to me in those first hard days when he was trying to realize that Dick's death was not the thing of yesterday that it seemed to him. It was all very hard for him. I helped him all I could. When his sister came it was easier for him, because it seemed to him only the other day that he had seen her last. Fortunately she had not changed much, and that helped him, too."

"It is all so strange and wonderful, Leslie. I think we none of us realize it yet."

"I cannot. When I went into the house over there an hour ago, I felt that it *must* be a dream—that Dick must be there, with his childish smile, as he had been for so long. Anne, I seem stunned yet. I'm not glad or sorry—or *anything*. I feel as if something had been torn suddenly out of my life and left a terrible hole. I feel as if I couldn't be *I*—as if I must have changed into somebody else and couldn't get used to it. It gives me a horrible lonely, dazed, helpless feeling. It's good to see you again—it seems as if you were a sort of anchor for my drifting soul. Oh, Anne, I dread it all—the gossip and wonderment and questioning. When I think of that, I wish that I need not have come home at all. Dr. Dave was at the station when I came off the train—he brought me home. Poor old man, he feels very badly because he told me years ago that nothing could be done for Dick. 'I honestly thought so, Leslie,' he said to me today. 'But I should have told you not to depend on my opinion—I should have told you to go to a specialist. If I had, you would have been saved many bitter years, and Poor George Moore many wasted ones. I blame myself very much, Leslie.' I told him not to do that—he had done what he thought right. He has always been so kind to me—I couldn't bear to see him worrying over it."

"And Dick—George, I mean? Is his memory fully restored?"

"Practically. Of course, there are a great many details he can't recall yet—but he remembers more and more every day. He went out for a walk on the evening after Dick was buried. He had Dick's money and watch on him; he meant to bring them home to me, along with my letter. He admits he went to a place where the sailors resorted—and he remembers drinking—and nothing else. Anne, I shall never forget the moment he remembered his own name. I saw him looking at me with an intelligent but puzzled expression. I said, 'Do you know me, Dick?' He answered, 'I never saw you before. Who are you? And my name is not Dick. I am George Moore, and Dick died of yellow fever yesterday! Where am I? What has happened to me?' I—I fainted, Anne. And ever since I have felt as if I were in a dream."

"You will soon adjust yourself to this new state of things, Leslie. And you are young—life is before you—you will have many beautiful years yet."

"Perhaps I shall be able to look at it in that way after awhile, Anne. Just now I feel too tired and indifferent to think about the future. I'm—I'm—Anne, I'm lonely. I miss Dick. Isn't it all very strange? Do you know, I was really fond of poor Dick—George, I suppose I should say—just as I would have been fond of a helpless child who depended on me for everything. I would never have admitted it—I was really ashamed of it—because, you see, I had hated and despised

Dick so much before he went away. When I heard that Captain Jim was bringing him home I expected I would just feel the same to him. But I never did—although I continued to loathe him as I remembered him before. From the time he came home I felt only pity—a pity that hurt and wrung me. I supposed then that it was just because his accident had made him so helpless and changed. But now I believe it was because there was really a different personality there. Carlo knew it, Anne—I know now that Carlo knew it. I always thought it strange that Carlo shouldn't have known Dick. Dogs are usually so faithful. But *he* knew it was not his master who had come back, although none of the rest of us did. I had never seen George Moore, you know. I remember now that Dick once mentioned casually that he had a cousin in Nova Scotia who looked as much like him as a twin; but the thing had gone out of my memory, and in any case I would never have thought it of any importance. You see, it never occurred to me to question Dick's identity. Any change in him seemed to me just the result of the accident.

"Oh, Anne, that night in April when Gilbert told me he thought Dick might be cured! I can never forget it. It seemed to me that I had once been a prisoner in a hideous cage of torture, and then the door had been opened and I could get out. I was still chained to the cage but I was not in it. And that night I felt that a merciless hand was drawing me back into the cage—back to a torture even more terrible than it had once been. I didn't blame Gilbert. I felt he was right. And he had been very good—he said that if, in view of the expense and uncertainty of the operation, I should decide not to risk it, he would not blame me in the least. But I knew how I ought to decide—and I couldn't face it. All night I walked the floor like a mad woman, trying to compel myself to face it. I couldn't, Anne—I thought I couldn't—and when morning broke I set my teeth and resolved that I *wouldn't*. I would let things remain as they were. It was very wicked, I know. It would have been a just punishment for such wickedness if I had just been left to abide by that decision. I kept to it all day. That afternoon I had to go up to the Glen to do some shopping. It was one of Dick's quiet, drowsy days, so I left him alone. I was gone a little longer than I had expected, and he missed me. He felt lonely. And when I got home, he ran to meet me just like a child, with such a pleased smile on his face. Somehow, Anne, I just gave way then. That smile on his poor vacant face was more than I could endure. I felt as if I were denying a child the chance to grow and develop. I knew that I must give him his chance, no matter what the consequences might be. So I came over and told Gilbert. Oh, Anne, you must have thought me hateful in those weeks before I went away. I didn't mean to be—but I couldn't think of anything except what I had to do, and everything and everybody about me were like shadows."

"I know—I understood, Leslie. And now it is all over—your chain is broken—there is no cage."

"There is no cage," repeated Leslie absently, plucking at the fringing grasses with her slender, brown hands. "But—it doesn't seem as if there were anything else, Anne. You—you remember what I told you of my folly that night on the sandbar? I find one doesn't get over being a fool very quickly. Sometimes I think there are people who are fools forever. And to be a fool—of that kind—is almost as bad as being a—a dog on a chain."

"You will feel very differently after you get over being tired and bewildered," said Anne, who, knowing a certain thing that Leslie did not know, did not feel herself called upon to waste overmuch sympathy.

Leslie laid her splendid golden head against Anne's knee.

"Anyhow, I have *you*," she said. "Life can't be altogether empty with such a friend. Anne, pat my head—just as if I were a little girl—*mother* me a bit—and let me tell you while my stubborn tongue is loosed a little just what you and your comradeship have meant to me since that night I met you on the rock shore."

XXXIV

The Ship o' Dreams Comes to Harbour

One morning, when a windy golden sunrise was billowing over the gulf in waves of light, a certain weary stork flew over the bar of Four Winds Harbour on his way from the Land of Evening Stars. Under his wing was tucked a sleepy, starry-eyed, little creature. The stork was tired, and he looked wistfully about him. He knew he was somewhere near his destination, but he could not yet see it. The big, white lighthouse on the red sandstone cliff had its good points; but no stork possessed of any gumption would leave a new, velvet baby there. An old gray house, surrounded by willows, in a blossomy brook valley, looked more promising, but did not seem quite the thing either. The staring green abode further on was manifestly out of the question. Then the stork brightened up. He had caught sight of the very place—a little white house nestled against a big, whispering fir-wood, with a spiral of blue smoke winding up from its kitchen chimney—a house which just looked as if it were meant for babies. The stork gave a sigh of satisfaction, and softly alighted on the ridge-pole.

Half an hour later Gilbert ran down the hall and tapped on the spare-room door. A drowsy voice answered him and in a moment Marilla's pale, scared face peeped out from behind the door.

"Marilla, Anne has sent me to tell you that a certain young gentleman has arrived here. He hasn't brought much luggage with him, but he evidently means to stay."

"For pity's sake!" said Marilla blankly. "You don't mean to tell me, Gilbert, that it's all over. Why wasn't I called?"

"Anne wouldn't let us disturb you when there was no need. Nobody was called until about two hours ago. There was no 'passage perilous' this time."

"And—and—Gilbert—will this baby live?"

"He certainly will. He weighs ten pounds and—why, listen to him. Nothing wrong with his lungs, is there? The nurse says his hair will be red. Anne is furious with her, and I'm tickled to death."

That was a wonderful day in the little house of dreams.

"The best dream of all has come true," said Anne, pale and rapturous. "Oh, Marilla, I hardly dare believe it, after that horrible day last summer. I have had a heartache ever since then—but it is gone now."

"This baby will take Joy's place," said Marilla.

"Oh, no, no, *no*, Marilla. He can't—nothing can ever do that. He has his own place, my dear, wee man-child. But little Joy has hers, and always will have it. If she had lived she would have been over a year old. She would have been toddling around on her tiny feet and lisping a few words. I can see her so plainly, Marilla. Oh, I know now that Captain Jim was right when he said God would manage better than that my baby would seem a stranger to me when I found her Beyond. I've learned *that* this past year. I've followed her development day by day and week by week—I always shall. I shall know just how she grows from year to year—and when I meet her again I'll know her—she won't be a stranger. Oh, Marilla, *look* at his dear, darling toes! Isn't it strange they should be so perfect?"

"It would be stranger if they weren't," said Marilla crisply. Now that all was safely over, Marilla was herself again.

"Oh, I know—but it seems as if they couldn't be quite *finished*, you know—and they are, even to the tiny nails. And his hands—*just* look at his hands, Marilla."

"They appear to be a good deal like hands," Marilla conceded.

"See how he clings to my finger. I'm sure he knows me already. He cries when the nurse takes him away. Oh, Marilla, do you think—you don't think, do you—that his hair is going to be red?"

"I don't see much hair of any colour," said Marilla. "I wouldn't worry about it, if I were you, until it becomes visible."

"Marilla, he *has* hair—look at that fine little down all over his head. Anyway, nurse says his eyes will be hazel and his forehead is exactly like Gilbert's."

"And he has the nicest little ears, Mrs. Doctor, dear." said Susan. "The first thing I did was to look at his ears. Hair is deceitful and noses and eyes change, and you cannot tell what is going to come of them, but ears is ears from start to finish, and you always know where you are with them. Just look at their shape— and they are set right back against his precious head. You will never need to be ashamed of his ears, Mrs. Doctor, dear."

Anne's convalescence was rapid and happy. Folks came and worshipped the baby, as people have bowed before the kingship of the new-born since long before the Wise Men of the East knelt in homage to the Royal Babe of the Bethlehem manger. Leslie, slowly finding herself amid the new conditions of her life, hovered over it, like a beautiful, golden-crowned Madonna. Miss Cornelia nursed it as knackily as could any mother in Israel. Captain Jim held the small creature in his big brown hands and gazed tenderly at it, with eyes that saw the children who had never been born to him.

"What are you going to call him?" asked Miss Cornelia.

"Anne has settled his name," answered Gilbert.

"James Matthew—after the two finest gentlemen I've ever known—not even saving your presence," said Anne with a saucy glance at Gilbert.

Gilbert smiled.

"I never knew Matthew very well; he was so shy we boys couldn't get acquainted with him—but I quite agree with you that Captain Jim is one of the rarest and finest souls God ever clothed in clay. He is so delighted over the fact that we have given his name to our small lad. It seems he has no other namesake."

"Well, James Matthew is a name that will wear well and not fade in the washing," said Miss Cornelia. "I'm glad you didn't load him down with some highfalutin, romantic name that he'd be ashamed of when he gets to be a grandfather. Mrs. William Drew at the Glen has called her baby Bertie Shakespeare. Quite a combination, isn't it? And I'm glad you haven't had much trouble picking on a name. Some folks have an awful time. When the Stanley Flaggs' first boy was born there was so much rivalry as to who the child should be named for that the poor little soul had to go for two years without a name. Then a brother came along and there it was—'Big Baby' and 'Little Baby.' Finally they called Big Baby Peter and Little Baby Isaac, after the two grandfathers, and had them both christened together. And each tried to see if it couldn't howl the other down. You know that Highland Scotch family of MacNabs back of the Glen? They've got twelve boys and the oldest and the youngest are both called Neil—Big Neil and Little Neil in the same family. Well, I s'pose they ran out of names."

"I have read somewhere," laughed Anne, "that the first child is a poem but the tenth is very prosy prose. Perhaps Mrs. MacNab thought that the twelfth was merely an old tale re-told."

"Well, there's something to be said for large families," said Miss Cornelia, with a sigh. "I was an only child for eight years and I did long for a brother and sister. Mother told me to pray for one—and pray I did, believe *me*. Well, one day Aunt Nellie came to me and said, 'Cornelia, there is a little brother for you upstairs in your ma's room. You can go up and see him.' I was so excited and delighted I just flew upstairs. And old Mrs. Flagg lifted up the baby for me to see. Lord, Anne, dearie, I never was so disappointed in my life. You see, I'd been praying for a *brother two years older than myself.*"

"How long did it take you to get over your disappointment?" asked Anne, amid her laughter.

"Well, I had a spite at Providence for a good spell, and for weeks I wouldn't even look at the baby. Nobody knew why, for I never told. Then he began to get real cute, and held out his wee hands to me and I began to get fond of him. But I didn't get really reconciled to him until one day a school chum came to see him and said she thought he was awful small for his age. I just got boiling mad, and I sailed right into her, and told her she didn't know a nice baby when she saw one, and ours was the nicest baby in the world. And after that I just worshipped him. Mother died before he was three years old and I was sister and mother to him both. Poor little lad, he was never strong, and he died when he wasn't much over twenty. Seems to me I'd have given anything on earth, Anne, dearie, if he'd only lived."

Miss Cornelia sighed. Gilbert had gone down and Leslie, who had been crooning over the small James Matthew in the dormer window, laid him asleep in his basket and went her way. As soon as she was safely out of earshot, Miss Cornelia bent forward and said in a conspirator's whisper:

"Anne, dearie, I'd a letter from Owen Ford yesterday. He's in Vancouver just now, but he wants to know if I can board him for a month later on. *You* know what that means. Well, I hope we're doing right."

"We've nothing to do with it—we couldn't prevent him from coming to Four Winds if he wanted to," said Anne quickly. She did not like the feeling of matchmaking Miss Cornelia's whispers gave her; and then she weakly succumbed herself.

"Don't let Leslie know he is coming until he is here," she said. "If she found out I feel sure she would go away at once. She intends to go in the fall anyhow—she told me so the other day. She is going to Montreal to take up nursing and make what she can of her life."

"Oh, well, Anne, dearie," said Miss Cornelia, nodding sagely, "that is all as it may be. You and I have done our part. We must leave the rest to Higher Hands."

XXXV

Politics at Four Winds

When Anne came downstairs again, the Island, as well as all Canada, was in the throes of a campaign preceding a general election. Gilbert, who was an ardent Conservative, found himself caught in the vortex, being much in demand for speech-making at the various country rallies. Miss Cornelia did not approve of his mixing up in politics and told Anne so.

"Dr. Dave never did it. Dr. Blythe will find he is making a mistake, believe *me*. Politics is something no decent man should meddle with."

"Is the government of the country to be left solely to the rogues then?" asked Anne.

"Yes—so long as it's Conservative rogues," said Miss Cornelia, marching off with the honours of war. "Men and politicians are all tarred with the same brush. The Grits have it laid on thicker than the Conservatives, that's all—*considerably* thicker. But Grit or Tory, my advice to Dr. Blythe is to steer clear of politics. First thing you know, he'll be running an election himself, and going off to Ottawa for half the year and leaving his practice to go to the dogs."

"Ah, well, let's not borrow trouble," said Anne. "The rate of interest is too high. Instead, let's look at Little Jem. It should be spelled with a G. Isn't he perfectly beautiful? Just see the dimples in his elbows. We'll bring him up to be a good Conservative, you and I, Miss Cornelia."

"Bring him up to be a good man," said Miss Cornelia. "They're scarce and valuable; though, mind you, I wouldn't like to see him a Grit. As for the election, you and I may be thankful we don't live over harbour. The air there is blue these days. Every Elliott and Crawford and MacAllister is on the warpath, loaded for bear. This side is peaceful and calm, seeing there's so few men. Captain Jim's a Grit, but it's my opinion he's ashamed of it, for he never talks politics. There isn't any earthly doubt that the Conservatives will be returned with a big majority again."

Miss Cornelia was mistaken. On the morning after the election Captain Jim dropped in at the little house to tell the news. So virulent is the microbe of party politics, even in a peaceable old man, that Captain Jim's cheeks were flushed and his eyes were flashing with all his old-time fire.

"Mistress Blythe, the Liberals are in with a sweeping majority. After eighteen years of Tory mismanagement this down-trodden country is going to have a chance at last."

"I never heard you make such a bitter partisan speech before, Captain Jim. I didn't think you had so much political venom in you," laughed Anne, who was not much excited over the tidings. Little Jem had said "Wow-ga" that morning. What were principalities and powers, the rise and fall of dynasties, the overthrow of Grit or Tory, compared with that miraculous occurrence?

"It's been accumulating for a long while," said Captain Jim, with a deprecating smile. "I thought I was only a moderate Grit, but when the news came that we were in I found out how Gritty I really was."

"You know the doctor and I are Conservatives."

"Ah, well, it's the only bad thing I know of either of you, Mistress Blythe. Cornelia is a Tory, too. I called in on my way from the Glen to tell her the news."

"Didn't you know you took your life in your hands?"

"Yes, but I couldn't resist the temptation."

"How did she take it?"

"Comparatively calm, Mistress Blythe, comparatively calm. She says, says she, 'Well, Providence sends seasons of humiliation to a country, same as to individuals. You Grits have been cold and hungry for many a year. Make haste to get warmed and fed, for you won't be in long.' 'Well, now, Cornelia,' I says, 'mebbe Providence thinks Canada needs a real long spell of humiliation.' Ah, Susan, have *you* heard the news? The Liberals are in."

Susan had just come in from the kitchen, attended by the odour of delectable dishes which always seemed to hover around her.

"Now, are they?" she said, with beautiful unconcern. "Well, I never could see but that my bread rose just as light when Grits were in as when they were not. And if any party, Mrs. Doctor, dear, will make it rain before the week is out, and save our kitchen garden from entire ruination, that is the party Susan will vote for. In the meantime, will you just step out and give me your opinion on the meat for dinner? I am fearing that it is very tough, and I think that we had better change our butcher as well as our government."

One evening, a week later, Anne walked down to the Point, to see if she could get some fresh fish from Captain Jim, leaving Little Jem for the first time. It was quite a tragedy. Suppose he cried? Suppose Susan did not know just exactly what to do for him? Susan was calm and serene.

"I have had as much experience with him as you, Mrs. Doctor, dear, have I not?"

"Yes, with him—but not with other babies. Why, I looked after three pairs of twins, when I was a child, Susan. When they cried, I gave them peppermint or castor oil quite coolly. It's quite curious now to recall how lightly I took all those babies and their woes."

"Oh, well, if Little Jem cries, I will just clap a hot water bag on his little stomach," said Susan.

"Not too hot, you know," said Anne anxiously. Oh, was it really wise to go?

"Do not you fret, Mrs. Doctor, dear. Susan is not the woman to burn a wee man. Bless him, he has no notion of crying."

Anne tore herself away finally and enjoyed her walk to the Point after all, through the long shadows of the sun-setting. Captain Jim was not in the living room of the lighthouse, but another man was—a handsome, middle-aged man, with a strong, clean-shaven chin, who was unknown to Anne. Nevertheless, when she sat down, he began to talk to her with all the assurance of an old acquaintance. There was nothing amiss in what he said or the way he said it, but Anne rather resented such a cool taking-for-granted in a complete stranger. Her replies were frosty, and as few as decency required. Nothing daunted, her companion talked on for several minutes, then excused himself and went away. Anne could have sworn there was a twinkle in his eye and it annoyed her. Who was the creature? There was something vaguely familiar about him but she was certain she had never seen him before.

"Captain Jim, who was that who just went out?" she asked, as Captain Jim came in.

"Marshall Elliott," answered the captain.

"Marshall Elliott!" cried Anne. "Oh, Captain Jim—it wasn't—yes, it *was* his voice—oh, Captain Jim, I didn't know him—and I was quite insulting to him! *Why* didn't he tell me? He must have seen I didn't know him."

"He wouldn't say a word about it—he'd just enjoy the joke. Don't worry over snubbing him—he'll think it fun. Yes, Marshall's shaved off his beard at last and cut his hair. His party is in, you know. I didn't know him myself first time I saw him. He was up in Carter Flagg's store at the Glen the night after election day, along with a crowd of others, waiting for the news. About twelve the 'phone came through—the Liberals were in. Marshall just got up and walked out—he didn't cheer or shout—he left the others to do that, and they nearly lifted the roof off Carter's store, I reckon. Of course, all the Tories were over in Raymond Russell's store. Not much cheering *there*. Marshall went straight down the street to the side door of Augustus Palmer's barber shop. Augustus was in bed asleep, but Marshall hammered on the door until he got up and come down, wanting to know what all the racket was about.

"'Come into your shop and do the best job you ever did in your life, Gus,' said Marshall. 'The Liberals are in and you're going to barber a good Grit before the sun rises.'

"Gus was mad as hops—partly because he'd been dragged out of bed, but more because he's a Tory. He vowed he wouldn't shave any man after twelve at night.

"'You'll do what I want you to do, sonny,' said Marshall, 'or I'll jest turn you over my knee and give you one of those spankings your mother forgot.'

"He'd have done it, too, and Gus knew it, for Marshall is as strong as an ox and Gus is only a midget of a man. So he gave in and towed Marshall in to the shop and went to work. 'Now,' says he, 'I'll barber you up, but if you say one word to me about the Grits getting in while I'm doing it I'll cut your throat with this razor,' says he. You wouldn't have thought mild little Gus could be so bloodthirsty, would you? Shows what party politics will do for a man. Marshall kept quiet and got his hair and beard disposed of and went home. When his old housekeeper heard him come upstairs she peeked out of her bedroom door to see whether 'twas him or the hired boy. And when she saw a strange man striding down the hall with a candle in his hand she screamed blue murder and fainted dead away. They had to send for the doctor before they could bring her to, and it was several days before she could look at Marshall without shaking all over."

Captain Jim had no fish. He seldom went out in his boat that summer, and his long tramping expeditions were over. He spent a great deal of his time sitting by his seaward window, looking out over the gulf, with his swiftly-whitening head leaning on his hand. He sat there tonight for many silent minutes, keeping some trysts with the past which Anne would not disturb. Presently he pointed to the iris of the West:

"That's beautiful, isn't it, Mistress Blythe? But I wish you could have seen the sunrise this morning. It was a wonderful thing—wonderful. I've seen all kinds of sunrises come over that gulf. I've been all over the world, Mistress Blythe, and take it all in all, I've never seen a finer sight than a summer sunrise over the gulf. A man can't pick his time for dying, Mistress Blythe—jest got to go when the Great Captain gives His sailing orders. But if I could I'd go out when the morning comes across that water. I've watched it many a time and thought what a thing it would be to pass out through that great white glory to whatever was waiting beyant, on a sea that ain't mapped out on any airthly chart. I think, Mistress Blythe, that I'd find lost Margaret there."

Captain Jim had often talked to Anne of lost Margaret since he had told her the old story. His love for her trembled in every tone—that love that had never grown faint or forgetful.

"Anyway, I hope when my time comes I'll go quick and easy. I don't think I'm a coward, Mistress Blythe—I've looked an ugly death in the face more than once without blenching. But the thought of a lingering death does give me a queer, sick feeling of horror."

"Don't talk about leaving us, dear, *dear* Captain Jim," pleaded Anne, in a choked voice, patting the old brown hand, once so strong, but now grown very feeble. "What would we do without you?"

Captain Jim smiled beautifully.

"Oh, you'd get along nicely—nicely—but you wouldn't forget the old man altogether, Mistress Blythe—no, I don't think you'll ever quite forget him. The race of Joseph always remembers one another. But it'll be a memory that won't hurt—I like to think that my memory won't hurt my friends—it'll always be kind of pleasant to them, I hope and believe. It won't be very long now before lost Margaret calls me, for the last time. I'll be all ready to answer. I jest spoke of this because there's a little favour I want to ask you. Here's this poor old Matey of mine"—Captain Jim reached out a hand and poked the big, warm, velvety, golden ball on the sofa. The First Mate uncoiled himself like a spring with a nice, throaty, comfortable sound, half purr, half meow, stretched his paws in air, turned over and coiled himself up again. "*He*'ll miss me when I start on the Long V'yage. I can't bear to think of leaving the poor critter to starve, like he was left before. If anything happens to me will you give Matey a bite and a corner, Mistress Blythe?"

"Indeed I will."

"Then that is all I had on my mind. Your Little Jem is to have the few curious things I picked up—I've seen to that. And now I don't like to see tears in those pretty eyes, Mistress Blythe. I'll mebbe hang on for quite a spell yet. I heard you reading a piece of poetry one day last winter—one of Tennyson's pieces. I'd sorter like to hear it again, if you could recite it for me."

Softly and clearly, while the sea-wind blew in on them, Anne repeated the beautiful lines of Tennyson's wonderful swan song—"Crossing the Bar." The old captain kept time gently with his sinewy hand.

"Yes, yes, Mistress Blythe," he said, when she had finished, "that's it, that is. He wasn't a sailor, you tell me—I dunno how he could have put an old sailor's feelings into words like that, if he wasn't one. He didn't want any 'sadness o' farewells' and neither do I Mistress Blythe—for all will be well with me and mine beyant the bar."

XXXVI

Beauty for Ashes

"Any news from Green Gables, Anne?"

"Nothing very especial," replied Anne, folding up Marilla's letter. "Jack Donnell has been there shingling the roof. He is a full-fledged carpenter now, so it seems he has had his own way in regard to the choice of a life-work. You remember his mother wanted him to be a college professor. I shall never forget the day she came to the school and rated me for failing to call him St. Clair."

"Does anyone ever call him that now?"

"Evidently not. It seems that he has completely lived it down. Even his mother has succumbed. I always thought that a boy with Jake's chin and mouth would get his own way in the end. Diana writes me that Dora has a beau. Just think of it—that child!"

"Dora is seventeen," said Gilbert. "Charlie Sloane and I were both mad about you when you were seventeen, Anne."

"Really, Gilbert, we must be getting on in years," said Anne, with a half-rueful smile, "when children who were six when we thought ourselves grown up are old enough now to have beaux. Dora's is Ralph Andrews—Jane's brother. I remember him as a little, round, fat, white-headed fellow who was always at the foot of his class. But I understand he is quite a fine-looking young man now."

"Dora will probably marry young. She's of the same type as Charlotta the Fourth—she'll never miss her first chance for fear she might not get another."

"Well, if she marries Ralph I hope he will be a little more up-and-coming than his brother Billy," mused Anne.

"For instance," said Gilbert, laughing, "let us hope he will be able to propose on his own account. Anne, would you have married Billy if he had asked you himself, instead of getting Jane to do it for him?"

"I might have." Anne went off into a shriek of laughter over the recollection of her first proposal. "The shock of the whole thing might have hypnotized me into some rash and foolish act. Let us be thankful he did it by proxy."

"I had a letter from George Moore yesterday," said Leslie, from the corner where she was reading.

"Oh, how is he?" asked Anne interestedly, yet with an unreal feeling that she was inquiring about someone whom she did not know.

"He is well, but he finds it very hard to adapt himself to all the changes in his old home and friends. He is going to sea again in the spring. It's in his blood, he says, and he longs for it. But he told me something that made me glad for him, poor fellow. Before he sailed on the *Four Sisters* he was engaged to a girl at home. He did not tell me anything about her in Montreal, because he said he supposed she would have forgotten him and married someone else long ago, and with him, you see, his engagement and love was still a thing of the present. It was pretty hard on him, but when he got home he found she had never married and still cared for him. They are to be married this fall. I'm going to ask him to bring her over here for a little trip; he says he wants to come and see the place where he lived so many years without knowing it."

"What a nice little romance," said Anne, whose love for the romantic was immortal. "And to think," she added with a sigh of self-reproach, "that if I had had my way George Moore would never have come up from the grave in which his identity was buried. How I did fight against Gilbert's suggestion! Well, I am punished: I shall never be able to have a different opinion from Gilbert's again! If I try to have, he will squelch me by casting George Moore's case up to me!"

"As if even that would squelch a woman!" mocked Gilbert. "At least do not become my echo, Anne. A little opposition gives spice to life. I do not want a wife like John MacAllister's over the harbour. No matter what he says, she at once remarks in that drab, lifeless little voice of hers, 'That is very true, John, dear me!'"

Anne and Leslie laughed. Anne's laughter was silver and Leslie's golden, and the combination of the two was as satisfactory as a perfect chord in music.

Susan, coming in on the heels of the laughter, echoed it with a resounding sigh.

"Why, Susan, what is the matter?" asked Gilbert.

"There's nothing wrong with Little Jem, is there, Susan?" cried Anne, starting up in alarm.

"No, no, calm yourself, Mrs. Doctor, dear. Something has happened, though. Dear me, everything has gone catawampus

with me this week. I spoiled the bread as you know too well—
and I scorched the doctor's best shirt bosom—and I broke your
big platter. And now, on the top of all this, comes word that my
sister Matilda has broken her leg and wants me to go and stay
with her for a spell."

"Oh, I'm very sorry—sorry that your sister has met with
such an accident, I mean," exclaimed Anne.

"Ah, well, man was made to mourn, Mrs. Doctor, dear.
That sounds as if it ought to be in the Bible, but they tell me a
person named Burns wrote it. And there is no doubt that we
are born to trouble as the sparks fly upward. As for Matilda,
I do not know what to think of her. None of our family ever
broke their legs before. But whatever she has done she is still
my sister, and I feel that it is my duty to go and wait on her, if
you can spare me for a few weeks, Mrs. Doctor, dear."

"Of course, Susan, of course. I can get someone to help
me while you are gone."

"If you cannot I will not go, Mrs. Doctor, dear, Matilda's
leg to the contrary notwithstanding. I will not have you
worried, and that blessed child upset in consequence, for any
number of legs."

"Oh, you must go to your sister at once, Susan. I can get
a girl from the cove, who will do for a time."

"Anne, will you let me come and stay with you while Susan
is away?" exclaimed Leslie. "Do! I'd love to—and it would be
an act of charity on your part. I'm so horribly lonely over there
in that big barn of a house. There's so little to do—and at night
I'm worse than lonely—I'm frightened and nervous in spite of
locked doors. There was a tramp around two days ago."

Anne joyfully agreed, and next day Leslie was installed

as an inmate of the little house of dreams. Miss Cornelia warmly approved of the arrangement.

"It seems Providential," she told Anne in confidence. "I'm sorry for Matilda Clow, but since she had to break her leg it couldn't have happened at a better time. Leslie will be here while Owen Ford is in Four Winds, and those old cats up at the Glen won't get the chance to meow, as they would if she was living over there alone and Owen going to see her. They are doing enough of it as it is, because she doesn't put on mourning. I said to one of them, 'If you mean she should put on mourning for George Moore, it seems to me more like his resurrection than his funeral; and if it's Dick you mean, I confess *I* can't see the propriety of going into weeds for a man who died thirteen years ago and good riddance then!' And when old Louisa Baldwin remarked to me that she thought it very strange that Leslie should never have suspected it wasn't her own husband *I* said, '*You* never suspected it wasn't Dick Moore, and you were next-door neighbour to him all his life, and by nature you're ten times as suspicious as Leslie.' But you can't stop people's tongues, Anne, dearie, and I'm real thankful Leslie will be under your roof while Owen is courting her."

Owen Ford came to the little house one August evening when Leslie and Anne were absorbed in worshipping the baby. He paused at the open door of the living room, unseen by the two within, gazing with greedy eyes at the beautiful picture. Leslie sat on the floor with the baby in her lap, making ecstatic dabs at his fat little hands as he fluttered them in the air.

"Oh, you dear, beautiful beloved baby," she mumbled, catching one wee hand and covering it with kisses.

"Isn't him ze darlingest itty sing," crooned Anne, hanging over the arm of her chair adoringly. "Dem itty wee pads are ze very tweetest handies in ze whole big world, isn't dey, you darling itty man."

Anne, in the months before Little Jem's coming, had pored diligently over several wise volumes, and pinned her faith to one in especial, "Sir Oracle on the Care and Training of Children." Sir Oracle implored parents by all they held sacred never to talk "baby talk" to their children. Infants should invariably be addressed in classical language from the moment of their birth. So should they learn to speak English undefiled from their earliest utterance. "How," demanded Sir Oracle, "can a mother reasonably expect her child to learn correct speech, when she continually accustoms its impressionable gray matter to such absurd expressions and distortions of our noble tongue as thoughtless mothers inflict every day on the helpless creatures committed to their care? Can a child who is constantly called 'tweet itty wee singie' ever attain to any proper conception of his own being and possibilities and destiny?"

Anne was vastly impressed with this, and informed Gilbert that she meant to make it an inflexible rule never, under any circumstances, to talk "baby talk" to her children. Gilbert agreed with her, and they made a solemn compact on the subject—a compact which Anne shamelessly violated the very first moment Little Jem was laid in her arms. "Oh, the darling itty wee sing!" she had exclaimed. And she had continued to violate it ever since. When Gilbert teased her she laughed Sir Oracle to scorn.

"He never had any children of his own, Gilbert—I am positive he hadn't or he would never have written such rubbish.

You just can't help talking baby talk to a baby. It comes natural—and it's *right*. It would be inhuman to talk to those tiny, soft, velvety little creatures as we do to great big boys and girls. Babies want love and cuddling and all the sweet baby talk they can get, and Little Jem is going to have it, bless his dear itty heartums."

"But you're the worst I ever heard, Anne," protested Gilbert, who, not being a mother but only a father, was not wholly convinced yet that Sir Oracle was wrong. "I never heard anything like the way you talk to that child."

"Very likely you never did. Go away— go away. Didn't I bring up three pairs of Hammond twins before I was eleven? You and Sir Oracle are nothing but cold-blooded theorists. Gilbert, *just* look at him! He's smiling at me—he knows what we're talking about. And oo dest agwees wif evy word muzzer says, don't oo, angel-lover?"

Gilbert put his arm about them. "Oh, you mothers!" he said. "You mothers! God knew what He was about when He made you."

So Little Jem was talked to and loved and cuddled: and he throve as became a child of the house of dreams. Leslie was quite as foolish over him as Anne was. When their work was done and Gilbert was out of the way, they gave themselves over to shameless orgies of lovemaking and ecstasies of adoration, such as that in which Owen Ford had surprised them.

Leslie was the first to become aware of him. Even in the twilight Anne could see the sudden whiteness that swept over her beautiful face, blotting out the crimson of lip and cheeks.

Owen came forward, eagerly, blind for a moment to Anne.

"Leslie!" he said, holding out his hand. It was the first time he had ever called her by her name; but the hand Leslie gave him was cold; and she was very quiet all the evening, while Anne and Gilbert and Owen laughed and talked together. Before his call ended she excused herself and went upstairs. Owen's gay spirits flagged and he went away soon after with a downcast air.

Gilbert looked at Anne.

"Anne, what are you up to? There's something going on that I don't understand. The whole air here tonight has been charged with electricity. Leslie sits like the muse of tragedy; Owen Ford jokes and laughs on the surface, and watches Leslie with the eyes of his soul. You seem all the time to be bursting with some suppressed excitement. Own up. What secret have you been keeping from your deceived husband?"

"Don't be a goose, Gilbert," was Anne's conjugal reply. "As for Leslie, she is absurd and I'm going up to tell her so."

Anne found Leslie at the dormer window of her room. The little place was filled with the rhythmic thunder of the sea. Leslie sat with locked hands in the misty moonshine—a beautiful, accusing presence.

"Anne," she said in a low, reproachful voice, "did you know Owen Ford was coming to Four Winds?"

"I did," said Anne brazenly.

"Oh, you should have told me, Anne," Leslie cried passionately. "If I had known I would have gone away—I wouldn't have stayed here to meet him. You should have told me. It wasn't fair of you, Anne—oh, it wasn't fair!"

Leslie's lips were trembling and her whole form was tense

with emotion. But Anne laughed heartlessly. She bent over and kissed Leslie's upturned, reproachful face.

"Leslie, you are an adorable goose. Owen Ford didn't rush from the Pacific to the Atlantic from a burning desire to see *me*. Neither do I believe that he was inspired by any wild and frenzied passion for Miss Cornelia. Take off your tragic airs, my dear friend, and fold them up and put them away in lavender. You'll never need them again. There are some people who can see through a grindstone when there is a hole in it, even if you cannot. I am not a prophetess, but I shall venture on a prediction. The bitterness of life is over for you. After this you are going to have the joys and hopes—and I daresay the sorrows, too—of a happy woman. The omen of the shadow of Venus did come true for you, Leslie. The year in which you saw it brought your life's best gift for you—your love for Owen Ford. Now, go right to bed and have a good sleep."

Leslie obeyed orders in so far that she went to bed: but it may be questioned if she slept much. I do not think she dared to dream wakingly; life had been so hard for this poor Leslie, the path on which she had had to walk had been so straight, that she could not whisper to her own heart the hopes that might wait on the future. But she watched the great revolving light bestarring the short hours of the summer night, and her eyes grew soft and bright and young once more. Nor, when Owen Ford came next day, to ask her to go with him to the shore, did she say him nay.

XXXVII

Miss Cornelia Makes a Startling Announcement

Miss Cornelia sailed down to the little house one drowsy afternoon, when the gulf was the faint, bleached blue of hot August seas, and the orange lilies at the gate of Anne's garden held up their imperial cups to be filled with the molten gold of August sunshine. Not that Miss Cornelia concerned herself with painted oceans or sun-thirsty lilies. She sat in her favourite rocker in unusual idleness. She sewed not, neither did she spin. Nor did she say a single derogatory word concerning any portion of mankind. In short, Miss Cornelia's conversation was singularly devoid of spice that day, and Gilbert, who had stayed home to listen to her, instead of going a-fishing, as he had intended, felt himself aggrieved. What had come over Miss Cornelia? She did not look cast down or worried. On the contrary, there was a certain air of nervous exultation about her.

"Where is Leslie?" she asked—not as if it mattered much either.

"Owen and she went raspberrying in the woods back of

her farm," answered Anne. "They won't be back before supper time—if then."

"They don't seem to have any idea that there is such a thing as a clock," said Gilbert. "I can't get to the bottom of that affair. I'm certain you women pulled strings. But Anne, undutiful wife, won't tell me. Will you, Miss Cornelia?"

"No, I shall not. But," said Miss Cornelia, with the air of one determined to take the plunge and have it over, "I will tell you something else. I came today on purpose to tell it. I am going to be married."

Anne and Gilbert were silent. If Miss Cornelia had announced her intention of going out to the channel and drowning herself the thing might have been believable. This was not. So they waited. Of course Miss Cornelia had made a mistake.

"Well, you both look sort of kerflummexed," said Miss Cornelia, with a twinkle in her eyes. Now that the awkward moment of revelation was over, Miss Cornelia was her own woman again. "Do you think I'm too young and inexperienced for matrimony?"

"You know—it *is* rather staggering," said Gilbert, trying to gather his wits together. "I've heard you say a score of times that you wouldn't marry the best man in the world."

"I'm not going to marry the best man in the world," retorted Miss Cornelia. "Marshall Elliott is a long way from being the best."

"Are you going to marry Marshall Elliott?" exclaimed Anne, recovering her power of speech under this second shock.

"Yes. I could have had him any time these twenty years if I'd lifted my finger. But do you suppose I was going to walk into church beside a perambulating haystack like that?"

"I am sure we are very glad—and we wish you all possible happiness," said Anne, very flatly and inadequately, as she felt. She was not prepared for such an occasion. She had never imagined herself offering betrothal felicitations to Miss Cornelia.

"Thanks, I knew you would," said Miss Cornelia. "You are the first of my friends to know it."

"We shall be so sorry to lose you, though, dear Miss Cornelia," said Anne, beginning to be a little sad and sentimental.

"Oh, you won't lose me," said Miss Cornelia unsentimentally. "You don't suppose I would live over harbour with all those MacAllisters and Elliotts and Crawfords, do you? 'From the conceit of the Elliotts, the pride of the MacAllisters and the vain-glory of the Crawfords, good Lord deliver us.' Marshall is coming to live at my place. I'm sick and tired of hired men. That Jim Hastings I've got this summer is positively the worst of the species. He would drive anyone to getting married. What do you think? He upset the churn yesterday and spilled a big churning of cream over the yard. And not one whit concerned about it was he! Just gave a foolish laugh and said cream was good for the land. Wasn't that like a man? I told him I wasn't in the habit of fertilizing my back yard with cream."

"Well, I wish you all manner of happiness too, Miss Cornelia," said Gilbert, solemnly; "but," he added, unable to resist the temptation to tease Miss Cornelia, despite Anne's imploring eyes, "I fear your day of independence is done. As you know, Marshall Elliott is a very determined man."

"I like a man who can stick to a thing," retorted Miss Cornelia. "Amos Grant, who used to be after me long ago, couldn't. You never saw such a weather-vane. He jumped into the pond to drown himself once and then changed his mind and swum out again. Wasn't that like a man? Marshall would have stuck to it and drowned."

"And he has a bit of a temper, they tell me," persisted Gilbert.

"He wouldn't be an Elliott if he hadn't. I'm thankful he has. It will be real fun to make him mad. And you can generally do something with a tempery man when it comes to repenting time. But you can't do anything with a man who just keeps placid and aggravating."

"You know he's a Grit, Miss Cornelia."

"Yes, he *is*," admitted Miss Cornelia rather sadly. "And of course there is no hope of making a Conservative of him. But at least he is a Presbyterian. So I suppose I shall have to be satisfied with that."

"Would you marry him if he were a Methodist, Miss Cornelia?"

"No, I would not. Politics is for this world, but religion is for both."

"And you may be a 'relict' after all, Miss Cornelia."

"Not I. Marshall will live me out. The Elliotts are long-lived, and the Bryants are not."

"When are you to be married?" asked Anne.

"In about a month's time. My wedding dress is to be navy blue silk. And I want to ask you, Anne, dearie, if you think it would be all right to wear a veil with a navy blue dress. I've always thought I'd like to wear a veil if I ever got married. Marshall says to have it if I want to. Isn't that like a man?"

"Why shouldn't you wear it if you want to?" asked Anne.

"Well, one doesn't want to be different from other people," said Miss Cornelia, who was not noticeably like anyone else on the face of the earth. "As I say, I do fancy a veil. But maybe it shouldn't be worn with any dress but a white one. Please tell me, Anne, dearie, what you really think. I'll go by your advice."

"I don't think veils are usually worn with any but white dresses," admitted Anne, "but that is merely a convention; and I am like Mr. Elliott, Miss Cornelia. I don't see any good reason why you shouldn't have a veil if you want one."

But Miss Cornelia, who made her calls in calico wrappers, shook her head.

"If it isn't the proper thing I won't wear it," she said, with a sigh of regret for a lost dream.

"Since you are determined to be married, Miss Cornelia," said Gilbert solemnly, "I shall give you the excellent rules for the management of a husband which my grandmother gave my mother when she married my father."

"Well, I reckon I can manage Marshall Elliott," said Miss Cornelia placidly. "But let us hear your rules."

"The first one is, catch him."

"He's caught. Go on."

"The second one is, feed him well."

"With enough pie. What next?"

"The third and fourth are—keep your eye on him."

"I believe you," said Miss Cornelia emphatically.

XXXVIII

Red Roses

The garden of the little house was a haunt beloved of bees and reddened by late roses that August. The little house folk lived much in it, and were given to taking picnic suppers in the grassy corner beyond the brook and sitting about in it through the twilights when great night moths sailed athwart the velvet gloom. One evening Owen Ford found Leslie alone in it. Anne and Gilbert were away, and Susan, who was expected back that night, had not yet returned.

The northern sky was amber and pale green over the fir tops. The air was cool, for August was nearing September, and Leslie wore a crimson scarf over her white dress. Together they wandered through the little, friendly, flower-crowded paths in silence. Owen must go soon. His holiday was nearly over. Leslie found her heart beating wildly. She knew that this beloved garden was to be the scene of the binding words that must seal their as yet unworded understanding.

"Some evenings a strange odour blows down the air of this garden, like a phantom perfume," said Owen. "I have never been able to discover from just what flower it comes. It is elusive and haunting and wonderfully sweet. I like to fancy it is the soul of Grandmother Selwyn passing on a little visit to the old spot she loved so well. There should be a lot of friendly ghosts about this little old house."

"I have lived under its roof only a month," said Leslie, "but I love it as I never loved the house over there where I have lived all my life."

"This house was builded and consecrated by love," said Owen. "Such houses *must* exert an influence over those who live in them. And this garden—it is over sixty years old and the history of a thousand hopes and joys is written in its blossoms. Some of those flowers were actually set out by the schoolmaster's bride, and she has been dead for thirty years. Yet they bloom on every summer. Look at those red roses, Leslie—how they queen it over everything else!"

"I love the red roses," said Leslie. "Anne likes the pink ones best, and Gilbert likes the white. But I want the crimson ones. They satisfy some craving in me as no other flower does."

"These roses are very late—they bloom after all the others have gone—and they hold all the warmth and soul of the summer come to fruition," said Owen, plucking some of the glowing, half-opened buds. "The rose is the flower of love—the world has acclaimed it so for centuries. The pink roses are love hopeful and expectant—the white roses are love dead or forsaken—but the red roses—ah, Leslie, what are the red roses?"

"Love triumphant," said Leslie in a low voice.

"Yes—love triumphant and perfect. Leslie, you know—

you understand. I have loved you from the first. And I *know* you love me—I don't need to ask you. But I want to hear you say it—my darling—my darling!"

Leslie said something in a very low and tremulous voice. Their hands and lips met; it was life's supreme moment for them and as they stood there in the old garden, with its many years of love and delight and sorrow and glory, he crowned her shining hair with the red, red rose of a love triumphant.

Anne and Gilbert returned presently, accompanied by Captain Jim. Anne lighted a few sticks of driftwood in the fireplace, for love of the pixy flames, and they sat around it for an hour of good fellowship.

"When I sit looking at a driftwood fire it's easy to believe I'm young again," said Captain Jim.

"Can you read futures in the fire, Captain Jim?" asked Owen.

Captain Jim looked at them all affectionately, and then back again at Leslie's vivid face and glowing eyes.

"I don't need the fire to read your futures," he said. "I see happiness for all of you—all of you—for Leslie and Mr. Ford—and the doctor here and Mistress Blythe—and Little Jem—and children that ain't born yet but will be. Happiness for you all—though, mind you, I reckon, you'll have your troubles and worries and sorrows, too. They're bound to come—and no house, whether it's a palace or a little house of dreams, can bar 'em out. But they won't get the better of you if you face 'em *together* with love and trust. You can weather any storm with them two for compass and pilot."

The old man rose suddenly and placed one hand on Leslie's head and one on Anne's.

"Two good, sweet women," he said. "True and faithful and to be depended on. Your husbands will have honour in the gates because of you—your children will rise up and call you blessed in the years to come."

There was a strange solemnity about the little scene. Anne and Leslie bowed as those receiving a benediction. Gilbert suddenly brushed his hand over his eyes; Owen Ford was rapt as one who can see visions. All were silent for a space. The little house of dreams added another poignant and unforgettable moment to its store of memories.

"I must be going now," said Captain Jim slowly at last. He took up his hat and looked lingeringly about the room.

"Good night, all of you," he said, as he went out.

Anne, pierced by the unusual wistfulness of his farewell, walked through the little gate hung between the firs.

"Ay, ay," he called cheerily back to her. But Captain Jim had sat by the old fireside of the house of dreams for the last time.

Anne went slowly back to the others.

"It's so—so pitiful to think of him going all alone down to that lonely Point," she said. "And there is no one to welcome him there."

"Captain Jim is such good company for others that one can't imagine him being anything but good company for himself," said Owen. "But he must often be lonely. There was a touch of the seer about him tonight—he spoke as one to whom it had been given to speak. Well, I must be going, too."

Anne and Gilbert discreetly melted away; but when Owen had gone Anne returned, to find Leslie standing by the hearth.

"Oh, Leslie—I know—and I'm so glad, dear," she said, putting her arms about her.

"Anne, my happiness frightens me," whispered Leslie. "It seems too great to be real—I'm afraid to speak of it—to think of it. It seems to me that it must just be another dream of this house of dreams and it will vanish when I leave here."

"Well, you are not going to leave here—until Owen takes you. You are going to stay with me until that time comes. Do you think I'd let you go over to that lonely, sad place again?"

"Thank you, dear. I meant to ask you if I might stay with you. I didn't want to go back there—it would seem like going back into the chill and dreariness of the old life again. Anne, Anne, what a friend you've been to me—'a good, sweet woman—true and faithful and to be depended on'—Captain Jim summed you up."

"He said 'women,' not 'woman,'" smiled Anne. "Perhaps Captain Jim sees us both through the rose-coloured spectacles of his love for us. But we can try to live up to his belief in us, at least."

"Do you remember, Anne," said Leslie slowly, "that I once said—that night we met on the shore—that I hated my good looks? I did—then. It's always seemed to me that if I had been homely Dick would never have thought of me. I hated my beauty because it had attracted him, but now—oh, I'm glad that I have it. It's all I have to offer Owen,—his artist soul delights in it. I feel as if I do not come to him quite empty-handed."

"Owen loves your beauty, Leslie. Who would not? But it's foolish of you to say or think that that is all you bring him. *He* will tell you that—I needn't. And now I must lock up. I expected Susan back tonight, but she has not come."

"Oh, yes, here I am, Mrs. Doctor, dear," said Susan, entering unexpectedly from the kitchen, "and puffing like a hen drawing rails at that! It's quite a walk from the Glen down here."

"I'm glad to see you back, Susan. How is your sister?"

"She is able to sit up, but of course she cannot walk yet. However, she is very well able to get on without me now, for her daughter has come home for her vacation. And I am thankful to be back, Mrs. Doctor, dear. Matilda's leg was broken and no mistake, but her tongue was not. She would talk the legs off an iron pot, that she would, Mrs. Doctor, dear, though I grieve to say it of my own sister. She was always a great talker and yet she was the first of our family to get married. She really did not care much about marrying James Clow, but she could not bear to disoblige him. Not but what James is a good man—the only fault I have to find with him is that he always starts in to say grace with such an unearthly groan, Mrs. Doctor, dear. It always frightens my appetite clear away. And speaking of getting married, Mrs. Doctor, dear, is it true that Cornelia Bryant is going to be married to Marshall Elliott?"

"Yes, quite true, Susan."

"Well, Mrs. Doctor, dear, it does *not* seem to me fair. Here is me, who never said a word against the men, and I cannot get married nohow. And there is Cornelia Bryant, who is never done abusing them, and all she has to do is to reach out her hand and pick one up, as it were. It is a very strange world, Mrs. Doctor, dear."

"There's another world, you know, Susan."

"Yes," said Susan with a heavy sigh, "but Mrs. Doctor, dear, there is neither marrying nor giving in marriage there."

XXXIX

Captain Jim Crosses the Bar

One day in late September Owen Ford's book came at last. Captain Jim had gone faithfully to the Glen post-office every day for a month, expecting it. This day he had not gone, and Leslie brought his copy home with hers and Anne's.

"We'll take it down to him this evening," said Anne, excited as a schoolgirl.

The walk to the Point on that clear, beguiling evening along the red harbour road was very pleasant. Then the sun dropped down behind the western hills into some valley that must have been full of lost sunsets, and at the same instant the big light flashed out on the white tower of the point.

"Captain Jim is never late by the fraction of a second," said Leslie.

Neither Anne nor Leslie ever forgot Captain Jim's face when they gave him the book—*his* book, transfigured and glorified. The cheeks that had been blanched of late suddenly flamed with the colour of boyhood; his eyes glowed with all the fire of youth; but his hands trembled as he opened it.

It was called simply *The Life-Book of Captain Jim*, and on the title page the names of Owen Ford and James Boyd were printed as collaborators. The frontispiece was a photograph of Captain Jim himself, standing at the door of the lighthouse, looking across the gulf. Owen Ford had "snapped" him one day while the book was being written. Captain Jim had known this, but he had not known that the picture was to be in the book.

"Just think of it," he said, "the old sailor right there in a real printed book. This is the proudest day of my life. I'm like to bust, girls. There'll be no sleep for me tonight. I'll read my book clean through before sun-up."

"We'll go right away and leave you free to begin it," said Anne.

Captain Jim had been handling the book in a kind of reverent rapture. Now he closed it decidedly and laid it aside.

"No, no, you're not going away before you take a cup of tea with the old man," he protested. "I couldn't hear to that— could you, Matey? The life-book will keep, I reckon. I've waited for it this many a year. I can wait a little longer while I'm enjoying my friends."

Captain Jim moved about getting his kettle on to boil, and setting out his bread and butter. Despite his excitement he did not move with his old briskness. His movements were slow and halting. But the girls did not offer to help him. They knew it would hurt his feelings.

"You just picked the right evening to visit me," he said, producing a cake from his cupboard. "Leetle Joe's mother sent me down a big basket full of cakes and pies today. A blessing on all good cooks, says I. Look at this purty cake, all frosting and nuts. 'Tain't often I can entertain in such style. Set in, girls, set in! We'll 'tak a cup o' kindness yet for auld lang syne.'"

The girls "set in" right merrily. The tea was up to Captain Jim's best brewing. Little Joe's mother's cake was the last word in cakes; Captain Jim was the prince of gracious hosts, never even permitting his eyes to wander to the corner where the life-book lay, in all its bravery of green and gold. But when his door finally closed behind Anne and Leslie they knew that he went straight to it, and as they walked home they pictured the delight of the old man poring over the printed pages wherein his own life was portrayed with all the charm and colour of reality itself.

"I wonder how he will like the ending—the ending I suggested," said Leslie.

She was never to know. Early the next morning Anne awakened to find Gilbert bending over her, fully dressed, and with an expression of anxiety on his face.

"Are you called out?" she asked drowsily.

"No. Anne, I'm afraid there's something wrong at the Point. It's an hour after sunrise now, and the light is still burning. You know it has always been a matter of pride with Captain Jim to start the light the moment the sun sets, and put it out the moment it rises."

Anne sat up in dismay. Through her window she saw the light blinking palely against the blue skies of dawn.

"Perhaps he has fallen asleep over his life-book," she said anxiously, "or become so absorbed in it that he has forgotten the light."

Gilbert shook his head.

"That wouldn't be like Captain Jim. Anyway, I'm going down to see."

"Wait a minute and I'll go with you," exclaimed Anne. "Oh, yes, I must—Little Jem will sleep for an hour yet, and I'll call Susan. You may need a woman's help if Captain Jim is ill."

It was an exquisite morning, full of tints and sounds at once ripe and delicate. The harbour was sparkling and dimpling like a girl; white gulls were soaring over the dunes; beyond the bar was a shining, wonderful sea. The long fields by the shore were dewy and fresh in that first fine, purely-tinted light. The wind came dancing and whistling up the channel to replace the beautiful silence with a music more beautiful still. Had it not been for the baleful star on the white tower that early walk would have been a delight to Anne and Gilbert. But they went softly with fear.

Their knock was not responded to. Gilbert opened the door and they went in.

The old room was very quiet. On the table were the remnants of the little evening feast. The lamp still burning on the corner stand. The First Mate was asleep in a square of sunshine by the sofa.

Captain Jim lay on the sofa, with his hands clasped over the life-book, open at the last page, lying on his breast. His eyes were closed and on his face was a look of the most perfect peace and happiness—the look of one who has long sought and found at last.

"He is asleep?" whispered Anne tremulously.

Gilbert went to the sofa and bent over him for a few moments. Then he straightened up.

"Yes, he sleeps—well," he said quietly. "Anne, Captain Jim has crossed the bar."

They could not know precisely at what hour he had died, but Anne always believed that he had had his wish, and went out when the morning came across the gulf. Out on that shining tide his spirit drifted, over the sunrise sea of pearl and silver, to the haven where lost Margaret waited, beyond the storms and calms.

Farewell to the House of Dreams

Captain Jim was buried in the little over-harbour graveyard, very near to the spot where the wee white lady slept. His relatives put up a very expensive, very ugly "monument"—a monument at which he would have poked sly fun had he seen it in life. But his real monument was in the hearts of those who knew him, and in the book that was to live for generations.

Leslie mourned that Captain Jim had not lived to see the amazing success of it.

"How he would have delighted in the reviews—they are almost all so kindly. And to have seen his life-book heading the lists of the best sellers—oh, if he could just have lived to see it, Anne!"

But Anne, despite her grief, was wiser.

"It was the book itself he cared for, Leslie—not what might be said of it—and he had it. He had read it all through. That last night must have been one of the greatest happiness for him—with the quick, painless ending he had hoped for in the morning. I am glad for Owen's sake and yours that the

book is such a success—but Captain Jim was satisfied—
I *know*."

The lighthouse star still kept its nightly vigil; a substitute
keeper had been sent to the Point, until such time as an all-
wise government could decide which of many applicants was
best fitted for the place—or had the strongest pull. The First
Mate was at home in the little house, beloved by Anne and
Gilbert and Leslie, and tolerated by a Susan who had small
liking for cats.

"I can put up with him for the sake of Captain Jim, Mrs.
Doctor, dear, for I liked the old man. And I will see that he
gets bite and sup, and every mouse the traps account for. But
do not ask me to do more than that, Mrs. Doctor, dear. Cats
is cats, and take my word for it, they will never be anything
else. And at least, Mrs. Doctor, dear, do keep him away from
the blessed wee man. Picture to yourself how awful it would
be if he was to suck the darling's breath."

"That might be fitly called a *cat*-astrophe," said Gilbert.

"Oh, you may laugh, Doctor, dear, but it would be no
laughing matter."

"Cats never suck babies' breaths," said Gilbert. "That is
only an old superstition, Susan."

"Oh, well, it may be a superstition or it may not, Doctor,
dear. All that I know is, it has happened. My sister's husband's
nephew's wife's cat sucked their baby's breath, and the poor
innocent was all but gone when they found it. And superstition or not, if I find that yellow beast lurking near our baby I
will whack him with the poker, Mrs. Doctor, dear."

Mr. and Mrs. Marshall Elliott were living comfortably
and harmoniously in the green house. Leslie was busy with

sewing, for she and Owen were to be married at Christmas. Anne wondered what she would do when Leslie was gone.

"Changes come all the time. Just as soon as things get really nice they change," she said with a sigh.

"The old Morgan place up at the Glen is for sale," said Gilbert, apropos of nothing in especial.

"Is it?" asked Anne indifferently.

"Yes. Now that Mr. Morgan has gone, Mrs. Morgan wants to go to live with her children in Vancouver. She will sell cheaply, for a big place like that in a small village like the Glen will not be very easy to dispose of."

"Well, it's certainly a beautiful place, so it is likely she will find a purchaser," said Anne, absently, wondering whether she should hemstitch or feather-stitch Little Jem's "short" dresses. He was to be shortened the next week, and Anne felt ready to cry at the thought of it.

"Suppose we buy it, Anne?" remarked Gilbert quietly.

Anne dropped her sewing and stared at him.

"You're not in earnest, Gilbert?"

"Indeed I am, dear."

"And leave this darling spot—our house of dreams?" said Anne incredulously. "Oh, Gilbert, it's—it's unthinkable!"

"Listen patiently to me, dear. I know just how you feel about it. I feel the same. But we've always known we would have to move someday."

"Oh, but not so soon, Gilbert—not just yet."

"We may never get such a chance again. If we don't buy the Morgan place someone else will—and there is no other house in the Glen we would care to have, and no other really good site on which to build. This little house is—well, it is and has been what no other house can ever be to us, I admit, but you know it is out-of-the-way down here for a doctor. We have felt the inconvenience, though we've made the best of it. And it's a tight fit for us now. Perhaps, in a few years, when Jem wants a room of his own, it will be entirely too small."

"Oh, I know—I know," said Anne, tears filling her eyes. "I know all that can be said against it, but I love it so—and it's so beautiful here."

"You would find it very lonely here after Leslie goes—and Captain Jim has gone too. The Morgan place is beautiful, and in time we would love it. You know you have always admired it, Anne."

"Oh, yes, but—but—this has all seemed to come up so suddenly, Gilbert. I'm dizzy. Ten minutes ago I had no thought of leaving this dear spot. I was planning what I meant to do for it in the spring—what I meant to do in the garden. And if we leave this place who will get it? It *is* out-of-the-way, so it's likely some poor, shiftless, wandering family will rent it—and over-run it—and oh, that would be desecration. It would hurt me horribly."

"I know. But we cannot sacrifice our own interests to such considerations, Anne-girl. The Morgan place will suit us in every essential particular—we really can't afford to miss such a chance. Think of that big lawn with those magnificent old trees; and of that splendid hardwood grove behind it—twelve acres of it. What a play place for our children! There's a fine orchard, too, and you've always admired that high brick wall around the garden with the door in it—you've thought it was so like a story-book garden. And there is almost as fine a view of the harbour and the dunes from the Morgan place as from here."

"You can't see the lighthouse star from it."

"Yes. You can see it from the attic window. *There's* another advantage, Anne-girl—you love big garrets."

"There's no brook in the garden."

"Well, no, but there is one running through the maple grove into the Glen pond. And the pond itself isn't far away. You'll be able to fancy you have your own Lake of Shining Waters again."

"Well, don't say anything more about it just now, Gilbert. Give me time to think—to get used to the idea."

"All right. There is no great hurry, of course. Only—if we decide to buy, it would be well to be moved in and settled before winter."

Gilbert went out, and Anne put away Little Jem's short dresses with trembling hands. She could not sew any more that day. With tear-wet eyes she wandered over the little domain where she had reigned so happy a queen. The Morgan place was all that Gilbert claimed. The grounds were beautiful, the house old enough to have dignity and repose and traditions, and new enough to be comfortable and up-to-date. Anne had always admired it; but admiring is not loving; and she loved this little house of dreams so much. She loved *everything* about it—the garden she had tended, and which so many women had tended before her—the gleam and sparkle of the little brook that crept so roguishly across the corner—the gate between the creaking fir trees—the old red sandstone step— the stately Lombardies—the two tiny quaint glass cupboards over the chimneypiece in the living room—the crooked windows upstairs—the little jog in the staircase—why, these things were a part of her! How could she leave them?

And how this little house, consecrated aforetime by love and joy, had been re-consecrated for her by her happiness and sorrow! Here she had spent her bridal moon; here wee Joyce had lived her one brief day; here the sweetness of motherhood had come again with Little Jem; here she had heard the exquisite music of her baby's cooing laughter; here beloved friends had sat by her fireside. Joy and grief, birth and death, had made sacred forever this little house of dreams.

And now she must leave it. She knew that, even while she had contended against the idea to Gilbert. The little house was out-grown. Gilbert's interests made the change necessary; his work, successful though it had been, was hampered by his location. Anne realized that the end of their life in this dear place drew nigh, and that she must face the fact bravely. But how her heart ached!

"It will just be like tearing something out of my life," she sobbed. "And oh, if I could hope that some nice folk would come here in our place—or even that it would be left vacant. That itself would be better than having it over-run with some horde who know nothing of the geography of dreamland, and nothing of the history that has given this house its soul and its identity. And if such a tribe come here the place will go to rack and ruin in no time—an old place goes down so quickly if it is not carefully attended to. They'll tear up my garden—and let the Lombardies get ragged—and the paling will come to look like a mouth with half the teeth missing—and the roof will leak—and the plaster fall—and they'll stuff pillows and rags in broken window panes—and everything will be out-at-elbows."

Anne's imagination pictured forth so vividly the coming degeneration of her dear little house that it hurt her as severely as if it had already been an accomplished fact. She sat down on the stairs and had a long, bitter cry. Susan found her there and enquired with much concern what the trouble was.

"You have not quarrelled with the doctor, have you now, Mrs. Doctor, dear? But if you have, do not worry. It is a thing quite likely to happen with married couples, I am told, although I have had no experience that way myself. He will be sorry, and you can soon make it up."

"No, no, Susan, we haven't quarrelled. It's only—Gilbert is going to buy the Morgan place, and we'll have to go and live at the Glen. And it will break my heart."

Susan did not enter into Anne's feelings at all. She was, indeed, quite rejoiced over the prospect of living at the Glen. Her one grievance against her place in the little house was its lonesome location.

"Why, Mrs. Doctor, dear, it will be splendid. The Morgan house is such a fine, big one."

"I hate big houses," sobbed Anne.

"Oh, well, you will not hate them by the time you have half a dozen children," remarked Susan calmly. "And this house is too small already for us. We have no spare room, since Mrs. Moore is here, and that pantry is the most aggravating place I ever tried to work in. There is a corner every way you turn. Besides, it is out-of-the-world down here. There is really nothing at all but scenery."

"Out of your world perhaps, Susan—but not out of mine," said Anne with a faint smile.

"I do not quite understand you, Mrs. Doctor, dear, but of course I am not well educated. But if Dr. Blythe buys the Morgan place he will make no mistake, and that you may tie to. They have water in it, and the pantries and closets are beautiful, and there is not another such cellar in P. E. Island, so I have been told. Why, the cellar here, Mrs. Doctor, dear, has been a heartbreak to me, as well you know."

"Oh, go away, Susan, go away," said Anne forlornly. "Cellars and pantries and closets don't make a *home*. Why don't you weep with those who weep?"

"Well, I never was much hand for weeping, Mrs. Doctor, dear. I would rather fall to and cheer people up than weep with them. Now, do not you cry and spoil your pretty eyes. This house is very well and has served your turn, but it is high time you had a better."

Susan's point of view seemed to be that of most people. Leslie was the only one who sympathised understandingly with Anne. She had a good cry, too, when she heard the news. Then they both dried their tears and went to work at the preparations for moving.

"Since we must go let us go as soon as we can and have it over," said poor Anne with bitter resignation.

"You know you will like that lovely old place at the Glen after you have lived in it long enough to have dear memories woven about it," said Leslie. "Friends will come there, as they have come here—happiness will glorify it for you. Now, it's just a house to you—but the years will make it a home."

Anne and Leslie had another cry the next week when they shortened Little Jem. Anne felt the tragedy of it until evening when in his long nightie she found her own dear baby again.

"But it will be rompers next—and then trousers—and in no time he will be grown-up," she sighed.

"Well, you would not want him to stay a baby always, Mrs. Doctor, dear, would you?" said Susan. "Bless his innocent heart, he looks too sweet for anything in his little short dresses, with his dear feet sticking out. And think of the saving in the ironing, Mrs. Doctor, dear."

"Anne, I have just had a letter from Owen," said Leslie, entering with a bright face. "And, oh! I have such good news. He writes me that he is going to buy this place from the church trustees and keep it to spend our summer vacations in. Anne, are you not glad?"

"Oh, Leslie, 'glad' isn't the word for it! It seems almost too good to be true. I sha'n't feel half so badly now that I know this dear spot will never be desecrated by a vandal tribe, or left to tumble down in decay. Why, it's lovely! It's lovely!"

One October morning Anne wakened to the realization that she had slept for the last time under the roof of her little house. The day was too busy to indulge regret and when evening came the house was stripped and bare. Anne and Gilbert were alone in it to say farewell. Leslie and Susan and Little Jem had gone to the Glen with the last load of furniture. The sunset light streamed in through the curtainless windows.

"It has all such a heart-broken, reproachful look, hasn't it?" said Anne. "Oh, I shall be so homesick at the Glen tonight!"

"We have been very happy here, haven't we, Anne-girl?" said Gilbert, his voice full of feeling.

Anne choked, unable to answer. Gilbert waited for her at the fir-tree gate, while she went over the house and said farewell to every room. She was going away; but the old house would still be there, looking seaward through its quaint windows. The autumn winds would blow around it mournfully, and the gray rain would beat upon it and the white mists would come in from the sea to enfold it; and the moonlight would fall over it and light up the old paths where the schoolmaster and his bride had walked. There on that old harbour shore the charm of story would linger; the wind would still whistle alluringly over the silver sand dunes; the waves would still call from the red rock-coves.

"But we will be gone," said Anne through her tears.

She went out, closing and locking the door behind her. Gilbert was waiting for her with a smile. The lighthouse star was gleaming northward. The little garden, where only marigolds still bloomed, was already hooding itself in shadows.

Anne knelt down and kissed the worn old step which she had crossed as a bride.

"Good-bye, dear little house of dreams," she said

LUCY MAUD MONTGOMERY:
A BIOGRAPHY

Caroline Parry

"I love books. I hope when I grow up to be able to have lots of them," Lucy Maud Montgomery wrote in her journal when she was just fourteen. This journal entry, made in 1889, is significant to readers today who know that when she grew up she not only owned and read many books, but also became the world-famous L. M. Montgomery. Maud, as she liked to be called by family and friends, wrote twenty-four books between 1908 and 1939. Her first was *Anne of Green Gables*, and her other works include seven more Anne books, the Avonlea stories, the Emily trilogy, two novels for adults, and the novel *The Story Girl*.

Lucy Maud Montgomery was always writing and reading and was quite a story girl herself, creating more than five hundred short stories. She also wrote many poems. One edition of her poetry was published during her lifetime, and today all her poems have been collected in a single volume.

L. M. Montgomery's favorite among her own work was *The Story Girl*, a novel about a young spinner of tales. What makes a person a "story girl"? Looking at the life of

Montgomery, it seems clear that being born on beautiful Prince Edward Island, Canada, inspired her. Having a literary family also fueled Montgomery's writing. But most important, she was simply full of stories, just like the characters she created: her beloved red-head, Anne; the autobiographical Emily of the Emily trilogy; and Sara, the central storyteller of *The Story Girl*.

In *The Alpine Path: The Story of My Career*, Montgomery wrote, "I cannot remember a time when I was not writing, or when I did not mean to be a writer ... I was an indefatigable little scribbler." Later she added, "Nine out of ten manuscripts came back to me. But I sent them out over and over again." She pursued her goals as a writer in a remarkably focused way.

Besides her literary endeavors, Montgomery wrote many letters; she and a childhood friend even wrote some letters to themselves, to be opened ten years later. As an adult Montgomery wrote extensive letters to two "pen friends," which were published in 1960 and 1980 as *The Green Gables Letters: From L. M. Montgomery to Ephraim Weber, 1905–1909* and *My Dear Mr. M.: Letters to G. B. MacMillan from L. M. Montgomery*. Besides her personal letters, Montgomery also made entry upon entry in what would become ten volumes of personal journals. She wrote:

> [Saturday] September 21, 1889. I am going to begin a new kind of diary. I have kept one of a kind for years—ever since I was a tot of nine. But I burned it today. It was so silly I was ashamed of it ... But I'm going to start

out all over new and write only when I have
something worth writing about. Life is
beginning to get interesting for me—I will
soon be fifteen—the last day of November.
And in this journal I am never going to tell
what kind of day it is—unless the weather has
something to do worthwhile. And—last but
not least—I am going to keep this book
locked up!!

She found much worth writing about; the journals run to
more than five thousand pages. Discussing anything from
geraniums with names to village gossip, from marriage pro-
posals to "great soul aches," Montgomery continued these
habits for most of her life, except during a period at the beginning of the Second World War when she was too depressed to
make her daily entries.

In January 1904, when she was almost thirty, Montgomery
wrote, "Only lonely people keep diaries." For all her rich
friendships, L. M. Montgomery was a lonely person. After
her mother died of tuberculosis in 1876, her father relocated
west, leaving Maud behind, and married again. Young Maud,
who was not yet two years old, was largely brought up by her
mother's parents. That side of her family gave her a love of
literature. For the lonely girl, books were important friends.

Although she did have cousins and schoolmates for company, she had no siblings, and she had no neighborhood play-
mates until she was eight. But being sensitive and imaginative,
she had two bookcase window companions, very much like
Anne Shirley's Katie Maurice. And just like Anne, Maud

named her favorite trees and plants, speaking to them as if they were friends.

As the years passed, Montgomery's journals became her best friend; she called them a "personal confidant in whom I can repose absolute trust." This was especially true during turbulent periods. In 1889 she traveled to Alberta to live for a year with her father and his second wife. Maud hated "Mrs. Montgomery," confiding, "I *cannot* call her anything else, except before others for father's sake." Maud's love for her father helped her survive her stay, as did being able to record her complaints in her journal. But she also had cause to celebrate in its pages. During that year, the first of her writings was published in *The Charlottetown Patriot*. She wrote on December 7, 1890: "Well, this has really been the proudest day of my life! ... there, in one of the columns, was my poem!"

In 1891 Montgomery returned to Prince Edward Island to finish her education. After a year in college and a stint as a journalist, she began work as a teacher. During that time, her love life became very tangled. While teaching at a school in Lower Bedeque, she boarded with Mr. and Mrs. Cornelius Leard. She soon became romantically involved with their son Herman, much to her own dismay. Not only was she already engaged to her second cousin Edwin Simpson, but she felt that Herman, an uneducated farmer, was not at all a suitable match for her. She had realized shortly after accepting Edwin Simpson's proposal that she did not love him, but breaking an engagement was a serious thing in her day, and she had not yet been able to end their relationship. Now she was tormented by her feelings for the two men.

When Edwin Simpson arrived in Lower Bedeque for an impromptu Christmas visit, Montgomery described the scene in her journal: "There I was under the same roof with two men, one of whom I loved and could never marry, the other whom I had promised to marry but could never love! What I suffered that night between horror, shame, and dread can never be told."

Despite her inner turmoil during this period, she never stopped writing; in twelve months between 1897 and 1898, she saw nineteen of her short stories and fourteen of her poems in print.

Her involvement with Herman Leard ended when she returned to Prince Edward Island after her grandfather's death in March 1898, and she broke off her engagement to Edwin Simpson a short time later. She remained on Prince Edward Island and became her grandmother's dutiful house-keeper and companion, carrying that heavy responsibility for many years.

In 1906 she became engaged to a minister named Ewan MacDonald, with the understanding that they would not be married until her obligation to her grandmother was fulfilled. She did not love MacDonald with any passion, but she respected him, and he was a more suitable match for her than any of her previous suitors. During their courtship, she began to write *Anne of Green Gables*, her first novel. When the book finally found a publisher, it became an almost instant success, selling more than nineteen thousand copies in five months. Surprised and delighted, Montgomery quickly completed a sequel. Little did she know that she would continue writing about the spirited Anne Shirley until 1939.

After her grandmother's death in 1911, Montgomery was finally free to marry Ewan MacDonald. They honeymooned in Great Britain, and then Montgomery accompanied her husband to his church in Ontario. They had three sons, one of whom, sadly, died at birth. From this period on, Montgomery always had two major roles to play: that of the internationally known writer, and that of wife, mother, and community figurehead.

Always juggling her duties and her creative work, she found satisfaction and joy in those years, but also great frustration as she strove to perform both roles successfully. Neighbors grew used to seeing the petite Mrs. MacDonald, as they called her, striding down the street to take care of shopping or Sunday school, muttering dialogue for her books as she went.

In her lifetime, Montgomery endured many strains: the horror of the First World War, her husband's severe depression, and deteriorating relations with her first publisher. But she kept up appearances as both a minister's wife and an author. Immensely productive both domestically and professionally, she maintained a daily routine of writing stories, poems, and letters, and personally replied to all of her fan mail. She continued to pour out her problems and the agonies of her inner life in her journal; she found the advent of the Second World War particularly horrible. Finally her days became so difficult that even her friendly old journal failed her. Sad and bitter, having neither written her pen friends nor unburdened herself in her journal for months, she died in 1942.

After her death, Montgomery's ambition "to write a book that will live" was fulfilled many times over, particularly through the Anne books. *Anne of Green Gables* has sold millions of copies and has been translated into numerous languages. Anne has also taken to the stage and screen, inspiring a musical and a ballet as well as many films and several television miniseries.

Ironically, despite the great popularity of all her books, L. M. Montgomery was ignored by the critics after the 1920s and was not recognized as a significant Canadian writer until the 1970s. At that time, scholars interested in female writers began to examine why people so enjoyed reading about Anne and Emily, as well as the other marvelous personalities Montgomery created. They questioned why a woman writer—whom a poll in 1947 showed to be almost as beloved as Charles Dickens—had been pushed to the sidelines of literature. At last Lucy Maud Montgomery's journals came to be seen as important resources for understanding both her own complex character and the characters she brought to life in her books.

Thanks to L. M. Montgomery's energy and genius, the people in her writing live on—especially the fiery-tempered Anne. The spirited independence of the small, red-headed heroine has endeared her to readers everywhere; Montgomery's keen sense of both beauty and justice, embodied in Anne and all her other heroines, has encouraged young people around the world.

HARDCOVER EDITIONS *also* **AVAILABLE**

REDISCOVER
the
WORLD
of
L. M. MONTGOMERY

EMILY

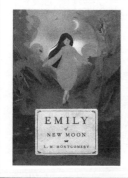

EMILY
of
NEW MOON
L. M. MONTGOMERY

EMILY
CLIMBS
L. M. MONTGOMERY

EMILY'S
QUEST
L. M. MONTGOMERY

ANNE

ANNE
of
GREEN GABLES
L. M. MONTGOMERY

ANNE
of
AVONLEA
L. M. MONTGOMERY

ANNE
of the
ISLAND
L. M. MONTGOMERY

ANNE
of
WINDY POPLARS
L. M. MONTGOMERY

ANNE'S
HOUSE OF DREAMS
L. M. MONTGOMERY

Spot and cover illustrations by Elly MacKay

ANNE
of
INGLESIDE
L. M. MONTGOMERY

RAINBOW
VALLEY

RILLA
of
INGLESIDE
L. M. MONTGOMERY

TUNDRA BOOKS
www.tundrabooks.com

LUCY MAUD MONTGOMERY (1874–1942) was born in what is now New London, Prince Edward Island, and raised by her grandparents after the death of her mother when she was just two. She worked for a time as a teacher and a journalist, then wrote her first novel, *Anne of Green Gables*, in the evenings while caring for her grandmother. She went on to publish twenty novels and hundreds of short stories, and she created, in Anne Shirley and Emily Starr, two of the most beloved characters in Canadian literature.

ELLY MACKAY is a paper artist and a children's book author and illustrator. She studied illustration and printmaking at the Nova Scotia College of Art and Design and at the University of Canterbury, in New Zealand. Her distinctive pieces are made using paper and ink, and then are set into a miniature theatre and photographed, giving them their unique three-dimensional quality. Elly lives in Owen Sound, Ontario, with her husband and two children.